S0-AHF-129

The SONG

JEAN JOHNSON

BERKLEY SENSATION, NEW YORK

THE BERKLEY PUBLISHING GROUP
Published by the Penguin Group
Penguin Group (USA) Inc.
375 Hudson Street, New York, New York 10014, USA
Penguin Group (Canada), 90 Eglinton Avenue East, Suite 700, Toronto, Ontario M4P 2Y3, Canada
(a division of Pearson Penguin Canada Inc.)
Penguin Books Ltd., 80 Strand, London WC2R 0RL, England
Penguin Group Ireland, 25 St. Stephen's Green, Dublin 2, Ireland (a division of Penguin Books Ltd.)
Penguin Group (Australia), 250 Camberwell Road, Camberwell, Victoria 3124, Australia
(a division of Pearson Australia Group Pty. Ltd.)
Penguin Books India Pvt. Ltd., 11 Community Centre, Panchsheel Park, New Delhi—110 017, India
Penguin Group (NZ), 67 Apollo Drive, Rosedale, North Shore 0632, New Zealand
(a division of Pearson New Zealand Ltd.)
Penguin Books (South Africa) (Pty.) Ltd., 24 Sturdee Avenue, Rosebank, Johannesburg 2196,
South Africa

Penguin Books Ltd., Registered Offices: 80 Strand, London WC2R 0RL, England

This book is an original publication of The Berkley Publishing Group.

This is a work of fiction. Names, characters, places, and incidents either are the product of the author's
imagination or are used fictitiously, and any resemblance to actual persons, living or dead, business
establishments, events, or locales is entirely coincidental. The publisher does not have any control over
and does not assume any responsibility for author or third-party websites or their content.

Copyright © 2008 by G. Jean Johnson
Cover art by Franco Accornero
Cover design by Annette Fiore
Text design by Kristin del Rosario

All rights reserved.
No part of this book may be reproduced, scanned, or distributed in any printed or electronic form
without permission. Please do not participate in or encourage piracy of copyrighted materials in
violation of the author's rights. Purchase only authorized editions.
BERKLEY SENSATION and the "B" design are trademarks belonging to Penguin Group (USA) Inc.

First edition: February 2008

Library of Congress Cataloging-in-Publication Data

Johnson, Jean, 1972–
    The song / Jean Johnson.— 1st ed.
        p.   cm.
    ISBN 978-0-425-21929-4 (trade pbk.)
    I. Title.
PS3610.O355S66   2008
813'.6—dc22   2007037458

PRINTED IN THE UNITED STATES OF AMERICA

10   9   8   7   6   5   4   3   2   1

ACKNOWLEDGMENTS

Once again, Stormi, Alexandra, and NotSoSaintly top the thank you list, who are one and all lovely, eloquent ladies. Alienor joins them; your linguistic talents are simply amazing—oh, and by the time this book comes out, happy birthday, again! Also, thanks to Macabre31 for cold reading this one; Amser, for being one of my guinea pigs; Yvonne, for yet again putting up with me moving around IV poles and rearranging visitor chairs; my sister Ny, for making me laugh over her reaction to reading about the scary mekha-whatsits; the Mob of Irate Torch-Wielding Fans for putting up with how I worked on *The Song* and not on the other stories they craved; and You, the readers who have been enjoying these books. Without you, there'd be no point in getting published!

If anyone is interested in joining the Mob of Irate Torch-Wielding Fans (and is eighteen years or older—sorry, but you have to be an adult to join), you can visit us at http://groups.yahoo.com/group/MoITWF, or you can come visit my website at www.jeanjohnson.net, where all are welcome!

Hugs,

~JEAN

ONE

The Fourth of Sons shall find his catch:
The purest note shall turn to sour
And weep in silence for the hour
But listen to the lonely Heart
And Song shall bind the two apart

*T*he owl leaped from its perch on the pylon, transforming back to its natural shape. Alys landed on the dock next to Evanor. He watched as his uncle-in-law's eyes widened in shock, remembering how Alys had told them she had faked her own death, magically, to escape this murderous, two-legged beast.

"Hello, Uncle," Alys greeted her kinsman, her face expressionless, but her tone dripping with loathing. Evanor was rather surprised by how calm she sounded; he had learned how much her uncle terrified her. "You're looking rather fat and bald, as usual."

"Insolent brat!" the balding mage snarled, tightening his hands into fists. "I wondered why your magics didn't come to me, when all my spells said you were dead! An oversight I will correct . . . skaren skaroth!"

Everything seemed to slow down now, though at the time, there hadn't been much more than an instant in which to react in pure instinct.

A lethal blade of reddish-white light flung itself from Broger of Devries' hand. None of them dared launch a counterattack. The foul man had wrapped himself in spells that would lash back at any attackers, whether they struck physically or magically. This, Alys of Devries had informed them of in advance. The solution had become the need to return his own lethal powers upon himself, should he come to their island home, which he had done. His goal was to destroy the eight brothers sent into exile, so that he could harvest their powers as well as secure his claim to their family seat. Broger would then be powerful enough to claim the throne of Katan, on the mainland.

But Alys didn't have one of the spell-reflective mirrors they had created to defend themselves with. There hadn't been enough time to make more than a few. One had already been used, and destroyed in the process; his outworlder sister-in-law still huddled over her injured hand, in shock from the shattering of her mirror. Evanor shifted between Broger and his target, the only one who could act. At the time, there hadn't been any time to think, only the instinct to protect the young woman who was in love with one of his elder brothers.

A single, reverberating note, and Evanor's magic flexed like a clear, rubber wall, bouncing the spell back at its caster. The spell hit Broger of Devries, nearly slicing his chest in half. Blood-red energies lashed back, spreading toward his attacker—

Evanor jerked himself awake, throat muscles flexing, trying to scream through the lingering dream-memory of burning, searing pain . . . and was met by an emptiness in his ears, an emptiness filled solely by the hissing of his breath. Curling up off the bed, he bowed his head over his thighs, elbows braced on his knees. Running his fingers through his sleep-mussed locks, the blond mage . . . ex-mage . . . struggled to slow his racing heart.

I don't know which way of waking up is worse, reliving the nightmare of losing my voice, or waking up having forgotten that I have lost it . . . until I try to speak. Rubbing his face with his palms, he shut out the early morning light seeping through his curtains. *I don't regret saving Alys' life. She's sweet and wonderful, and deserves to live. And it could have been far worse, though Kata knows this is bad enough . . .*

Staving off depression wasn't easy. So much of his post-puberty life had revolved around the intertwining of his voice and his magic that the loss of one had triggered the loss of the other. His brothers all believed that if they could just restore his vocal cords, his magic would return. Ev harbored greater doubt than that. There were some spells a mage learned so well and so thoroughly, spells that were so easy and commonplace, that they could be performed without any component other than the mage's will. No words, no enhancements from herbs or runes, and some that didn't even require a gesture.

He didn't have that, anymore. Not reliably. A few times since the accident, he had cast such magic instinctively, out of pure, thoughtless habit . . . but when he thought about it consciously, his powers refused to flow.

Evanor was now about as magicless as his outworlder sister-in-law, Kelly, and it was not a comfortable thing to be. Not after more than a decade of being a fully trained mage. He could admire Kelly's original efforts to clean her chambers by hand when she had arrived among them several months ago, but it wasn't something he wanted to do for the rest of his life.

Trevan, his next-youngest brother, had managed to come up with a few ways for Kelly and Evanor to use magic, without having any of their own. There were some things that were already in place, of course; the lightglobes were touch-activated, and the faucets and refreshing room facilities could be used by anyone. Trevan had gone a step further, enchanting a pumice-stone that his next-eldest sibling could run over his chin each morning, removing his facial hair that way rather than through a highly unreliable attempt at a shaving cantrip. The fifthborn brother had also created a crude system of bells in the halls that could ring throughout the palace complex, each with a tone representing a wing, a floor, and a distance from the donjon, the octagonal hall at the heart of the palace.

It was an attempt at replacing the gaping hole Evanor's silenced voice had left. Before, Ev had simply Listened with a special spell:

Anytime one of his brothers sang out his name—not just spoke it—Evanor would hear it and be able to respond. That had vanished along with his magic, leaving them without a central point of communication. The bells, recently installed every dozen body-lengths or so in the corridors, were a somewhat awkward system, but they were learning how to use them.

The bells' biggest drawback was that they only told the others that someone was needed in such-and-such place. It didn't say who was needed, or who needed them, or even why. Trevan claimed it was a work in progress. Evanor secretly hated it; he missed being the center-point for their communications. He *appreciated* the effort his sibling was taking to try to refine the system, but it was like being given a handful of coppers to spend after having a lockbox fat with treasure stolen away.

Trevan had also cobbled together a washtub that agitated, rinsed, and wrung out their clothing during Dominor's absence from the family. It was a lot more practical than bells that required a person to know which tone meant what. Of course, Ev's twin wasn't very impressed with the machine, since it couldn't dry their clothes as well, and it threatened more wear and tear on the fabric and seams than the thirdborn's own spell-enhanced methods did. But when Dominor had been kidnapped several weeks ago, they'd been forced to make do without their self-designated launderer . . . and Evanor had lost his voice shortly after that. His own laundry skills relied mostly on magic. Which he didn't have, anymore.

This self-circling isn't getting you anywhere . . . You have work to do, Evanor.

Breakfast wasn't his chore today, but it was almost time for the morning meal. Sliding his hands from his face, he blinked blearily at the golden shades of wood that dominated his bedroom. With his bedchamber tucked into the southern-facing side of the wing his quarters were located in, he didn't get direct sunlight in the mornings. There was enough indirect light coming in through the gauzy curtains to illuminate the parquetry in the walls, furniture, and floor.

Let his twin have a bedroom with stone walls and a stone-paved floor. He liked the comfort of wood. There were a variety of chambers in the castle-like palace that was their home-in-exile, far more variety than Corvis Castle had boasted. This one had appealed to him too much to give up, though it was at the farthest end of the wing from everything else.

But the exercise, as Mother would have said, is good for your body . . . and the fact that this room is your sanctuary is good for your soul. That was Father's advice, when he caught Koranen and Morganen arguing about decorating their room, as boys. Make your bedroom your sanctuary . . .

He missed his parents.

Running his hands through his blond locks again, he breathed deeply to let go of another source of potential depression. When Evanor finally rose, he grimaced at his bed for a long moment, then made it with a few tugs of his hands here and there. It just wasn't the same as being able to snap his fingers and have the thing as neatly made as if an army of servants had invaded. Not that they had an army of servants . . .

Oh, now there's an idea; I can talk to Kor and Dom about enchanting some of those glass-bead people they came up with for the Mandarites, and see about turning some of them into actual servants. It doesn't take that much in the way of enchanted intelligence to sweep a floor or make a bed . . .

Making a mental note to remember to speak—well, whisper—to them about the idea, he headed for the refreshing room. A wash, a stone-shave, a fresh set of clothes. Maybe he'd feel normal by breakfast time. Maybe not.

T here you are, Evanor! Good morning," Kelly called out to him as he entered the dining chamber. "Come on over here; Mariel has some good news!"

Curious, the blond mage crossed to join his eldest sister-in-law. The dark-auburn-haired Koranen slipped out of the way, leaving room for Evanor to join the strawberry-blond woman in front of the oval mirror. Mariel, shorter and curly-haired, and a middle-aged woman clad in white, her hair covered by a veil, stood on the other side. Mariel smiled as soon as she saw him through the mirror.

"Hello, Evanor. I've managed to copy the Healing tomes I needed, with the Mother Superior's help," Mariel stated. The middle-aged woman nodded her head slightly in acknowledgment. The Healer continued with an encouraging smile. "I have several options available that should be able to take care of your problem. More than that, the last of our things are all packed up and ready to be shipped across. If you're ready for us, that is."

"Your son and you are both more than welcome," Kelly reassured her, smiling back. "Just to warn you, it usually seems like there're a lot of bodies over here, and it can get very confusing, sorting out who's who. But you'll get the hang of it."

"We've finished preparing a couple of suites of rooms for you to choose from, in the southwest wing," Morganen, the lean, light brown–haired mage standing on Kelly's other side added. "They're the best of those currently furnished."

Evanor arched his brow, leaning forward so he could stare at his youngest sibling. Morg smiled, but Ev wasn't fooled. The youngest of them was the Destined Matchmaker of the others, after all. Ev's quarters, with their lovely wooden parquetry, were in the southwest wing, and he was considered to be the next brother in the "Song of the Sons of Destiny."

Glancing back at the woman in the mirror, Evanor felt his mouth curving in a smile of his own. *Not that I'll protest too hard against my Destiny. Certainly we'll be thrown together long enough for her to come to know me, and I, her.*

She certainly is beautiful . . .

Unable to speak loudly enough to be easily heard through the twinned scrying mirrors spanning the distance between Nightfall Isle and the heart of Natallia on the other side of the Eastern Ocean, Evanor contented himself with watching Mariel. It was hard to gauge size through a mirror, but he was fairly certain she was shorter than Kelly and Alys, who in turn were shorter than Serina, the newest of his sisters-in-law. She possessed vigorously curly hair that was almost the same shade of light brown as Morganen's, only just a little richer and darker. Or maybe that was due to the lighting in her location; there were strange crystals embedded in the ceiling that illuminated the dining hall with a golden white light. It put little golden highlights and darker brown shadows into her shoulder-length ringlets. Evanor liked the effect.

Her eyes were hazel; in the occasional shaft of light as she shifted her stance, they looked greenish with hints of amber, and when she was in less direct light, they appeared to be a speckled brown. Her nose turned up just a little bit at the end. And it had a dusting of freckles that extended just a little bit onto her cheeks. They were faint, but then Evanor was studying her very thoroughly. What little of her ears that he could see suggested they were small. And her neck was maybe a little short, but he thought there was enough room for a man to nibble if so inclined.

Since most of her torso lay below the rim of the mirror's edge, he could only see the slope of her breasts under her sleeveless top. It was more than enough to tell they were quite generous. He had seen more of her figure on previous occasions, though; she had looked deliciously plump. Full-figured. Unlike her tall, willowy, pale-haired friend, this Mariel was curvaceous and very enticing to him. Evanor really couldn't see what attracted Dominor to Serina, when this was the true beauty of the two wom—

Kelly's elbow jabbed him in the side, breaking off his musings. He blinked and glanced at his sister-in-law. The amusement in her aquamarine eyes told him that she knew he had been daydreaming and not paying attention. Blushing, Evanor tried to figure out what his response was supposed to be.

Thankfully, Kelly took pity on him, leaning over to whisper in his ear rather than speaking loudly enough for the others to hear. "Stop drooling and pay attention, Ev. The Mother Superior, there, just asked you if you're willing to share Mariel's Healing abilities with the nuns, at least until they can contact one of the other nun-neries to send them a Healer to replace her."

Blinking, he considered her words for a moment, then nodded. *"Tell her I can certainly understand her concern and would be willing to permit this . . . provided Rydan is willing to permit it, since he's the one who controls whatever method of transport they're using."*

"He says he understands your concern perfectly and is willing to share her services until they can be adequately replaced," Kelly translated for him. "Provided, of course, that she can indeed cross back over as needed, that his own recovery isn't jeopardized severely by her temporary loss, and that she will be allowed to return."

"I'm still a little bit reluctant to let her go," Mother Naima demurred. Her smile said she wasn't very serious. "Not to mention the cost in magic and effort to send her across. I think, for the services of such an exemplary Healer, we should be given some sort of trade compensation . . . wouldn't you agree?"

Ev watched Mariel narrow her eyes, but Kelly only laughed. "We have a crate of fresh-picked *toska* fruit that I think we can spare. If you like, we can send it across as a thank you for all your trouble."

"Never heard of it. Is it any good?"

"The rind is hard, and the inner seed is equally inedible," Saber replied, standing behind his redheaded wife, "but the flesh is very sweet and tangy. I think you'll like it."

Evanor nudged Kelly, whispering in her ear. *"Tell her it's good served both fresh and cooked and makes a sweet spread when turned into a jam."*

She complied. "It's good either fresh, cooked, or served as a jam. I've also had it frozen as a sherbet, mixed with honey and other things. It's quite good, really."

Grateful Kelly was willing to be his voice, Evanor returned to studying the Healer framed by the mirror. He discovered that she was studying him, too, and blushed. But he didn't look away. He knew what he looked like; handsome enough, at least by Katani standards. If that appealed to her in any way, he wasn't going to be upset in the least. Of course, she would be his Healer first and foremost, but she would be staying for quite some time afterward, if he—and her friend Serina, plus Morganen the matchmaker and the rest of his large family—had anything to say about it.

There would be plenty of time for the two of them to get to know each other; it was their Destiny, after all.

Brown eyes. She couldn't get over the fact that he had brown eyes, and yet had blond hair. Serina had amber eyes and pale blond hair, but she was from the Moonlands. The tall, slender mage had admitted at one point over the past two years that most of her people had pale blond hair and light brown eyes. But this was more of a buttery shade of blond, and brown eyes the rich color of *cinnin*, that exotic spice from the Draconan Empire. Even having been Serina's friend for more than two years, Mariel still wasn't used to seeing brown eyes with such light hair. Nor could she get over the fact that, however much their bone structure was very much alike, his twin brother, Dominor—Serina's new husband—had blue eyes and dark brown hair. Like night and day.

Most Natallians had darker hair, come to think of it. She had the curly hair of a Gucheran, thanks to a grandmother on her father's side. Her son, Mikor, had inherited those curls, though his hair was the darker brown of his father, Milon. Mariel sighed, waiting for the same wistful thoughts to rise up in her at the thought of her late husband, but the blond male on the other side of the mirror was looking at her again. Staring, really, but not in a bad way.

It was actually rather flattering that such an exotic, handsome man could find her so fascinating. His build was lean, much like her late husband's, and his hair about as straight, but there really weren't any other comparisons to make between the two men. Milon had been a bit hairy under his tunic; she could see a bit of this man's chest through the vertical slit at the front of his tunic neckline, and he didn't look very furry at all. Not like the broader-shouldered fellow standing behind him.

Evanor, the name of her admirer if she remembered it right, had a face that was longer, more rectangular than Milon's rounded features, and his nose was straight and long, not slightly snub at the tip. Despite his blond hair and brown eyes, and his twin brother's brown hair and blue eyes, he looked remarkably like Dominor, whom Mariel had come to know over the past few months. Those brown eyes had a slight slant to them just like his brother's, enough to make him look subtly exotic. The expression in them, masculine, fascinated, with a hint of gentleness rather than his twin's firmer gaze . . . reminded her of her husband. Mariel still missed Milon in some ways, but two years was long enough to mourn, really. Surely her husband wouldn't want her to deny herself the chance of finding happiness with another man?

Of course, there was still a corner of her heart that wanted to scold herself for such thoughts. She had known her late husband for most of her life, had been childhood sweethearts with him since turning sixteen, had married at nineteen, and borne their son at the age of twenty. She had lived the last decade of her life here in the Retreat at Koral-tai, simply because Milon had said the Goddess had shown him a vision of the two of them moving up into these mountains.

Born a lowlands child with a distinct dislike of heights, moving to the mountains had been an act of sheer faith on her part, as much as an act of marriage. But she had moved here, overcome her fears, and had remained here, despite her husband's fatal fall from the mountain path. And now—today—she was going to move else-where. The Retreat was where she had spent most of her married life. Moving away from it meant moving away from the last re-minders of her husband, other than for a few mementos she couldn't quite bring herself to leave behind.

It was also going to be a transition for her son. Mikor had never known anything but the mountains around the Retreat and had rarely gone on trading journeys. He was familiar with the labyrinthine cor-ridors and the dangers of living literally on the side of a mountain. Mariel worried over what sort of dangers might await her and her son in this new place, this Nightfall Isle. She hadn't asked about such things, and it was a bit late to backpedal out of the commitment to go, now.

Mikor was certainly eager to go. She had given up getting him to sit still this morning and had instead tasked him with overseeing the nuns digging up and bundling several herbs to take with them, so that she would have access to many of the same medicines she was used to using as an adjunct to her Healing magic. He had a list of how much to bring of each kind, and was—politely—bossing around the nuns with an air of importance that made all of the women watching him hard pressed to not chuckle about it.

Having stressed how important the job was, Mariel had left it in her son's care. He was perhaps a bit young for the responsibility, but the nuns would know what needed to be done. And they would treat his "responsibility" with respect, so long as he attended to his task politely. The Order of Koral-tai might not care for adult males as a matter of both principle and practice, but Mikor had endeared himself to most of them literally from before birth.

As the Mother Superior drew her trade negotiations to a close, Mariel spoke. "I will be bringing a large number of living plants with me—medicinal herbs and such. Will there be a place for me to replant and tend them?"

The freckled redhead on the other side of the mirror craned her head, looking up at her golden-blond husband. He was broader-shouldered than the one Mariel had been admiring, muscular and sort of intimidating in a physical way, but he had proven so far to be intelligent and polite. He frowned a moment in thought, then nodded.

"Yes, I believe the northwest gardens will have some space available for your needs. That's where we've planted most of our culinary herbs, but as there aren't that many of us to feed, we haven't been growing anything in truly large amounts," Saber said.

"Good. Then I suggest we get going," Mother Naima finished. "Guardian Rydan is ready with his end of things, and it will only take me a few minutes to secure mine. I'll be taking this mirror into the nunnery half of the Retreat and hanging it in my outer study. Leaving it here would be awkward for future communications, as I will still be taking my meals with my fellow Sisters, thus leaving this section of the Retreat abandoned. If these fruit of yours are as tasty as you say, I'll consider other forms of trade as well, and we'll need to talk about it."

"A good idea," Kelly agreed. "We definitely want to consider discussing trade items with you, in the future."

"We'll await you in the courtyard," her husband offered. "Start sending things through as soon as you're ready."

Mother Naima tapped the edge of the mirror, restoring its normal reflection. She turned to Mariel with a sigh and a wry smile. "Everything is settled, then. I've known you for the last ten years, Mariel; I'll miss you. And that impertinent scamp you call your son."

"We'll miss you, too," Mariel agreed, embracing the older woman. She looked one last time at the mirror, but it only showed her curly-haired reflection. A sigh escaped her. "Well. Off I go into another adventure. I had one in coming here, and I'll have one in going there."

"And you're very nervous about it," the Mother Superior pointed out sagely. At Mariel's sharp glance, she smiled. "Which is only natural to see."

"I thought I was hiding it better than that," Mariel muttered.

"I've known you for ten years, a frightened young wife who couldn't even look out the windows when you first arrived. You're stronger than you know," Mother Naima counseled her. "And blessed with an opportunity to find more love in your life. Guardian Milon was a good man, but there are others out there who could give you equal love, if not greater. May the Goddess bless you with another chance at love. Even if it must be with a male."

Mariel couldn't help the laugh that escaped her at the Mother Superior's wry, teasing caveat. "Sorry, Mother Naima, but I'm just not the nunnery type. Come, let us check on my son before he wreaks any further havoc in the herb beds."

Mikor emerged from the whirling excitement of the Fontway with a jolt, as the cart he was sitting on landed in the midst of bright sunshine. The mare whickered and moved forward, while Mikor was still trying to blink and clear his eyes. Once he could focus, he found himself surrounded by pale, white granite, cheerful blue roof tiles, and several strangers. Male strangers.

They all looked similar enough to his new uncle to be the mage's brothers, but the only one Mikor really knew was Dominor. The rest were a profusion of large bodies in too-short tunics and loose leggings. Each one had different-colored hair, too, not the dark brown of his Uncle Dominor's locks. Some were talking in a small group, while the others were unloading the carts that were being sent back and forth through the mirrors that had been set up in some highly complicated way of transporting him and his mother a gazillion miles to wherever this warm, sunny place might be.

"Come here, Mikor."

The familiar voice was accompanied by familiar hands, as his aunt—honorary, not blood-kin, but still his aunt—reached up to lift him down from the cart. He jumped down, allowed her to steady him on his feet for a moment, then pulled away, eager to investigate this new place. Within moments, he spotted his mother chatting with a big, tall, muscular fellow, the one with the S-name. Saber, that was it. There were so many men here! It was rather confusing and yet exciting to the youth.

The other man standing next to him, the one with even lighter blond hair, though not quite as light as his aunt's, that was the man Evan-something, the one his mother was supposed to Heal. Mikor spotted him near the short woman with the strawberry blond hair and the freckles, Queen Kelly. She didn't look much like a queen. Mikor wrinkled his nose doubtfully at her, then turned to watch the others. There was a youngish man with light brown hair who was making all the boxes of plants levitate out of the cart he had ridden in, and one with deep reddish hair who was levitating the crates and trunks of their belongings out of a previous cart, sending them floating through one of the doorways into the big, four-storied building surrounding them on two sides.

One of the men had more coppery-colored hair, somewhere between the queen's shade and the darker redhead's; he was working with a woman whose hair was about as curly as Mikor's own, but a light brown in color, not dark brown. They were calming the mares of the carts that were being turned around and sent back by his new Uncle Dominor. Grateful for a familiar face, Mikor waited until the last cart and horse floated through the enlarged mirror-Gate, then darted forward to greet the dark-haired mage, one of only a few truly familiar faces in this strange place. The other familiar face, Aunt Serina, had just joined her husband; Mikor wanted to be with her, too, since his mother was busy talking with the others.

A hand grabbed him by the back of his tunic, yanking him off his feet. Startled, Mikor yelped, then staggered as the arm responsible returned him to the ground. Twisting, he looked up at a man with even more muscles than the one married to the queen; he had thick brown hair and a voice that rumbled like a growling dog, frightening him. "*Don't* run in front of the mirror. Something else could be coming through."

Gulping, scared by all those flexing muscles, Mikor nodded quickly, hoping the man wasn't going to shake him or anything.

"Mikor, come here!"

As soon as the somewhat scary-looking man let him go, Mikor dashed off to the side, making an exaggerated arc around the area in front of the mirror. He quickly placed his aunt between him and the big fellow, only then noticing that the man had eyes sort of like his honorary aunt's, only more golden than amber. Those eyes followed him for a moment; then the man was distracted by another cart being sent through, this time with one of the nuns at the reins. Mikor took advantage of the distraction of the cart landing and being unloaded to tug on his new uncle's sleeve.

Dominor glanced down. He had to keep an eye on the process; two carts would come through, be unloaded, then sent back, while two more were being loaded on the other side. It was his responsibility to wrap the carts in a protective sphere for the return journey, since he had experience with the task. There were a few moments he could spare for the boy, though. "Yes? What did you want?"

"Who's the scary one?" Mikor asked in a near whisper, pointing furtively at the big-muscled fellow. It wasn't easy, keeping them all separate, but that one looked too big to be ignored.

Following his gesture, Dominor spotted his next-elder brother and almost laughed out loud. Struggling, he suppressed the urge into a mere snort and smirk. "Wolfer, the second-eldest of us. And he's not that scary."

"You're a grown-up mage, and almost as big as *he* is," Mikor retorted. "You don't have to be afraid of anything! I'm just a boy, and he's four times as big as me!"

The second cart came through, diverting Dominor's attention. Distracted with the need to protect the enchanted mirror from the nervous mare, who was balking and trying to back up after suddenly finding herself in a strange place, he offered, "Well, just go up to him and tell him you're not afraid of him!"

The mare squealed and tried to rear, despite the rigging tying her to the cart. As Mikor watched, the big man with the golden eyes grabbed her bridle, yanked her onto all fours, and growled at her, his face mere inches from her muzzle. Mikor's eyes widened almost as much as the quickly subdued mare's. When the muscular man tugged on her bridle, the mare moved forward docilely, though her ears flicked back and forth in lingering discomfort.

A hand tapped his shoulder, making him squeak. It was just his aunt, who smiled down at him. "Come along, before any of these people trip over you. Let me show you where your new room is going to be." Lifting her gaze, she raised her voice slightly. "Mariel, are you coming? I'm going to go show Mikor his new room!"

"I'll be with you in a few moments!"

"She'll catch up," Serina confirmed, ruffling Mikor's curls, which made him wrinkle his nose and push at her hand. "We actually have *three* rooms prepared for you to choose from, and your mother has agreed that you get to have the first pick of those three."

That made up for the hair-tousle. "I get to choose? Really?"

"You certainly do. Come on!" Beckoning for him to follow her, she headed for one of the doors that didn't have boxes and bags floating through it.

Inside, Mikor could see the walls, which were slowly shifting with color. It took him a moment to realize the walls had been painted with clouds. "Wow—did you see the walls, Aunt Serina?"

"What? Oh, yes. Dom told me about that. They had someone trying to pick a war with them a while back, using scrying to send them nasty creatures, and they foiled the scrying attempt by making the paint on the walls change color. That made it too hard for the mage to peek at them from afar," she told him as they entered a stairwell and started climbing.

"A war? Is it still going on?" Mikor asked eagerly.

Serina stopped and faced him. She moved down a few steps until her head was almost level with his, and leveled his eagerness with a flat look. "War is never fun, Mikor. You've been sheltered at the Retreat all your life, but war is all about being hurt, bleeding, and quite possibly dying. That includes both you, your mother, me,

Dominor . . . anyone who gets in the way of danger could be seriously hurt.

"In fact, one of the brothers almost lost his life, in defeating their foe. He's lucky he only lost his voice. One of the other brothers was shot by a Mandarite weapon, though he has since healed. And Queen Kelly lost her finger, though at least the others could find it and reattach it in time so that she could keep it—and don't go asking her which one she lost," Serina added quickly, catching the gleam in his green eyes. "That would be rude. If *she* brings it up, *then* you may ask. But not until then. Got it?"

"Yes, Aunt Serina," Mikor responded, subdued. He followed her up the stairs again. They had reached the third floor when he finally asked, "The one that lost his voice—that's the really blond one, kinda like you, right? Ev-something?"

"Evanor, and yes, that's the one."

Mikor considered that, and considered what he'd seen his mother doing from time to time, during their mirror-talks with these people. He rubbed the side of his nose. "I think Mother likes him."

Humor colored his aunt's voice. "I think she does, too. And I think he might like her, just as much."

"Do you think *he'd* be willing to be my new father?" Mikor asked her, joining her as she emerged in a longish corridor where the walls showed butterflies flittering over rolling fields of gently swaying flowers. It reminded him of the times he'd traveled down into the lowlands at the base of the mountains holding the Retreat.

"I don't know. Maybe, but then maybe not. Why don't we finish getting moved in, here, and let things settle a bit. You can get to know everyone, like your mother and I have been doing, and they can get to know you in turn. Then you'll know whether or not any of them are interested in that sort of thing, alright?" Serina offered.

"Okay. So, which room is going to be mine?"

"One of these three," she told him, pointing at three open doors. There were four, here at the end of the wing, two on each side, but one of the four doors was closed.

"Why not that one?" Mikor asked her, pointing at the fourth. Its door was fancy, decorated with eight-pointed stars made from carved and inlaid wood. The other doors had different patterns on them, one with crescent moons, one with a sun-in-glory, and one with flame-like curlicues.

"Because that one is Evanor's room, and you're not allowed to go in there without his clearly expressed permission," Serina told him. "Now, take a look inside these other three rooms and see which one you want for your room and which one you think your mother would want."

"Will the third one be your room?" Mikor asked her.

"No, mine is in the next wing over, on the other side of the courtyard from where you arrived," Serina told him. "I'm married to Dominor, so I'm living with him in his quarters, now."

"Oh. So who lives in all those other rooms?" Mikor asked, gesturing at the other doors leading down the hallway.

"No one, they're empty. Your mother wants you to be close to her so she can keep an eye on you, and you can be close by if you need her in the middle of the night. Though you still get your own room, at least. She also needs to be close to her patient, Evanor, which is why Dom and I spent some time last night tidying up these rooms so that you could pick from among them."

"Why didn't we get rooms by you an' Uncle Dominor?" Mikor asked. He liked the dark-haired mage, liked the fact that Dominor talked to him like a real person, not just a boy. Mikor had only known the adult male for a month or two, ever since Dominor had come home with his honorary aunt to help her with some special piece of magic no one had ever actually explained to the youth, but he liked him.

"Because Dominor and I are newly married, and newly married people like to have time alone, away from interruptions. Because that's where Dominor's bedroom is, and his twin's bedroom is over here," Aunt Serina explained to him, tugging briefly on the end of her braid, though she smiled as she did so, letting Mikor know it wasn't her usual worried kind of tug. "Because Evanor is going to be your mother's patient, and she'll need to keep an eye on him as well as on you . . . and because we're hoping the two of them become friends as well as Healer and patient . . . which could lead to him wanting to be your mother's new husband, and your new father. *If* the two of them can get along well enough, of course."

"Oh. Well . . . Mother's really nice. I can't imagine anyone not getting along with her. So this Evanor had better be nice to Mother and me, 'cause I want a new father, but I want a *nice* new father." With that piece of wisdom stated, Mikor stepped into the room next to the one the man Evanor was using. He missed the twitch of Aunt Serina's lips as she struggled not to laugh. Instead, he explored the first suite.

There were three chambers beyond the first door, half in stone and half in painted wood: a sort of solar with tables and padded chairs; a bedchamber with a big canopied bed, some empty bookshelves, and a tall wardrobe; and a refreshing room. It had a bathing tub instead of a rain-shower stall, but it was as nice a refreshing room as the ones back at the Retreat, otherwise.

The rooms beyond the next door, across the hall from Evanor's, were done entirely in wooden wainscoting and painted, sculpted plaster, which made the whirling snowflakes of the paint ripple over the sculpted bits in an odd sort of way. It had four rooms, with the extra one lined in shelves like Aunt Serina's changing room, back at the Retreat. It looked like some sort of changing room, bare of all but shelving and a padded bench in the center, while the remaining rooms had furniture similar to the first suite. The refreshing room tub was big, too, with plenty of shelf space around it. Mikor could easily picture his mother's bottles of softsoap, perfumes, and other female-stuff sitting around the edge of the tub. If she didn't want to use the extra chamber as a changing room, he decided she could dry her healing herbs in there since it was out of direct light with lots of shelf space.

He checked the third suite, which was almost entirely lined in plastered walls covered with the color-shifting paint, this time showing a slowly panning view of water trickling down over moss-covered rocks. It was bigger than the first one, though it only had the three rooms, solar, bedchamber, and refreshing room. The solar was long enough to need a fat, rectangular stone post in the middle.

Hammered into that fat quasi wall were several pegs. It took Mikor a few moments of scratching his head through his curls as he peered at them to figure out what they were for. It finally came to him, though: They were very much like the posts used to hang up armor and weapons in the armory attached to the salle back at the Retreat.

That helped him make up his mind. Turning around, he found his honorary aunt standing in the doorway, polite inquiry in her amber gaze. He grinned at her, remembering that her husband, his new uncle, had promised him sword work lessons. Now he had not only Uncle Dominor, but a bunch of others who could teach him all about fighting, and maybe even get him some armor and real weapons. When he was big enough, of course; he knew his mother wouldn't put up with him having anything bigger than an eating knife before proving he could handle a real weapon safely . . . which only made him want sword work lessons even more.

"I'll take this one," he stated confidently. "And Mother can have the one next to it, on this side of the hall. That bathtub has space around the edges for her scented stuff, and the room with the shelves can be used for storing herbs or clothes, whatever she wants."

"Good choice. Excellent reasoning, too, and very considerate of you," Serina praised him, making him flush with pleasure. "I'll start moving the boxes up from downstairs, then. You'd better come out of there and wait in that room you didn't pick—I don't want anything to accidentally hit you in the head, if you dodge the wrong way."

TWO

·✦·

A nd I was getting paid two gold coins a day, on top of room and board. Of course, that was to care for a nunnery of more than one hundred women, and not . . . what? Eleven of you, not counting my son and myself?" Mariel asked to confirm. "A single gold a day would be sufficient, with a much smaller population base."

"A gold a day!" Saber scoffed, scowling at her.

Evanor listened silently to the argument going back and forth between the other three, Saber, Kelly, and Mariel. He couldn't have been heard even if he tried, between the racket of the carts arriving and leaving, the mares whinnying as they were guided back and forth across unimaginable distances, the boxes and trunks creaking as they were levitated out of the way, and the vociferousness of the argument between his eldest brother and his possible future bride. Contenting himself with watching the curly-haired Healer, he let them work out the problem. Having drunk Ultra Tongue months ago, Evanor understood every word of Natallian she said, though they sounded more like exotically accented Katani to his ears.

The combination of potion and spell that was Ultra Tongue made it easy for any of his brothers to reply in kind, just by putting that same "accent" into their own language. Kelly had drunk the potion, too. Serina had apparently imbibed her own version, but he didn't think Alys had drunk any; her magic didn't seem strong enough for the task, and he doubted she had the training for it, either. That left Wolfer's bride speaking only her native Katani. He wondered if Serina had given Mariel Ultra Tongue to drink, or Mariel's son, Mikor. If so, it would be convenient . . . but the problem with Ultra Tongue was that the listener couldn't *tell* if someone else had drunk it, unless they started talking in a wide variety of dialects.

The Healer wasn't averse to arguing her point, he noted, approving of her standing her ground in the face of his eldest brother's skepticism.

"Most of my expenses go right back into purchasing medicines and other Healing supplies, and as I don't know what will be available here, I have to assume that what I'm used to using will cost proportionately higher because of the greater distance and trouble spent in obtaining whatever it is," Mariel argued. "A gold a day will cover those expenses."

"It would cover the medical supplies for fifty people, maybe, but we don't even have a quarter of that!"

"*I* think it's worth the expense."

Saber switched his scowl to his wife. "Kelly, do you have any idea how much a gold coin costs, in terms of spending power?"

"Evanor told me once that it's roughly twenty coppers to a silvara, which are the silver coins, and ten silvaras to a gilder, a gold coin. Alys also told me that the average cost of a room at a decent inn and an edible bowl of stew are six and three coppers, respectively. *Without* any stout or ale," the freckled outworlder asserted. "Which is a copper a mug. And that the average day's wage for a farmworker is a silvara, in Katan. Which doesn't leave a field hand much in the way of a profit, once you factor in other expenses. Paying her a retainer to work for us will be expensive, yes, but it would be far more expensive to try to entice a Healer to come out here whenever we needed something done."

"Yes, but we're not going to pay such an absurd amount!" he argued. "We don't get injured *that* much, on the Isle—no offense, Evanor."

"None taken," the fourthborn brother whispered wryly.

"True, but we're paying her *to be available*, in addition to actual services," Kelly stressed. "Prompt and competent medical attention is worth the extra cost. And it's not like we'd be paying a traditional retainer, which doesn't cover expenses beyond the most basic services. All expenses would be considered covered by this fee—isn't that correct?" she asked the Healer.

Mariel nodded. "Unless it's an exceptionally rare ingredient for a cure, I would be covering the expenses out of my own pocket, based on the pay I'd be given. And we're talking . . . essence of lilith root, or ground-up rainbow pearls. The odds of one of you catching a disease or being hit by a curse needing something like that for its cure is highly unlikely, however."

"Yes, but we're *not* made of money," Saber stated curtly. "We do most of our trading *in* trade. We literally do not have the gold to pay you a coin a day!"

"Well, then Serina can just keep track of a running tally on the Exchequery books," Kelly compromised. "And whatever our Healer needs to order can be paid for out of that running tally, when the merchant ships come around."

"Well, I *would* like to have some actual coins, to do some of the buying for myself," Mariel interjected.

"We don't exactly have a reliable market, other than once every new and full of Brother Moon. The goods vary from trip to trip, unless we order something well in advance. And the traders aren't supposed to trade with any woman found here, by Katani law," Saber admitted reluctantly, his skin reddening at the admission. "They're under orders to take exception to a woman's presence with, ah, extreme prejudice, in fact."

"Though we are working on that," Kelly interjected firmly. "I fully intend to open the Isle to not only a wider variety of trade opportunities, but also to settlers from the mainland and from other places as well. We *will* be increasing our population base, and with that increase, we will definitely need the services of a Healer living full-time on Nightfall itself. Which means we will have the need for a market economy, in time. Not just for buying things, but for selling the things that we'll be making, whether it's salt blocks, magic swords, fruit, cheese, or maybe even grain from our own fields, one of these days."

"Kelly, in order to do something like that, and truly be independent from Katan, we would need to be able to mint our own coins," Saber reminded his wife. "Nightfall Isle is very mineral-poor! We have all the granite we want for stone carving, sand from the beaches for glassmaking, even some marble deposits to the south, but there are no deposits of iron, no copper, no silver, and *no gold*."

"Well . . . what about the ocean?" Kelly offered. Her husband quirked his brow, as did Evanor.

"What do you mean, the ocean?" Mariel asked her, equally puzzled. "Are you trying to see if you're rich in sea-pearls or something?"

"No—though that would be a good idea to check. I meant that seawater is rich in dissolved minerals. You can extract not only blocks of salt and fertilizer-algae, but with the right spells, you could actually strain the ocean's water for gold." At Saber's skeptical look, Kelly amended, "Well, you would have to strain a *lot* of water to get the gold, but it should be there. I cannot imagine the oceans around here being that much different from the ones back home. In fact, back home, there are nodules at the bottom of the ocean floor that contain magnesium and iron, bauxite and copper, just to name a few possibilities. We have the right to claim all of the resources of the sea near our shores, so why not claim them?"

"What about gemstones?" Mariel offered. "Aren't there deposits of precious or semiprecious minerals on the Isle? Lapis, amethyst, citrine, quartz, anything like that? Colorful coral from the sea can be highly prized in some areas, too. I know that blue coral is prized in Guchere, and red coral is valued to some degree in Natallia. You don't have to *mine* the metal to make the coins—you could always take the coins you make in trade, smelt them down, and remint them under your own stamp and seal. All you'd need to do that is find a local natural resource that would be a highly valued commodity in other lands, and then find a way to export that commodity and trade it with those who value it most."

Evanor wanted to praise her intelligence when she made that offer, but he didn't know if it would be appropriate. Mariel was going to be his Healer, which meant he would be her patient. Healers and patients weren't encouraged to flirt, traditionally. He also didn't know if it would be welcome. She did seem to like the look of him, but that could simply be a casual sort of appreciation.

Still, it was good to know the woman could think so well. After just a few days in Serina's company, he knew he didn't want a woman quite *that* intelligent—or that absentminded—but he definitely knew he didn't want a village idiot as his Destined bride, either. No matter how pretty a woman might be when she was young, her looks would fade with time, leaving only her personality and her wits to keep her man interested in old age. A brilliant mind lasted longer than a brilliant body.

The same could be applied to a man, of course. Intelligence, humor, and kindness were the key traits he wanted to see in a partner, and they were the key traits he had to give in return. The problem was how to get her to notice these things when he still couldn't make himself heard in a conversation.

"We do have the salt and algae blocks to trade, as our natural resource," Saber admitted. "But in order to sell enough to make a true profit, we'd have to process far more water than we currently do now and widen our range of trading partners from just a few ships a month to at least a few ships a day. That would require workers who can be paid to spend their time hauling the blocks from the processing halls to the warehouses, because frankly, the rest of us have better things we could be doing with our time and energies, being artificer-mages."

"Which means importing workers from the mainland and other regions—" Kelly returned, only to be interrupted by her husband.

"Kelly, the Council of Mages is not going to allow anyone to migrate from the mainland to this island!" Saber protested.

"Then we'll take them from Natallia, and Guchere, and God

knows where else they'll be coming from!" she countered. "The point is, we have plenty of room to offer land to those who want it, and work for those who want it, and *trade* for those who want it! And one of the *enticements* we can offer is the free services of a Healer, paid for *by* the nation of Nightfall! *That* is worth a gold a day, for . . . for up to *fifty* residents on the Isle at a time."

Mariel thought that was a reasonable amount. She was also briefly sidetracked by the curiosity of *which* God the redheaded woman was referring to like that. She herself had grown up worshiping Natua, the patron Goddess of Natallia.

"Of course, if we get fifty-one citizens, then we increase it to two gold a day. And if we get one hundred and one, three gold, and so forth, until we need another Healer—and by that time, we'll probably *have* another Healer willing to move here. They don't *have* to come from Katan, to settle here," Kelly stated firmly.

"Well, I won't accept just anyone coming to live here. *Certainly* not any of those misogynistic Mandarite bastards," Saber reminded her. "Do *you* want someone like that coming to live here?"

Kelly snorted. "Definitely not! I won't put up with anything that absurd in my kingdom. Men and women may be different physically, but in all other regards, they are equals, end of subject," she digressed briefly before returning to the subject at hand. "The point is, we don't *have* to rely on Katan for anything. In order to do so, however, we'll need to be able to trade far and wide for whatever we need.

"To do that, we'll need to have products to sell, and to do *that*, we'll need workers and artisans crafting more than just what the few of us here can make. To get the workers and artisans interested in moving here," Kelly continued, "we'll need amenities that are attractive to them. Food, lodging, health care, the chance to own and work their own plot of land, to earn a respectable wage . . . which comes back to the need to have coins to pay the people who live and work here.

"Which means this is turning into a very cyclical argument," Kelly sighed roughly, running a hand through her strawberry-copper hair. "Saber, I am going to make a sovereign decision, here.

We *are* going to pay her the *equivalent* of a gold coin a day. That will cover the cost of her being available for all of our health-care needs, up to a total of fifty of us per gold coin, and restoration of Evanor's voice and missing magic, *and* will give us an incentive for recruiting settlers to come populate the island. Somehow, I don't think all that many kingdoms have state-sponsored, *socialized* medical services, out there."

"They don't," Mariel agreed, catching the gist of Kelly's comment, even though the slightly taller woman had used a foreign word somewhere in there. "But it worked quite well between the nuns and me. I can see it working just as well for a small but prosperous kingdom, with the Healers' services being paid for by taxes. Not just on the populace, but on imports and exports—Serina would know far better about such things than I, of course. But it would have to be a prosperous kingdom, and eventually it would need more than just a single Healer. I do need to sleep at some point in time."

An image formed in Evanor's mind, of her brown curls spilling over his pillow, of his bedding draping itself tenderly over each of her curves, her mouth quirked up at the corner in sated slumber, hinting at the dimple that showed whenever she smiled in full. The image held him in its thrall, making him ache to see it come true. It also made him miss whatever was said for a few moments. Until Kelly elbowed him in the ribs, that was.

"*Sorry—what?*" he whispered, blinking away from his daydream.

"I said, why don't you show her up to her rooms, now that we've settled her Healer's fee," his sister-in-law repeated. Before he could even nod his head, one of the palace windows opened and a dark curly head poked itself through.

"Mother?" Mikor waved down at them. "*Moootherrrr!* Come see the rooms I picked out for you!"

Grinning, Kelly pushed Evanor at the mother in question. "Go on, show her how to get up there, Ev."

Not needing to be told twice, Evanor bowed and offered Mariel his hand. She slipped her fingers into his, blushing and offering him a smile that definitely displayed the dimple lurking on one side.

"I do hope he won't be too much of a bother for all of you—my son, I mean," Mariel clarified as he arched a brow at her. "He's getting to that age where he's full of energy and curiosity and knows just enough to get himself into danger from the combination, but not enough to get himself safely back out again. And suddenly having all these male role models in his life . . . well, I have a feeling you and your brothers are going to be plagued by a curly-haired bump of curiosity."

"So long as he stays out of our private quarters, and especially out of our work towers, I think we'll get along just fine. It wasn't all that long ago that we were young boys ourselves."

"Oh? How old are you?" Mariel asked him.

"Twenty-seven, plus almost half a year. We were all born on the same day, you see, but each set of twins was born two years apart from the next."

"Interesting—were you all born on some auspicious day, like Midsummer? Or a holy day?"

"Not quite. Three days after the Spring Equinox, which isn't exactly auspicious. Just . . . four sets of twins, each of them two years apart, born on the same day."

"No other siblings? Just the eight of you?" Mariel asked.

"Mother . . . we had a stillborn sister," Evanor related. *"Both of them died in birth, and Father followed both of them within a month, from a combination of fever and broken heart. Or so the Healer said."*

"It's very rare for someone to actually die of a broken heart," Mariel admitted. "Not entirely unheard of, but rare."

Evanor shrugged. The pain had faded with time, though he and his brothers still missed their parents. *"Well, he did have a cold . . . and we think a heart attack. And he had just . . . lost the will to go on without her."*

"I myself have never met someone who felt that strongly about their beloved. Don't get me wrong, I was devastated when my late husband died . . . but I had Mikor to give me a reason to get up every day and keep going. And Serina." The petite woman smiled ruefully. "She kept me going. In fact, she called it revenge for every single time I had bullied *her* into remembering to eat, and bathe, and do other normal sorts of things that were just getting left on the wayside in my grief, as they had been occasionally lost in her passion for mathemagics."

Her frank admission gave Evanor hope, even as her comments about her late husband made him uncomfortable. *"And do you consider yourself recovered from your grief? Not to diminish your loss, of course, but . . ."*

"But you mean to ask, am I a one-man woman, or am I open to the possibility of someone else in my life?" Mariel finished for him, slanting him an amused look with those hazel eyes of hers. Evanor opened the door into the palace for her, a courtesy she appreciated. Especially coming from a handsome man like him, absent vocal cords and all. "Thank you . . . I'd say I'm ready. *If* the man is worthy of my time, of course . . . and if he doesn't mind the fact that I *am* a mother, and as such, concern for my son will always be one of the uppermost thoughts on my mind."

"Why wouldn't he be?" Evanor asked her, confused by her comment.

"Oh . . . a few times, when I'd accompany the nuns on their trading expeditions down into the lowlands in the last couple of years, I'd run across men who were interested in a widow . . . but not in a mother. They thought I should just hand Mikor off to the nuns to take care of while I dallied longer with them. It wasn't so much the dallying with them part that was the problem, so much as it was the fact that they thought my son was a hindrance. That he could be set aside like . . . like a toy. Something to put on a shelf when it's not being played with. They wanted me to put my 'toy' on a shelf so that *they* could play with *me*."

"Children are not toys. They are a lifelong responsibility. And you don't just hand them off to anyone who can watch them for an hour or so," Evanor asserted, pausing at the foot of the stairs. *"I remember Mother firing one of our nanny-tutors when we were young, because the woman had fobbed us onto one of the kitchen maids so that she could dally with a stable hand, instead of teach us our lessons for that morning. But the kitchen maid still had to get her work done, and couldn't watch all of us while doing so. Kor was only three at the time and cut himself grabbing for a*

knife in the scullery, which was where she had to watch us while she was working."

Mariel had to lean close to catch every word that he hissed, but she didn't mind. He smelled nice, this close. A hint of perfume, soap, and that underlying musk that was the scent of an adult male. He looked nice, too, clad in a light blue tunic and darker blue trousers. They were a little odd looking to her Natallian eyes, since she was used to seeing longer, knee-length tunics on men, and fitted hose, not loose pants, but she didn't *have* to know what his legs looked like, she supposed. *No, wait—yes I do . . .*

Regathering her wits, Mariel responded to his revelation.

"I'm glad your mother fired that tutor. But I'm curious as to what your mother did with her own time. Not that I can blame her in wanting a nanny to help take care of eight boys. I'd certainly hire some help, if it were me that had that many sons," she admitted.

"She did spend a lot of time with us, but she was also the Countess of Corvis and had many responsibilities, assisting our father with his duties in overseeing the demesne." He smiled at her. *"Much like the things Kelly and Saber were doing with you, just now."*

"Ah, that's right! Dominor did say he was a noble-born son." A thought following that statement made her flush. "I'm afraid I'm just a commoner, by birth. The only thing special about me is my affinity for Healing magic. My mother was just an herb-healer, and her father before her, though my great-grandmother had a small touch of magic, according to family history.

"Of course, my parents were very proud of me when I started showing signs of magic at the age of eleven. My father came from a long line of farmers, but he was very proud to have a mage in the family, and a mage-Healer at that. My mother was a little jealous at first; she was a farmer's daughter, too, though she had a bit of herb-healing knowledge. But after I went to the Healing College when I was twelve and showed the teachers there all that she had taught me about herbal medicines, I told her how impressed they were with her herbal lore, and she felt a little better."

"Being able to heal without magic is just as important, in some ways," Evanor demurred.

"Yes, but it's not the same as being able to do so with magic. You can do so much more with magic."

"The place where Kelly is from, they don't use magic to heal," Evanor said, guiding her up the steps.

"They don't?" That startled Mariel. "Why ever not?"

"She's an outworlder, from a universe where magic is extremely rare. Instead of spells, they use nonmagical means to cure all sorts of illnesses and injuries. She knows more about it than I, but she did mention her own people could reattach severed limbs, if it was done quickly enough. The healing rate isn't as swift as magic, though, and they cannot regenerate lost organs or limbs. But it's still impressive for a realm without spells."

"Goodness!" Mariel exclaimed, eyeing him askance. "She's from a place without magic? Of any kind? And she's your *queen*? However did she manage that?"

He grinned at her. *"She declared herself our queen, that's how."* His grin turned into a wry smile, wrinkling his nose a little. *"I'm afraid I couldn't quite keep my brothers civilized enough, during the three years of our exile from the mainland. Just before she arrived . . . not to scare you, but we had let our chores lapse. In fact . . ."*

He hesitated a moment, then shrugged and finished his statement.

"In fact, you could say we were very much like pigs rooting in a pen. Well, they were like pigs rooting in a pen; I tried to keep everything neat, but I'm only one man. My twin only ever bothered with tidying his own quarters, and very little effort anywhere else, and the rest were even worse. When Kelly arrived, she bullied us into scrubbing the palace from top to bottom, and the difference really showed, comparing the slovenly sections to the recently cleaned.

"The way I figure it, if she could bully the eight of us into being civilized again—including my sometimes stubborn twin—she's definitely strong willed enough to be our sovereign."

"I suppose a foreign outlook on life might help, too," Mariel admitted as they emerged on the third floor, "so long as she keeps a sensitivity to local customs and how things work in *this* world, as opposed to her own." She paused as a trunk came floating past them, forcing her and Evanor to move up against the wall of the corridor to avoid the levitating object. "But it does make me wonder, if she's from another universe, who does she follow as her chosen deity? She did say *God*, during our conversation, but she said no specific name."

"You're lucky I can answer this one," Evanor said. *"She calls herself 'agnostic.' She believes in a Divine Creator of some sort, but that it is by its very nature unknowable, beyond the grasp of mortal man. And, as she said it herself, since she hasn't met any of* our *Gods and Goddesses personally, and probably won't ever meet any personally, the Divine remains unknowable to her. Apparently, the Gods and Goddesses of her own universe don't manifest themselves very often, nor display very many overt miracles, so there are a sizeable number of her own people who feel the same way."*

"How sad," Mariel murmured. "Of course, I haven't personally seen a manifestation of the Goddess Natua, but still—"

"There you are, Mother!" Mikor popped out of one of the doors up ahead, grinning at them. He pointed at the room the chest was floating into. "That's your room! I picked it out for you. And *that* one will be mine," he added, pointing at the door next to it. "I'm supposed to stay in this one so Aunt Serina doesn't clobber me with a stray box or something. *That* one is *your* room, right?"

Evanor, finding himself the center of the youth's attention, nodded in confirmation. He didn't bother to speak, though; he was beyond whispering range with the boy. The woman at his side spoke up, though, addressing her son.

"Yes, Mikor, that is his chamber, and you're not allowed to go in there without Evanor's permission. *Or* into any of the other places that will be pointed out to you as off-limits," she asserted. "This is just like the Retreat, in that there are rooms you aren't allowed to go into. They might not be the nuns' cells, or their temple sanctum, or exactly like the other places that were off-limits there, but they're off-limits *here* all the same. Got it?"

Mikor nodded, his cap of curls bouncing with the motion. "I know. But that's okay, 'cause Uncle Dominor is going to keep giving me sword lessons—right?"

"*Be*cause he will keep giving you sword lessons, yes," Mariel agreed. Another box floated up the corridor, this time swerving into the room Mikor had pointed out to be his own. She gave Evanor a wry smile. "I think it would be wise to join my son in that spare room, there, while whoever it is continues to float things upstairs. It's probably Serina and that fellow with the light brown hair, the youngish-looking one."

"Morganen," Evanor filled in for her. *"You'll meet everyone formally soon enough."*

"I look forward to it. Do I get to meet *you* formally, or shall we remain informal in our interactions?" Mariel found herself teasing.

In a leap of faith, the blond mage decided that her gently teasing query was an opening between them, a doorway through which he could hopefully find his Destined bride. Picking up her hand, he pressed a kiss to her knuckles, unwittingly echoing what his twin had once done to her. Straightening, still holding Mariel's hand in the warmth of his, Evanor shifted close enough to lean down and dare to whisper into her ear, *"You may interact with me any way you desire . . ."*

Heat flooded her body, but not from her face down, as normal. Instead, it rushed from her womb up. Mariel resisted the urge to flap her free hand at her cheeks to cool them down. Her other hand tingled from her knuckles to her neck, from the touch of his lips to the touch of his breath, making her feel weak with excitement. Making that comment had been her way of testing the waters, like touching bathwater with the littlest finger of her hand. His reply, however, made her feel as if he'd immersed her arm halfway to her elbow instead.

It had been a long time since she last flirted with a man. Well, a man she was drawn to as much as she felt drawn to this one. There had been a few lighthearted exchanges after her husband's death, those times she had descended from the Retreat. But that was all they had been, lighthearted and ephemeral, since she would only be in that town for a few days, with no guarantee she'd come back to that particular place any time soon. This time . . . she was here for a good long stay in a place with several available men, including the one whispering into her ear.

"Motherrr," a familiar voice demanded impatiently. "Aren't you coming in here?"

Clearing her throat, Mariel checked the corridor for floating objects before moving to join her son. "I'm coming, son." She glanced over her shoulder at the blond, voiceless mage. "Will you join us?"

"Of course." How could he say anything else? Evanor wasn't blind, nor had he been deaf to her earlier comments. Mother and son were a package deal; for a man to have the one in his life, he had to accept the other. With open arms, preferably. Ev was tempted to try to win the boy over immediately, but two things stopped him. One, the lad was probably smart enough to see through any attempts to charm him, and two, Evanor couldn't exactly impress anyone without a fully functioning voice.

The best he could do was to be himself—or what little there was of him, without his voice—and hope that it would be enough for a favorable impression, where both mother and son were concerned.

"Mikor, this is Evanor, your Uncle Dominor's twin brother. Younger twin, am I right?" she asked him. Evanor nodded, and Mariel continued the introductions. "Evanor, this is Mikor, my son."

Evanor held out his hand. Mikor eyed it for a moment, then clasped and shook it with good manners. "A pleasure to meet you, milord. And, um, thank you for letting us stay near you—how big is this place anyway?"

"Very big. We'll go on a tour, later," Evanor promised him, releasing the smaller hand. Mikor narrowed his green eyes and tilted his head in confusion, so Ev repeated himself in a louder whisper. *"We'll go on a tour, later!"*

"That's right—you can't speak, 'cause you lost your voice, didn't you?" the youth asked him.

"*Be*cause he lost his voice, yes," his mother corrected him gently. "Consider it a lesson in learning how to listen carefully."

Mikor rolled his eyes, looking away from his mother. Evanor managed to catch his gaze and rolled his own eyes as well, silently commiserating with the boy. That made the youth snort, but only softly. Mikor eyed him a moment, then asked boldly, "So . . . what do you do? For a living, I mean. What's your job? Do you make a lot of money?"

"Mikor!" his mother protested.

Smiling, Evanor quieted her with a lift of his hand. *"That's a good question. I'm the Chamberlain. That means I manage the household for my family. I make sure everyone gets fed, assign all the chores such as when all the rooms are to be cleaned, that everyone has new clothes to wear, that they remember to go out and harvest the various fruits when the orchards are ripe, or hunt deer, or catch fish for freezing or salting when we're running low, that sort of thing. I also create magical things in my spare time, just like the rest of my brothers."*

"Really? Like what?" Mikor asked him.

"Most recently, a magical box that sings different sorts of songs." Evanor glanced at Mariel as he said that, wondering if Kelly would object to him borrowing her wedding gift. Somehow, he didn't think his sister-in-law would mind. More than that, there was a perfectly sound reason for him to borrow it. *"Actually, I should borrow the one I made from my sister-in-law. You might need or want to know what my voice sounds like normally, in order to be able to restore it fully."*

"I take it this box is enchanted to sing its songs in your voice, then?" Mariel asked him, curious to know what he normally sounded like. As it was, she didn't know if he was a tenor, a bass, or a baritone. His twin's voice was a low, soothing tenor, but the others ranged all over, with no two of them exactly alike, even if they were each from a set of twins. These brothers were all similar to some degree, but not entirely identical.

Evanor nodded. *"It was a wedding gift to Her Majesty. Her own people have something very similar. They don't have magic like we do, but the things they can do seem like a kind of magic anyway. I got the idea from her descriptions of their music boxes, and I think they will sell very well. Unfortunately . . . I lost my magic right along with my voice, not more than a week or so after I created the first box. There's a second one waiting for me in my workroom out in my tower, but it's unfinished."*

"Then we'll put it on the list of things to do. But not today," Mariel sighed, eyeing her son. Mikor looked eager to investigate. "Today . . . we have to unpack some of our things, once your aunt has finished floating them into our rooms. And I really should get my herbs planted as soon as possible, too. You can stay up here under Aunt Serina's supervision while I do that, young man."

"Awww," Mikor moaned. "I wanted to go exploring!"

"Not today. We have to unpack today, and plant things in the garden. Tomorrow, we can go exploring. Even if there's still a lot of things left to unpack," she added with a small smile, granting him that much of a compromise. "But no going off and exploring on your own until we've had the grand tour. Otherwise you won't know what's off-limits, nor what's unsafe. And *no* going outside the walls of this place without an escort from one of the brothers. That includes running off out of their sight even if they are escorting you. I want you to stay close to one of these men if you go outside, so they can keep you safe."

"But, Mother—"

"No buts, or I'll paddle your behind," Mariel asserted firmly. "Until we know what is safe and what is dangerous among the local life-forms, you're not allowed outside the palace walls. The last thing I want to do is have to treat my own son for a poisonous snakebite, or something."

She shot Evanor a hard look at that. He had been about to reassure both of them that there were no poisonous snakes on the Isle, or any other sort of lethal mobile creature—though there were some nasty plants to avoid—but decided to skip that admission under her stern gaze. It was apparently the right thing to do, for she nodded her head ever so slightly. Figuring that any protest otherwise at that moment would undermine her authority over her son, Evanor chose to bolster it instead.

"*My next-youngest brother, Trevan, knows all the various life-forms on the island, both plants and animals. I'll make sure he takes the time to tell you what to look out for, both good and bad. And your Aunt Serina, too. She hasn't actually left the castle grounds yet, so it hasn't come up,*" he added diplomatically. If he made it seem like all the newcomers had to learn such things, it wouldn't be singling the boy out for special restrictions. "*None of you should wander outside the perimeter walls without an escort, the first few times. Nor go into any of the tower chambers, along the outer wall.*"

"Well, we can just get together for a lesson on the island's flora and fauna, and where we can or cannot go, and get it over with in one go," Mariel agreed. "Do you think your brother would be willing to give us some examples? And maybe a quiz after his lecture?"

"Motherrrrr!" Mikor groaned, rolling his eyes again.

"For *all* of us, young man—including your Aunt Serina, as well as you and me. You always said you'd love to see *her* tortured with a test or two," she added shrewdly, smiling at her offspring.

His green eyes narrowed, then gleamed at the prospect. A gamin grin stretched his lips. "I can't wait to see her grumbling over some dumb essay question—just keep all the vases away from her while she's taking it, okay?"

"*Vases?*" Ev asked Mariel.

Mariel nodded sagely. "She likes to throw them when she gets frustrated."

Contemplating that fact, Evanor imagined his normally dignified twin attempting to dodge bits of flying pottery and snorted with amusement.

THREE

❦

"*Aaaaigh!* Ow ow ow! *BACK!*"

Evanor, startled, dropped the trowel he was using to dig a hole for one of the plants Mariel had brought. Shoving to his feet, he ran for the chicken yard, arriving just in time to see the curly-haired woman beating back one of the squawking, feathered devils. She managed to get the gate closed, the hen beating its wings on the wire penning it inside, a couple of loose feathers fluttering to the ground.

The disheveled Healer scraped her hair back from her face, panting. She winced at her arms, then twisted to look down at her legs. Evanor could see the holes pecked in her tights and winced in sympathy.

"*Are you all right?*" he asked, touching her shoulder gently. Her son was unpacking some of his things in his room, under his honorary aunt's supervision; Mariel planned to unpack hers later that evening, since they had plenty of lightglobes to spare for illumination. The others had scattered to do their own chores, including the preparation of lunch. Mariel had wanted to work on her plants right away, to get the most delicate of them planted before the day's end, so Evanor had offered to help her. Planting didn't require magic, after all.

When she realized she could check on the chickens at the same time, Mariel had decided to do so, to see if she could bring herself to perform regeneration experiments on them. Of course, Dominor had warned her about the nastiness of the poultry on this island, but Mariel hadn't believed him. Now she did.

She grimaced at her injuries, then glared through the wire fence. "Damned creatures . . . they're not chickens! They're demonic beasts from a feathered Netherhell!"

"*BkAW!*"

She jumped back a little as the last hen to attack her fluttered at the walls of its cage, squawking its opinion rudely. The hen cocked its head sharply, its red eyes bead-bright and its comb flopping with the motion, then strutted off without further concern. Sticking out her tongue, Mariel let Evanor tuck his arm around her, guiding her to a low section of stone wall. Once seated on the granite block, she hissed at the blood welling up from the scrapes and gouges on her skin.

"I have *never*, in all my life, met with such . . . such *ornery* beasts!"

Evanor's ears twitched, meaning the Ultra Tongue he had drunk was working to translate the word. "*Ornery . . . that translates as 'mean,' doesn't it?*"

"Stubborn and mean, yes," she agreed. "It's a Gucheran word. I grew up on the eastern border of Natallia in a trading town about five miles from Guchere. Naithong City. Rolling hills, golden with wheat and green with orchards. And *nice* chickens!"

The chickens in the coop clucked quietly to themselves. Evanor chuckled, but it only came out as puffs of air. "*I sometimes think the Council deliberately exiled us here with the nastiest poultry on the whole of the mainland as further punishment for simply being born who and what we are. Either that, or they exiled the chickens, and we were just an afterthought, playthings for the feathered little monsters to torment.*"

"Probably. I should Heal myself, in case their claws and beaks left an infection." Making a face, Mariel eyed her injuries one last time, then breathed deeply, settling her mind in a slow exhale so that she could concentrate. Evanor shifted back a little, no longer touching her. She appreciated the space in which to think, even as she missed the warmth of his touch. Another deep inhale, and she unfurled her powers through her fingertips with a thread of pure sound.

Evanor's eyes widened. He barely breathed, listening to her Sing—his own magic might be gone, but he knew Singing when he heard it. When he felt it, for that matter. Most mages used words to unlock their powers, and many of them used gestures as well. Some needed herbs, or runes, others needed crystals. A few used sound to focus their powers. He had been one of those, before literally losing his voice.

Hers was a beautiful voice, too. She was a mezzo, somewhere between an alto and a soprano . . . though she could dip into the lower registers, he noted. All but holding his breath, Evanor listened raptly, as her voice flexed into a simple arpeggio tune, following the back-and-forth movement of her fingers over the injured spots on her flesh.

The scrapes sealed themselves as she worked, some bleeding a little more freely before drying and turning pink with newly formed tissues. He might not have a true affinity for Healing, but Evanor had studied enough of the basics to know that making the punctures bleed helped to cleanse the threat of infection from each wound. Finished with her arms, she moved her hands and the power behind her voice to her legs, starting down at her ankles. The tears in her hose knitted themselves back together in the wake of her flesh closing and restoring itself whole.

Entranced, Evanor swayed slightly, following her self-ministrations as she worked. Longing built up within him, the more he listened to her Sing. The odds of encountering another Singing Mage weren't all that high under normal circumstances, but to have one come here to the island, *and* come at a time when it was logical for her to be *his* Destined, foreseen bride . . .

Mariel, aware that he was watching her avidly, nervously let her fingers caress one final sore spot on the back of her thigh. Her voice trailed into silence as the Healing finished; clearing her throat, she smiled at him. "There. That should do it. And it's not that different from—"

He couldn't help himself; Mariel had inadvertently seduced him, just by Singing. Unable to contain his excitement, his fascination, the thrill of meeting someone who clearly *knew* the importance of vocal cords to a Singing mage, someone who could Heal him and restore his powers, Evanor caught her face and pulled her into a soft kiss.

With her lips parted mid-speech, he had full access to the sweetness of her mouth. Sighing, Evanor tasted her with his tongue. The kiss—an expression of his surprised, exuberant joy—quickly became an end in and of itself. She hesitated only for a moment out of shock, then surprised him by responding within a heartbeat or two. That encouraged him to delve even farther into her kiss.

Instinct ruled between them for several more seconds, until Evanor slowly drew back, sighing and ending the kiss. He felt sated, pleased in a bone-deep sort of way. She had returned his kiss, and that was pleasure enough for him. Except that, with the kiss over, he suddenly realized he hadn't even *asked* her if she would let him kiss her. Instead, he had technically forced himself upon her. Even if she had reciprocated willingly enough, that was an inappropriate thing to do. Blushing, he released her face and quickly returned his hand to his lap.

"Ah . . . *sorry. If you didn't want that, I mean. And that it was without invitation. I just . . .*" He sought for something to say to explain himself to her as she blinked at him, then let his shoulders slump. "*It's your voice. It's truly beautiful. Like the rest of you.*"

Her face flamed at the double compliment. Flustered, Mariel wasn't quite sure how to respond. It had been an awfully long time since she had last been courted. Awkward though this was, it was more like being courted than the few rare times she had found a lover to flirt with and exorcise her physical needs since her husband's death. And though Milon *had* courted her in their youth, they had settled into a very pleasant but somewhat routine marriage in their later years together.

When she didn't respond, other than blushing and looking at the ground, Evanor swallowed. *"I've offended you, haven't I? I'll, um, not do that again—"*

"Oh, no!" Mariel quickly retorted, scrambling to correct his mistaken impression. "I just . . . It's been a while since someone complimented me like that. Not just with words, but with that . . . with a kiss. It was . . ." She broke off with a soft laugh. "I was about to say 'it was very nice,' but *nice* is such a bland, spiceless word, isn't it?"

"So then what would you call it?" Evanor asked her.

"Enjoyable. It was unexpected," she said, meeting his gaze with a smile, "but definitely enjoyable."

Relieved, pleased, Evanor shifted forward, intending to kiss her again. Her palm interposed itself between them, stopping him. He lifted one of his brows in silent inquiry.

"I'm your Healer, Evanor. Or I will be, for a little while. I think we should wait to get to know each other in *that* way. It's not as if I'm going anywhere for a good long while, you know," she added, shrugging. "At the very least, I wouldn't think of going elsewhere until after we know just how long it will take to get your problem cured. Which will be after I know if I can bring my skills back up to where they'll need to be." She leaned past him, eyeing the chickens inside their pen. "Though I see now why your twin wasn't at all distressed with the thought of someone experimenting with regeneration techniques on those *things* pretending to be poultry, over there."

A soundless laugh escaped Evanor. It faded quickly; he wanted to put his arm around her, to hug her close, but she was right. As his Healer, it would not be appropriate for them to have a relationship.

Except, if the Prophecy is correct and she's supposed to marry you, a corner of his thoughts proposed, *she'll have a relationship with you for the rest of your lives together, even if she has to be your Healer ever again . . . so why not start that relationship now?*

But on the other hand, she was right. They should take some time to get to know each other, first. Small steps would be best, Evanor decided. He wouldn't retreat, nor let her retreat . . . but he would only take small steps. So, though he longed to tuck the petite, plump Healer into the curve of his arm, Evanor settled for sliding his hand over hers where it rested on her lap. *"Then let's just get to know each other."*

She looked up at him and blushed, but didn't push his hand away. The corner of her mouth twitched up in a small smile, too. "That would be nice—*pleasant*. That would be very pleasant."

He grinned at her self-correction.

Mariel smiled back, then eyed the fenced poultry yard again. She sighed, considering it. "I think I'm going to have to brush up on my immobilization spells. I don't think I want to deal with those things if they're free to move around."

Parting his lips with an offer to petrify them with a spell, Ev shut his mouth, stifling a grimace. He couldn't do that, anymore. Not unless both his voice and his magics were restored to him. Frustrated, he didn't realize his free hand had curled into a fist on his thigh until Mariel glanced at it.

"Is something wrong?"

He hesitated, not wanting to admit a weakness in front of a beautiful woman. Of course, she wasn't just a beautiful woman; she was going to be his Healer, and Healing wasn't just about the physical problems. The whole of a person had to be treated, for them to completely heal. Breathing deeply, he forced himself to confess. *"I'm very frustrated, at the moment. I could have offered to immobilize them for you . . . had my magic still been functioning. But it isn't."*

Mariel looked up from their clasped hands with a curious look. "You've lost your magic?"

"I Sing, like you do," Evanor explained, holding her gaze. *"It's not Healing-related, except for the minor medical spells, but my magic lay in my voice. Without it . . . even the most instinctual cantrips are unreliable, beyond my conscious reach."*

"Well, then we'll just have to see what we can do about that." Mariel started to say more, but a series of bells rang in a set of odd, unpatterned notes, echoing across the compound. "That sounds strange . . ."

Evanor knew what it was and smiled. *"Those are the bells for the dining hall. It means lunch is ready."* His lips twisted in wry regret. *"I used to be the communications point for my brothers, receiving and sending messages across the island, wherever any of us were. Now . . . well, we had to come up with something different."*

"So you picked bells?" Mariel asked, rising with him from their impromptu bench.

"It's a work in progress," Evanor hedged, leading her toward the nearest door into the castle-like palace, since their hands were still intertwined. *"Trevan—my next-youngest brother, the one with the copper hair—is working on it."*

"I see. Well, if you'll pardon my saying, it literally sounds a bit awkward," she warned him. "And what if someone turns out to be tone-deaf? There are people out there who cannot tell one note from the next. They could end up migrating here."

He had to concede her point. *"Perhaps you should speak with Trevan about that. He admits it's a work in progress, and that he's looking for input."*

They met up with her son and friend outside the door to the dining hall, along with several others. There was a bit of confusion before they managed to get everyone into the room and sorted out. Saber directed his siblings to organize themselves into a line—all except for Evanor, who stayed next to Mariel, their hands still linked together—and cleared his throat.

"Now that we're all here, save for Rydan," the tall, muscular blond stated, addressing the Healer in their midst, "we should introduce ourselves formally. Would you like to start?"

"I'm Mariel Vargel, Healer, and this is my son, Mikor Vargel, son of the late Seer Milon, formerly one of the Guardians of Koral-tai," she said, touching her son briefly on the shoulder.

"I am Saber, the eldest brother of the males on this island," he returned, giving her a polite half-bow. "I was formerly the Count of Corvis over on Katan and am now Consort and husband to Her Majesty."

"Don't forget, you're also Her Majesty's Lord Protector, and General of the Armies," the darker of the two redheaded males interjected. He was standing near the end of the line, off to the left.

"Wait your turn; there are too many of us to introduce all at once," Saber admonished his second-youngest sibling. He gestured at the freckled redhead standing next to him. "This is my wife, Kelly, the Queen of Nightfall."

"Hello," Kelly offered with a grin and a little wave as she looked at Mikor and Mariel. "I believe we've already met."

Mariel chuckled and bowed, Natallian-style. "A pleasure, again, Your Majesty."

"You don't have to be that formal all the time," Kelly demurred. "Call me Kelly."

"Or virago," someone muttered; that was the brother whose hair was light copper, similar to Kelly's, though somewhat brighter than her strawberry blond shade.

"Hush," Saber reproved, frowning briefly at his sibling. "Next to her is my younger twin, Wolfer, Master of the Hunt and Captain of the Armies."

"Such as they are," Wolfer rumbled, folding his muscular arms across his equally broad chest.

Mikor touched his mother's wrist for a moment, then took a deep breath, squared his shoulders, and stated boldly, "I'm not afraid of you!"

Wolfer blinked his golden eyes. Saber arched a brow, exchanging puzzled looks with the others. Mariel, flushing with embarrassment, cleared her throat. "Um . . . that's nice, dear."

"Well, I'm *not*," Mikor mumbled, most of his courage having been used up.

Wolfer studied the youth, arching one of his brown eyebrows; he didn't comment, however.

"And next to Wolfer is his wife, Alys, Mistress of Herds," Kelly stated quickly, smoothing over the awkward moment.

"*Vara sudra ni'esketh,*" the curly-haired, gray-eyed woman stated, craning her head to look at her companion.

"I'm sorry; what did you say?" Mariel asked as the other men and women blinked.

Wolfer raised his other brow, his voice rumbling with surprise. "You didn't understand that?"

She gave him a bemused look. "No, was I supposed to?"

The woman Alys said something else, touching her husband's forearm. One of the others spoke up, the one with straight, light brown hair at the far end of the row. "Ah. I think I know what's wrong. Neither of them have drunk Ultra Tongue. We never got around to making it for Alys. She's the only one of us who hasn't taken any. Aside from the newcomers, of course."

Mariel instantly knew what he meant by that. With understanding came confusion. "But—I talked with her through the mirrors! I didn't need a translation potion then, so why would I suddenly need it now?"

The brothers eyed each other, shrugging.

"Of course!" The youngest mage-brother smacked his forehead with his palm. "I forgot about that! Rydan dusted the mirrors during their construction with the very last of the *myjiin* powder, in an attempt to extend how far their communication ability could be stretched. It wasn't enough to be used in brewing Ultra Tongue, but he thought it would help, and it did. It also seems to have added some translative ability to the mirrors." He grimaced and gave Mariel an apologetic look. "I'm afraid we won't be able to brew up a new batch until we can get our hands on more of it, and it's very rare and expensive."

"Not that rare," Serina scoffed. "I can sell you some, myself. I can't *give* it away, since I have a limited supply, but I can sell it to you for cheaper than you'd get it elsewhere."

"*You* have *myjiin* powder?" Dominor asked his wife. "Why didn't you tell me this, before?"

"Because it never came up?" the willowy blond retorted.

"Then we'll simply buy some, so that we'll all be able to understand each other," Wolfer stated. "Problem solved."

The young woman at his side nodded sharply in agreement, making her dark blond curls bounce.

That confused Mariel. She glanced between Wolfer and his wife, Alys. "Wait—did she understand what you said, just now? But . . . how is that possible, if you're talking in Natallian, yet she doesn't understand it?"

"Because we're *not* actually talking in Natallian," the same young mage as before explained to her, the one with light brown hair and aquamarine eyes. His words confused her, even as he drew her attention back to the end of the line. At her puzzled look, the mage continued, his aqua gaze studying her with a gentle, friendly expression. "Ultra Tongue makes you *hear* other languages as if they were your own, and allows you to *speak* other languages as if they were your own, only it's all done as if you were hearing or speaking the words in your own language, if with a slight accent. It's very much like breathing, too: You can do it consciously, choosing to speak in a specific accent for a specific language, or just speak normally and let the potion translate for all within range. Just like how you can control how fast or slow you draw air into your lungs consciously . . . or just let yourself breathe normally, without any conscious effort at all."

"Once you've drunk it and been properly enchanted, Mariel, your ears will twitch whenever you encounter a different language. Or your eyes will blur for a moment if you're trying to read something," Serina added, explaining it to her friend. "You see, when we just *talk*, we're speaking in *our* native language, but all of our listeners are hearing us in *their* native tongue, whatever it is. However, when we consciously adopt a particular language-accent, we're speaking in *that* language, and that language alone. That's how it works. I made some for myself back when I was in Guchere, so I came to the Retreat already able to speak and be understood by everyone, but since I didn't think you'd be leaving Natallia, I never bothered to make you any."

"And that's why some of the words and terminology *I* use aren't translated," Kelly offered. "My homeworld and culture are so different from this one, that there are terms and ideas that just have no parallel. The same goes for some of the local words the brothers have used, leaving *me* occasionally confused."

"Ultra Tongue does the same for reading and writing, as it does for hearing and speaking," Serina continued. "When you read, your brain interprets the other language as it would your own, only you see it in a specific style of writing—block print versus cursive, angular versus scrolled. And when you write, you write it as if it were

your own language, but in whatever particular style of penman-
ship you *intend* the words to be written in, with the language guiding
your hand. Your body will only write the words in the language you
concentrate on, or if you don't, in your own language, and once it's
written down, it stays in that language, regardless of who reads it . . .
which makes it unlike the spoken version.

"But it will respond very readily to any translation charms that
are applied, even if you don't personally know the language that was
used for the writing, as a result of the lingering magical residue from
the Ultra Tongue. That's why it's both a potion and a spell. The
mage applying the potion binds it to your own magics so that it is a
permanent part of you," Serina concluded.

"Wait—I'm from a universe without any magic. How does it
work for me, then?" Kelly asked the others.

"But your world *does* have magic, Kelly," the aqua-eyed mage
stated confidently. Mariel realized suddenly that he and Kelly both
had aquamarine eyes. "It just has such a tiny amount that your people cannot tap into it, under most circumstances."

"It's like a small scrap of sea sponge that has been compressed
between your fingers until it is almost completely flat," Dominor explained for her. "When it is that flat, it cannot hold a lot of magical
moisture, for lack of a better term. Here, in this universe, the
'sponge' has room to expand, and can hold enough to empower the
Ultra Tongue. You can also interact with various pre-spelled artifacts, such as amulets and lightglobes, and benefit from the magic of
a Healing spell . . . but that's the extent of your capacity. You just
don't have a big enough sponge to be a mage."

"Ah." Kelly pondered that for a moment, then shrugged. "Okay,
so I'm not a mage. I wasn't one before, and I'm not one now. I can
live with that. Just remember, I can still make you eat dirt!"

Mariel choked on a laugh at that. She grinned at the next brother
waiting to be introduced, enjoying the way his cheeks flushed. "I
remember you mentioning that ability of hers, Dominor. I look
forward to seeing it in action!"

"*Not* on me," Dominor quickly denied, slashing a hand through
the air.

"Yes, well, I'm sure you've more than met Dominor, thirdborn brother, and our Lord Chancellor and Master of Ceremonies," Kelly said, resuming the introductions. "Plus his wife, Serina, who is now our Royal Exchequer."

"*Royal* Exchequer?" Mariel repeated, arching an amused brow at her friend.

The tall, willowy mage grinned at Mariel. "I may not be the Guardian of Koral-tai anymore, but at least I'm still gainfully employed."

"I already figured that much. I was mocking the fancy title," Mariel quipped, winking. She returned her attention to Saber as he continued.

"The man next to you, of course, is Evanor, our Lord Chamberlain, your impending patient."

Evanor gently squeezed her fingers with his, smiling at her. Mariel blushed. She enjoyed the introduction more when he held out his free hand to Mikor, who shook it, grinning.

"Next is Trevan," Saber stated, gesturing at the coppery redhead.

"We aren't sure what he does, so we made him our Lord Vizier," Kelly quipped, teasing the mage.

Trevan gave her a dirty look. "Says the woman who was summoned here by my bells . . . A pleasure to meet you," he continued, bowing to Mariel and Mikor both. "I'm actually a lot more useful than she implies."

Evanor narrowed his brown eyes, a silent warning to his sibling that the younger mage had better not be *too* useful where Mariel was concerned. She was *his* Destiny . . . or at least had the potential to be. As far as he was concerned, his next-youngest brother could wait for his own bride to show up.

Or until Mariel says, flat out, that she doesn't want you and will never love you, Evanor's conscience forced him to admit. *Just because she's holding your hand doesn't mean she's going to fall into your arms that easily . . . or that some other disaster isn't going to crop up and threaten your attempt at a relationship with her.*

After all, his twin hadn't had an easy time in wooing his own mate, with Dominor first being bought as a war slave, then oath-bound to help Serina with a complex piece of magic, and then all the misunderstandings that had happened between the two of them from simple miscommunications. Saber and Kelly hadn't even liked each other at first, and had argued vociferously until an attack by magically poisonous snakes had forced the two of them together during their hours-long recuperation. Even Wolfer and Alys had suffered a few troubles along the way. Of course, they had been friends throughout most of their childhood. The renewal of that friendship had shortened the length of their courting considerably, but Alys' uncle had threatened all of them . . . and stolen Evanor's voice.

Mariel eyed the coppery-haired mage while Evanor was thinking. "You're the one that was injured by the Mandarite gun, aren't you?"

Teeth flashing in a grin, Trevan admitted, "That was me, yes. Would you like to look at my scar?"

"He'll take any chance he can to strip off his tunic for a lady," Kelly interjected wryly as Mariel's brows rose. "Even if she's not interested."

"Ow, a hit! I've been unfairly wounded again," Trevan mock-complained, pressing his hand to his heart. "I meant for our *Healer* to look at it in a purely *professional* sense. Frankly, I don't trust my own brothers to have done the best job possible. I know them too well."

"Then on a purely professional level, I will," Mariel agreed as the mage with the aquamarine eyes leaned over and whapped his elder sibling on the arm. "Another time, however. I don't know about your customs, but where we come from, men do not come to the dining table half dressed."

Trevan started to reply, then closed his mouth, catching Evanor's pointed stare. He rubbed at his shoulder, glared at the last in the line, and subsided. Wolfer, the big fellow with the golden eyes, folded his arms across his chest, clearly struggling against an urge to smile at his younger sibling's expense.

"Unfortunately, Trevan's twin, Rydan, isn't very fond of daylight hours," Saber told Mariel. "You'll see him this evening. He joins us for breakfast and supper, but not for much else."

"Except for storms," Kelly interjected. "Then he just wanders all over the place. He's a little strange at times, but mostly harmless . . . I think."

Her hedge made Mariel wrinkle her nose. "I'll take your word for it. So long as he won't make a fuss over my or my son's presence, it should be fine."

"Does *he* have a title?" Mikor asked Kelly. "The one who's not here? All the others have a title, so far."

Kelly smiled at him. "Yes, he does. Lord Protector of Nightfall."

"But stay out of his tower," Trevan warned the boy. "That's the one that's due north. In fact, you're not allowed in any of the towers along the outer wall, without an escort. Go where you're not allowed, and we'll turn you into a toad for a week."

Mariel noticed the gleam of interest in her son's green eyes and quickly cleared her throat. "What he *means* is that you'll be punished for a solid week. If you *like* being turned into a toad, then you'll be put to scrubbing floors and washing clothes instead."

Subsiding, the boy pouted silently, crossing his arms. Peering at Wolfer, Mikor refolded his arms just so, visibly attempting to look like the larger, intimidating male. Biting back a smile, Mariel turned her attention to the next one in line, the auburn-haired fellow. "And you are . . . ?"

"Koranen, Lord Secretary to Her Majesty, and Pyromancer extraordinaire," he introduced himself, giving her a bow and a smile. "Seventhborn of the eight of us."

"A pleasure to meet you, Koranen," Mariel returned, smiling back at him.

"And the last one down there is my Royal Mage, Morganen," Kelly introduced, nodding at the mage with the aquamarine eyes and the light brown hair.

Morganen nodded to Mariel and her son, giving each of them a pleasant smile, his arms lightly folded across his chest. He was the one who had been full of helpful comments. "Welcome to Nightfall, both of you. Now, since I was given the task of preparing lunch today, and I'd rather not see all my hard work wasted, if you'll take your places over here, we can get to it before it turns cold. It's chicken pie and a green salad, and sticky buns for dessert, which I think our youngest new citizen will thoroughly enjoy pecking at."

Mariel bit her lip in an effort to not laugh. She turned her head into Evanor's bicep, shoulders shaking with mirth. Evanor's eyes gleamed as well, though no sound passed his parted, grinning lips.

"Alright," Mariel said. "Let me see if I've got this right. The eldest is Saber, with the golden blond hair. His twin is Wolfer, the muscular fellow. Then Dominor, of course, and Evanor. Trevan is the lighter redhead, the one named, um . . . Rydan, that's it," she managed, smiling, "has hair blacker than Dominor's, and he's sixthborn and not here. Then Koranen, the darker redhead, and Morganen at the end."

"That's all of us males," Morganen agreed. "And the females?"

"Easy," Mikor snorted, answering for his mother. He pointed at them. "That's Kelly, the queen, and Alys, who talks funny."

His honorary aunt reached over and whapped him lightly on the back of his head, mussing his curls more than anything else. "What about the rest of us, scamp?"

"Fine. You're my Aunt Serina, and she's my mother, Mariel," he added, rolling his eyes at having to name everyone. "*Now* can we eat?"

"Yes, now we *may* eat," his mother corrected him, nudging him toward one of the seats.

The meal was interspersed with questions about the island. Mikor immediately wanted to know where he could go—which was almost anywhere in the four main wings, excepting only the chamber at the very top of the donjon—and where he couldn't go—which was into individual bedchambers and the eight towers and their attached workshops along the outer wall. Or outside the palace compound, without an escort. Mikor pouted a little, but not for long; he had sticky buns to eat, after all.

Mariel asked Trevan to tell them about the dangerous flora and fauna of the island, which he did by showing them illusions of the toxic plants in question, plus a few stinging and biting insects that would be a good idea to avoid. There weren't many, thankfully. Mikor teased his honorary aunt with an impromptu quiz, making the pale blond woman in turns annoyed and amused, until she threatened to steal away his sticky bun. At that point, Mariel threatened to separate the two of them and send them to their rooms, making the other adults laugh.

It wasn't until Evanor caught and squeezed her hand for her attention that the final important matter was broached. Leaning in close, she let the blond mage whisper in her ear, while the others joked among themselves. His breath against her neck was just as distracting as it had been earlier that morning, but she firmly reminded herself to pay attention to his words, not his proximity.

"So . . . you said there were three possible ways of curing my problem. What are they?"

"Ah, that. Yes," Mariel agreed, leaning back again so that she could nod her head without hitting him. "There are indeed three ways to restore your lost voice, each with its own risks and rewards."

Her words caused the others to fall silent, making her the center of their attention. Evanor nodded to her, his whisper audible in the quiet. *"Go on . . ."*

"The first way to restore your voice would be to literally replace it with the vocal cords of someone else. Of course, this presumes that there is a blood relative who is willing to give up his own voice for you," Mariel admitted.

Judging from the dismayed looks on his brothers' faces, Evanor didn't think that was an option. Not that he'd ask them to do so if there was another way, of course. It also didn't sound like it would give him his magic back. *"Even if one of them agreed, would that restore my powers?"*

"Probably not, since you are a Voice mage, yet none of your brothers are Voice mages themselves," Mariel replied, wrinkling her nose at the admission. "But it would take only a single day of preparation and an hour's worth of actual enchanting to complete."

"What are his other options?" Saber asked her, speaking for his fourthborn brother. "I sincerely hope that one isn't the best of the lot."

"Option number two would be to regrow Evanor's voice box

over a span of about six to eight months, depending on several factors. The good news is that you would gradually be able to speak above a whisper. The bad news is, the more you speak and use your vocal cords, the longer it will take for them to regrow," the Healer told Evanor, meeting his brown gaze honestly. "And if you stressed them too much . . . it *might* affect your ability to Sing. This wouldn't be a concern for any other type of magical affinity, but in your case, it could be."

"And option number three?" Trevan asked her. Across the table from him, Wolfer was murmuring into Alys' ear, repeating and thus translating what the Natallian Healer was saying.

"A forced regrowth of the vocal cords that would only take about three weeks . . . but both his ability *and* his desire to speak would have to be spell-blocked," Mariel confessed. "Any attempt to try to form a word would warp the regeneration process, because it would make the nerves attempt to twitch the muscles while they were still growing. That means you wouldn't even be able to whisper, and I mean *able to* whisper. Nor could you shape words with your lips, so no lipreading by others. What the mind desires, the vocal cords would twitch with the urge to produce. I would have to entirely block your ability to communicate verbally. That's the bad news.

"The *good* news is that this method has the greatest chance of restoring his lost powers," Mariel told the others. She looked at Evanor. "Personally, I think this is your best option. I did find a pair of records of it being used successfully on Voice mages in the past. Their magic, which had been damaged along with their voices, was restored concomitantly with the regeneration of their throat tissues.

"Of course, those were from wounds, not an absolute absence of vocal cords, but the spell can regenerate the whole thing just as easily as a part of it. Though it will take correspondingly longer, thus the three weeks of being utterly wordless. I'll give you time to make up your mind, since the restoration won't happen immediately. I'll still have to practice whichever spell form I'd need to use."

"*Third option.*" Evanor didn't even have to think about it. Three weeks of not being able to communicate would be even more frustrating than what he suffered right now, but if it could restore his voice and powers in whole, it was the only viable option. *"Silence me completely. I want my voice and my magic back in full."*

"It won't be that bad, surely," Serina asked her friend, glancing between Mariel and Evanor. "I mean, he can still communicate by writing on a slate or something, right?"

"Well, yes, he should still be able to do that, but he wouldn't even be able to form a word with his lips. Just with his fingers."

"Ay Ess Ell!" Kelly exclaimed, unsettling most of the others. At their puzzled looks, she explained. "ASL, short for *American* Sign Language; it's what the deaf people in the country where I come from use. I know a little bit of it. If I can remember how it goes, will the Ultra Tongue be able to translate that for all of us? It *is* a language, after all." She frowned for a moment in thought, then smiled and touched her chest, tapped her first two fingers on each hand together, then shifted the fingers of one hand slowly and awkwardly in some sort of pattern. "There! Did anybody get that?"

"I think you would have to be a native speaker, Sister," Morganen stated, quelling her enthusiasm. "Not because it's a hand language as opposed to a voice language, but rather because you just don't *know* it. You have to truly *know* a language, for the Ultra Tongue to recognize it . . . and since I couldn't make sense of what you just 'said,' I don't think you know it well enough. It's like the way the words of a spell aren't translatable."

Her shoulders slumped. "Rats. I hoped it would work."

"Thanks anyway," Evanor praised her.

Kelly nodded and picked at the nuts decorating the top of her sticky bun, shrugging philosophically. "Well, I'm sure our newest sister-in-law can spare a chalkboard or two for you to use, in the interim."

"*If* I can find one that isn't already infused with arithmancy equations," Serina muttered. At Dominor's pointed look, she sighed. "Alright, alright, I'll clear one for him!"

"Well. I'd like to get started on practicing the spell in the next couple of days," Mariel said. "I still have to put the rest of my herbs into the ground and unpack enough of my things to find the book with the Healing rite in it. I'll also need a place to work—oh, and Evanor said something about a music box that plays the sound of his voice. If I know what to aim for as the end result, it might help ensure a fuller Healing, speeding up the process a little."

"I'll bring it to supper," Kelly promised her.

Evanor squeezed Mariel's hand, giving her a very warm, pleased smile. *"Thank you."*

She blushed and nodded her head. "You're quite welcome. Um . . . after having visited the, ah, chickens, I don't think I'll have any qualms about practicing on them. It shouldn't take me too long to be confident enough to regenerate your voice, but since it's such an important part of you, I want to take my time and get it right on them before I attempt the spell on you."

"I appreciate it."

Kelly snorted. "Trust me, you can practice on the damned citizen-chickens *all* you want. I'll even make it a Royal Decree: I hereby proclaim that our resident Healer may torture the citizen-chickens all she likes, in the pursuit of perfecting her medical skills. Just so long as there's enough of them left to lay eggs afterward, of course. *And* so long as *I* don't have to collect said eggs from them."

Her mock-shudder made the others laugh.

FOUR

Like most empires, Katan was technically run by its Sovereign and his or her Council of Mages. But, like most empires, in reality it was run by its bureaucracy. And like most bureaucracies, it was in turn run by paperwork. Paperwork that took time to file, sort, collate, process, digest, and figure out whom to pass it along to next. If it was important enough to be passed along, of course.

Thus, despite the speed at which verbal information could travel with the advent of modern magical communications such as scrying mirrors and mirror-Gates, it took literally months for the dutifully filed paper accounts of what the exiled Corvis brothers had bought from the trader-captains to collate and trickle their way up to the desk of one Lord Consus of Kairides, Councilor of Sea Commerce.

This was, to some extent, a fortuitous event. It could have been Duke Finneg, Councilor of Conflict Resolution. The Duke hadn't been a member of the Council at the time of the Corvis brothers' exile; if he had, he would have been more inclined to just kill them outright rather than exiling them. So long as his version of

Conflict Resolution ended the impending conflict immediately, the Duke didn't care about the vague mutterings of ancient Seers. Lord Consus, on the other hand, believed that there was no way to escape Destiny, save by removing oneself as far from it as possible.

Fortunately for the exiles, he had been the only Councilor in range of the Hall of Mirrors the day that the Count-in-Exile, Saber of Corvis, contacted the mainland about some sort of spurious "invasion" from across the Eastern Ocean, and thus the only one to have learned of the presence of a woman among the eight mage-born sons a few months ago. It hadn't sounded like much of a disaster, to him. Being the Sea Commerce Councilor, he knew that there was no way the decades-old civil war raging across the sea would spill onto Katani shores.

Once the . . . what were they called? Mandarites, that was it . . . once the Mandarites tried to trade with us and the Natallians got wind of it, they'd just cut off their foe. It had happened a few decades before, after all, according to the logs of his predecessors. No, it was the same as the futility of trying to send their own ships across the Eastern Ocean; it just wasn't worth the cost to either side to attempt any trade, given the ferocity of the ongoing war. *If the Mandarites had come to plunder Nightfall Isle, that was the problem of the exiled brothers. Let them bear the brunt of the forays and distract the plunderers from coming close enough to bother Katan. So long as the Empire stays as far away from the matter as possible, how could we possibly be drawn into any conflicts?*

Thus he had put the matter of that mouthy, copper-haired woman out of his mind as much as possible and focused his efforts on keeping Katan's coastlines safe and prosperous. Certainly, he didn't seek to stir the Council pot until it boiled over by mentioning the incident to any of the others. And, thankfully, the brothers hadn't bothered to contact the mainland again, making it easy to keep the matter quiet and let the distant Threefold God of Fate unfold things however They willed. By preference, far away from Lord Consus, the Council, and all of mainland Katan.

Until, reading his way through the quarterly reports, he ran across the collated report from the Sea Commerce suboffice in Orovalis City. Lord Consus read the report of yards of trims and ribbons, silk, cotton, and so forth, the bottles of softsoaps and perfume oils, with an increasingly furrowed brow. There were the usual requests in the lists of supplies, cheeses, preserved beef, kegs of grains, barrels of flour, the occasional tool or rare ingredient for one of the Artifacts they sold in exchange for more of the same. Basically, all things that the brothers couldn't produce for themselves wound up on these quarterly report lists . . . but those extra items bothered him.

Turning to the mirror on the wall behind his desk, Consus tapped the rim, muttered the activation words, and added the destination. "Orovalis City, Sea Commerce Suboffice."

It only took a few moments for the mirror to make the connection, shifting first to rippling blue. The patterns of color were designed to prevent anyone from scrying into a government office without permission, a security precaution against having state secrets stolen. When the woman on the other end touched her own mirror, banishing the pattern and displaying her tanned face, she blinked in surprise to see her topmost superior staring at her. "Councilor Consus! Er . . . what an honor. Puzzling, but an honor. How can the Orovalis Suboffice assist you?"

"I need the most up-to-date information on the items being traded on Nightfall Isle, if you please," the Councilor said.

The woman, Meredin if he remembered right, lifted her dark brows in surprise, but turned away, rummaged through a drawer just at the edge of the mirror's angle of view, and came back with a handful of papers. At his nod, she started reading through the lists of supplies. Standard staples, the occasional tool . . . more requests for cloth, perfumed soaps, largish quantities of paint pigments of all things, high-grade silica from the Glazier's Guild in *very* large tonnage . . . a whole herd of dairy cattle, including two bulls for freshening? Enquiries about acquiring a flock of sheep in a future trade? Requests for crates of chalk stones and panes of raw slate large enough to be turned into chalkboards? *Chalkboards?*

The list—which included an increasing number of nonstandard

items—thoroughly puzzled him. It *was* possible that the brothers had requisitioned these things for a new line of artifacts. Consus picked up the quarterly report at his side, checking the items being sold by the brothers. Magical weapons, lightglobes, warding amulets . . . the usual. He eyed Meredin. "Is there anything of note in the papers you haven't forwarded yet, regarding the objects that the brothers are now selling?"

She nodded and flicked through the sheaves in her hand. "Yes . . . there's a notation by the sea merchants that the exilees are now demanding payment for the salt and algae blocks, which were previously taken for free. As you may remember, it was decreed that half the net profit from the sale of those blocks was to be considered the export-import tax for the sea traders being able to do business with the brothers on the Isle. That profit margin has been cut down to roughly a quarter of what it originally was, because of this change in sales policy, sir. The report also indicates that the traders refused to buy the salt blocks the first time this happened, but they have since given in and paid the demanded price.

"Between this and the purchase of those trims and perfumes, I'm beginning to think something very strange is happening on Nightfall, sir," Meredin stated, as the door to Consus' office opened behind him. "The captains say they haven't seen any sign of women on the Isle, but my instincts—"

"*Women* on the Isle?" a voice interrupted, forcing Consus to swivel his chair around.

Duke Finneg stood on the other side of his desk, scowling at the older man. Where Consus was ordinary, nondescript, average in height, weight, and skin tone, with thinning grayish brown hair, hazel brown eyes, and a body of middling fitness for his middling years, Duke Finneg was a broad brick wall of dark hair, dark eyes, and dark skin over strong muscles. And a strong, dark attitude. On the one hand, internal rebellions had been put down more swiftly and decisively in the last two years than in the whole of the last two decades under his auspices, but on the other hand, the warrior-mage had a very bad habit of poking his nose into his fellow Councilors' business.

"What's this about *women* on Nightfall Isle? Women aren't allowed on that island, and for good reason!"

"I didn't say that!" the woman on the other side of the mirror said hastily. "I said there's been no *sign* of women on the Isle."

"But I heard something about perfume," he said, casting both of them a suspicious look. "Men don't buy perfume!"

Consus arched one of his brows, but carefully kept to himself his opinion that Finneg would smell a lot better if he were to use a scented soap. A heavily scented soap. The man was in the halls of the Council Chambers, not in some practice salle, yet he still insisted on wearing a boiled-leather breastplate. Sweaty leather was only attractive to other sweaty men, in Consus' opinion. Not refined mages of higher hygienic standards. But as it would be political suicide to say as much, Consus merely demurred, "Some of us do, Your Grace. And some Artifacts require the use of essential oils in their construction."

"If it involves anything unusual and that Isle, I want it investigated," Finneg asserted, leaning on his fellow Councilor's desk. "*Has* there been anything unusual happening on Nightfall Isle?"

Having survived three times as many years in bureaucracy and politics as the younger mage-warrior, Consus wasn't nearly as intimidated as his colleague undoubtedly wanted him to be. "If there is, it is *my* department that shall investigate it."

Unfortunately, at the same time he said that, Meredin on the other side of the mirror-connection said, "Just the fact that they're insisting on selling the salt blocks to the traders, instead of letting them be taken away for free."

His Grace narrowed his dark brown eyes. "Isn't that *our* income, not theirs?"

"Well, yes," the woman in the suboffice agreed hesitantly.

"If they think they can do that, they will be taught to rethink the error of their ways. I will not stand by and watch the Council's funds being appropriated by a bunch of exiles. Councilor Thera needs to know about this outrage!"

The duke headed out the door, making noises about visiting the woman himself, to get her to pay attention to the seriousness of the matter. Consus thought it was over the top, but then any excuse to go after the brothers was apparently a good excuse, to the duke's way of thinking.

Consus winced in realization, picturing the last bit of tranquility for his day vanishing from his office along with His Grace. It looked like he would have to take some of these reports home to finish reading them. *If* he had enough time to do that. Viscountess Thera, Councilor of Tax Collection, was likened to a pookrah when it came to tax evasion, biting down and refusing to let go until her prey was limp and dead. She was proportioned like one, too; overly large, long-jawed, sharp-toothed, and quite deadly when she ran in a pack of her fellow financialists, the Councilor of the Exchequery and the Councilor for the Imperial Budget.

Since news of the incident had come through *his* Department, Consus knew he'd not only have Finneg's sweaty-leather scent breathing down the back of his neck, but Thera's flowery fumes as well. Technically, his department was an adjunct of the Councilor of Commerce's, not the Councilor of Tax Collection, but sea-based import and export taxes were gathered through his branch's auspices. He was thus more acquainted with the tenacious arithmancer than he cared to be.

Between the two of them, Finneg and Thera would probably take this matter to the whole of the Council for investigation . . . and that meant Consus would no longer be able to hold to his nice, comfortable, let-*them*-deal-with-it attitude, regarding the Corvis brothers and their Curse. One thing he knew for absolute certain: He was *not* going to tell his fellow Councilors that he himself already knew about a woman being present on the island.

Sighing roughly, he directed Meredin to send him all the data she had collected to that point on the brothers' trading habits, and anything else she could collect in the way of gossip. He gave her a deadline of a week to track down the various sea captains to question them about any and all incidents they might have observed, then closed the mirror, restoring his own reflection.

He hated having to start something that would surely draw the

Prophesied Disaster into Cursing the mainland, too, but he was a Councilor, and he would do his job. If he had to.

Kelly brought the music box to supper. Demonstrating how the levers activated the magic and how each of the squares contained two songs apiece, she set it to play quietly, providing background music during the evening meal. The others talked and laughed over the noise, once the demonstration was complete. They had heard Evanor singing in the past and thought nothing more of it, save for pity that he couldn't sing right now.

Mariel, hearing the voice of her patient for the first time, felt a shiver race down her arms and spine. It was quite possibly the most *beautiful* voice she had heard, if such a word could be applied to a man. Clear, strong, yet deft enough to be delicate in the quieter passages. There was a touch of vibrato on the lower notes, making her want to press her ear to his chest to feel as well as hear the vibrations. Once he had his voice back, of course; pressing her ear to his chest right now would only reveal the rhythm of his heart. When the recording lifted his voice in an arc of melody, it sent more goose bumps prickling along her skin from the sheer emotion invested in the words . . . of a love song, she realized, flushing.

Hoping no one noticed the heat in her cheeks, Mariel felt the urge to sequester herself in her new bathing tub. She had brought her collection of unguents and felt an urge to have a "feminine moment," as Milon used to call them. Her late husband had gently teased her about wanting to be all flowery-scented and soft-skinned for him. Mariel missed doing that for a man. Once in a rare while, Milon had joined her, but most of the time when he had caught her bathing in softsoap bubbles and essential oils, he had retreated to their bedchamber, changing the linens, lighting candles, and preparing himself for her in his own way.

It was the romance she missed most. Once in a while, after her husband's passing, she had left the Retreat, gone down to some town or city, and found a willing bed partner for a few hours. But that was just sating one's lust. Flirtation had been fast, blunt, and to

the point, since she rarely had much time to devote to such pur-
suits. Being much more interested in men than in women, it just
hadn't been the same when one of the Koral-tai nuns had flirted
with her, though she could have spent a lot more time flirting with
one of them, seeing as how they had all lived in the same place. It
was nice to be flirted with; Mariel hadn't ever denied that. But flirting with a woman just wasn't the same as flirting with a man, in her
opinion.

She wasn't cut out to be a nun. They were forbidden congress
with men, and she was too interested in the pleasures one could
share with a man to give that up. Since she wasn't interested in the
pleasures to be shared with a fellow woman, that hadn't been a viable alternate outlet for her sexual frustrations, either. Mariel
wanted it all. Sex, romance, love. All of it.

Eventually, the libido would fade; as a Healer, she knew there
was only so much one could do to keep it alive as the body aged. If
one didn't have a true companion, someone to share an emotional
bond as well as a physical one, then one didn't have anything to fall
back on as they aged. She *had* thought she'd found the right companion for her in Milon . . . but Fate had taken him from her.
Mariel suspected that Milon had known well in advance that he
wouldn't live long enough to grow old with her. He had done little
things, made certain comments, that suggested he knew she would
one day move on without him. That she should not cling to his
memory forever, but be willing to open her heart and fill it with a
new love.

Such as reminding her that the more a person loved, the more
they *could* love—if she loved Milon, she would love their son. If she
loved Milon and Mikor, she would love Serina as well, and so on and
so forth. Not that Mariel *loved* Evanor. Yet. His *voice*, maybe . . .

That thought made her smile.

Warmth caressed her ear, as the source of her smile whispered
into it. "*Are you enjoying the music, or is it something else that makes you
smile?*"

"Both," Mariel admitted with a touch of diffidence. Turning her
head, she almost bumped noses with him, he had leaned that close to

her. She smiled again, looking into his tawny eyes. "You have a beautiful voice. I can see why everyone is so eager to restore it."

"So, what else makes you smile?" Evanor wanted to know. Unfortunately, his twin said something at the same time, drowning out his words. At Mariel's puzzled look, he tried again. This time, Koranen laughed loudly at some jest of Trevan's. Frustrated, he sighed heavily, closing his eyes in a bid for patience. A warm palm touched his cheek, snapping them open again. Mariel angled her head, leaning her ear as close as she could to his lips. *"I asked, so what else makes you smile?"*

That made her blush. Mariel knew it would be proper to remain reserved in her interactions, while she was his Healer. She met the aquamarine eyes of the island's youngest brother as she figured out what to say. Something in the younger mage's gaze reminded her of Milon, oddly enough. A sort of *knowing* in those eyes. *But he's not a Seer*, Mariel reassured herself, looking away. *The Gods decreed that Seers could channel energy into Curses and Prophecies, but not that they could be Mages and cast spells. And that Mages could channel magics into spells and objects, but not that they could predict or mold the future as a Seer can . . .*

Aware of Evanor waiting patiently for a reply, Mariel ducked the issue with a murmured, "I might tell you later."

Across the table, Morganen quirked one of his brows, but said nothing. Having amplified his hearing for picking up his fourthborn brother's whispers, he had also heard Mariel's reply. Morg had seen her reaction to the longing in the song Evanor had preserved in the music box, moments ago. She didn't look entirely comfortable thinking such thoughts, yet. Not when confronted by their source. Unfortunately, today was too busy, filled with other things that needed to be done. Like settling her and her son into the routines of the castle and its inhabitants. Tomorrow would be busy, too.

He would approach the Healer in their midst with certain things she needed to hear, and soon. But not just yet. The two hadn't spent enough time together yet to form real opinions about their impending, predestined relationship. Morg smiled to himself; he knew that Evanor could be quite charming, and very sweet when he was interested in a woman. Hopefully, the youngest of them wouldn't have to interfere too much to nudge these two together.

ℳariel gently brushed one of her son's wayward curls from his brow. He yawned sleepily, his murmurs about what he was going to do to make his new suite even better degenerating into wordless mumbles. It had been a long day for both of them, filled with excitement, hard work, and extra hours added because of their westward change in position around the giant globe of their world. She thought she heard a mumble about sword practice, and smiled wistfully.

He's getting so big. Thinking about becoming a man. Milon, you'd be proud of him . . . and thank Natua we're now in a place where he can have some positive male influence as he makes that transition. At least, I hope *they'll be positive male influences*, she allowed herself to hedge. So far, the brothers had been noisy, inquisitive, polite, and helpful. Time would tell if those latter two qualities would remain, once the shiny patina of "new arrivals" had worn off and things returned to whatever passed for normal around this place.

Exiled to an island just for having a Seer mention them. Mariel wanted to call it silly, but after eight years of marriage to a Seer, she knew how people could sometimes overreact to the things that were Prophesied about them. She also didn't know the full text of this "Curse" of theirs. Serina had told her a little about it, after learning of it from Dominor, but she hadn't learned much. Mariel had the impression that the brothers weren't comfortable talking about it. Resolving to speak with Kelly, since the redhead seemed a rather straightforward type who wouldn't hedge—perhaps not the best approach for a political figure, but not a disaster either, with a population as small as the thirteen of them, sans those hideous citizen-chickens—the Healer gently rapped the lightglobe by the bedroom door down to its lowest glow and left her son to sleep.

These lightglobes were a bit different from the suncrystals favored in Natallia; they weren't controlled by a single rune on the wall per chamber, and they had to be adjusted individually, but they *could* be adjusted. It would be nice to wake up in the middle of the night, tap one of these things softly, and *not* be blinded by a sudden burst of light for once. Of course, it would be nice to not have to wake up in the middle of the night at all.

Tired from a long day of planting herbs and sorting through her belongings, Mariel debated that bath she had thought about, earlier. On the one hand, she was a bit stiff and sore from all the work she had done. On the other hand, she was worn out from said work. Her shoulders in particular were rather stiff. Closing the outer door to her son's new quarters, she rubbed at her muscles, padding over to the door to her own chambers.

"Are you all right?"

The harsh whisper startled her. Whirling, Mariel grimaced as her too-tight muscles protested. Evanor stood in the doorway across from her. "Oh, hello! My shoulders are aching, that's all."

He smiled, crossing the hall so that he didn't have to try so hard to be heard. *"If you need any oils or softsoaps for a hot bath, I do have some I could share."*

That made her arch her brow; she wasn't accustomed to *men* who kept such things on hand. But as much as a hot bath sounded nice, Mariel was afraid she'd fall asleep in the middle of it. "No, I'm too tired. Too sore to not think it's a lovely idea, but I also don't want to drown."

Evanor hesitated for a moment, then licked his lips and offered, *"If you like . . . I could give you a massage. You could already be tucked into your bed, so you wouldn't have to worry about falling asleep in a chair, or walking to your room."*

Myriad responses whirled through her head. On the one hand, he was her patient, she was his Healer, not the other way around; on the other, why couldn't *she* be the patient for once and allow herself a little massage therapy for her poor, aching body? There was the fact that she'd be letting him into her bedchamber while she was clad only in a nightgown, but there was also the fact that she'd bedded near strangers, after being propositioned for something far less innocuous than a backrub. Not that she hadn't been careful or selective in making her bed partner choices, but then she hadn't lived within shouting distance of those men, either. Conflicted between propriety and need, she found herself asking wistfully, "Are you any good?"

He smirked at the challenge. This was something he had done for his mother, back when he was young; Lady Annia had suffered from tension headaches from time to time, and Evanor had wanted to know how to make his mother feel better. When he had grown old enough to be interested in women, and had realized massaging could be a part of love play, he had added it to his repertoire of ways to get the castle maidservants interested in dallying with him.

Even after their exile, when one of his brothers strained something in their back, they usually came to him to make it feel better. A massage could be platonic, sensual, or somewhere in between, in his hands. With that wistful little question, Ev knew he held the power to seduce her literally in his hands.

Slipping behind her, he laid his hands on her shoulders, just touching her for a moment, then gently pressed down and in, and caressed. Gradually increasing the pressure, he grinned outright when she moaned, her head lolling back a little. Gentling his touch, he rubbed her back and patted it. *"Into your room, and into your nightgown, milady. You have ten minutes to be in bed, before I'll be by to put you to sleep."*

"Make it five, or I'll already be asleep," she muttered, disappointed that he had stopped. "Better yet—wait in the solar; I'll call you as soon as I'm in bed."

Following her into the front room, which still had trunks and chests scattered across the space, Evanor waited patiently while she disappeared through the next doorway. This suite had a changing room, but he didn't know if she would continue to use it to do so. Mikor had said something when he was helping his mother move her clothing in there earlier, about how it might be good for storing dried herbs, too, but she needed a better place, a dedicated herb room. There was already one in the palace, of course, down in the basement level by the kitchen and buttery; he made a mental note to introduce her to it.

"Evanor? I'm ready."

His heart thumped, stumbling into a faster pace. It was a strange reaction—he was no untried virgin—but he felt flushed and nervous at the thought of seeing her in bed, even if she would be decently clothed. Of course, that was presuming she *would* be decently clothed, in there. She did have a son, and in Evanor's admittedly limited experience, mothers and fathers tended to wear nightclothes in case they were woken up by a needy child in the middle of the night.

Moving into her bedroom, he found her lying facedown in her bed, the covers lowered to her hips, clad in a loose, sleeveless tunic. Her hands were tucked under the pillow cradling her cheek. She looked ready for a massage, in the sense that he could see the tension in her stiffly held shoulders. Crossing to the bed, Evanor seated himself next to her and rested a hand on her back.

She definitely wasn't as skinny as a post, like his twin's willowy wife; there was a distinct layer of softness overlying the muscles under his palm. It reminded him of how curvaceous she was, and how much he used to enjoy exploring the lush body of a woman, back before being exiled to the Isle. He felt his own muscles tensing, felt a certain *interest* stirring within him as he slowly caressed her spine with his hand.

"*Relax,*" he whispered, as much for his own benefit as for hers. It was too soon to expect an invitation to join her in her bed. Dom had confessed to his twin that his own wooing of the Arithmancer in their midst had been tumultuous, full of misunderstandings. Saber and Kelly had fought stubbornly against their fate. Evanor was determined his own courtship would progress much more smoothly. Like Alys and Wolfer had managed. The only drawback was that there was no preexisting friendship between him and Mariel, like the one Wolfer had shared with Alys when they were younger. Evanor would have to start from scratch with his wife-to-be.

Shifting onto the bed, Evanor balanced on his knees and rubbed his palms up the length of her spine, starting at the dip that was the small of her back, and not stopping until his fingers were half-buried in her shoulder-length curls. Dragging the pads of his fingers in a raking motion back down to their starting point released a moan from the woman under his touch. The sound, raw with pleasure, speared straight through his ears to his groin.

Evanor leaned himself into the massage, working his way up either side of her spine in soothing circles, then back down again. The pads of his fingers raked diagonally across her back from shoulders to hips, crisscrossing her muscles, stretching them out. He pressed the edges of his hands along either side of her vertebrae, sliding them all the way up toward her scalp. Then he kneaded her shoulders, stroking his thumbs up into her hairline and back down again, loosening the tension lurking there.

More moans rewarded him for his efforts.

Eyes shut, body melting, Mariel tried not to let herself drool too much. The man had the hands of a god, and he was using them to do utterly delicious things to her body. She could feel her nipples tightening, and other places tingling. The last time she had let a man run his hands over her body was definitely more than half a year ago; her body missed physical pleasure. But she was exhausted from the move, and his ministrations were just sooo gooooood . . .

With the release of her tensions came the release of her consciousness, tipping her into sleep.

Evanor slowed his touch when she stopped responding. Stroking her back gently, soothingly, he whispered, *"Mariel? Are you awake?"*

The soft sound of her breathing was her only reply. Giving in to temptation, Evanor leaned over just long enough to press his lips to her linen-clad back, then shifted off the bed and drew the covers up over her body. They were headed into autumn, which could get a little chilly at night, even this early in the season. Adjusting the lightglobes, he left one softly lit in the refreshing room and left the door ajar, providing enough illumination to hopefully help her find her way in the as-yet unfamiliar suite.

Retreating to his own quarters, Evanor shut his bedchamber door, stripped off his clothes, dimmed the lightglobes, and slid into his own bed. His own, big, lonely bed. Staring at the shadows of the ceiling, he waited for the *interest* in his groin to go away.

Unfortunately, his mind kept replaying the sounds of her moaning under his touch. It insisted on turning her over in his thoughts,

so that his hands could massage the fullness of her breasts, the softness of her belly . . . the plumpness of her thighs, encased as they
had been in those odd but attractive, fitted Natallian hose all day
long. There, that was something safe to think about: fashion. Between Kelly's insistence on wearing trousers most of the time, Alys
copying her with shy delight in the mobility they provided, and
Serina echoing Natallian fashions with their fitted hosiery and
panel-skirts, he almost missed seeing women in the full folds of an
honest gown . . . but not enough to ignore the way those same hose
showed off Mariel's delicious thighs.

No, don't think about her thighs . . . Mariel would look gorgeous in
something corseted, he decided, pulling his mind up off her legs. He
could picture it now, her waist cinched in a bit, her breasts lifted up
until they were generously spilling over, her hips flaring out . . . in
green, Ev decided. That would go well with her hazel eyes. Green,
with a cream chemise to help restrain her cleavage. *No, don't think
about her breasts* . . .

Firming his concentration, Evanor turned his mind toward organizing the chore list for the next half-moon. That was one of his
jobs, after all. And it could be done with or without a voice, since all
he had to do was write it out. Unfortunately, there were now thirteen inhabitants on the island. That was going to be harder to keep
track of than eight had been, considering Mikor was too young for
handling some chores, yet had to be given plenty of things to do to
keep his youthful energies occupied, without making him rebel at
not having enough playtime, too.

Maybe if he borrowed one of Serina's chalkboards, and made a
grid, it would be a little easier. Posting it in the hallway next to the
dining chamber would be a start. But that dining table was starting
to get a little crowded. There was a large dining hall on the ground
floor, suitable for seating upwards of two hundred people, if they
could get the tables and chairs dug out of storage and repaired. That
was a little too big for right now, though. Some of the more modest-
sized salons could be converted . . .

*No, what we need is a longish table. Not the octagonal thing Trevan
and Morganen built for us. I suppose it was too much to think it would be*

neat pairs of husbands-and-wives only, he thought, twisting onto his side as his loins relaxed under the non-lascivious bend to his thoughts. *With the addition of Mikor, we'll need room for more than just sixteen people. And who knows if any of the other wives will arrive with their own relatives in tow, save for maybe Fate Themselves?*

If he was going to be the Lord Chamberlain, Evanor was going to do a good job of it. That meant planning not just for their immediate needs, nor for their needs for the next year, but their needs five and ten and even twenty years from now. Maybe if he got his head together with Koranen, their "Lord Secretary," and Kelly to plot out where she wanted this sovereign kingdom stuff to go, what goals she wanted to set for resettling the island, it might help with those plans.

They needed to figure out what buildings down in the western cove were still salvageable, which had to be rebuilt before they could be reinhabited, which orchards were reclaimable from the wild, what fields could be cleared for plowing . . . and for the people who would come to inhabit those buildings and tend those fields and orchards, they might come with families, and families meant children, and children meant lessons, and clothing that they constantly outgrew, and playmates for Mikor . . . And someone for the youth to court, when he grew up to be of that age. They *had* to encourage people to migrate to the island, Curse or not. Every single child born of the eight brothers' unions would be related to every single other child. Even Mikor to some extent, if Mariel and Evanor married and had more children. He wouldn't be directly related to the others' offspring, but he'd be related to his half-siblings.

Part of managing a household was family planning. Evanor knew that Serina was already pregnant, as a direct result of the complex magic she was attempting to correct back in Natallia with his twin's help. Kelly wasn't, for all she and Saber hadn't exactly done anything to prevent it from happening—at least, that Evanor knew about—but it was only a matter of time. In fact, the only person on the whole Isle who he knew wore a contraceptive amulet was Alys, and that was because she was still working with Morganen to free herself from the last of her late uncle's enchantments.

They didn't tie her powers to the unmourned Broger of Devries, swallowed by the Netherhells during his thwarted attempt to destroy the brothers once and for all, but they did still tie her magics to her cousin, Barol, Broger's son. If she died, her powers would be drawn to him, along with the powers of any of her blood kin and her kin by marriage. Morganen said he was working on it in his spare time.

Evanor vaguely remembered Barol as something of a brooding boy, something of a bully. Not nearly as cruel as his father had turned out to be, in the end, but still an unpleasant fellow. He didn't want the youth gaining the upper hand by draining the brothers' magics through the continuation of his father's mad schemes for enough power to challenge the Council and rule all of Katan.

Which led Ev back to the thought of Nightfall breaking away from the empire, declaring itself independent, and maintaining that independence. Somehow, he didn't think King or Council would take it lightly, or give in graciously. That was another worry on his mind.

The circuitous nature of his thoughts frustrated him. At this rate, he wasn't going to get any sleep. Rolling onto his back, Ev contemplated the problem of getting his mind to relax enough to sleep. Only one thing came to mind. Grabbing one of his feather-stuffed pillows, he twisted onto his side, hugged it to his chest, and pictured himself in bed with Mariel, holding her plump curves in his arms. The pillow was a poor substitute, but it allowed him to imagine spooning with the Healer.

The only problem was that his groin tightened again, even as the rest of him relaxed. Evanor did his best to ignore it, concentrating on the image of Mariel in his arms. He did so by focusing on the remembered warmth of her skin under his palms, the soft-crisp texture of her curls, the way she sighed near-silently as she slept. Eventually, each of his muscles relaxed, dropping him into slumber.

FIVE

The moment he woke, Mikor felt excitement rush through his blood, chasing away the last dregs of sleep in his mind. Pushing aside the covers, he crawled out of the largish bed and hurried into the refreshing room to use it, rubbing the granules of sleep from his eyes.

Once he was more or less clean—surely his mother wouldn't check to make sure he'd scrubbed his back, just his face, hands, feet, and behind his ears, so long as he didn't smell too dirty—he pulled on tan tights and a brown, short-sleeved tunic, tugged on a pair of half boots, tightened the laces around his ankles and a belt around his waist, and left his suite. Yes, there were still chests and boxes to unpack, things to settle, and places to select for them to be settled into . . . but he had a whole *castle* to explore.

To that end, he raced down the stairs and pushed open the door that he remembered led to the outside. The morning air was crisp in the courtyard; maybe a longer-sleeved tunic would have been better, this early in the day. The sun was only just up. It lit the top of the dome at the heart of the sprawling structure and some of the tower tops, too. It hadn't quite reached the rooflines of the four-story palace, but that was alright; there was plenty of light to see everything around him.

Heading to the left, sun-wise, he followed the outer wall, eyeing the massive white stones that had been set in place who knew how long before, and the big, rounded towers where the brothers worked their magics. Mikor wished he could go inside, but he didn't have permission, yet. He had discovered with Uncle Dominor that he liked being around other boys, even if they were adults. They were much more interesting than a bunch of girls, like the nuns, his mother, and his aunt.

There were more buildings than just the wings of the palace, the great hall at the center, which these people called a *don-jon*, and the towers spaced evenly around the great, arcing outer wall. There were buildings built up against the outer wall. Mikor spotted one that wasn't locked with ropes and runes, and it had smoke rising from a large chimney in the center of its blue-tiled roof. It was also constructed entirely of magic-fused stone, almost a seamless piece of stone, though he knew it hadn't been carved out of a mountainside like the Retreat had been.

Curious, he approached cautiously, unsure if a building attached to the outer wall qualified as something he couldn't go into. It wasn't a tower, though it was next to the base of one. The doorway stood open, a broad thing with metal panels hanging back to either side. Used to seeing wooden doors, Mikor edged close enough to touch the iron, fingering the eight-pointed stars that formed the rivets fastening the hinges to the metal pane. Voices murmured inside, male voices, making him jerk his fingers back, in case he wasn't supposed to touch.

The voices weren't directed at *him*, however. Realizing that, Mikor edged farther into the doorway, straining to hear. Eyes adjusting to the dimmer light inside, he realized the largish outbuilding was some sort of workshop. Tools of all sorts hung on pegs set into the stone walls, from small files and rasps to great forceps large enough to have picked up the nine-year-old boy, if needed. The voices also grew clearer, as one of the two conversing males chuckled.

"And what a *rump* she has. If I didn't have respect for the damned

Prophecy, Evanor would be facing some very tough competition for her hand."

"Don't you mean some very *stiff* competition?" the other male enquired. There was a lilt in his tone that Mikor didn't quite understand.

He peered past the entryway, toward an orange glow off to the left, where the voices were coming from. The two men in the place were the two redheads. The coppery-haired one was grinning at the darker-haired one, who was blushing and rubbing the back of his neck. The coppery-haired one, Trevan was his name, was clad in loose trousers and a thigh-length tunic, very odd and foreign to Mikor's eyes, used to the fitted hose and longer tunics of proper Natallians.

The other man, the one with the auburn hair, was clad only in a loincloth. His body was a lot more muscular than it had looked, yesterday, and his skin all but dripped with sweat, gleaming in the light of the forge fire, and glowing with the pinkness of either a full-body blush or a sunburn. As Mikor watched, clutching the corner of the wall in surprise, Koranen—that was his name—reached into the glowing pit with his bare hand and pulled something out. It was all twisty and squiggly, and it gleamed with a yellowish light at the center that faded to orange, then red, then to a dull sort of metal gray at the edges. The redhead held the object between his fingertips, arms fully extended. That centered the metal thing over the flames burning up through the coals in the forge pit.

"*Subakoth, di ess Eth!*"

Blue fire crawled up over Koranen's back, lashing down his arms as it raced into the thingy. Mikor's gasp was lost in the roaring of the flames. After several seconds, the flames started to die down. The mage wiped at his brow with the back of one hand, sweating visibly. He muttered to himself, or perhaps to the twisty-thing, and the yellowish red glow turned blue, then winked out under a flutter of his fingers.

Koranen sighed and set it off to one side, on the flat of an anvil. "That's all I can do, until after breakfast. I still have to fuse them with their warding-tiles, plus add a few more spells before they're done."

"You didn't answer my question," Trevan reminded his sibling. He followed Koranen away from the anvil.

"I know I didn't." The nearly naked mage touched the edge of the lumps of rock lining the forge pit, burrowing his fingers into the material. They started to glow after a moment. Some of the flushed look to his skin faded. Extracting his hand, he moved over to the back wall, where a length of more of the nubbly fabric hung. He scrubbed his body, muttering a cleansing cantrip, as Trevan and the unnoticed Mikor watched.

Trevan folded his arms across his chest, giving his younger brother a sardonic look. "Admit it, Kor. You're just as much an adult male as the rest of us. Don't deny that you have certain *needs*."

"I *don't* deny it," Koranen returned defensively over his shoulder.

"No, but you deny yourself."

Mikor, seeing the thingy on the anvil was unattended, found himself drawn away from the shelter of the wall. He wanted to see what it was, to try and make sense of it. Creeping closer, he peered at the twisty bit of metal. It looked a little different, now, like it had picked up a reddish tint to the dark gray of the iron. It also had a strange, almost velvety texture to it. He wondered if it really was as soft as it looked.

"What would you have me do, burn another woman?" Koranen asked his elder brother sardonically. "I will touch no woman until Destiny brings me the one woman I cannot harm."

"But you admired her rump," Trevan prodded him. "You admitted it yourself."

"Of course! I'm Cursed, not dead—"

"*Ow!*" Yanking back his hand, Mikor shook out his fingers, blowing on the pain in their tips. Not even the two mages whirling to confront him could distract him from the pain. "Ow ow owie ow!"

"What are *you* doing in here?" the coppery-blond mage demanded.

"He's burned himself on the sigil," Koranen muttered, crossing the space between them. "Hold out your hand, Mikor."

"Ow, ow, ow . . . I'm sorry, I didn't think it would hurt me! You didn't say this place was off-limits, just the towers, and it *really* hurts!" Mikor said, conflicted between the pain in his hand and the knowledge that he was going to get into a lot of trouble for this. Tears prickled at his eyes, threatening to leak and spill the moment he realized his fingertips were blistering.

"Yes, well, you're going to have to think about the consequences of your actions," Trevan scolded him.

Koranen flipped his hand at his brother, silencing the older mage. "Give me your fingers, Mikor," he directed, his tone gentle as he crouched in front of Mikor. "That's it . . . *mahala mahui-ie* . . . You probably saw me handling the sigil with my bare skin, and thought you could touch it, too, didn't you?"

The pain easing in his fingers, Mikor nodded. Sparks were rising up from the red-haired man's fingers as he enchanted the pain of the burn away. "It . . . it didn't *look* hot, anymore."

"Well, now you know better. I am a Fire Mage, like your mother is a Song Mage. *Mahala mannana* . . . there, see? Already the blisters are fading. They'll be gone by the end of breakfast. I'm very good at healing burns," Koranen added, giving him a smile. "I've had even more practice at it than your mother, I should think. *Mahala numa lu.* There. Your fingertips will still be sensitive for a little while, but consider it a lesson in thinking before touching. Especially in a forge. There is a lot of danger here, if you don't think things through."

"Yes, and you should stay *out* of here," Trevan scolded him.

Twisting, Koranen gave his brother a hard look. "You know, it wasn't so long ago that *you* were getting into trouble in the wood-wright's shop, back home. I seem to remember an instance where you sliced open your knee as a youth, playing with a set of chisels?"

Trevan had the grace to look away, at that.

"Mikor, if the doors are open to this place, you may come inside," Koranen instructed the youth. "But only just far enough to see if I am in here, and *ask* me if it's okay to be in here. If I say no, or am too busy to answer, then you'll need to go away.

"But other than that . . . well, a young man has to start somewhere when it comes to figuring out what tasks he'll want to learn, in order to make his way in the world as an adult. If I'm not busy, and you're interested," the auburn-haired mage added with an easy smile, "I could always teach you the basics of the smith craft."

"But . . . I'm not a mage," Mikor admitted, glad his fingers were barely smarting, now. "I'm too young to have magic . . . and even then, it might be Healing magic, like my mother's. Or I could turn out to be a Seer, like my father, or probably not have anything at all."

"I didn't have any magic of my own when I first was drawn toward the smith on our property, when I was still growing up," Koranen admitted. "And I learned everything the nonmagical way. Even after my power and its affinity manifested, I continued to learn the nonmagical ways. Magic can do many things that bare hands and plain tools cannot accomplish on their own, but it is only another sort of tool. You have to know *all* of the tools at your disposal to know which is the best tool for a particular task, and that means learning the nonmagical ways. That goes for *all* crafts and disciplines . . . right, Trevan?"

Rising, he elbowed his brother in the arm.

Trevan rolled his eyes, sighed, and nodded. "Yes." Another nudge from his brother, and the lighter redhead added, "And . . . you can have the same ruling for my own workshop. You come, knock on the door frame to see if I'm in there, and if I'm not busy with something delicate, I'll let you come in and show you some of the things I do when I'm working with wood and leather. Though Wolfer is the better tanner, of the two of us."

"I'm *not* afraid of him," Mikor muttered, thinking of the big, intimidating mage with the deep, growly voice and scary way of handling recalcitrant mares.

"That's . . . good to know," Trevan replied diplomatically, exchanging an amused look with his sibling. "He can be scary at times, I'll admit."

"But he's also kind, underneath all the growls," Koranen reassured the youth. "In fact, if there's ever any danger, you just hide behind *him*, and he'll take care of it."

Mikor considered the scary secondborn mage being scary at something scaring *him*, and nodded. That was a far better use of

such overgrown fearsomeness than having it aimed at his own, un-
dergrown self. Changing the subject, he lifted his chin at the thingy
on the anvil. "So . . . what are you making?"

"Warding sigils, for you and your mother to hang on your bedposts. They'll protect your bedchambers against fire and other dangers, guarding you while you sleep," Koranen admitted. "I have to
incorporate your names into their creation, plus some knowledge of
who and what you are, to get the most protection out of the spells
imbued into them. That's why I couldn't start them until after you
came here, when I could learn something about you."

Bells rang in the distance, clanging in an odd, dissonant pattern.
Trevan winced. "I don't think those summoning bells are working
out very well. If we keep expanding our population base, we'll need
something more than just Evanor to keep an eye on everyone in this
place, even after he gets his voice back . . . but I'm beginning to
think those bells aren't going to be it."

"You don't have to work in emptiness, Brother," Koranen reminded him. He motioned for Mikor to head out the door ahead of
them. "Why not ask all of us for more ideas on how to keep tabs on
each other? Say, over breakfast?"

Trevan picked up Koranen's outer clothes from one of the workbenches. "I think I'll take you up on the offer—but only after you
get dressed. The only naked flesh I want to see at the dining table is
either a beautiful woman sprawled eagerly before me . . . or a
freshly roasted chicken. Preferably the chicken."

Koranen arched a bemused, questioning brow while stepping
into his trousers. "Isn't it usually the other way around?"

"Not when I have chicken-feeding and egg-gathering as one of
my chores, today," the fifthborn brother admitted, grimacing.

And so I'm open to suggestions at this point," Trevan concluded,
setting down his mug of fruit juice. "Those bells are *not* working."

His twin, Rydan, poured more of the juice into the half-empty
cup. Aside from a muttered hello at the previous evening's meal, he
hadn't said much at all. Or even during the past week or two, saying

no more than five or six words ever since Dominor had come back from Natallia; Rydan had become very taciturn, even for himself. Thus it surprised the others when he said, "They also do not work beyond the hearing distance of the carillon. If one is down on the beaches, they're useless for summoning."

"Well, I'm not going to let you make them louder," Saber stated, giving Trevan a firm, gray-eyed stare. "Not when the carillon was installed directly over *my* bedchamber."

"*Our* bedchamber, and I quite agree," Kelly said, cutting into the jam-smeared pancakes she had helped make for breakfast. "You know, it's a pity this is a world of magic, not technology. I mean, it's not as if we could suddenly install *cell phone* technology. Not even the tech level of the Mandarites could manage duplicating that."

"Um . . . what has commerce to do with communication?" Serina asked, arching a pale blond brow in confusion.

"What?" Kelly asked, fork halfway to her mouth.

"You said something about installing some sort of selling technology. What has selling things to do with communication?" the Arithmancer clarified.

Kelly chuckled, lowering her fork back to her plate. "Not *selling* things. Cell phones. Cell, as in a defined area, and *phone*, from the root word *phonic*, an old term for *sound*."

"So, what are they?" Morganen asked her, joining the inquiry.

"Well, to put it into 'magical' terms, since I couldn't even begin to explain the scientific ones," the freckled outworlder began, "you start with a network of cell towers, dispersed over a populated landscape as evenly as you can manage. These towers route the messages from the sender to the receiver. The units used to do the sending and receiving are very much like audio-only scrying mirrors . . . hey—you *could* replicate the technology, using mirrors! *Little* mirrors," Kelly emphasized abruptly, forming a circle between her thumb and forefinger with her fingertips not quite touching. She looked at the others, interest brightening her aquamarine eyes. "You could install them on bracelets that people could actually wear!"

"But *you* wouldn't be able to use one," Saber reminded his wife. "You'd have to be a mage to activate the scrying spell. *And* you'd have to know where to connect the image to, even if having a contact-friendly mirror on the other end helps expand the communication distance involved. That's assuming that the mirrors aren't enspelled against incoming scrying attempts to spy upon us ... against which, we've enchanted all the mirrors on this island."

"And if a person is wearing the mirror on the far end, and they're moving around, that makes it nigh impossible to hit the right target, even if you do know the location it's supposed to be in, which we likely would not. This may not be the mainland, but fifty miles long is still fifty miles long," Trevan told her bluntly. "Why do you think we had so much trouble trying to find Dominor in utterly unfamiliar territory, of an unknown size and distance from here?"

"But that's the point of the cell towers," she told him, including the others in an earnest glance around the table. "They're constantly aware of each cell phone's location within their sphere of influence by using passive sensors. In turn, each cell phone has a specific 'phone number.' If you want to contact that person, you have to know their exact phone number, dial it—that is, input or *program* it via a series of numbered buttons that you touch—and your unit links to that other unit through the interconnected cell towers. It's all *automated*."

"*Otto-mated?*" Morganen asked her. He wasn't the only one uncertain of the foreign word.

"Pre-enchanted, if you will," Kelly amended. "What Serina does with runes and mathemagical equations, with spell-parameters and magical energies, my people do with *electrons* and *computer* languages, *binary* codes and logic gates. There are certain parallels between the two universes. Our means of doing similar things is in some ways a lot more complicated and machinery-based—we cannot just wave our hands, concentrate our willpower, and enchant something into changing—but we have achieved greater levels of advancement all the same. I think there's quite a lot that could cross over, if we find ways to parallel what my old world does with what we can do similarly in this one."

"Go on," Dominor encouraged her, visibly intrigued. "Try to put these outworlder ideas into terms we can understand."

"You'd need a routing spell capable of handling several different calls being made at once, not only for a bunch of different bracelets being used all at the same time, but also for contacting a group of phone numbers, or rather, bracelet numbers for a group discussion, and some sort of chiming spell to indicate when a bracelet is being activated by an incoming call, maybe a hinged top with the mirror on the inside of the lid and the numbered buttons on the bottom half, so that it isn't accidentally set off if the bracelet is bumped. Plus a way of recording the calls that you aren't able to answer for some reason, so that you can go back and watch the message at a more convenient point later on." At the blank looks of the mages seated around the table, Kelly smiled. "Hey, it's not *that* complicated. I mean, if *my* people can figure out how to do it—I mean, my *old* people—then so can we, here and now."

Serina fished a piece of chalk out of her pocket with one hand, using the other to push her breakfast dishes out of her way. Dominor rolled his eyes and muttered something; a snap of his fingers brought a small chalkboard sailing into the dining hall, as his pale-haired wife started scribbling her ideas on the surface of the table. She tapped the frame, muttering a spell of her own, and the figures leaped into the rectangle, settling themselves onto the gray slate surface in time for her to begin writing again.

Evanor whispered as loudly as he could. *"I have a tome detailing some of the spells that the Council uses to keep in touch with their various offices. I believe this would just be a variation upon that theme."*

"Yes . . . yes! But rather than specific mirrors that have to be painstakingly interconnected in person to each of the others," Koranen offered with rising enthusiasm, "we would have this number-system Kelly mentions! That would be far easier and cheaper in terms of labor and magic to imbue into each bracelet than personally interconnecting them! In order to personally interconnect them in the way the Council does, the ones out there in common use would have to be brought in each and every time a new mirror-bracelet was made. Or you only disperse a single set of them, or you know the exact location of the exact mirror that's within your range and confined to a specific area. If we instead enchant them to send and receive coded number sequences, all we'd have to do is assign it an incoming number of its own and an ability to send out coded signals."

"It would *definitely* require these interconnected 'towers,' all imbued with the same interlinked spells for awareness of each unit and its designated number, and the ability to relay messages onward to the correct unit or units," Dominor said, as his wife scribbled with the chalk in her increasingly white-dusted fingers. The thirdborn brother nodded to himself. "Yes . . . each bracelet could be empowered with a tincture of *comsworg* oil, to have the same lasting power source as a lightglobe, or perhaps a channeling crystal that the owner could pay a mage to recharge every so often, though we'd have to import the crystals for that.

"And it would require some means of recharging the magic within those towers as well, since we should plan for centuries' worth of use. Lightglobes fade within three to five years of steady use, and we'd have to assume that the bracelets have a limited life span between re-enchantments, but those towers would have to be lower maintenance than that, yet sturdy enough to handle all the taxing demands that will be placed upon them. Which means we're either looking at some sort of Permanent Magic, or something with a renewable source of . . ."

The thirdborn mage trailed off, staring at the sixthborn brother. Rydan narrowed his eyes. "Don't go there."

"Oh, please, we all know you have it!" Dominor scoffed. "You're the Guardian of a Fountain, Brother. Pledged to protect its vast magical energies from misuse, *and* to use them wisely for the betterment of the surrounding land. What better use could we have, than to ensure instant communication across the length and breadth of the Isle?"

"That Fountain is *mine* to decide what to do with it!" Rydan snapped. "*Not* yours!"

"Rydan."

The softly spoken name made the black-haired mage glance at the outworlder seated among them. She had clasped her hands together, resting her forearms on the edge of the dining table. Aquamarine eyes gazed into jet black. A strange tension passed between them as she held his attention. The others stayed still, wondering what the magicless woman was doing.

"Do you believe I hold the best interests for Nightfall in my heart and mind?" she finally asked him, her voice quiet.

He paused for a long moment before answering grudgingly. "Yes."

"Am I your queen?" she asked next. When he stayed silent, she repeated herself. "Rydan, am I your undoubted, sovereign queen?"

His second answer was no more—or less—grudging than the first. "Yes."

"The amount of magic required to power a grid of towers is a small price to pay to ensure communication across the length and breadth of this Isle. If these scrying bracelets had already been established when the Mandarites had struck, we could have coordinated a much better counterattack to Dominor's kidnapping. We could have gotten medical aid to your twin a lot faster, rather than waiting until he had been carted all the way up the pass, allowing him to lose that much more blood on the journey. He could have been met halfway down the mountainside that much sooner." She held his gaze by force of personality alone as she continued, one finger tapping lightly on the tabletop for emphasis. "I am instructing you, as your sovereign queen, to set aside some of the power of this Fountain-thing toward the defense of this island . . . to *include* the empowering of an efficiently enspelled communications network.

"We did discuss the possibility of setting up a network of scrying mirrors to watch our shoreline for unexpected visits. We've already been invaded by the Mandarites via ship, and Alys' uncle via that Dark Gate thing, out on our docks," she reminded him. "There's a phrase that suits this moment, where I come from: 'Knowing is half the battle.' We can use the same cell towers to not only form a permanent communications relay, but also to function as a scrying network. Used in conjunction with detection wards, we'll be able to tell when foreigners come here, and have that much more advanced warning to study them, to see if they're potential friends or possible foes. In time . . . we could even imbue those towers with protective, defensive measures, such as shields to screen out incoming spells or Gated beasts of the sort that used to plague the eight of you, before I came here.

"You are the Protector of Nightfall. It is your duty to lend whatever aid you can toward the preservation of this land. Are you going to cooperate?" she asked him, still holding his gaze.

He brooded for a moment, then nodded. Grudgingly.

"Good. I'll leave the empowerment of the towers in your hands. If magic works anything like technology, I would suggest a hexagonal deployment grid across the landscape, since that's the most efficient pattern when operating within a literal sphere of influence. Work with your brothers to come up with not only a communication network, but also the necessary alert spells and protection wards." Kelly turned her attention to the others, expanding on her orders. "The first priority will be here at the palace, then the road down to the western cove and especially the western docks, then the road down to the eastern beaches. From there, we can work our way north and south, adding to the network as time and available materials permit.

"I expect all of you to work together, since I'm sure there will be mathemagics involved for calculating the most efficient and effective ratio of coverage provided by each tower, fire spells and smithcrafting for the forging of the mirror-bracelets, and who knows what else will be involved. The only ones exempted from this task will be Mikor, of course, Mariel, and her patient, Evanor. I'm *tired* of the bells," she finished, giving Trevan an apologetic look. "They're inefficient and discordant."

"You didn't exclude yourself?" Dominor asked her.

"I'm the one you'll be needing to question about cell phone capabilities," she admitted, shrugging. "They can do a lot more than just contact each other, unit to unit."

"I'm hesitant to make this our priority," Saber warned his wife, grimacing slightly. "We still have goods we need to produce for the traders."

"We have salt and algae to sell," Kelly countered. "We *also* have a young gentleman in our midst who *is* going to go wandering off into the jungle one of these days." She gave Mikor a wry smile as she said it. "I'm not so old that I cannot remember the lure of the unknown, at your age. I'd rather you had one of these communication artifacts to take with you when we do let you roam all over, in case you fall and break a leg or something—I'd rather *I* had one of these things, in case I'm out picking fruit from the overgrown orchards, and *I* fall and break my leg, or something."

"Then we'll complete our morning chores and reconvene here in roughly one hour," Saber agreed, giving in to his wife's logic.

Evanor noticed the pout on Mikor's face, as the boy scraped the tines of his fork over one of his half-eaten pancakes. *"What's wrong, Mikor?"* His question was lost in the murmur of voices from his brothers, who had begun discussing the various requirements for the task ahead of them. Rolling his eyes, Evanor nudged the youth, leaned over, and whispered in his ear. *"Hey, what's wrong?"*

"I *thought* I'd be getting more sword lessons, once we came here. But Uncle Dominor doesn't have *time* for me, anymore!"

Evanor remembered his own bout of interest in such things, at that age. There really wasn't much to entertain a young lad on the island, unfortunately. At least, not one who wasn't allowed outside the castle compound just yet. Since Mariel would be wrapped up with her practicing on the chickens in preparation for his Healing, Evanor was the only one left to keep an eye on Mikor, let alone entertain him.

It was also, he admitted to himself, an excellent opportunity to bond with the boy. *"I can teach you."*

"You can?" Mikor asked him, surprised. "But . . . well, you don't seem like the kind who goes around swinging a sword, not like . . . not like Uncle Dominor, or Saber. You're too nice!"

That made Evanor smile externally, even as he winced internally. He did his best to correct Mikor's mistaken impression. *"Nice fellows get picked on by bullies, because bullies hate the fact that nobody likes someone who's mean, while they really like someone who's nice . . . so we nice guys have to learn how to protect ourselves. I assure you, I'm not the worst swordsman in the family."*

"He's right, you know," Morganen spoke up, addressing the

youth. Mikor blinked and turned to face him. "*I'm* the worst
swordsman in the family. I can defend myself physically, and even
hold my own against my older brothers for at least a few minutes
apiece, but I'd rather not waste my breath in doing so, if I have other
means to protect myself. Such as my magic. Or hiding behind
Wolfer, here."

He flashed a grin at the second-eldest, who smirked. Morganen
continued.

"Of course, Ev isn't the absolute *best* in the family, either . . . but
he does know the basics, and knows them solidly enough to teach
you, if you're interested. He can bring you up to speed to the point
where 'Uncle Dominor' and later, your Uncle Saber can take over
your training."

"*Gee, thanks,*" Evanor muttered voicelessly, giving his youngest
sibling a dirty look.

Morganen's offer caught Saber's attention. "You really want sword
lessons, Mikor?"

The boy nodded emphatically, curls bouncing across his forehead. "Yes, please!"

Saber's gray eyes met Evanor's brown, reading his younger sibling's earnest look. The corner of his mouth quirked up. "I'll admit
Evanor isn't me, but he does know the basics very well. He's exceptionally good at dodging blows, rather than meeting them head-on.
At your age and size, with your current strength, you're far better
off learning how to avoid being hit than learning how to parry and
block. You don't have the muscles to meet an opponent head-on, just
yet. Ev can teach you how to avoid breaking your arm in a fight . . .
or your head . . . which is what would happen if you tried to parry a
full swing with those half-grown limbs of yours."

"*I can also show you around the palace,*" Evanor offered. If
Prophecy had arranged for Mariel to come to him and be his future
bride, then it had also arranged for him to become a second father to
the boy. He wasn't going to force his company on the youth, since
that would only lead to resentment, but he would be there if Mikor
wanted to spend time with him.

"That reminds me," Morganen interjected before Mikor could

reply. "Serina promised to give me some *myjiin* powder to make Ultra Tongue for our three newest members. I trust you have it with you, Sister?"

The blond Arithmancer nodded. "I can have it ready within an hour. I just have to desiccate and grind the nutmeat into a powder."

"*Myjiin* comes from a nut?" Dominor asked his wife, curious.

"Yes—from the *myjii*, the Sacred Fruit of the Moonlands, my homeland," she told him. "The same fruit whose liqueur we drank when we married. There's six nuts in every fruit. When eaten raw, they have enough magic to permit you to hear and understand every language spoken, chirped, or squawked in your presence, provided the creature communicating has a brain bigger than the nutmeat was. And it will do so for a full week. But if you dry it and grind it up, and prepare it in the correct manner, it becomes a very small piece of Permanent Magic, allowing you to speak any language that comes from a sentient mind. That's the catch, of course," Serina added with a wry twist to her lips. "The trade-off is that you lose the ability to communicate with the birds and the beasts, at least until you can eat a raw nutmeat."

"Isn't that the same fruit you have a whole stinking chestfull of, up in our quarters?" the thirdborn mage asked his wife pointedly. "And I do mean that literally. When you opened that one fruit, back at the Retreat, it made your whole study smell like a backed-up refreshing room on a hot summer's day."

"I have *thoroughly* warded that chest for stasis suspension *and* odor control, Dom, and you *know* that!" Serina retorted, rising to her feet in her indignation.

"Hey! If the two of you are going to argue, take it up to your quarters," Mariel interjected firmly as Dominor stood also, ready for a rebuttal. "Especially if you have any plans to kiss and make up in the middle of it."

"An excellent suggestion, Mariel," Dominor praised. "You heard her, wife. Go to our bedroom!"

Serina stuck out her tongue at him but moved quickly for the door when he swatted at her backside.

"Do *you* woo like that?" Mariel found herself asking Evanor, eyeing him askance.

He snorted. *"Hardly. I'm far more romantic than my twin."*

The smile and blush that spread across her face made him glad for his candid reply.

Off to one side, Saber leaned over, murmuring in his wife's ear. "Kelly, however did you get Rydan to back down, like that?"

She smiled and shrugged, speaking under her breath. "I've noticed he's a lot easier to deal with if you just approach him calmly, with a firm but gentle hand. I think I'm beginning to understand him, a little."

"If you *can* understand Rydan, and can explain him to the *rest* of us, I'll call you a miracle worker," he muttered back. And received an elbow nudge in his ribs for the jest.

SIX

❧❧❧

Evanor showed Mariel and Mikor the indoor salle, which was located on the ground floor in the west wing. The two Natallians discovered it was much like the one at the Retreat, with mirrors along one wall, high windows that wouldn't shine sunlight directly into the eyes, and racks holding weapons and armor. It even had pells—rope-wrapped wooden posts, vaguely man-shaped—designed to be hacked and poked at with weaponry for practice purposes.

The floor was wood laid over stone, not sand laid over stone, but age had sanded the surface, leaving it splinter-free. There was also a small drinking fountain trickling water into a basin, a shelf with several horn cups next to it, and not one, but two doors in either narrow end of the hall. Each led first into a changing room, then into a refreshing room, replete with bathing tub.

"*The two changing rooms, we think were separated for men and women to use,*" Evanor explained. "*Kelly wanted a separate room for practicing her kung foo—it's a sort of weaponless fighting form. This one is designated for men, and the other one for women, in case you want to learn weapon forms.*"

Mariel was intrigued by the idea of an unfamiliar style of weaponless combat, but her son responded first. Mikor rubbed at the side of his nose, staring at the tub. "Don't you have any rain showers?"

"*Rain showers?*" Evanor asked, glancing at Mariel for explanation.

"We use tubs for soaking, not for bathing," she told him. "For cleaning ourselves, we have tiled stalls with a pipe that stretches overhead. The pipe is pierced in several places, allowing the water to 'shower' like a rainfall. It's very efficient. You can ask Dominor how nice they are; I know he used the one in Serina's quarters while he was at the Retreat."

That was something his twin hadn't told him. Evanor shrugged. "*It sounds efficient, but depending on how long this phone-bracelet project takes, and how involved it will be, it might be a little while before one of the others will have enough time to make the necessary alterations. If no one has by the time my voice is back, I'll look into it myself.*"

"Thank you." Mariel smiled at him, her hazel eyes holding his brown ones.

Mikor shifted restlessly, bored. "Are you gonna stare at each other, or am I gonna get a sword lesson?"

"We are *going to* stare at each other, not 'gonna'," Mariel chided her son. "I swear, I should never have let you hang around that group of nuns that came from the Lofrei-tai nunnery, last year. You have picked up some very bad verbal habits."

"Well, are you *going to* just stare at each other?" Mikor challenged his mother. "Or do I get my sword lesson?"

" 'May I please have my sword lesson'," she instructed him.

Rolling his eyes, he sighed and folded his arms across his chest before complying. "May I *please* have my sword lesson now, Mother?"

"Since you asked so nicely, yes, you may." Turning to Evanor, she smiled wryly at him. "If you need me, I'll be busy shielding myself against a foray into the chicken coop. Oh—I'll need a place to work."

"*You can use the herb room, and the room next to it. I'm not sure if the room was used as an infirmary, since it has a refreshing room but no furniture, but it's yours if you like it. The herb room is in the basement, near the kitchen. I'll show you both where that is, then Mikor and I can come back and start our lesson."*

Impatient at the delay, but eager for a tour, Mikor trudged grudgingly for the first four or so steps in their wake, before skipping to catch up with them.

Deeming the dining hall to be unsuitable—that, and Wolfer shooed them out of the chamber, since it was his turn to clear the table and wash the dishes, with Alys' help—Kelly directed the others to one of the ground-floor rooms in the north wing. It had an odd, *V*-shaped table, so massive it must have been constructed within the room itself, since there was no way it could have been carried inside.

Kelly suspected the room had once been a sort of council chamber. There were aging but still stout wooden chairs with armrests, wrought-iron stands suitable for holding several lightglobes each—though only a few globes were actually present—and large blank walls painted with the color-changing pigments Morganen had invented. She suspected the walls had once held large maps of the island, its surrounding waters, and the Katani mainland, but the castle had been abandoned more than two centuries ago, long enough for the maps to have fallen down from age and been removed by the occasional exiled group of occupants.

Currently, the view on the painted walls was that of a forest-edged beach, with circling gulls, lapping waves, and swaying branches. If one looked closely enough, little sand crabs could be seen scuttling here and there. While Kelly took the seat at the center point of the *V*, which was actually a flat edge and not a point, the walls shifted, gradually darkening into a night sky with silhouetted mountains. Morganen ducked out of the room, coming back with several lightglobes floating in his wake. As in many of the ground-floor rooms, the windows in this one were higher up on the outer wall than normal. They provided some light, but with the walls darkening to star-studded indigo and black, the lightglobes were needed to dispel some of the corresponding gloom.

The night-loving Rydan had reluctantly followed them there, rather than retreating to his bed. Wolfer and Alys had kitchen duty, Evanor was elsewhere with Mariel and Mikor, and Dominor and Serina had yet to return. Koranen helped his twin place and rap the lightglobes, while Saber seated himself to Kelly's right. Trevan had vanished somewhere between the second and first floors.

Finished helping with the globes, Koranen gave the others a rueful smile. "Since I'm supposed to be the Lord Secretary, I'd better go get something to write with. I'll be right back."

"I'll be right back, too," Morganen added, following his twin to the door.

"Where are you going?" Saber asked him.

For a moment, it looked almost as if a faint blush tinted Morganen's cheeks. His words, however, sounded like his usual cheerful, helpful self. "I thought I would fetch my outworld-attuned mirror, so we can question Kelly's friend about these cell phone things. She may have one of her own, so she might be willing and able to demonstrate one for us."

Kelly wasn't fooled. That *was* a blush. She tried not to smirk outright, though she smiled in encouragement. "That's an excellent idea, Morg. Bring it here, by all means. We'll wait for both of you to return."

Saber waited until his youngest sibling's footsteps had faded down the hall before commenting. "I wonder just how much of a coincidence it was for him to pick you out for me, out of the five candidates he said he had been watching. The one woman whose friend just happens to be named 'Hope,' which is the nickname of the bride listed in our youngest brother's Prophecy verse."

"The other four outworlder women could've also had friends named 'Hope,'" Kelly defended. "Besides, we know why he picked me to haul across, thanks to those prejudiced, wanna-be arsonists trying to burn down my house while I slept."

Saber covered her hand. "You're on Nightfall, now. No one here is going to let you die. Certainly not by fire, if Koranen has anything to say about it."

"If I have anything to say about what?" the auburn-haired brother in question asked, reentering the room. He had a tray in his hands, piled with a sheaf of papers, an inkwell, and a metal-nibbed pen.

"We're just expressing our gratitude at those antifire amulet things you made for us, for our wedding present," Kelly explained.

Koranen nodded. Then snorted. "Like the ones I'm making for our two newest guests; I was going to get back to doing that after breakfast. Speaking of which, our youngest islander was curious enough to touch it right after I set it down, just before the breakfast bells rang, and burned his finger." The Fire Mage gave Kelly a rueful look. "I fixed his burns like I did yours, but he's going to need a lot of careful watching, and a lot of reminding of what's appropriate to do and what's not so appropriate. Like remembering to *ask* for permission before entering our nonmagical workshops, outside of the towers."

Saber grimaced. "None of us thought to ban him from them, just from our magical workplaces."

"Actually . . . I'd rather not," Kor offered, taking the seat across from his eldest brother, at Kelly's left elbow. "He needs to have an eye kept on him whenever he's in one of those places, yes, but he's also much like we were at that age: being eaten alive with curiosity and wanting to try all sorts of new things. He's also old enough that, if we give him some supervision, he can actually start trying those new things. We just have to *teach* him to be more cautious, ask for permission, and be suitably careful even when he has permission to do things."

"Having a child on the Isle is going to take a lot of our energy," Saber stated, sighing heavily. "We can't just fob him off onto Mariel and Evanor all the time. They need time alone together, if she's the woman mentioned in Evanor's verse. As much as Mikor would be a part of their family, having a child around can be rather . . . inhibiting, to some degree."

"Ah, yes," Kelly agreed. "My people have a saying for that: *childus interruptus.*"

"Amusing." The one-word comment drew their attention to Rydan, who had seated himself at the far end of the *V* from Kelly, on the same side as Saber. "Can we get this going, so I may sleep?"

"We need to wait for Serina, who needs to know what a cell phone can do, so she can work up the right magical formulas for enchanting the cell towers," Kelly reminded him. "And for Morganen to come back with his mirror, so Hope can demonstrate for us how they work."

"Then let us discuss these cell towers of yours," Saber offered. "How far do the ones in your world work? What is their range?"

Kelly gave him a blank look for a moment, then shrugged. "I'm not really sure—a couple of miles in radius, maybe? All I know is, the farther away you are from the tower, the weaker your reception. And sometimes the signal is dropped when traveling between towers, or because of bad weather, or from interference as it bounces around large building structures. There's also a limit on how much energy the towers can safely use, too. Too much, and it can start to interfere with other equipment. Too much, and it can even start to interfere with your health. But I don't know if magic carries the same risks or not."

"There are some risks," Rydan admitted, shifting into one of his infrequent talkative moods. "Nonmages and mages of lesser power can only handle up to a certain amount of magical radiation. The more power you yourself radiate, the more you are able to handle." He shifted his gaze to Saber briefly, then muttered, "That's why I hadn't told the others about the Fountain. Only three of us are strong enough to handle its energies. Morganen . . . doesn't need it. And I *didn't* want Dominor thinking he could tell me what to do with it."

"Dominor is going to tell you what to do with it, anyway," the dark-haired mage stated, entering the room. His hands were full of stacks of slateboards in their smaller, more manageable size. Serina followed him, carrying a mortar and pestle.

Trevan came last, looking smug. "I thought I'd go fetch them and make sure they participated."

Dom set the stack of chalkboards on the table, then held out the chair in front of them for Serina. He took the mortar and pestle from her and something small and brownish that she had been holding in her palm, and seated himself next to her.

"Is that the seed-thing you need for the Ultra Tongue potion?" Kelly asked him.

"Yes," Serina answered for Dominor, who was putting the mortar in his lap so that he could grind the seed under the pestle at the best angle. "And someone in this family owes me twelve gold for it, too. Probably you by default, Your Majesty, since it's going to facilitate communication among your populace."

Judging from the lack of protest out of the other mages, Kelly guessed that was a reasonable price. "Oh. Well . . . just out of curiosity, how much Ultra Tongue can be brewed from each seed?"

"Six brewings, with two to three doses a brewing," Serina answered, busy sorting through her chalkboards. "Normally I'd charge three times that for a seed, but you're family, now."

"And how many of these seeds do you have?" Trevan asked her.

"Six seeds per fruit, a couple dozen fruit. Enough to last a little while," the platinum blond mage replied absently, chalk appearing in her fingers magically. She didn't even look up when she continued. "Then we'll have to import more from the Moonlands, and the price will go up correspondingly. I got the chest of fruit from an idiot sailor who fished it out of a shipwreck and didn't know its true value. Paid only fifty in Natallian gold for it, too," Serina added, glancing up at the others with a smirk. "All I have to do is check the stasis charm periodically to make sure it stays fresh, and they'll keep indefinitely."

"Well, if you have fresh fruit, and the seeds are in the fruit, not dried and desiccated yet . . . why don't you just plant some of it?" Kelly offered. "That way we won't have to import it."

That lifted Serina's head from her calculations. She blinked and eyed Kelly askance. "Because it's the *holy* fruit? It is sacred to my people, and sacred to our beliefs, and sacred to our land. It only grows in the Moonlands. I don't even think it *can* grow anywhere else—certainly not on unsanctified land, and only the Moonlands worship Brother and Sister Moon as their God and Goddess, as far as I know."

"Oh. Well, please forgive any offense I might have given in asking that question," Kelly apologized.

"I take no offense." Shrugging, Serina returned to her work. "You didn't know. Now you do."

"Good. Then my only crime is ignorance," Kelly stated wryly. "At least ignorance can be cured. Stupidity can't be."

"That does bring up a good question," Trevan said. He had settled himself next to his twin and now leaned back in his chair, putting one booted foot on the tabletop. "The subject of the Gods, that is. Most of us worship Jinga and Kata, but we've two followers of the Natallian deity—"

"Natua," Serina offered, carefully drawing a diagram on one of her slates. "Goddess of the family, home, hearth, children, that sort of thing."

"Thank you . . . and a worshipper of the two Moons. And an outworlder who claims the Divine is unknowable . . . yet it is often the responsibility of the monarch to ensure that a kingdom's Divine Patron is worshipped properly," the fifthborn brother reminded the others. "Usually by setting a good example, attending and being a patron to the local religious services, festivals, and holy days, and encouraging the priesthood or clergy to perform their duties properly, hopefully without falling into the pitfalls of corruption and greed," Trevan offered. "If we make a break from Katan, we make a break away from Jinga and Kata. Yet we're not a part of Natallia, or of the Moonlands, so worshipping either this Natua or Brother and Sister Moon are also out."

"Why should they be 'out'?" Kelly challenged him. "If we repopulate this island, our new citizens are probably going to come from a lot of different places. They'll have a hard enough task ahead of them without us asking our influx of farmers, ranchers, fishermen, dock workers, and assorted craftspeople to give up their beliefs. Faith is a source of great comfort to many. Why shouldn't they be free to worship as they please, provided they don't try to prevent others from doing the same, as *they* please? As far as I'm concerned, and provided it harms no one, they could even worship the citizen-chickens if they wanted!"

Everyone else at the table, save for one, eyed her with mixed horror and disbelief at her suggestion. That sole exception startled the others even further by erupting with laughter. Hearty laughter. Trevan dropped his boot from the table, staring slack-jawed at his younger twin.

Wiping tears from the corners of his eyes, Rydan subsided into chuckles, then *snerk* sounds as he struggled to control his amusement . . . but every time he glanced Kelly's way, he started laughing again, until he was reduced to keeping his head turned in the opposite direction.

Saber gave his sixthborn sibling a wary, wide-eyed look, before addressing his wife. "It isn't a matter of giving up their beliefs, Kelly; when people move to new lands, and not just travel, they are expected to worship whichever God is the patron of that land."

"It's a part of being a citizen," Trevan stated. "You support your Patron, who in turn blesses your homeland, makes it fruitful, quells the damage from horrible storms, and so forth . . ."

Koranen eyed Kelly as well, lifting his gaze from the few notes he had made so far. "Doesn't it work that way in your old land?"

"Well, no . . . not exactly. Faith happens wherever you are in the world," Kelly tried to make them understand. "You carry your version of Divinity with you. There's this one religion, the faith of Islam. Its followers, who call themselves Muslims, must pray to their God, Allah, five times a day, if they are to be faithful to their religion. And each time a Muslim prays, they must pray in the direction of their most holy city, Mecca.

"But since the world is so big and round, if they cannot pray to the exact direction of Mecca, they must pray facing east, toward the rising sun. Thus they can go anywhere in the world and still pray faithfully, so long as they know which way is east," she told the others. "Because of this, you will find Muslims living literally thousands of miles away from Mecca, yet they still worship Allah. The same goes for other religions, for those who worship Vishnu, and Yahweh, the followers of Taoism and Paganism, and the other faiths. Wherever they go, they continue to pray to their version of the Divine."

"Yes, but do these Gods of your world—these Allah, Yahweh, Taoism, and Paganism—do They answer Their followers' prayers,"

Trevan asked, "even when Their followers are far from Their patroned lands?"

Considering she'd never seen a miracle in person, but had heard rumors, Kelly shrugged. "Well . . . yes, and no. Not all prayers, of course, but there are a few that I've heard of. My *point* is, on my old world, faith isn't limited by geographical location."

"Then it is definitely a different world than here," Serina observed, lifting her gaze from her work. "Travelers can attempt to invoke the names of their Gods, but it is harder for Them to hear the prayers of someone so far away from Their power base." At Kelly's puzzled look, she explained. "Prayers have a kind of power, sort of like magic. But unlike a spell, even a nonmage can make a prayer powerful, if their desire is true and worthy enough."

"It doesn't matter if their prayer is not answered in the end," Dominor contributed. "That energy is invested into the landscape. The more who worship a particular Deity—whether or not their prayers are worthy—the easier it is for that Deity to draw on the power of those past prayers to grant some truly worthy miracle."

"It's all a circle of energy," the platinum blond mage finished with a sort of logical dismissal in her voice and the shrug of her shoulders. "We give the Gods our faith, and They use the energy of that faith to perform miracles, causing us to believe in Them all the more strongly, providing Them with even more power to perform miracles on our behalf. Which makes it important to pick the right God or Gods when starting up a new kingdom."

"Which brings us back to the point of which God and/or Goddess to pick," Trevan repeated, looking at Kelly. "As the monarch, the final word is yours . . . and it *has* to be yours, as the monarch, if you are to cement that final bit of your power."

A large cheval mirror floated in through the doorway as Trevan spoke, followed by Morganen; the youngest mage gave the others a bemused look.

"But I don't *want* to limit the worship of the people who live here," Kelly protested. "It goes against everything I was raised to believe in. The separation of Church and State, the absolute right of an individual to determine whatever they themselves want to believe in . . . if I *tell* someone what to believe, by picking a specific Deity, it's like I'm *telling* them who they can or cannot have sex with—it's that intimate a choice, to me! We should be free to choose *anyone*."

Setting the mirror down at the open end of the *V*-shaped table, Morganen eyed the others. "You're discussing the worship of Gods?"

"Yes—I think it's completely wrong to limit everyone's choices to a 'State Religion' here on Nightfall," Kelly repeated. "In fact, if I didn't realize it was so important to the rest of you, I'd declare that there is *no* one, single, official religion here on Nightfall. I mean, what makes the worship of Jinga and Kata more important than the worship of Brother and Sister Moon?" she asked Trevan. "Your faith and your belief are no less valid than Serina's, Trevan. And hers is no less important than yours. Yes, there's eight of you to only one of her, but her faith is just as strong as yours, whether it's one or all of you."

"But we can't *be* a kingdom without a Patron!" the copper-haired mage protested.

"Relax, Trev," Morganen urged his brother. "The Bell hasn't been rung, yet. We have plenty of time to settle this debate. *Another* time. Right now, we're keeping Rydan from his bed, waiting for us to finish our cell phone debate."

"What do you mean by 'the Bell'?" Kelly asked the youngest of the brothers.

Saber answered for him. "Whenever a new kingdom is formed . . . which isn't often, I'll admit . . . a bell is rung by those challenging the right for that new kingdom to be formed. If a Patron God or Goddess does not immediately answer the summons, the new monarch has a year and a day to find a Patron to defend their land's claim to sovereignty. In seceding from Katan, a bell would have to be rung on Nightfall soil and a formal challenge presented to us to produce our chosen Patron, most likely by a representative of the King of Katan. Since that hasn't happened yet, we have time, as Morg says, to debate all of this later."

"*That's* an odd custom," Kelly muttered, bemused. "Ringing a bell to summon a God?" Shaking it off, she looked at Morg. Gods and bells and Divine Patrons would have to wait for another time. "You're right. We need to focus on cell phone technology. I've lost track of what day of the week it is back home, but it's early enough, Hope should still be at home and not out running errands."

Nodding, Morganen reached into a leather pouch slung on his belt and pulled out a small box. Forewarned by experience, Kelly stuck her fingers in her ears. She wasn't the only one; Morg's brothers quickly followed suit. Words of power thundered out of the young mage, forcing even Serina to drop her chalk and cover her ears. When the greenish powder inside the box had been dusted over the surface four times and the glass had flared with light, the noise ceased.

Now, instead of a reflection of herself and the *V*-shaped table, Kelly could see into her best friend's kitchen. There was a butcher's block to the left, a bit of wall to the right, and a fridge directly ahead. The whimsical magnets stuck to Hope's refrigerator made the redhead feel a bit homesick, as did the chrome curve of a toaster, and the sleek black plastic of a microwave oven. Standing to one side, Morganen muttered under his breath and gestured with one hand. A brass bell hanging from a magnet-hook on the fridge jangled in response, disturbed by his magic. The sound was a bit faint, so he did it again, harder.

No doubt it was louder on the other side, for they soon heard the muffled thumping of footsteps, and a woman in jeans and a pink plaid shirt skidded into view, the plain pink socks on her feet allowing her to slide across the linoleum. Her skin was naturally tan, but a hint of a blush could be seen in her smiling face. With her dark brown locks swept up into a somewhat untidy ponytail, her sleeves rolled up past her elbows, and her hands holding a rag and a can of furniture polish, it was clear she had been in the middle of housekeeping chores.

Quickly setting the rag and polish on the counter, she turned to face the mirror's intersection plane. Her left hand rose in front of her, palm out, and her right hand rose to cover her breasts, centered over her heart. She waited with an expectant, breathless look as she did so.

Morganen blushed. Vividly. There was no denying how red his face was. Turning away from the others, careful not to meet anyone's gaze, he reached through the surface of the mirror and pressed his own hand to hers, his right to her left. His other hand rose somewhat self-consciously to his chest, hesitated, then pressed against his sternum. Even his ears were distinctly pink.

"My goodness, Morg," Trevan drawled, watching the act. "Who knew you were such a romantic?"

"Yes, do you *always* do that with my wife's friend?" Saber inquired archly.

"How cute," Dominor added, amused. "We're not even all married yet, and already you're courting!"

"Shut up!" The sharp retort came from Rydan, not Morganen. Scowling, he shoved to his feet, glared at all of them with a fierce black gaze, then stalked out of the room. The door opened without a touch, as it always did for him—and *slammed* behind him.

In the silence that followed, no one said anything for a long, awkward moment . . . until Kelly spoke.

"How dare you." Her aquamarine gaze met the eyes of the three brothers who had dared to tease the youngest among them. The quiet admonishment made them blush and look away, including her own husband. "The three of you owe Morganen an apology. I'll remind you that *some* of you wouldn't care to have your own romances laughed at. So why should you laugh at *his* chance for happiness?

"Destinies or not, we have work to do, so I suggest you get your juvenile sniggering under control, while I go get Rydan back." Pushing her chair back, she rose and left the room, seeking the sixthborn brother. She had to open and close the door by hand, but her slam was every bit as forceful as Rydan's had been.

Morganen, extracting his hand, gave his brothers a dark look. "You're lucky sound travels from her world to ours far better than it does from ours to hers. Otherwise, you'd owe Hope an apology, too."

"We're sorry, Morg," Trevan offered contritely. "It's just that you're our Prophesied matchmaker, and it's nice to see *you* having to court someone, rather than just meddling in our own lives, one at a time."

"I think Trev is a little jealous that he hasn't had his turn, yet," Dominor offered. He quickly held up his hand as the fifthborn brother shot him a dirty look. "That's not to say some of the rest of us haven't suffered along the way, in our own way . . ."

"A *lot*," Serina muttered, glancing at her dark-haired husband. Their own courtship hadn't gone smoothly, thanks to misunderstandings both deliberate and accidental.

"The point is, we're sorry, and we apologize," Saber stated, cutting through any reply Dominor might have made.

Looking at his siblings for a long moment, Morganen finally nodded, accepting their apologies. He turned back to the mirror, where Hope was busy erasing something from a stretch of shiny white material hung on the wall next to the refrigerator. "I've gotten rather good at writing messages to her, with that odd, fat writing tool, there. I'll use it to ask her to fetch a cell phone thing for us, while we wait for Kelly and Rydan to return."

Instinct sent Kelly down to the basement level, where the web-work of corridors extended under the courtyards all the way to the towers, to special stairwells that spiraled up to the rampart levels, opposite the stairs spiraling past the inner rooms. Not that she'd been into those towers, aside from Morganen's and Saber's, but she knew Rydan preferred avoiding sunlight. Sure enough, she spotted him leaning against one of the walls, half constructed from huge granite blocks, half carved from the speckled white bedrock itself.

It was a relief to not have to chase him all the way to his tower, at least.

Arms folded across his chest, back pressed to the wall, Rydan flicked her what seemed like a resentful look. But when she closed the last few yards between them, stopping an arm's length away, he confined his irritation to a heavy sigh. Staring moodily at the far wall, he waited for her to make the first sound.

A twist placed her back to the same wall, echoing most of his pose, save that, whereas his arms were folded across his black-clad chest, hers were tucked lightly behind her back. "I told them to knock it off. They *will* behave, now."

A rough sound escaped him, not quite a snort, but not quite a laugh, either. "Or Else?"

"Or Else," Kelly promised him, capital letters and all. Shifting her left hand, she reached for his elbow. "Come along, back to work—"

He flinched away from her touch. Not exaggeratedly, but distinctly all the same. Kelly didn't quite know what to make of that, other than that he didn't want to be touched. There was clearly something more going on with the sixthborn brother than just plain moody irritableness. Whatever it was, though, it was going to take a lot more attention to pry it out of him than she could spare.

Dropping her arm, Kelly mentally shrugged and repeated herself lightly. "Come along. We still have work to do."

He followed, reluctantly, but he followed. "I will not let the others near the Fountain."

"Considering I'm still not clear what a Fountain is or does, other than spew magic like an artesian wellspring," Kelly admitted, "so long as you agree to share some of that power—for the betterment of the Isle—then they don't have to get anywhere near it."

Another sound escaped him, this time closer to a laugh than a snort. "Or Else?"

"Or Else," Kelly agreed, grinning. Figures emerged from the door to the spiral stairwell, Evanor, Mariel, and young Mikor. She smiled and lifted her hand in greeting. "Hello, again!"

"Hello! Evanor is showing us where the herb room is located," the curly-haired Healer said, gesturing vaguely at the basement level around them. "I hope you don't mind if I take it over?"

"So long as you share its resources with the brothers, since I understand they process a lot of raw spell components in there, too, I won't have any problems," Kelly cautioned the shorter woman.

"There's a room next to it, I think it was the infirmary," Evanor whispered as loudly as he could. *"She could use that, too."*

"A good idea. You get her settled, while we get back to the great cell phone debate." Gesturing for Rydan to precede her, Kelly lingered a moment while the trio headed up the corridor toward the herb room and the kitchens. As she watched them, she saw Evanor touch his hand to Mariel's back, guiding her to a specific door. His palm slid down her back in a little caress, making the petite woman glance up at him. Seen in profile, her smile was unmistakable, though the lightglobes down here were spaced too widely and rapped too dimly for Kelly to be able to tell if Mariel blushed or not.

"Are *you* coming?" Rydan asked her, his voice floating down from the stairs.

"Coming!" Hurrying after him, Kelly decided she really liked having more women around this place. The sprawling, palace-like castle was finally beginning to feel like a home.

SEVEN

* ❧❦❧ *

n o. Absolutely not!" Saber braced his palms on the table, glaring at his freckled wife.

"But, Saber, it's the best way to demonstrate!" Kelly protested. "I can ask Hope all the right questions, and she can demonstrate them, rather than go through this tedious writing-on-the-whiteboard crap!"

"I don't want to lose you!"

"You're not *going* to lose me, you big lummox!"

"Why not let *her* cross over *here*?" Koranen asked, seeking a compromise.

"Because the cell phones won't work, over here—" Kelly answered. At the same time Morganen said, "—Because she refuses, until she says it's the right time."

The others glanced at their youngest sibling, confused. Trevan arched one of his coppery brows, repeating Morg's statement. "Until it's the right time?"

"She's a psychic," Kelly explained quickly. "It's sort of like being a Seer, I think—she can sense things, like when someone is lying to her, or where someone has lost their keys, that sort of thing. Look, Saber . . . there are things that I *miss*, in that universe. Is it so much to ask to let me hop over for just a couple hours' visit? I promise to come back!"

He glowered at her. Sulked, actually, since there wasn't quite enough heat in his gaze to be a full glower. Kelly gave him first a coaxing look, then when that didn't work, a pointed one.

"Look, it'll stop me from whining about wanting to go and have a visit in my old universe. At least for a little while."

"Oh, for Jinga's sake—would you just let her go?" Dominor demanded. "She's not the least bit like *my* wife."

"What is *that* supposed to mean?" Serina challenged him, lifting her gaze from one of her slateboards.

"It means that she won't go off in a daze, immersed in her work, and forget to do normal things, like eat, sleep, and come back." Lifting his hand to Serina's face, Dominor rubbed a stray smear of white from her cheek. "If it were me, I'd have to go with my wife, to make *sure* she remembered to come back."

Serina stuck out her tongue at Dominor and swiped a chalky finger down his nose as he quickly pulled back, wincing.

"Fine. We'll *both* go across. I've survived a nearly magicless realm once; I can do it again," Saber muttered. "Besides, *I* can ask questions from a mage's perspective."

"Poor baby," Kelly pretended to commiserate, touching her husband's cheek.

"Don't call me baby," he groused. "Let's get this over with. Morg?"

Satisfied with the arrangement, Morganen gestured, and the pen hovering in the grip of his powers marked the smooth board hung on the wall in the other world. *Prepare for two guests.*

On the other side of the mirror, Hope nodded and moved to one side, behind the butcher's block. *How* she knew where the intersection plane was, Morganen still didn't know. Surely it wasn't enough for her to be *sigh-kick* in order to notice it, as Kelly called it, or whatever the odd term was. There was so little magic in the other realm that one would have to be exceptionally sensitive to notice its presence, but *sigh-kicks* were supposedly like Seers, not like mages. Surely the Gods of this realm didn't operate in such a far-flung realm? *But if she is sensitive to magical energies, that makes me wonder just how she would react to coming here, where magic radiates from our very selves and permeates the world . . .*

Saber, escorting Kelly to the end of the *V*-shaped table, eyed the mirror for a moment, then stepped through. He sank down half a foot and stumbled, since the intersection plane was higher than he expected. Hope caught him by the elbow, helping steer him clear. "Easy, there," she said, her voice crossing the barrier faintly. "Saber, isn't it?"

"That's right." Turning, Saber searched the air, his gaze not quite finding the right spot, and held up his hand. "Watch the floor. It's a few inches lower."

Kelly stepped through, reaching out and taking his hand, letting him assist her back into her homeworld. "Thanks. Hello, Hope, it's great to see you again!"

"Kelly! Long time no see, literally!"

The two women embraced, muttering and exclaiming and pulling back to examine each other before hugging again. Saber sighed and leaned back against the counter, staring vaguely in the direction of the spot in the air where the mirror should be.

"Once they're done being female, we can get to work," he said, knowing his brothers and sister-in-law could hear him.

"Don't be silly," Hope admonished him, releasing her friend with a flip of one tanned hand, first at him, then at the whiteboard on the wall. "You want to know about cell phones and how they work, for who knows what reason. Whatever that reason is, I don't mind explaining it to you. You're also very much in luck, because I just happened to have switched carriers two days ago, and I still have both phones."

At the puzzled look on Saber's face, Kelly chuckled. "A 'carrier' is a company who specializes in maintaining the cell towers and transmitting, or 'carrying' their signals. Like any other commodity or service, there is more than one carrier-company, because it's a profitable business, one well suited to some healthy competition.

And there's more than one type of cell phone, and more than one type of service provided."

"Not to mention, improvements are constantly being made to the systems," Hope added. "The technology has only been around for a couple of decades, but it's progressed by leaps and bounds in that amount of time. Here," she said, turning to a leather satchel on the counter next to the sink, which had been out of the range of the scrying mirror. She rooted around in the purse and fished out two small objects. One was hinged, which she flipped open. "This is the new one. This other one is the old one. The old one had a shorter range, a signal that was less clear, and it couldn't transmit images, just text and sounds. The new one can take pictures—instantly painted images, sort of—and transmit them from this cell phone to any other cell phone that can receive and display images."

"Or to a computer, which is sort of like a magical artifact-box that can record words, calculate numbers, paint pictures, play music, and exchange information with others of its kind, sort of like a scrying mirror," Kelly tried to explain, taking the old phone from her friend. "But that's a really complicated explanation for another day. Hope, why don't you call this one, and we can demonstrate how it all works?"

"Sure. First, you turn on the power by pressing this button," the dark-haired woman explained. She stood by the intersection-plane, so the others could see as well as Saber. "Then you push the right numbers in the right order . . . there . . . and you hit this other button, here, which starts the call. It takes a few seconds to relay the signal to the nearest tower, and for that tower to find the old—and there we go!" Hope crowed as the gray blue object in Kelly's hand beeped. "Contact has been made."

"When that happens, I, the recipient, touch this button here—it's tinted green, like that one—to activate the call." Kelly put the phone up to her ear and said, "Hello!"

Hope had done the same, and responded. "And hello, right back. Now *you* try," she said to Saber.

Kelly showed him the red button. "You push this one to end the call, which is very important to remember to do. That frees both phones from the connection and makes them ready to be used again, as well as conserves their energy."

Turning the phone toward Saber, Hope pointed at the display screen. "On this model, if you look at the screen, the glowing bit, I can just hit this button here . . . and this button, here, and it recalls the last number I called, and automatically dials it again, so I don't have to hit all the buttons again."

Taking Saber's hand, Kelly put the cell phone into his palm. He twitched a little as it beeped, unsettled by the noise. Under her encouraging look, he gingerly pressed the green button, making it beep again, then lifted it to his ear.

"The holes here are where the sound comes out, on that end, and the holes on *this* end are where the sound goes in," Kelly encouraged him, turning the phone around in his hand.

Flushing, he adjusted it and said, "Hello?"

"Hello!"

He heard it both in his uncovered left ear, given Hope's proximity, and from the device pressed to his right ear. "Jinga! That's loud and clear. It doesn't quite sound like you, but it's very close. Scrying mirrors are a bit clearer, more natural-sounding," Saber observed. "Not completely perfect, but better."

"That may be because that's an older model," Hope suggested. "Anyway, that's how they work. Push the red button to end the call. Actually, let me push it on my end . . . there. Doing that on either side usually ends the call, but sometimes the signal gets crossed and tangled, so hit it on your own side—there, like that. And then, to conserve power—or for that model, to keep from accidentally hitting the buttons while the phone is in your purse or pouch or whatever—you turn it off with the same power button that was first pushed."

"You have to hold it for a few seconds, turning it on and off," Kelly instructed him. "If we use a flip-top model, we won't have to do that, since we can design a latch to keep the top from flipping open and the buttons from being accidentally touched."

"Ah. It's sort of like a lightglobe, then. But, if it's off, does the tower still know how to contact it?" Saber asked Kelly.

"No . . . no, it doesn't," she admitted, glancing at her dark-haired friend, who shrugged.

"Then what is the point of turning it off?" Saber asked her. "Shouldn't it stay active all the time?"

"Do you really want to have a lightglobe constantly glowing all the time?" Kelly countered. "It's the same principle."

"Listen to your wife," Hope told him, lifting the folded phone in one of her tanned hands. "These things become annoying after a while, especially if you have a lot of people wanting to call you. Trust me, you'll want to be able to turn them off, from time to time."

"Imagine your brothers making one of those things beep while we're in the middle of a 'royal conference,'" Kelly added with dry persuasiveness. "*I'd* have it turned off at that point, because otherwise, I'd want to smash it for the untimely interruption."

"Good point," Saber agreed. He stared at the phone in his hands, then turned and glanced at one of the objects on the counter. He pointed to it. "That thing has its numbers in a different pattern. What is its function?"

"The microwave? It quickly reheats food placed inside of it," Kelly explained. "Don't ask me how it works, since I don't know enough to explain it in any depth."

"Oh! I have some books that might help with that!" Hope exclaimed, and dashed out of the kitchen . . . carefully dodging around the area where the mirror's invisible boundary was located. She came hurrying back after just a few moments, arms cradling several books. "Presuming you can read English, these are full of articles and drawings on all sorts of technology, from the simplest kinds of machines, like the ramp and the pulley, to some of the most current and complex, including microwaves and cell phones. They're all 'How Things Work' books. Here, take them. I don't need them anymore."

Saber arched a sandy blond brow at that. "You don't need them anymore?"

She flushed, glancing at him with a strange mix of embarrassed scorn. "What, you think we're all *born* knowing this stuff?"

"Hope was caught up in a tornado, four years ago—no, almost five years now, wasn't it?" Kelly asked her friend. Hope shrugged and looked away. The redhead continued. "Four and a half, then. She was swept up when the tornado crashed through half of her house, and dropped miles away."

"And she survived?" Saber asked, impressed. "Tornadoes are more common up in the northern plains than where I grew up, back on Katan, but I've heard of them. Straws driven through tree trunks, houses lifted whole or smashed to rubble, people stripped of their clothes with not a scratch or a bruise, while others . . . don't survive. Most don't survive, when stolen by a whirlwind."

Hope blushed and looked away, so Kelly answered for her, filling the gap in the conversation. "Well, she did. Hope told me she escaped with a minor concussion physically, but with major amnesia. She couldn't remember her own family when they finally found her at a nearby hospital, where one of the workers recognized her from school—couldn't remember half of anything, really, even the stuff many of us take for granted on this world. It took you, what, a year to get back to normal?" Kelly asked her friend. "And you still don't have most of your childhood memories back?"

"Something like that," the curly-haired woman mumbled. "Look, just take the books. I honestly don't need them anymore," Hope said. "A quarter of that stuff is really simple, kid's stuff that an adult should already know, and a quarter of it will be easy to translate across, but the rest of it will probably take a lot of time and effort to make work, according to the ways of . . . wherever it is you're living now. If you even can. Some of it's pretty specific to the way this world works, I think."

"It probably is, but the brothers are rather clever," Kelly defended lightly.

"Let's get back to the subject of cell phones, shall we?" Hope stated briskly. "If I get what you're trying to do, you're trying to replicate something like a cell phone for your own use, yes? Then you should know all of the different things cell phones can do, so you can figure out which features you want to duplicate and which you don't want to bother with, just yet. Calling other people for a chat and retaining a memory of the most recently dialed numbers are only the start of all the features they have, these days."

So this is how you break away your wrist, always pulling toward the spot between fingers and thumb," Evanor demonstrated, gently tugging his own arm out of the handhold he had instructed Mikor to use. He broke free easily, though Mikor tightened his young fingers reflexively. *"That spot is the weakest in someone's grip. And by turning inward to face them, you're automatically putting your arm into the best leverage position to get free."*

Mikor wrinkled his nose. He was *expecting* a sword lesson, not this weaponless stuff. "When do we get to the swords?"

"Later. First, you need to know how to get away. Now, since I'm a lot stronger than you, obviously you can't just pull your arm away on its own. So when I take your wrist, I want you to make your caught hand into a fist, and grab it with your free hand as you turn to face me."

"Later?" Mikor questioned. "But, I wanna learn sword work *now!*"

"You'll be living here a long time, plenty of time to—"

"I wanna learn sword work *now!*" Mikor protested, drowning out Evanor's whispers. He frowned at Evanor, suspicion coalescing in his mind. "The others say you're good with a sword, but you won't show me anything—I don't think you're any good! I'm gonna go find Uncle Dominor! *He* knows what to do!"

Whirling, the boy stalked toward the door. Evanor lunged forward and managed to catch his wrist. Manacling it firmly but not bruisingly with his fingers, he allowed himself a smirk as Mikor tugged fruitlessly, trying to free his young, thin arm.

"Leggo! Let go of me! Evanor, let go!" Mikor ordered, tugging with his arm, as if trying to slip his hand through the circle of the older male's grasp. He tried kicking at Evanor, but the mage dodged the blow with just a shift of his leg. "Let go of me, now!"

"No."

The smile accompanying his denial was smug on the outside, though inside, Evanor worried that he'd just ruined his chances of getting to know the boy. Mikor tugged on his arm again, then scowled. He couldn't wriggle free, however. "Leggo! You're being mean!"

Evanor waited until he had the boy's attention again, then whispered, *"You realize, of course, if you had paid attention to what I was trying to teach you, just now . . . you would already be free? I'm not trying to be mean. I'm just trying to make a very good point."*

Mikor gave him a wary, skeptical look.

"Why do you think I was trying to teach it to you?" Evanor asked him rhetorically. *"Mikor, people a lot meaner than me are going to try to grab you, at some point in your life. You need to know how to get free and get away from them."*

"If I have a sword, I can fight them!" Mikor half-boasted, half-protested.

Ev arched one of his light blond brows, showing the youth his skepticism. *"Are you going to spend the rest of your life with your sword in your hand? It would be very awkward when using a refreshing room, and I don't think your mother would let you use it instead of a fork at the dinner table. And even if you do carry a sword all the time . . . someone could still sneak up on you from behind and grab your wrist . . . and then he'd have control of your sword arm. And more than just your sword arm . . ."*

He emphasized his whispered words by moving Mikor's arm around, and with it the rest of his body, though the Natallian boy tried to resist. Evanor made sure to not move the boy too roughly, just strongly enough to make his point. Subsiding, he allowed the boy to face him again, though he kept his fingers around Mikor's wrist.

"Are you gonna let me go?"

It occurred to Evanor that he *should* be helping Mariel correct the boy's language. But a lecture wouldn't help at the moment. Instead, he shrugged and merely spoke with the clear diction his voiceless state demanded of him. *"Are you going to pay attention to my lessons?"*

Mikor considered Evanor's words. Finally, he sighed roughly, the kind of heavy exhalation that only a youth being put out by the demands of an adult could emit, and rolled his green eyes expressively. *"Fine.* I'll listen. Are you gonna let go, now?"

"No. But I am going to tell you how to get yourself free," Evanor compromised. *"Ready?"*

Intrigued in spite of himself, Mikor nodded, eyeing the blond mage.

"Make a fist with the hand that is in my grip," he directed the boy. *"Good. Now grab it with your free hand . . . very good. Now, pretend your caught arm is a lever, and pull up and away with both it and your free hand, in the direction where my thumb and fingers—yes! Like that! Exactly like that!"* Evanor praised as Mikor wrenched his arm free.

Of course, he wasn't holding the boy really tightly, just firmly, but Mikor got himself free. Mikor grinned. "Yes!"

"Useful, isn't it?" Evanor asked him.

"Well, yeah . . . *Now* can we get to the swords?" Mikor asked him hopefully.

Closing his eyes briefly, Evanor silently counseled himself to be patient. Opening them again, he reached out and grabbed the back of Mikor's tunic. *"And if I held you like this, how would you get free?"*

The dirty look he received from the boy was enough to let Ev know his point had been driven home.

Releasing Mikor, Evanor nodded at the door. *"Come with me."*

Uncertainty crossed the youth's face, wrinkling his nose. Mikor followed, trailing after Evanor, who headed for the kitchens, one wing over and one floor down. Unfortunately, just as they were about to enter the kitchen, an unmistakable, feminine moan met their ears. Evanor quickly stopped, holding out his arm to stop Mikor from entering the arched doorway.

"Oh yes, Wolfer . . . yes!"

"Mmm, Alys, so *sweet* . . ."

Mikor tried to peer past Evanor's arm, whispering, "What are they doing in there?"

"Shh." Pursing his lips, Evanor whistled. Sharply. Two voices exclaimed, there was some bumping noises, mutterings, and then the clearing of a voice, before Wolfer spoke.

"Who's there?"

Cautiously, Evanor leaned his head forward enough to peer into the kitchen. Both his secondborn brother and his second sister-in-law were decent, though Alys still had her back to the doorway, fiddling with something on her front side. Probably the lacings to the odd garment Kelly had come up with, a compromising cross between trousers and a sort of demi-skirt, high in the front and low in the back. Both women liked wearing it because it was sort of feminine, thanks to the skirt-like ruffle, but very practical for moving around in, thanks to the pant legs.

Wolfer, spotting his fourthborn sibling, folded his arms across his chest. "What do you want?"

Since they were decent . . . though his brother's chin looked suspiciously damp . . . Evanor walked inside, allowing Mikor to trail after him. Stopping when he was within whispering distance, he tipped his head at the boy. *"I need your help demonstrating something."*

Arching a brow, Wolfer eyed the two of them. "What?"

"Wrestling. I want to demonstrate holds and escapes, in specific."

Not too happy with the request, Wolfer rubbed the back of his neck, glancing at his wife. She looked to be too embarrassed to turn around and face them. The secondborn brother sighed, his deep voice rumbling reluctantly. "Right now?"

"Yes, now. Before my young student, here, loses interest."

Grimacing, Wolfer sighed again—the kind of heavy exhalation a male being pulled away from his choice of female might heave—and nodded. "Fine. But only for a short while."

Evanor didn't protest. He had what he wanted, his elder brother's cooperation, so he turned to lead the way back upstairs to the salle in the west wing. It hadn't escaped his notice that Mikor found Wolfer to be . . . intimidating. If Evanor could *show* the boy how to escape from a clearly stronger opponent, then perhaps it would capture and hold the youth's attention long enough for the lessons to take hold.

If he and Mariel were Destined for each other, then it was his responsibility to make sure Mikor knew how to protect himself. The threat of Katan finding out there were women on the Isle still loomed, as well as a possible return of the Mandarites. Even if the only ones who came to the island were immigrants hoping to settle and start new lives here, some of them would have children of their own, after all.

Some of those children might not have learned the value of being nice, polite, and civilized. Some might be younger and thus not yet fully taught, while others would be older and might be the kind to reject their parents' teachings. Or the kind with parents who didn't have the time to teach them right from wrong, the value of accepting responsibility for one's actions, that sort of thing. Or parents who just didn't care; it happened sometimes.

That thought led to him thinking of the need for some sort of screening process to weed out the undesirable sorts of immigrants from the ones who would actually make good new citizens. Not that they were likely to get new citizens in a huge rush anytime soon, but it was better to be prepared in advance . . . which was the point of today's lesson with Mikor. Which Evanor would teach to the boy, even if it meant going up against his second-eldest brother, who out-massed him by at least twice as many muscles.

Mariel dropped into the seat next to Evanor, heaving a rough sigh. "I swear, if I weren't such a compassionate, kindhearted person, I'd do away with the pain-blocking spells I've oh-so-compassionately been using. *Please* tell me we're having chicken for lunch. I could do with a little vengeance for all the blood I lost, trying to separate individuals from the flock."

"Sorry, we're having beef," Trevan apologized, passing over a platter filled with tender, pink gray slices. "I wanted roasted chicken, but Alys had the cooking chore for lunch. That reminds me, Morg wants to see you and your son after you're through eating," he told Mariel. "He'll be ready to administer the Ultra Tongue to the two of you and Alys, once we're through here."

Koranen made a face. "Couldn't they have it before they ate? That stuff tastes nasty."

"We were all too busy to bother preparing it, up until now. But Alys baked a sweet bread and promised to set aside a few slices for you to have afterward. Something nice to get the bitter taste out of your mouth," Dominor promised Mikor and his mother.

Mariel bumped Evanor's arm, passing him a bowl of fried roots.

She heard his quiet, indrawn hiss, though the others were still gathering at the table, making enough noise to drown out the sound from more than a few feet away. Leaning over, she whispered into his ear.

"Are you all right?"

Evanor managed something like a smile of reassurance for everyone else, since he didn't want his brothers—especially Wolfer—to worry. *"I'd tell you no, but I'll live. I pulled three muscles in my arm . . . and two in my ribs . . . and I think I twisted my ankle. I'll tell you about it later. Worst is . . . I was in the mood to play one of my instruments this afternoon, for the first time in weeks . . . and now I'm not sure I can pick one up."*

Goodness. Mariel blinked, wondering what her son had done to the poor man. Speaking of which, she had to get the two of them back into their usual patterns. She was determined to give her son a good education, even if they were far from any organized schools. "Mikor, after we take our doses of that potion, it'll be time for you to settle down into some lessons."

Her son grumbled. "Motherrrr! Ev was showing me magical stuff he'd made. I was hoping to see the rest of it!"

"That's no reason to neglect the other areas of your education. We'll start with a review of all the dangers on the island to watch out for and then review your multiplication tables. We haven't worked on your mathematical skills lately."

Moping over his food, Mikor glanced at his honorary aunt, who hadn't served herself any food, yet. "Is Aunt Serina going to be testing me?"

The blonde mathemagician gave him a wan smile, even as she swayed back from the bowl of fried roots being passed in front of her. "Aunt Serina . . . isn't feeling very good, right now. I think . . . I think I'll just have a bowl of salad . . . and eat it elsewhere."

Mariel's brows rose at that. She watched her friend push away from the table, forgoing the salad. Dominor split his attention between his plate of food and his wife, then grabbed her empty plate, dumped some garden greens on it, and rose to follow her. Catching his elbow, Mariel added a piece of flatbread. "You might want to give her weak juice or tea, too, but don't force it on her. Definitely give her some water, though."

Nodding, Dominor followed his wife.

"Morning sickness?" Kelly asked, sympathy in her tone.

"Most likely. I'll examine her later," Mariel offered. *And Evanor.* She still didn't know what her son had done to the poor man. Knowing how rambunctious and energetic Mikor could be, she could only imagine.

So, how *did* you injure yourself today?" Mariel asked Evanor, closing the outer door to her son's suite. She had just tucked Mikor into bed, sleepy but happy.

He had done better with his math than either of them had expected, given the turmoil and excitement of the move. He had, however, earned a lecture on proper use of language, when she'd asked him to give an oral report on the flavor, use, and effects of Ultra Tongue, using a couple of books borrowed from the castle's library to test its efficacy with the written word for both of them. Plus she had instructed him to write a thank-you note in the Katani script to Koranen, in gratitude for the enchanted metal tiles that the seventhborn brother had given each of them. The Artifacts were supposed to protect them against the threat of fire and other disturbances as they slept, and Mariel had used the gifts as a chance to reinforce proper manners in her son.

In some ways, being a Healer was a lot easier than being a mother; once she Healed someone, they usually stayed healed until injured again. With her son, it was a case of herding cats at times, trying to get him to remember certain lessons, whether it was common courtesy, or multiplication, or simply how to speak properly. Now that Mikor was in bed, Mariel could relax and be a woman again, as well as a mother.

Evanor, having seen her disappearing into her son's room to say goodnight, had lingered in the hallway rather than going into his bedroom. It had been a longish wait, but worthwhile. Seeing her in the hallway like this had reminded him of last night, giving him reason to wait. His soreness gave him an excellent excuse to reenact last night, if with a twist.

"If you promise to give me a backrub . . . and maybe a little touch of Healing . . . I'll tell you about it," he offered.

Mariel chuckled. She hadn't seen much of him after parting company at lunch, but she had seen him moving stiffly. "Opportunist. Well, go on inside. I'll follow. I'm presuming you want this backrub to take place on your bed, in case you fall asleep out of sheer bliss just like I did?"

Nodding, Evanor opened the door to his suite and escorted her inside.

"Oh, how lovely!" Mariel stared wide-eyed at the elaborate parquetry that greeted her. Both the floor and the walls of his salon had been inlaid with different colors of wood, forming geometric patterns in bands of narrow and broad trim, eight-pointed stars, sinuous curves, and repeated patterns. All of the wood gleamed as if well oiled. Even the furniture matched, much of it looking almost new. "Did your brother, Trevan—the one who works with wood and such—make any of this?"

Evanor shook his head. *"No, but he did repair much of it, when we first moved in here. I traded several chores with him, to have this room restored to its best. I love the warmth of wood, even if I have no skill for working with it."*

"I can see why you love it," Mariel agreed. She tipped her head back, staring at the ceiling, while Evanor retired to the next room. The ceiling was plastered, and not very ornately at that. Though, where the ceilings of the other rooms were often plain and white, this one had been covered with the color-changing paint. The sun had set outside, but overhead, a flock of birds swooped and soared in a clear blue sky. Of course, they were illuminated awkwardly by a trio of lightglobes in a wrought-iron stand near the door.

Accustomed after years of living at the Retreat at Koral-tai to having suncrystals shining down from overhead, not from the side like torches, lamps, or these round lightglobe things, she sometimes found the different direction of the light to be a little disorienting. Especially coupled with that painted ceiling. Yet the exotic nature of this chamber appealed to her. She longed to see it in daylight, when it was at its best.

A soft whistle broke her reverie. Padding over to the door, Mariel opened it and stepped inside. More parquetry greeted her, along with another painted ceiling. This time, the view seemed like one was looking up through a canopy of autumn trees. Every once in a while, an unfelt tug of painted wind would send a few red and golden leaves swirling free overhead. Instruments hung on the walls and rested on shelves, ranging from a broad, flat drum to a deep-bellied lute, a lap harp, and a set of panpipes crafted from glass. If he had finally felt in the mood to play his instruments, but had been thwarted by sore muscles, then it was her duty as a Healer to get him back into the mood. Music had been too rarely heard at the Retreat—aside from formal religious pieces—for her to not encourage it now.

Lowering her gaze to the bed as she approached, she spotted her patient lying on his stomach on the right side, near a lightglobe mounted on one of the tall bedposts. The covers had been drawn back, leaving him outlined in crisp, bleached linen. A long, lean expanse of lightly tanned back met her gaze, lighter than his arms, but definitely gilded compared to the paleness of the skin visible at the small of his back. His legs weren't tanned, either, until about mid-calf, and his ankles weren't nearly as golden as his arms.

Mariel could tell all of this very easily, because he wasn't wearing anything, other than a scrap of that nice, nubbly fabric they used for toweling cloths in this place. She stopped when the realization hit, staring at all that masculine skin on display. All that very nice, masculine skin. Very, very nice . . .

A blush washed over her, heating her whole face. Her only saving grace was that his head was turned away from her at the moment. That, and when she dragged her mind out of its salacious gutter, she realized she could see a few bruises here and there. The sight of those darkened spots acted like a dash of cold water on her warm skin, reminding her sharply that she was here to Heal and massage the man, not leap all over him like an animal in heat.

However much she wanted to.

EIGHT

❧❧❧

vanor heard her stop when she was only halfway across the
room. Heart pounding in his chest, as it had since the moment he decided to strip himself completely bare, he hoped he
hadn't offended her. It was a daring, bold thing to do . . . but he did
hurt in several different locations, and she was a Healer. He just
wanted her to *see* him as a man, too.

Of course, it was a good thing he was lying facedown. If Ev had
been forced to lie on his back, no amount of fuzzy toweling cloth
could've hidden his eagerness for her touch. In specific, the eagerness of his masculinity; the thought of being naked in the presence
of such a beautiful, lush beauty as she, after more than three years
of celibacy, followed most recently by having to listen to his elder
brothers courting their own women, the idea of having her hands
willingly touching and caressing him . . . it was heart-pounding, in-
toxicating, heady stuff.

She moved again, and his ears pricked, taking in every sound she
made. The soft pad of her leather-slippered feet on the inlaid wood
of his floor. The gentle inhale, exhale, of her breath. The creak of

that one floorboard near the foot of his bed. He heard her speak before he felt the bed dip next to his waist, felt her hand gently touch his shoulder.

"You were going to tell me how this happened?"

"Lessons for your son. He wasn't paying attention," Ev whispered, and had to admonish himself silently to *pay attention* as well. To what he was supposed to be telling her, and not just the feel of her palm sliding gently over his back. *"So I asked for Wolfer's help and demonstrated some wrestling tricks, how to escape various holds and traps."*

"And so he wrenched your muscles and gave you bruises?" Mariel asked dryly. "I thought you were just demonstrating, not actually wrestling."

"No, that was my fault," Evanor confessed with a huffed breath for a laugh. He hissed as her fingers prodded at the far side of his ribs. *"Wolfer always holds back against me, but to match even that . . . well, it takes more of my strength than it does of his. I wanted to put on a good show."*

"Did it work?" she asked him, moving down onto his legs. "Was my son impressed?"

"I believe so. He practiced with the two of us with a lot more enthusiasm than before. Then we did basic sword drills against the pells, like my twin has apparently been teaching him. I think I've got his—ow!—his respect, now."

"Sorry, that's a deeper bruise than the rest." Extending her inner senses all the way to his feet, Mariel knew he'd recover on his own soon enough—nothing was worse than a few pulled muscles, a few deep bruises, after all—but a little judicious Healing wouldn't hurt. She did owe him a backrub, too. Healing four chickens of their deliberately destroyed vocal chords hadn't taken that much of her strength, just a lot of her concentration. "There's a lot of tension in your muscles, a lot of twitches and spasms. I'll give you a Healing first, then the massage."

"Please." The whisper was more of a sigh. Of course, Evanor knew the reason for at least half that tension, and most of those little muscle spasms. They were from the touch of her hands, warm, smooth, feminine. If he hadn't lain himself carefully on the bed,

pertinent parts adjusted just so before whistling for her, he might have injured himself by now.

Pertinent bits that hardened even further, the moment she started Singing. It was a soft sound, a little too lively to be a lullaby, yet gentle enough to help coax his body into relaxing. Heat poured out of her palms as she Sang the magical words, seeping into his aching muscles, soothing strained ligaments and tendons. It didn't take long for Mariel to infuse her Healing magic into Evanor's body, allowing her to reduce the tune to a soft, wordless croon and permitting her to firm her touch from a sliding caress to a deeper knead.

If Ev had any sort of voice at all, he would have been groaning in sensual pleasure by the time she was merely humming. As it was, when she stopped Singing and just massaged him from ankles to nape and back, he was breathing heavily with each exhalation. Finally, her hands stopped, one of them giving him a pat on the middle of his back.

"Time to turn over," Mariel instructed him.

Evanor shifted, starting to comply, and stopped, reminded abruptly of what her touch had done to him. There was no way he could turn over. Not without grossly offending her. She patted his back again when he didn't move.

"Come on, turn over."

"*Uh . . . no, that's alright. Thank you,*" he added politely, glad his face was turned away from her, hiding most of his blush.

"Don't be ridiculous. I can tell you still have several bruises and a couple of strains on your front half. It's time to take care of those," Mariel countered. "Come on, roll over."

"*No, really—*"

She swatted the curve of his rump lightly, knowing the toweling cloth would absorb most of the sting. "Roll over, Evanor! This is your Healer talking."

Reluctantly, one hand furtively catching the edge of the cloth still draped over his hips to make sure it continued to cover him, Evanor carefully edged onto his side, facing away from her. Inching away from her, in fact. But no farther; if he rolled any farther, his problem would be all too apparent. And since he really, really did not want to offend her on this, her second day in this place—

Impatient with his reluctance, Mariel pulled on his shoulder and hip. He resisted, but she managed to roll him onto his back anyway. He had a couple bruises on his front, a rampant erection, and a . . . rampant . . . Heat flooded her face. In fact, it not only flooded her face, it flooded her womb, too, making her lower abdomen *clench*. There was no disguising what, exactly, tented that nubbly-soft fabric, causing his reluctance.

Dragging her gaze away from his barely covered loins, she found his face as red as her own must have been, though unlike her, his eyes were tightly shut. Undoubtedly, he was mortified at being caught out like this. Mariel could imagine and sympathize with his mortification, but she could also understand his reaction.

As a Healer, she had been trained in a Gucheran Sanitorium, which had included lessons in the physical healing arts as well as the metaphysical ones. One of her classes had covered the healing properties of massages. It had included a lecture on how pain and tension could sometimes cause impotence in both men and women . . . and how the release of pain and stress could induce a corresponding, sudden sexual response just like this one.

Of course, the class had implied that such reactions weren't usually very strong, just enough to let the affected patient know that functionality had returned to their sexuality. A partial enhancement and display of desire, as it were. This, however, was a full-blown engorgement. A jutting spike of man-flesh, ripe and ready for a good, solid nailing. Just looking at how excited he was made her think of whipping off that towel, yanking down her hose, and straddling him lasciviously. Even if that wasn't normally how she approached sex, that was what she wanted to do, for one wild, impulsive moment.

Her womb clenched again, voting in favor of that idea. Blushing, Mariel cleared her throat, dragging her mind back out of its sex-starved gutter. He was her *patient*. She would keep that in mind, above all else. "Um . . . once again, first the Healing, and then the massage."

I can do this I can do this—I can do this without leaping on him like a cat in heat . . . Oh, sweet Natua, give me strength, he's so Gods-be-damned sexy!

Drawing in a deep, bracing breath, she let it out in a thread of Song, caressing him down at his ankles. It seemed the safest place to start, really. Except even his feet were attractive. At least, she had the odd urge to suckle on his toes. It was something Mariel hadn't even done with her late husband, nor had ever felt an urge to do before, but these particular toes looked tasty. His calves looked lickable, too; unconsciously, Mariel moistened her lips with the tip of her tongue before going back to crooning a trickle of her power into his flesh.

Evanor wanted to groan in protest when she carefully detoured around his groin, working her way up onto his stomach and the bruises that had gathered there. Yes, she was relieving him of the aches of his injuries, all the way up to the strained tendon over his collarbone. But she was building up a different ache in his body. It rose with every gliding caress of her soft hand and fell with each wave of her power, soothing his hurts but denying him relief. Easing his tension but doing nothing to give him release. And all the while she touched him, teased him involuntarily, her voice wove itself through his senses as surely as her touch, digging into his nerves only to sensitize them further.

Feeling rather warm, breathless, even sweaty, Mariel studied her patient. She was breathing almost as heavily as Evanor was, with his head tilted back and his mouth parted to allow each panting breath. The last of his bruises were fading away, with no more strains, no more aches left to Heal. Save for one, but Healing magic wasn't what that ache needed.

Technically, her work was done. A Healer fixed whatever the injury or illness was, and this was neither an illness nor an injury. A Healer held compassion for his or her patients, but remained aloof from them, for to care too much was as bad as to not care enough. A Healer . . . *Oh, toss it!* Mariel ordered herself, giving up on reciting the litany of what a Healer was or wasn't. *It's odd, how they prattle on in all those classes about maintaining a certain objectivity, but they never address what to do when it's your own flesh and blood that's in need. They cover the warnings about not falling in love with your patients, just because*

*of the intimacy of Healing someone, and the gratitude of being Healed . . .
but they never cover caring for your beloved!*

He's not going to be your patient forever, Mariel Vargel, she lectured
herself. *You're here on a burgeoning island nation with five bachelors, and
this is the one that you're drawn to, like you haven't been drawn to anyone
since first meeting Milon all those years ago . . . so stop tormenting both of
you!* she ordered herself.

She jumped a little when his hands came up to cover hers, which
had stopped kneading the muscles of his chest. Those hands pushed
her palms lower, onto his abdomen. She glanced at his face, meeting
his tawny brown gaze.

Evanor looked feverish, but wasn't fevered. In agony, but not
injured. *Technically,* she should leave the room right now. Right now,
in fact. Right about now . . . right now . . .

*Right. And trees will fly! Sod it . . . do I, or don't I? Should I, or
shouldn't I?—Bright Heavens, this is hard to decide!*

His touch was light enough, she only had to twitch her flesh under his to be freed. Letting his arms fall to the bed on either side, he
watched her, chest rising and falling in shallow breaths. Dragging
her hazel eyes down to his loins, she noticed the damp spot on the
toweling cloth draped over the blatant peak made by his flesh. It riv-
eted her gaze in place.

A dry corner of her mind managed to observe, *You do realize, for
all the times you nagged Serina about releasing her sexual tension with a
fellow, she nagged you, too? And here you have a man who—if he still had
a voice—would be begging for your touch. Forget your teachers! They're
all dried up old biddies and bachelors! You are a woman, Evanor is a man,
and you're attracted to each other. Bright Heavens, go for it!*

Sliding her hands down to his hipbones, Mariel plucked up the
toweling cloth, lifting it free of his loins. He grabbed for it belat-
edly, but she flicked it over her shoulder, out of his reach. The sight
of his erection, rampant and proud, took some of her breath away.
He wasn't longer than Milon had been, but he was thicker. And erect
enough that the little cowl of his foreskin had stretched itself out,
baring the reddened, seeping tip of him.

Evanor couldn't breathe, he wanted her to touch him so much.

He tried, gulping air in short, sharp gasps, but he was so on the edge, he was forced to close his eyes against the sight of her staring at him, in case he flew over the edge. Or worse, in case she didn't like what she saw.

The feel of her fingers encircling him was startling. Twice, in fact—once for the aching beauty of her touch itself, and again for the way that touch shattered the tightly gripped control that had been stealing his breath. Arching his back, Evanor cried out in pleasure. Nothing escaped him but a long, drawn-out hiss of air, of course. Well, that, and the *splat* of his semen striking his stomach . . . and the heavy gasps of lungs that followed as she gently stroked him, milking his seed. Prying open his eyes, he watched her gazing at him with rapt attention, cheeks flushed, lips glistening in the glow of the lightglobe as she moistened them with her tongue.

The thought of that tongue kept him from softening. Combined with her touch, with the reality of her *touching* him . . . Evanor covered her hand with his, showing her how to stroke more firmly. It was said that lightning could strike in the same place twice, if the energies weren't dissipated with the first stroke. *His* energies certainly hadn't been sated, and he definitely wanted her to keep stroking him.

Thankfully, the shy, pleased smile curving her mouth reassured him that he wasn't forcing himself on her. Indeed, when he let his hand fall from hers, she kept stroking him of her own volition. She even experimented a little, twisting her hand on the downstroke, tickling him with the lightness of her fingertips on the upstroke, pausing to smear her palm through the moisture on his abdomen so that her skin slid over his without too much friction.

But there was enough friction to lift him back up again. Literally, as his back muscles and buttocks tensed, driving himself up through the tight clasp of her fingers. Once, twice, thrice . . . she worked with his rhythm, bringing up her other hand to gently stroke the sack of flesh at the base of his shaft. Evanor clutched at the bedsheet with both hands; the sweet torment went on and on, rising higher inside of him.

Those beautiful hazel eyes shifted to his face, meeting and holding his gaze, but it was too intense. Forced to close his eyes, to try to block out the vivid sight of her enjoying giving him pleasure, Evanor panted and bucked. Hissing a second time in his release, shuddering with the strength of it, this time he struggled so heavily for air, he couldn't hear the sound of his seed striking his skin. Though he could feel it.

Her touch gentled, thankfully. He was now quite sensitive, and when she withdrew her hands, it was the warmth of her skin he missed, not the stroking of her fingers over his flesh. But he did miss her. Heart slowing, gasps subsiding, he struggled against his body's post-bliss lethargy. The bed shifted, but it was a few more moments before he could find enough energy to open his eyes.

Mariel wasn't in the room with him anymore. Before he could do more than blink and frown, worried, he saw her emerging from the refreshing room, a damp scrap of cloth in her hand. A washcloth. Returning to his side, she sat on the edge of the bed and gently cleaned his skin, wiping up the mess of his fluids with the warm wet fabric.

If she hadn't still been smiling as well as blushing, he might have been horribly embarrassed. As it was, he struggled to find something to say. Withdrawing from the side of the bed, she returned to the re-freshing room for a moment, then came back to him. But not to join him; instead, she reached over his body and pulled the covers into place, tucking them around him with a gentle touch. A dip of her head brushed her curls against his cheek, and her lips against his temple.

"Sleep well, Evanor."

That made him narrow his eyes, but she had already turned away. He was *not* a child, to be tucked into bed like that. Pursing his lips, he whistled, a short, sharp sound that caught her attention before she was more than halfway to the bedchamber door. Freeing a hand from the covers, he curled a finger, beckoning her back to his side.

Curious, Mariel returned. "Yes?"

Evanor caught her hand, tugging her closer. Lifting it to his lips, he pressed a kiss to her knuckles. As much as he wanted to do more . . . prudence and blissful exhaustion modified what he wanted to say.

"Tomorrow night . . ."

"Yes?" Mariel asked, breath catching and holding with curiosity.

"I'll return the favor."

Heat burned her face. Managing a nod, she freed her hand and escaped. Smirking, Evanor snuggled into his bedding and sighed. Blissfully.

Lord Consus had a headache. So did half the Councilors in the Chamber, he suspected. Rubbing at his forehead, he peered at the clock on the wall. Two hours past supper time. One would think the starvation of the Council would cause them to come to *some* sort of swift conclusion of the matter, but it didn't seem to be making any sort of dent.

Mainly because of Duke Finneg of Conflict Resolution and Viscountess Thera of Tax Collection. Both were tenacious when it came to promoting their own ideas. Of course, Finneg was as warlike as his department, though at least he had forgone his breastplate in favor of a crimson silk tunic that warmed and complemented his brown skin. Thera was icy-cold in comparison, her pale southlander skin looking even paler, because the gray satin of her corseted gown accented the streaks of gray in her dark brown hair. She looked like a pookrah carved from ice, with her long jaw and intense stare.

The rest of the Council, looking like a scattered clutch of pompous jewels in their riot of colors, were growing tired of the debate. Most had managed to attend, as soon as they heard that one of the new topics to be discussed was Nightfall Isle. Even Her Majesty, Queen Samille, was in the Council Chamber. She wasn't a mage like her husband, and thus not qualified to serve as a Councilor, but she did possess a broad practical streak. As Consus watched, she touched her husband on the back of his tanned hand, leaning over to whisper in his ear. Her dark hair swung in front of her pale cheek, obscuring whatever words she spoke.

Oh, please, let that be her telling His Majesty that this nonsense has gone on long enough . . .

He didn't really think his wish was going to be answered, until

King Taurin grasped the black marble ball resting in its little dish at his seat. Unlike other nations, whose Council undoubtedly sat at a long, angular table, some *V*-shaped, others *U*-shaped, and still more shaped like rings and rectangles, ovals and other things, the Council Chamber was filled with individual little tables. The oval hall was also tiered in four different layers, so that there was plenty of room for the Councilors to spread out, yet still see over each other's heads. That allowed everyone in the oval-shaped room to keep an eye on their leader, the strongest mage among them.

A few others among those arguing with Finneg and Thera noticed where their king's tanned hand now rested and stopped speaking. The drop in volume caused the others to notice as well. Even Finneg ceased his diatribe on teaching the exilees to respect Katani law, lowering himself back into his seat with a disgruntled but respectful look. Releasing the dark sphere, His Majesty spoke.

"What we have here is a consensus among the majority of us. Strange items for purchase are *not* reason enough, in and of themselves, to engage your department's particular services, Councilor Finneg. We do not even know whether these items *should* be a cause for concern," Taurin added, pausing only briefly before continuing. "But, in the interest of averting any possible Disaster . . . they should be investigated. *Properly*. Councilor Consus."

Consus jerked his head out of his hand, with which he had been trying to massage away his headache. "Yes, Your Majesty?"

"You know which glass in the Hall of Mirrors is connected to one of the Corvis brothers' mirrors. Please bring it here."

"Yes, Your Majesty."

Rising from his seat, Consus retreated through the door in the wall behind and to his right. The Hall of Mirrors was next door to the Council Chamber for just this reason. Orienting himself in the room, he selected a mirror that was a rounded-cornered rectangle and lifted it from its hanger. Carefully, he carried it back into the Chamber. Lady Apista, Councilor of the Temples, was already setting up a stand for the mirror on the bottom level, facing their ruler. Most of those who were positioned behind or too shallowly to either side shifted out of their seats, joining the others in the other half of the room for a better view, though a few remained in place, not interested in having a look.

"Shall I activate it, Your Majesty?" Consus offered as soon as the mirror was settled safely in place on the tripod. A glance behind him showed King Taurin nodding, his sun-streaked brown hair sliding across his shoulders. Touching the mirror, Consus muttered under his breath, focusing the spell on the mirror that had been linked to it and left in the brothers' possession for just such a need. Blue rippled across the surface, and a faint chiming noise could be heard, letting them know the contact-spell was working.

She was very beautiful. Full of life, laughing and giggling and eating that fluffy stuff Kelly had told him was called "popcorn." Ignoring the fingerprints he was leaving on the glass, Morganen leaned on the surface of his extra-dimensional mirror, watching the object of his scrying affections. She had invited two friends over for a box-mirror play. At least, that was the best way Morganen could describe the device, since it was shaped like a box, had images almost as clear and crisp as a mirror-scrying, and it depicted scenes from some sort of drama. It wasn't live-action; he recognized at least two of the participants from other productions and knew they were actors portraying some sort of land-spanning story, though the various transportation Artifacts used in that world looked very little like the ones he knew in this world.

Of course, without opening up the mirror, he couldn't *hear* what was going on, but Morg didn't want to do that. For one, she had guests over, and it would be rude for him to interrupt that. Not to mention dangerous, given how Kelly's neighbors had reacted poorly to the mere *thought* of magic. For another, she would undoubtedly want to touch his hand. As much as he longed to do the same, it wasn't a wise idea while her friends were in the house.

A chiming noise startled him. Pulling away from the mirror, he glanced around his workroom, trying to locate the source. It came, he realized after a moment, from behind a bit of cloth shrouding one of his other mirrors. The one connected to the Council of Mages. Curiosity warred with annoyance. Here he was, enjoying the voyeurism of watching the woman he hoped was his Prophesied bride, and the Council had to stick their stupid noses into his life. Morg didn't want to deal with them, but if he didn't answer the damned mirror—

A brilliant idea came to him, widening his eyes. Allowing himself a brief snicker, Morganen struggled his features into a semblance of polite neutrality and pulled the shroud from the mirror. A mutter under his breath set up an illusion spell to record his image. Touching the rim, he activated the blue-glowing surface . . . but didn't give the mages on the other side of the connection a chance to speak.

"Greetings," Morganen stated cheerfully, barely pausing for breath. "You have reached the mirror for Nightfall Isle, home of the Corvis brothers. Unfortunately, my siblings and I are busy at the moment and are unable to respond to your attempted link. If you feel you have reached this mirror in error, please check your spell and try your scry again. If you have reached the correct mirror and wish to leave a brief message, please state your name, your mirror-coordinates, and a time at which we might be able to get back to you."

A subtle flick of his finger behind his back, and a gong shimmered softly. He held his polite smile for a silent, slow count to fifty, while Councilor Consus blinked and spluttered, and the others in the background started arguing, then flicked his finger again. The gong sounded again.

"Thank you for contacting Nightfall Isle—have a good day!" With his pleasant, friendly smile still in place, ignoring the ongoing sputterings of the Council, Morganen reached up and touched the edge of the mirror again, breaking the link. A quick mutter, and a misty veil of light lifted off of his body and sank into the mirror's gilded frame, imbuing the scrying device with an exact duplicate of what he had just done. Now, every time the Council called . . . they'd get that exact same message once again, without having to bother him.

He grinned wickedly. The message said the mirror would record their complaints and attempts to contact the brothers . . . but he hadn't enchanted it to do so. Yet. As he watched, the mirror chimed, flickering with the blue holding pattern of before. It shifted to yellow after a moment, and Morganen could hear his own voice, if faintly, repeating his previous "answering machine" message.

Unfortunately, as amusing as it would be to just let the mirror ignore the Council's reactions to this new piece of magic, he knew better. In order to keep his brothers prepared for whatever may come, he had to record the damned Council and their damned complaints. Picking up a piece of chalk from one of his tables, Morganen scraped a set of runes onto the rim of the mirror, just as his little speech came to its end. The waves of pulsing yellow on the screen picked up pink undertones, turning it peach when the gong resounded inside the recording.

Faintly, as dimly as his recorded voice had been, he could hear the Council protesting the insult of being ignored and attempting to get ahold of a real, live mage. A last rune as the faint tone of the gong sounded again, and the spell was complete. Now it would function as the magical equivalent to that "answering machine" thing he had seen Hope using.

Setting the chalk back down, Morganen dusted off his fingers and returned to the cheval mirror, whistling, happy with his improvisation. The view on the mirror no longer showed the sitting room where the scrying-box was located, but that was alright; he had set it to follow Hope around her house, and it had followed her from the couch to the kitchen, where she now stood in front of the whiteboard thing they used to communicate.

There was a curious, blank expression on her tanned face. Morganen frowned, bemused. He watched her pick up the writing pen, uncap it, and mark something on the surface. A number—44.

She blinked, seemed to come out of what he realized must have been a trance, eyed the number, then shrugged and capped the pen, returning it to its tray. Whatever it meant, she didn't explain it to him, though she had written to him on that board a time or two in the past. Of course, it might not have anything to do with *him*, but Morganen decided he would keep an eye on the number all the same, in case she explained it later, or if he had a chance to question her about it.

Even if Evanor was working on courting their newest female, it would be a little while before Mariel became his bride. And only the Gods knew how much longer before Trevan's bride came, and Rydan's bride, and Koranen's, whoever they were destined to be. Mindful of the long wait before he could court his own woman, Morganen reluctantly ended the scrying.

If he tried to court her now, beyond occasional question-and-answer sessions and the occasional palm-to-palm touch, their impatience to be together could mount until it threatened to ruin his Prophesied task. Worse . . . he could lose her, if she wanted to join him before he was ready for her. *If* she was his Destined Bride. Since rushing the point ran that risk, he wasn't going to try. Morg liked women, and there was no doubt in his mind that he liked this particular woman.

The mirror chimed again, telling him the Council was calling again. The faint but demanding babble of voices on the other end of the link cut off as the creamy gold surface of the mirror shifted to peach, to yellow again, then from yellow to clear, ending the scrying link. A few moments later, it chimed again, flaring blue, then turning yellow . . . and returned to clear, indicating the Council had ended the attempt. That left him staring at his own reflection.

Grinning at himself, Morg lifted the drape-cloth back into place, shrouding the mirror in a second layer of protection against scrying. Most of the mirrors in their exiled, palatial home were enspelled against scrying attempts, and those that weren't were enspelled with the same shades-of-blue privacy illusion that prevented anyone from peering into a room uninvited. Certainly, none of his siblings wanted the Council to spy upon them without their consent.

The only one that didn't work that way was the mirror linking them with the Retreat at Koral-tai in the heart of Natallia, on the far side of the Eastern Ocean, but then it was a twinned mirror, designed to contact only its twin and no other. Neither mirror had been hung in a sensitive location on either side, so there was no point in blocking its view. But since Morganen didn't fully trust the Council to not have some sort of one-way cancellation spell, since they had invented that blue-privacy-hue idea themselves, he covered their mirror whenever it wasn't in use.

Satisfied they couldn't scry on him, Morganen tidied up his workbenches and headed for the stairs spiraling up out of his tower. Behind him, the Council-linked mirror chimed again. It was conceivable that they could negate both the privacy spell and his little prerecorded illusion . . . but if he wasn't there to answer the mirror anyway, there was nothing they would be able to do. Certainly, they couldn't use the mirror as a Gate—they themselves had forged countercharms against that possibility into the mirror during its construction. Any attempt to do so would not only thwart them, it ran the risk of shattering both mirrors.

Amused by the thought, he smiled and retired to his rooms.

Frustrated by their failure to break through the repeating illusion, the Councilors returned the mirror to the Hall. Head throbbing, Consus settled back into his seat. Finneg was arguing that this recorded illusion was a deliberate insult, while others were countering with the argument that yes, it was annoying, but it *had* been politely worded. The Councilor for Sea Commerce winced at the sharp double-rap of the King's Sphere in its matching marble holder, then sighed quietly as silence descended. Until His Majesty spoke, of course.

"Enough. We will draft a list of questions for the traders to take with them, the next time they sail for the Isle. Councilor Consus, when is the next trade ship due to leave for Nightfall?" King Taurin inquired.

Caught once again with his forehead in his palm, Consus jerked himself upright. He grimaced as he tallied up the days in his head. "I'm afraid the next ship has probably already left, Your Majesty. Tomorrow is the full of the moon, and they sometimes set sail with the tide of the day before, which would have been today."

"Then we shall wait for their report of what the latest requests in trade items shall be. If this was a temporary aberration, lasting only a few months long, perhaps long enough to complete some odd project or other, their purchasing list will return to something more like their previous lists," the King of Katan said. Finneg opened his mouth to protest, and was silenced as Taurin raised his hand. "There is no indication that these items are being purchased for women. You know as well as I that there are thousands of enchantments requiring tens of thousands of components, some of them quite ordinary. *However* . . . we will also keep an eye on any continuing demands they may make of payment for the salt blocks. That is not their property—they are merely exilees. If they continue to do so with this next shipment, we shall chide them for their arrogance at the next opportunity."

"Like we'll chide them for their refusal to answer our call, Your Majesty?" Finneg asked him sardonically.

Queen Samille answered the duke's pointed query. "Nightfall Isle is farther east than we are. They may have simply gone to bed already. I suggest that, as this is technically a question of Sea Commerce, we direct Councilor Consus to attempt to contact them tomorrow and interrogate them with a list of questions."

"I second my queen's motion," her husband stated, ensuring no one could thwart the idea. The king nodded to his right. "Councilor Consus, take care of it. Try contacting them at least twice a day, at different times if need be, until they respond. When they do, ask them what those nonstandard purchases were for and remind them that the salt and algae blocks belong to the Empire of Katan. Do so politely, at least for this round in the negotiations. Politeness costs nothing, save for the reining in of our tempers. Conflict has more tangible costs.

"In the meantime, we shall wait for the trader's report to come back to us. We will *not* engage in conflict resolution, so long as there are more peaceful ways of getting the Corvis brothers to comply," King Taurin added firmly, fixing Duke Finneg with a hard stare before the other man could do more than draw breath to protest. "I need not remind most of you how powerful the brothers are, both individually and as a whole."

"Majesty," Finneg tried to protest, "there are but eight of them! They are no match for the force I would bring."

"If it *does* come to conflict resolution, it will take far more spell power than your own department can muster to settle the matter,

Councilor Finneg. Not without risking more lives on our side than I care to see expended. You were not there when we went to evict them from the County of Corvis," Taurin added, giving Finneg a quelling look. "You did not see the strengths that were displayed, nor how closely it came to an outright war. We will *not* waste the precious resources of this nation on what could turn out to be just a petty squabble for attention." A sharp bang of the black marble ball ended the subject. "As this session has gone on more than long enough, I am calling it at an end. We'll meet again in three days. Councilor Consus, prepare us a report by then."

Forced to nod in acquiescence, Consus waited until the king banged his marble sphere again, then dropped his forehead back into his hand. It looked like his preferred neutrality regarding the Sons of the Song of Destiny was going to be pressured and tested in the next few days. Hopefully, he wouldn't be pushed to the point of breaking. He hated confrontations.

NINE

❦

Evanor awoke with an incredible sense of utterly relaxed lethargy. The sun wasn't up yet, but it had lightened the gloom beyond his curtains just a little bit, letting him know breakfast would be served soon. If it hadn't already started. But he didn't want to get up, just yet.

Not normally an indolent sort of man, Ev found the mere act of stretching under the covers to be that intriguing mix of exhausting and satisfying that occasionally struck him in the mornings. When that happened, he usually ignored it; today, however, it was very tempting to just close his eyes and go back to sleep. Managing to roll onto his back, he breathed deeply and stretched again, seeking enough energy, enough caring, to crawl out of his bed. It didn't come, but it felt good to lie on his back and blink sleepily at the ceiling, which was currently patterned in slowly fluttering veils. He considered it rather refreshing, not having had his sleep disturbed by a nightmare about his lost voice.

Of course, there was the question as to *why* he felt so good this morning. With the mental query came an equally silent answer in the memory of Mariel, lovely, beautiful, talented Mariel putting her hands all over his body . . . *all* over his body. Already a little hard from the usual morning stiffness, Evanor wormed one hand down under the covers, stroking his fingertips across his abdomen. Brushing his shaft, he touched himself lightly, teasingly, remembering how she had looked while touching him. He'd spent half the experience with his eyes squeezed shut from the sheer intensity, but he remembered.

The curves of her body surfaced in his mind. Soft and rounded, not angular and hard. Womanly, not girlish. Hers was a body that had all sorts of handfuls for a man to cup and caress. He could easily picture himself burying his face between the soft mounds of her breasts, or the soft flesh of her thighs.

Gripping himself more firmly, Evanor stroked himself, aroused by that thought. Tonight, it was his turn to give her a massage. His turn to caress her all over, and not just her back as he had done the first time around. His turn to touch her, to arouse her, to excite her and satisfy her. He wouldn't go too fast, nor too far . . . but he'd definitely get his hands *all* over her lush figure. The thought of it had him pushing the covers down quickly with one hand, the other stroking faster. As soon as the bedding was clear, Evanor imagined the feel of her feminine folds beneath his fingertips, the crinkly curls, the soft skin . . . the warm wetness . . .

His back arched, his hips convulsed, and wet warmth of his own spilled over his skin, dampening his abdomen. All accompanied by the hissing of her name. It was a bitter edge to such a pleasurable moment, being reminded that he had no voice with which to groan. Panting as he slowly relaxed, refreshed and awakened by the stimulation, Evanor wondered when Mariel would be done testing her spells on the chickens and ready to test her skills on him.

Mariel eyed the other woman, Alys, as she finished examining the current hen in their mutual grip. Or rather, the hen immobilized by Alys' magic and prodded at by her own powers. These chickens were too ornery for her to hold them quiescent with one spell *and* examine them with another. It was also nice to finally be able to talk *with* the other woman—that dose of Ultra Tongue potion was very helpful.

"So let me get this straight. Morganen kidnapped Kelly from another universe and dumped her in Saber's lap. While she needed rescuing because of some sort of Mandarite-like persecution against magic. The two of them fought, until *your* uncle sent magical war beasts in an attack—one of a long series of attacks that you knew about, but couldn't do anything to prevent at the time—and as a result of their injuries, they were forced to spend time together cooperatively, instead of arguing?"

Alys nodded. "Yes, and that's when they fell in love. They're both very stubborn and arrogant at times. Like a pair of horses fighting for dominance. It took dragging them into the same harness to make them learn how to work together, from what Wolfer told me."

"I see." Murmuring a thread of sound-woven magic, she closed up the bloodless gap she had created in the chicken's neck. When the wound was sealed, she released the feathers she had been holding back out of the way and nodded at the hen. "You can put that one back, now. The numbing spell will wear off in a few moments. Thank you for your assistance, by the way."

"You're welcome. I'm glad we can talk, now." Scooping up the bird, Alys headed over to the coop. With the quiescent chicken tucked into one arm, she snapped something firm-sounding that pushed the other clucking hens back from the wire-woven door, then opened it long enough to toss the hen inside before latching it again. "These are much nicer to try to feed than the beasts my uncle kept. May he rot and fester in his chosen Netherhell."

"Yes, tell me about that," Mariel encouraged her. "You were saying that your uncle grew restless at being thwarted in his one-way scrying attempts, thanks to the color-changing paint on the walls, and that was the point when you escaped?"

Alys nodded. Her hair wasn't quite as curly as Mariel's, but it was very close in color, being just a few shades lighter. That made her curls dark blond, whereas Mariel's were light brown. Beyond their hair, though, the two women weren't very similar. Mariel's face was round, while Alys' was more oval; Mariel's frame was stocky, petite, and plump, and Alys was taller and more slender. Alys *was* curvaceous—more so than Kelly, who was thin but had womanly breasts and hips, and definitely more than the tall, slender Serina—but Alys was not nearly so motherly in figure as Mariel.

"Yes. I escaped and came here, met up with Wolfer, and then things happened very fast," Alys explained. "My other uncle, Donnock, tried to get onto the island, we think at Uncle Broger's direction, so he could get a personal fix on the Isle for scry sendings. Wolfer beat him up and sent him away, and then Uncle Broger called him back and used him in a Dark Gate sacrifice."

"A what-what sacrifice?" Mariel asked her, confused.

"A Dark Gate . . . it's a thing where you sacrifice someone close to you, and you open a sort of warding-circle version of a mirror-Gate, only it uses the powers of a Netherhell to do so, because you're murdering someone," the younger woman explained, gesturing vaguely, diffidently. "Uncle Broger brought a whole bunch of his beasties across, onto the dock down in the western cove, and Wolfer and I spotted him. Wolfer ran to warn the others, and I trailed after him in disguise—I followed my uncle, that is—and then the attack happened. Only Morg had researched what my uncle had done, so he ran in and grabbed him and somehow transported *all* of us out to the docks again.

"You have to close a Dark Gate a specific way, you see, or it weakens the Veil between this world and the Netherhells," Alys added. Mariel shivered, listening to her; the younger mage nodded, confirming the narrowly avoided disaster. "Exactly. Since we didn't have a priest on the island, we had to make my uncle sacrifice himself on the spot where he opened the Gate. But that was okay, because we couldn't attack him directly anyway; he had too many protective spells that would backlash on the person trying to harm him, physically or magically.

"I . . . I confronted him, provoked him into a killing rage, and Evanor rebounded my uncle's spell back on himself, killing him. The Dark Gate reopened, the demons or whatever dragged him into the Netherhell, and that sealed both ends of the Gate with his death.

And may his soul be tormented for all of Eternity!" Alys added with
a brief touch of firmness in her otherwise gentle voice.

Arching one eyebrow, Mariel studied the younger woman.
"Pardon me, but you don't seem, well . . . you don't seem *brave*
enough to have done that. Confronted him like that. I know you *did*,
but it must have taken all of your courage to do so. You seem a
bit . . . reticent."

"Shy, retiring, and quiet?" Alys quipped, flashing the older mage
a grin. "I am. Sometimes. And sometimes I screw up my courage and
can be very brave and bold. When I need to be." She hesitated for a
moment, then curved her mouth into a smile somewhere between
shy and wicked. "Especially when pouncing on my Wolfer."

Mariel chuckled at that, joining her by the coop. "Yes. It's good
to have a man chase you around the bedchamber, but sometimes it's
even better to chase *him* around. *Zootrath peless*, number four!"

One of the roosters flapped its wings, attempting to squawk in-
dignantly as it was yanked off its clawed feet and pulled up toward
the door. Of course, having no vocal cords—even as primitive as a
chicken's voice box was—it made no sound beyond a vicious sort of
hiss. Alys knocked it unconscious with a numbing spell, while Mariel
kept it afloat, both women working quickly before the other chickens could reach the door. They extracted their victim, made sure the
door to the wire-enclosed coop was secure, then retreated to the
small table Mariel had brought out for her examinations.

"Anyway, that was how Ev lost his voice," Alys told her, watching
as the Healer muttered her examination spell, opening up the feathered neck of the fowl under their hands. "And then we had to wait
to try and find Dom, because of the Prophecy."

"Prophecy?" Mariel glanced up at her sharply. "Which Prophecy?"

"Didn't anyone . . . ? *Men*," Alys muttered, in the way of annoyed females everywhere. "The brothers have this Prophecy laid
upon them, the Curse of the Sons of Destiny, though it's turning
out to be not so big a curse, after all. Or rather, their birth fulfills a
really old prediction by the Seer Draganna, who was a very famous
Seer of Katan about a thousand years ago. Back when Saber and
Kelly got together," she added, "there was this bit about how if he

has sex with a maiden, some unspecified disaster would happen, and at that point, Katan would 'fail to aid' . . . and everyone on the mainland thought that *that* meant some huge Disaster was going to befall the whole empire, rendering it *unable* to aid."

"I take it this was a mistaken impression?" Mariel asked, glad that the rooster's vocal cords were growing back nicely. Since chickens were a lot smaller and less complex than humans, their vocal cords would be regenerated in a handful of days. She'd be interested in trying it on one of the cows, but the amount of tissue to be regrown in a cow would take as long or longer than regrowing a human voice, and she didn't want to make Evanor wait that long. Her success with the chickens should be enough to satisfy her that she had the technique right.

"Very mistaken. There was a Disaster, of course," Alys admitted. "The Mandarites came out here, looking for some land to conquer—this was before my uncle attacked, but after the changing paint thwarted him from scrying on them—and Kelly got the brothers to cobble together the idea of a powerful, magic-drenched 'kingdom,' with herself as the queen, and these little glass pebble-things as illusionary courtiers and such. The premise being that the whole island was capable of cloaking itself in illusion, 'hiding' whenever anyone unwanted was nearby . . . which would supposedly explain why they didn't see any signs of habitation until they reached the palace walls," Alys revealed. "It was a bit complicated, but the Mandarites fell for it, or so I was told.

"They thought we were too powerful for them to attack, but they were also tempted by the thought of male mages, so when Dominor—in his guise of Lord Chancellor—escorted them back down to their ship, they traded a bunch of *comsworg* oil for our salt blocks, and lured Dom onto their ship to get him to use his magic to ensure the salt wouldn't be sullied by ship's tar, or whatever. Then they somehow drugged him and dragged him off. Without any ships of our own, and what with Wolfer being afraid of heights, and Trevan being shot by their weapon-thing when he tried to go after the ship as it departed . . . well, they couldn't get him back."

"*Wolfer* . . . is afraid of heights?" Mariel asked, amused by the thought. The most muscular of the brothers, the mere sight of Wolfer of Nightfall was rather intimidating, as proven by her son's constant mutters of *not* being afraid of him.

Alys laughed. "Oh, yes. Anything above wall-height or tree-height, and he can't handle it. He has an affinity for shapeshifting in his magic, like I do, but he definitely prefers ground-bound forms. Walking, climbing, running, swimming . . . but nothing that goes up in the air, if he can help it."

"So, the part about Katan failing to aid?" Mariel asked, getting the subject back on track. "What was that really about?"

"The brothers contacted the mainland to warn them and ask for help, but the Council of Mages said they were on their own—*that's* how Katan 'failed' to aid. Um . . . that was when the Mandarites first showed up," Alys added after a moment of thought. "Because that was when Kelly said she declared Nightfall to be independent and proclaimed herself queen, after Katan disavowed any help for them, and then they all ran around, throwing together what they hoped would look like a suitably prosperous and powerful kingdom, before the Mandarites finished walking up from the shore."

"I'll bet the others weren't too happy about a woman claiming rulership over them, having been bachelors for so long," the Healer chuckled. "Especially Dominor."

She finished examining the bloodless examination wound. It wasn't an easy spell to master, requiring more power than one might think, because it sealed off the blood vessels without cutting off the blood supply, but she'd mastered it back at the Sanitorium. It was also the kind of spell that separated a lesser Healer from a greater one. Not that it could be used frequently, since that ran the risk of scarring the tissues involved, but it was an excellent diagnostic tool, and all but required for a good teacher to know, in a Healing School.

"Actually, Wolfer said Dom accepted her almost right away, though he himself was a little leery of the idea for a bit," Alys admitted. "But just the other morning, Kelly got even Rydan to cooperate—you saw it yourself—and if anyone is truly stubborn and antisocial in this family, it's him. If she can do *that*, she can do just about anything. That's a kind of magic that has nothing to do with spell power, and everything to do with willpower. Not even the Gods can give a person that; it has to come from within."

Nodding, Mariel hummed, closing the wound in the somnolent rooster's neck. "Here, toss this fellow back into the coop. It looks like it's going to start raining shortly, and all the vocal chords are regenerating nicely, so no point in dragging this out."

"Alys?" a feminine voice called out. It belonged to Kelly, who had poked her strawberry blonde head out one of the doors in the nearest wing of the palace. "Time for your next kung fu lesson!"

"Kung foo?" Mariel asked, curious. Alys waited until she had tossed the rooster back among the hens and latched the coop door before replying.

"It's a sort of weaponless fighting thing she's been teaching me," Alys admitted with a touch of shyness. A grin curved her mouth. "I use it to pin Wolfer to our marriage-bed, sometimes."

"That sounds like the kind of fighting I learned from the nuns at the Retreat. Are you going to take over the salle and oust Ev and Mikor from their lessons?" Mariel asked Alys.

"Oh, no, we have a room of our own upstairs, in one of the wings. With felt-padded floors and a bathing room for soaking out any bruises," the younger woman told her. "I don't think Kelly would mind showing you, if you'd like to see. Here, grab that edge of the table, I'll get this end."

Droplets of water splattered the courtyard flagstones, urging them into hurrying for the castle door, an awkward task, given the table they were hauling between them. It was somewhat small and thus lightweight, but still burdensome. The leaden sky looked like it was going to cast down a fair amount of rainfall. Happy to get inside, Mariel nodded to Kelly, who held the door for them, then addressed the part-time, self-proclaimed royal as soon as the women had returned the table to the room across from the door. "I understand you and Alys practice some sort of weaponless fighting style?"

"Yes, kung fu. I'd be happy to teach you, too," Kelly offered. "I'd like to see all the women on the Isle trained in self-defense, so that would include you."

"I know a Natallian form of weaponless fighting called *tai,* some-

thing the nuns of Koral-tai teach each other for self-defense,"
Mariel offered. "In fact, why don't I go grab Serina, drag her away
from her chalkboards, and make her join us? It's important that she
gets some physical exercise as well as mental, and there are charms
we can apply to her abdomen to protect her baby while we're practicing."

Kelly grinned. "Sounds like a great idea. The practice room
we're using is in the northwest wing, third floor, seventh door down
from the *Y*-split on the left side. It's in what used to be Saber's old
quarters, before he moved in with me up at the top of the donjon.
Grab your friend, and we'll make it into what my people call a 'hen
party,' full of laughter and plotting against our menfolk, as well as a
fight practice."

Closing the door to the courtyard, shutting out the rain that was
now pattering down in greater amounts, Kelly led Alys toward the
nearest stairwell, while Mariel headed for the wing with the chambers Serina had picked out for her workspace.

Captain Thorist paused in his negotiations to peer out the windows
of the chapel. "Jinga's Tits. It's starting to rain. That'll ruin the salt."

He was one of the three or four traders visiting the Isle who preferred using the chapel halfway up the first hill from the western
cove for his trades when the weather didn't look good. For one, the
exiled brothers weren't allowed onto any ship, by Katani law. For another, the boathouse wasn't big enough to display his wares. For the
third reason, he was a suspicious, superstitious sort. Holy ground
was far more reassuring than some old, abandoned dwelling. Sailors
were usually a suspicious lot, but the northern-bred ones weren't
normally quite so nervy as the southern-born ones tended to be;
Thorist was an exception to the rule.

Saber nodded patiently. "And if you'll buy the salt blocks, we'll
put the usual anti-humidity charms on them and shelter them from
the rainfall until they're in your hold, free of charge."

"I don't see *why* we have to buy the damned things. When I heard
through the grapevine what you told Captain Melkin, I thought the

gossipers were drunk," Thorist complained. "Those salt blocks belong to the Empire, and the Empire demands its share of the profits. If I pay *you*, that cuts into my profits, and *that* cuts into theirs. And who are they going to come complaining to?"

"Us. Far more than you," Saber stated, knowing it was the truth. The eldest of the brothers also knew a stand had to be taken.

"You're just doing your job, Captain, plying the sea and trading with everyone you meet, hauling prenegotiated goods to and from the island at our request," Morganen observed. "We're the ones who are insisting on raising the price of some of those goods—technically it's being raised from nothing to something."

"I know. But I want to know *why*," Thorist said, wincing as the rain started falling heavily around them, turning into a sort of rhythmic hiss. It wasn't quite a storm, since there wasn't any wind, nor lightning and thunder, but it fell heavily, pattering against the paned and tiled roof, splattering against the leaves of the trees surrounding the chapel, and splashing into quickly forming puddles on the road outside.

The four sailors who had come with him to help carry the goods their captain wanted to display grimaced at the weather, but otherwise ignored it. Koranen, not needed at the moment, padded outside into the rain, where he turned his face up to the falling drops, spread out his arms a little, and just stood there for a few moments, smirking. The sailors eyed him like he was crazy until the mage started visibly steaming. Then they muttered among themselves and looked away, shaking their heads.

Saber couldn't blame his second-youngest sibling for playing in the rain, though sometimes he did wish Kor would grow up just a little more. Turning his attention back to the trader, he repeated, "*Why* are we selling the salt, rather than giving it away? Because it's ours, not Katan's. We're the ones who cleaned out the pipes and started the water flowing again. We're the ones who shift the blocks off of their processing ramps and stack them up in the old warehouses. We're the ones who make sure those warehouses are dry and clean, and we're the ones who build and maintain the mage-carts that ship them from building to warehouse to dock."

"We're the ones who cast our magics to ensure the salt blocks stay dry and clean from the moment they come off the ramps to the moment they leave your holds," Morganen added, backing up his eldest brother. "Let's just say we got tired of doing all the work and getting none of the reward for our efforts."

Thorist eyed the younger mage with a shuttered, unreadable look. "Melkin says you've declared yourselves independents. That you no longer recognize the authority of the empire. Now, he didn't put that into any official report—none of us would be that foolish, letting something like *that* reach the King and Council's ears—so it's 'only hearsay,' since you didn't mention it to Captain Reganon on his visits, from what I've heard . . . but . . . is it true? *Have* you gone independent?"

Morganen answered when Saber hesitated. "Katan abandoned *us* when they exiled us out here. No women, no visitors, no entertainments, no free market trading, just 'authorized' trips every two or so weeks. We're tired of it. We want traders to come here when they like. We want *people* to come here when they like . . . and if the empire doesn't like it, they can stuff it where—"

"Morg," Saber interrupted, giving his youngest sibling a sardonic look. "You don't have to be crude to make our point. And our point, good Captain, is that we're not going to play by the empire's rules anymore. Now, you don't have to break those rules if you don't want to, since I know they'll come down hard on anyone who sails here without authority . . . but you can spread the rumor that we'll be looking for traders outside of the full and the new of Brother Moon. It's *just* a rumor, after all."

Thorist's brown eyes narrowed a bit, making his gaze all the darker in his already dark face. "Out of curiosity . . . since it's *just* a rumor . . . would there be a discount for anyone sailing here at a non-authorized time, someone who was interested in buying all that salt?"

No idiot, Saber caught on to his meaning. The captain wanted to know, if he did it under the table, would he get a price cut, rather than having to report it to the Empire, and lose tax money as the government took its cut of his profits. Smuggling salt, in other words. Nodding slowly, he admitted cautiously, "If there *were* such an intrepid purchaser willing to take such a risk, I suppose a *small* discount could be granted to them. Not much, per block . . . but it would add up."

"Of course, to make it further worth our while, since we'd be running a risk, too . . . I suppose it might be helpful if such a person also came loaded with things not normally permitted on the Isle," Morganen added in a casual-seeming drawl.

"Smuggling women would be too risky," Captain Thorist stated bluntly. "You'd have to give me the salt for free for a year, before I'd consider that."

"We're not looking for women," Koranen dismissed, stepping back inside the chapel. His clothes continued to steam for a few moments more as they finished drying against his heated skin. "We're looking for farmers and their chattel. People who know how to reclaim orchards run wild, as well as how to cut and plow a field. Carpenters and stonemasons who can reclaim and rebuild houses and other buildings."

"In other words, settlers from Katan," Thorist observed. "All men? No women? You won't get many men willing to come join without any women, unless they're of a mind to enjoy each other's company in full . . ."

"Settlers can be of either gender," Saber dismissed. "And of any useful age . . . and they *don't* have to come solely from Katan. Families will be welcomed, third or fourth sons and daughters who want a bit of their own, rather than their elder brothers' or sisters' leavings. But we don't want the lazy or the shiftless here. If they're not willing to work hard to earn a plot of land, whether it's for a house, a farm, an orchard, or a workshop, we're not interested in having them, and we won't support them."

"It also doesn't have to be settlers, at first," Morg pointed out. "We could do with more supplies, first. Things that could entice people to come here. Iron barstock to turn into plowshares, ingots of other metals and alloys, bolts of cloth, bars of soaps, stacks of pottery, pots and pans, barrels of oil, sacks of dyes and mordants, and especially bags of seed for the planting season," Morganen told the trader captain.

"And coins; we'd like to be paid at least a quarter of our trade in coins, rather than most of it in barter," Koranen stated, as much to remind his two brothers of Serina's comment about needing coins to melt and re-mint into their own money. "In return, you can get salt blocks, algae blocks—though I know there's not much call for those as autumn sets in and shifts to winter—plus lightglobes, hand mirrors, spell-preserved fruit, the usual sort."

"But only for the intrepid, and the smart. It wouldn't be in anyone's best interests to let the Council get wind of this sort of rumor," Saber finished.

Thorist snorted. "You think I don't know that? Melkin talked to each of the other captains and me privately in person, rather than putting this rumor of your independence down on paper, and I've chatted with them since. *Something's* going on here. You say it's that you want to recolonize a dead and Cursed island, that you're tired of being exiled and shut out of contact with the rest of the world. *I* say there's something more going on, here."

Morganen smiled wryly, folding his arms over his chest. "Let's just say that Curses *do* lift eventually and leave it at that, shall we? So. Are you going to buy the salt now, or later?"

The sea trader rubbed his chin. "Now," he said after a moment of thought. "*If* these rumors are true, then it'll take a bit of time on the mainland end of things to set things up, find warehouses and the trustworthy merchants who own them to handle sales on the mainland. It would also help if the salt came in a different, less-recognizable form. The algae blocks break down easier; they can be turned into bags of mulch either in transit or as soon as they're offloaded, but the salt is a bit more problematical.

"Of course, transporting settlers is out of the question . . . at this point in time, same as any women . . . but I could spread the word of that possibility slowly. And perhaps, in time . . . if a careless, brand-new sailor neglects to get back to the ship in time to be aboard when she leaves, and the bo'sun doesn't count noses closely enough before

the anchor's weighed . . . well, accidents do happen," Captain Thorist pointed out with a smirk. "And a ship with a schedule to follow
just might not have enough time to turn around and pick up the
missing crewman, by the time their absence is noted."

"I'd jump ship," one of the sailors muttered. The others glanced
at him, and the man shrugged. "Well . . . if I had promise of a moor-
ing spot on the docks for a fishing boat, I'd at least think about it."

Saber eyed the sailor, who was clad in brown-and-cream striped
trousers, sturdy brown boots, and a long-sleeved, faded green tunic.
His skin was halfway between the darker hue of Thorist's nut-
brown hide and Saber's own golden tan, his eyes were hazel green,
and his dark brown hair was parted and plaited in two thick, waist-
length braids. Like most Katani men, he was clean shaven, which
allowed Saber to gauge his age at around his mid-thirties, maybe a
little older.

"What's your name?" Saber asked.

"Marcas. From Sommerie."

That was a city on the far western coast of Katan. Saber considered the other man, taking in his muscles and calluses. "What skills
do you have, Marcas?"

"I can handle any size of ship, and make repairs on 'er. I've done
everything seaworthy, from fishing to sea-pearl diving, sailing to
boatwrighting. I'm not *good* at being a boatwright, not enough to
make it a career, but I can keep a longboat or a fishing smack sound,"
Marcas admitted with a somewhat diffident shrug. "I've also put
away a bit, so I could buy a fishing boat, sail 'er here, and start earning my keep with fish-hauls. *If* I were to jump ship, that is," he
added, glancing at his captain. "Which would be after I found a man
to take my place, back at a mainland port, since I wouldn't want to
leave our good captain in the lurch."

"You'd better not," Captain Thorist ordered his crewman, before glancing back at Saber. "Marcas is a good man to have on a ship.
He's not a designer, but he is a repairer, and he does have a knack for
fixing things. Of course, *if* I were to let him retire . . . I'd have to be
sure he'd be adequately taken care of: food, housing, getting ade-

quate pay for his catches. Including a promise of protection from the Council's displeasure. You're not allowed long-term visitors, just short-term ones."

"He'd have that, if he were to stay and be a productive citizen," Saber stated, glancing at his two youngest brothers. "In exchange for vows to obey the laws of the Isle, not betray its people, so on and so forth. There are other advantages that would come with settling on the island, but he'd have to earn them."

"Advantages?" Marcas asked skeptically. "Like what?"

"We're considering having any settler who can prove they're an asset to the island and worthy of being allowed to stay dosed with Ultra Tongue, which grants the recipient the instantaneous ability to speak and read any known language," Morg stated, making all five sailors blink. "And that's just the start. We're also crafting unusual Artifacts for our own personal use; they'd be made available to those who moved here, provided you put in an equal amount of effort in making the island inhabitable."

"We'd probably even help you pick out a spot for a house, and help you build it. Something good and weather-tight," Koranen offered. "And definitely negotiate a space on the docks for your ship, and probably take the rent of it as a portion of your catch."

"And would you help in processing it?" one of the other sailors asked. "You high and mighty mage-types would be willing to get up to your elbows in fish guts?"

Koranen answered that one, dismissing it. "There's ways to gut and prep fish with magic. And ways to preserve them that don't require salting everything . . . though we do have the salt to spare."

"That, you do," Thorist agreed dryly as two of his men chuckled. "But I'm not letting him go just yet. This is all just speculation, at the moment . . . because I don't see any intact houses on this island, nor so much as a rowboat tied up to that dock, let alone a shipyard to make one.

"So, since we've got most of the trade worked out, I'll need your list of things for the warehouse in Orovalis to stock up on for the next ship's visit, then some help getting our pay goods down to the ship, without getting them wet. Not to mention all those salt blocks we'll be buying. Do you want the pay for that in coin, or in trade, this time around?"

Giving it a moment of thought, Saber looked at the goods spread out around the chapel. Some of it might be worth the trade, baskets and rugs, stacks of leather hides . . . but Koranen's comment about wanting coins was a good idea. They needed to start accumulating copper, silver, and gold so they could restamp it into their own currency. "Coins, by preference. The other goods, we'll continue to trade item for item as usual, but you can start spreading the word we'll sell the salt and algae for solid coin only. Unless there's something truly worthwhile in exchange."

Thorist grimaced, but nodded. "I think I have enough for the price you're asking . . . though if the market for salt weren't so high right now, thanks to the harvest season, I'd wait to come back 'later,' when the price just might drop a little bit."

"We'll think about uncorking a few more pipes in the meantime," Saber offered. "Morg, go on down to the warehouse and help Wolfer get the blocks ready for loading. Kor, go put rain-wards on the wagons, while I help these gentlemen pack up their unpurchased wares."

The men shifted. Saber found himself working next to Marcas after the first load went downhill with Koranen. The sailor eyed him in curiosity.

"So . . . if I *were* to come here, you'd be wanting an oath given to you that I'd follow you, is that right?"

"An oath, yes. But not to me," Saber corrected.

"But, I thought you were the eldest. You're the one who conducts these trade negotiations; I've seen you doing it before, the times I've been here and helped out on shore," Marcas pointed out. "Who leads the lot of you, if it isn't you?"

"*If* you choose to come here and settle, you'll find out soon enough. And you'll swear to follow that person as a law-abiding citizen, or you'll be tossed off the Isle."

The threat didn't faze Marcas. "Fair enough. If you're making a bid for independence, you'll want those willing to be loyal to stand with you. But if you don't mind my asking, do you have a Patron Deity picked out yet?" Marcas asked, gesturing at the chapel around them and its eight altars. "Because I remember my old schooling lessons, how Katan was two lands that became one, and the God and the Goddess joined up together, making it one land under Their combined protection, one of the few lands around that did it that way. But you're not joining up, you're breaking away."

Aware just how awkward this was going to be if his wife continued in her outworlder way to insist that everyone should be free to worship whatever Gods they wanted, Saber confined his reply to a simple, terse, "We're working on it."

TEN

An' then he gave me a lesson in writing Katani-style . . . and loaned me one of his books from when he an' his brothers were little," Mikor told his mother, yawning sleepily. "A story with magical beasts that were smart enough to talk. I was gonna read it before goin' to bed, but I'm gettin' tired . . ."

"You are *going* to read it tomorrow, then, because you are *getting* tired," Mariel corrected her son automatically. "And you will be very careful with Evanor's book, just like you were very careful with the books in the Retreat Library."

Mikor nodded, shivering a little and snuggling deeper into the blankets. It was still raining, and the temperature had dropped noticeably. She had built a fire in the small fireplace, double-checking to make sure the charm on the fire grate would keep sparks and cinders from flying out of the hearth, but it didn't warm the sheets, just the air. A soft knock at the door made her rise from the bed.

Opening the stout panel, she let in Evanor, his arms laden with bedding. Mariel had asked him if there were extra blankets around. Apparently, he had found some. Setting the stack on a chest at the foot of the bed, Evanor shook out the top blanket and carefully laid it over the others covering the youth in the bed. Mikor gazed sleepily at him and curled up one side of his mouth in a smile.

"You're kinda like my father. He did that for me," Mikor said, yawning again. He blinked a couple of times, then eyed Evanor. "You don't look like him . . . but if you wanna be my next father . . ."

"Mikor," Mariel chided her son, coloring at his forwardness. She glanced at the man standing beside her and witnessed his own blush in the dim glow of the lightglobe by her son's head.

"What?" Mikor challenged, giving his mother a soft frown. "I don't like the others as much as I like him! Don't *you* like him, too?"

Flushing, Mariel didn't know what to say. She *did* like Evanor, but her son really shouldn't push like that. Of course, she couldn't blame Mikor for wanting a father in his life. Milon had passed away just as Mikor was getting to know him. Having had no other men in his life for the last two years, her son was clearly craving a father figure. One who would be around for a good, long time. But it wasn't his choice. Nor was it entirely hers. She glanced up at Evanor.

"Mother?" Mikor prompted. "Don't you like him?"

Cheeks hot, she nodded. She had never lied to her son before, and she wasn't going to lie now. "Yes, I do."

"Evanor . . . do you like my mother?" Mikor asked, interrupted by another yawn.

"Yes." His reply came without hesitation. As did the hand that caught hers, lacing their fingers together.

"Good. Then you should make him my new father." Mikor sighed happily, closed his green eyes, and smiled. "Goodnight . . ."

And within three steady breaths, he was limply asleep, content in his belief that the two adults by his bedside would agree with his assessment of the matter.

Hot-faced and flustered with embarrassment, Mariel said nothing, just grabbed the stack of extra blankets to carry them to her own room. Evanor followed her into the next suite, all the way to her bed, where he took one of the blankets from her and flicked it out over the bed with a practiced snap of his wrists. She set the last blanket aside and cleared her throat.

"Um . . . you don't have to . . . that is . . ."

"*Shh.*" For once, Evanor was grateful he had no voice. This was not a subject meant to be discussed aloud. To be discussed, yes, but not in a way that would lead to loud arguing. Catching her hand, he lifted it to his lips. She smiled shyly, and tried again.

"I know Mikor's got it in his head that he needs a father, but I don't want you feeling pressured into taking the role, just because of him."

That made the voiceless mage smirk. "*I'm not pressured.*"

She blushed even more. In fact, it felt like her face had been flaming from the moment her son had made his first father-hunting comment, tonight. At this point, she wasn't sure she'd need that extra blanket to stay warm, if her face kept burning like this. Evanor leaned close, but didn't dip his head down far enough to kiss her mouth. Instead, he brushed his lips against her forehead.

"*Go get ready for bed,*" he directed her, enjoying the way she swayed toward him a little when he pulled back. She opened her eyes and he smiled. "*I owe you a massage.*"

That reminded her of his promise to reciprocate the special, extra touch she had given him at the very end of his massage, last night. "You don't have t—"

Evanor silenced her with a finger laid on her lips. "*I know I don't have to. I want to. Will you let me pleasure you?*"

Oh, dear Natua . . . Mariel wondered how her legs were still managing to stand under the seduction of that simple, straightforward question. Managing a nod, she forced herself to move toward the refreshing room. Once away from his lean frame, she felt cooler; perhaps not all of her blushing had been from embarrassment. Perhaps some of it had come simply from being in close proximity to a handsome, intelligent, charming, attractive male. Whose touch she wanted very, very much.

Watching her close the refreshing room door, Evanor released his self-restraint long enough to raise clenched fists in victory. It was a very good thing he didn't have a voice right now; hissing in triumph was bad enough, but if she *heard* his triumph through the closed door . . . He didn't want her thinking he was some callow youth just interested in luring her into his bed for some temporary fun. Ev was very much interested in luring her into his bed for some *permanent* fun.

Thank you, Jinga, for getting Mikor on my side! Every ache and pain I had from sparring with Wolfer yesterday was worth it . . .

He heard the flushing of water, the splashing as she washed her hands. The air was still a little nippy in the room. She had built up a fire in her own hearth, he noted, but hadn't laid it with as much care as she had her son's, and it was threatening to go out. Crossing to the fireplace, he shifted the grate out of his way and used the tongs from the holder next to the hearth, poking the coals back to life. He heard her return to the bedroom, but concentrated on laying a few more logs just so, ensuring there would be warmth for some time.

Restoring the grate, he rose and turned, in time to see her pulling her tunic-dress over her head. As much as he wanted to go to her, however, his hands were a little sooty. Detouring around her, he retreated to the refreshing room and scrubbed his fingers in the sink. He'd be a poor, inconsiderate lover if he left smudgy handprints all over her skin.

When he came back to the bedroom, Evanor found the lights had been dimmed. Not only that, but Mariel had tucked herself into the bed. Not pretending to be asleep, at least, but she was holding the bedsheet over her breasts and was propped up on one elbow. *Her tunic-less breasts*, he realized, taking in the sight of those softly rounded shoulders bare of anything other than the fall of her shoulder-length curls.

In that moment, Evanor realized he was falling in love with her. It was inevitable, since it was Prophesied that he would fall for *someone*, but he knew it was definitely Mariel that he would love. Approaching the bed, he seated himself on the side she wasn't using. They both hesitated for a moment, then she sat up farther, he leaned in, and their lips met. It was soft, gentle, dry . . . sweet.

Her tongue flicked out as they parted, wetting her lips. It also caught the tip of his upper lip, tickling him. Teasing him inadvertently. Ev leaned back in, pressed his dry mouth to hers . . . then licked both of their lips.

She giggled. Pulling back with a smile, she eyed him, then reached up to touch his hair. And winced. Concerned, Evanor gave Mariel a questioning look.

"I pulled a muscle, practicing against the other three ladies this morning," Mariel confessed. "I Healed most of it, earlier. Your eldest sister-in-law definitely knows that outworlder weaponless fighting form of hers. It's quite comparable to the one I learned from the nuns. Different, but comparable. I'm going to enjoy learning more of it from her."

"Would you like me to massage away the last of it?" Evanor asked her.

A slow smile spread across her lips. "Yes. Please. If you don't mind."

"My pleasure," he reassured her.

Shifting back to give her enough room to sprawl in the middle of the bed, Evanor slipped off the low, soft-soled boots he wore around the castle. Mindful of the chill in the room, that it would take several more minutes before the heat from the fire warmed it suitably, he leaned over and grabbed the last, soft gray blanket from the stack he had fetched. Turning back, he caught sight of a familiar, carved wooden box on the nearer of the two bedside tables.

Carefully draping the blanket over her naked back, he leaned forward, snagging the box. Sorting through the brass squares, he selected the ones he wanted, organized them into the order he wanted, then flicked the lever that activated it. A flute began playing, followed by a drum. Evanor adjusted the volume lever to provide soft accompaniment, then set the music box back on the nightstand, allowing it to do all the vocal work for him. The rest of his seduction would be up to his hands. Rubbing them briskly together, he brushed back the blanket sheltering her against a chill and began a slow knead up the length of her spine.

This was different from the first time. For one, he touched nothing but her flesh, rather than the flesh and soft cotton of her sleeveless tunic, like he had last time. For another, he knew he was going to touch more of her body than just her back, neck, and shoulders. But he didn't rush, just kneaded and stroked her back from nape to waist throughout the first song, which was about a man noticing the beauty of a particular woman, her hair, her eyes, her smile. Most of the descriptions didn't match, of course, but the feeling of the song suited Evanor's purpose.

Mariel melted into his fingers, and into his voice. He really had a fabulous voice, and knew how to sing a tune with deft phrasing and definite emotion. When it ended, he covered her back in the soft wool blanket, then shifted on the bed, pulling the covers down to her knees. Mariel squeaked in surprise and embarrassment, worrying about her rump.

It wasn't a small rump; she'd given birth to her son, after all, and that had spread her hips a bit. Living in the Retreat, with all of its stairs going every which way, had kept her in some shape, as had her martial exercises with the nuns, but her body—especially her rump—was still rather plump. When he placed his hands on her buttocks, fingers spread and palms cupping her flesh, she worried about her attractiveness.

But he stroked her flesh, cupped it, squeezed it, and caressed it . . . then lowered his head and kissed one of her nether-cheeks. Evanor did so with a soft exhalation that, if he'd had a voice, Mariel realized would have been a full-blown groan and not just a sigh. A groan of appreciation, no less.

He saluted the other curve, then kneaded in earnest. Not bruisingly hard, but thoroughly, leaving no inch of her backside untouched, from her waist to the crease delineating the backs of her thighs, from the dimple of her spine to the flare of her sides. Mariel felt him shifting farther down the bed and enjoyed the hands stroking the outsides of her legs. Working one, then the other, he relaxed her hamstring muscles . . . and tensed her feminine ones, for he massaged from the outside to the inside and did not neglect the uppermost inch or two of her inner thighs.

But he didn't touch her sexually, not deliberately. She wanted to whimper in disappointment when he moved down to her calves. Then giggle in ticklishness when his fingers slid from her calves to the soles of her feet. She squirmed a little until he left her alone, but that was only to readjust the blanket so that it covered her legs, keeping her warm.

When he returned his fingers to her feet, he touched them firmly this time. That helped cancel out the ticklishness, though it reduced her to moaning helplessly into her pillow. There shouldn't have been any way the nerves in her feet were connected to the nerves in her womb, but they were.

It took Mariel a few moments to realize the song the box was now singing was one about a man wanting to touch a beautiful woman. Nothing truly improper, but Evanor's thorough, talented hands and the sound of his true voice combined made her shiver with pleasure. His fingers finally left her feet somewhere around the second or third time she had to swallow her saliva to keep from drooling on her pillow. Shifting up on the bed, he leaned over her, his light blond hair tickling the curve of her shoulder where the blanket didn't completely cover her.

"Roll over."

Roll over? Mariel blinked at the suggestion, waking up enough from her massage-induced bliss to be embarrassed by the idea. She wasn't covered by the bedding anymore, just a blanket draped over her body. "Um . . ."

"Please."

It was difficult to resist such a polite request. And really, she didn't want to resist. Giving in to her want, Mariel squirmed onto her back, shifting to keep the soft gray blanket in place over her body. He didn't remove it; in fact, he helped adjust it so that it was covering everything from breasts to feet, and then carefully straddled her hips. Leaning over, he gave her a reassuring smile and began massaging her left arm, working from her shoulder all the way down to her hand.

The current song was now something about walking by a riverbank with one's beloved lady, admiring the pairs of waterfowl building their nests, not about holding hands or anything similar, but he did stroke and knead in time to the music. When he reached her hand, he spent about as much time on it as he had on her feet, then shifted to start all over again at her right shoulder. The whole experience was turning her limp, yet wasn't putting her to sleep; Mariel was too aware of the blond, voiceless mage to feel the least bit sleepy. Indeed, with him straddling her body, she had a good view of his groin, and the proof that he was finding this just as arousing as she was.

Rather than moving to her upper torso next, Evanor decided to move back down to the foot of the bed. Placing his hands on her feet, he kneaded them again, massaging until she moaned softly, then worked his way up her shins, up over her knees. The blanket got pushed up every time he stroked and caressed a little higher, until it was bunched up over her mound. By that time, she was panting rather than just breathing . . . and by that time, he could smell her. Warm, feminine, musky . . . needy.

As much as Ev wanted to part her thighs even farther, to inhale more directly from the source of that natural perfume, he still had the rest of her body to do. Reluctantly, he tugged the blanket back down into place, then crawled up to the head of the bed. Kneeling next to her, he stroked her forehead gently, making her open her hazel eyes in curiosity. Her tongue flicked out, moistening her lips and drawing his attention to them.

Ironically, the next song began just as he was debating whether to give in and kiss her: a song about kissing a lover. Seeing the anticipation in her eyes as soon as she puzzled out the lyrics, he gave in just enough to lean over and brush his mouth against hers. Once . . . twice . . .

He pulled away before she could do more than lift her head a little, seeking more. Shifting back, giving himself room to work, Evanor peeled down the edge of the blanket, baring her breasts. They sagged, of course; she was lying on her back, after all. But they were soft and generous, and she arched up into his touch as he cupped them, rippling his fingers in a slow, gentle knead.

Her nipples beaded, begging for his mouth; somehow he found the strength to resist. Smoothing his palms up over her shoulders, he stroked down her ribs to her abdomen, where he caressed gently, enjoying the softness of her skin, and feeling the tiny ripples of faded stretch marks. Her hand shifted down, covering his for a moment; a glance at her face showed her blushing again, this time in discomfort. Evanor guessed she was self-conscious about the signs of motherhood on her body.

Wanting to reassure her, he dipped down, pressing a kiss to the swell of flesh below her waistline. More than a single kiss; he pressed a string of them in a spiral around her navel, then daringly licked the soft, warm skin. Her hand shifted to his head, her fingers tangling briefly in his hair. She stroked down to the ends of it, which she rubbed over her belly. The sensuality of the act encouraged him into shaking his hair across her stomach. It made her chuckle. But when she pushed on his shoulder and parted her legs, patently wanting him to work his kisses farther south, Evanor resisted.

Disappointment washed through Mariel, making her wonder if she should've bathed so that she was fresh. Or worse, she wondered if he just didn't like that aspect of lovemaking. Not all men enjoyed licking and kissing their partners everywhere, after all. She knew as a Healer that, so long as both partners were in good health and kept themselves clean, scrubbing their teeth and bathing thoroughly everywhere, it wasn't an unhealthy act. In fact, it was part and parcel of a healthy love life. Milon had thankfully enjoyed it, and she had enjoyed reciprocating. But there was no telling whether this man did, and she felt a little awkward just blurting out the question.

Covering her carefully with the blanket, Evanor leaned over her long enough for a slow, sweet kiss, and a whispered order. *"Don't move."*

Curious, Mariel craned her neck, watching him leave the bed and pad over to the hearth. He stacked two more logs on the fire behind the grate, then disappeared into the refreshing room for a moment. She heard him washing his hands, then he reappeared. Seeing her still lying as he'd left her, he smiled and returned to the bed. But not to remove the blanket, nor to kneel at her side. Instead, he climbed onto the bed and stretched out beside her.

Propped up on his elbow, Evanor leaned over Mariel, taking a moment to admire the curly-haired healer before continuing. Her nose was slightly snub and as charming as her son's. Her mouth was full along the bottom, perfectly bowed along the top, and quirked up slightly at one corner, making him want to tongue it, to try and taste whatever secretly amused her. And her eyes . . . those captivated him. Of all of his brothers, only Koranen had hazel eyes, but his were more golden, with flecks of green. Mariel's were green with flecks of brown, rimmed in blue gray around the edges and golden toward the center.

Aware that he could easily stare into her eyes for a long time, Evanor reminded himself that he didn't have that luxury, yet. Sliding his free hand under the soft wool covering her, he stroked her stomach. She twitched a little, smiling, and he knew he'd tickled her.

That was fine by him. Smiling back, Evanor let his hand glide upward, across her ribs. That allowed him to cup her breast. All he did was cup it, that and trail the edge of his thumb over the nipple at its crest. Slowly, back and forth. He could feel her areola shriveling, felt her nipple tightening, and felt his loins hardening in tandem.

Not that he hadn't been hard already—Evanor was touching a beautiful, alluring, sensual woman, after all—but now he could feel his own heartbeat pulsing in his unsated flesh. Not quite to the point of pain, but definitely to the point of decision, one of how far to go. Aware that this was only their third night together, he made up his mind to not take any personal satisfaction, tonight.

This was about Mariel, about *her* pleasure. About her learning to trust him and coaxing her into falling for him. With that in mind, he nuzzled the edge of the blanket away from her nearer breast and replaced it with the warmth of his lips.

The feel of his mouth against her flesh, of the slight rasp of stubble from his chin sliding against her skin, pleased Mariel. As did the hand still cupping and stroking her other breast. With the room now comfortably warmed from the fire, she felt bold enough to push the blanket down, baring herself to the hips. The soft sigh of his breath let her know he appreciated the view, but she wished he already had his voice back; the glorious tenor issuing from the music box made her wonder what he would sound like if he groaned in the heat of passion. It would be a different sort of love song, the kind that came without words. Or at least, without words that rhymed.

Wanting to encourage him, Mariel touched his hand, the one

cupping her breast. Gently, she pulled it from her flesh and slid it down her belly. Only that far, though—like his hand on hers the previous night, she didn't demand more than he would be willing to give. She did, however, suggest what he should do simply by moving his palm down her body.

He lifted his head from her other breast. Staring into her hazel eyes, he read her silent request, and the need that prompted it. Allowing his lips to quirk into a slight smile, he lifted his hand from her belly just far enough to tease her navel with his fingertips. Her stomach quivered with a suppressed laugh, and when he did it again, she slapped lightly, playfully at his fingers.

Ev just smirked and shifted his fingertips farther down, tickling just above her mound. She squirmed and giggled and pushed at his hand—and he slid his middle two fingers down into her curl-dusted folds. Slick warmth met his touch, as well as the satiny softness of her flesh. Mariel moaned, arching her head back into her pillow.

Her thighs splayed a little wider, shifting the blanket over the top of his wrist. He didn't mind; if he *watched* what he was doing to her, he might lose control over his own arousal . . . and he didn't need to see her flesh to feel his way across that little peak and down into the soft folds below. Careful to not scrape anything with his fingernails, he rubbed her turgid flesh in slow, leisurely circles.

Mindful that he hadn't known nearly as many lovers as his next-youngest brother, Trevan, and that it had been more than three years since his last encounter, Evanor wanted to go slowly, to get it right the first time. When he felt her hips beginning to move, circling in subtle counterpoint to his touch, he increased the speed, and a little bit of the pressure. That made her sigh; a glance at her face showed her lashes against her cheeks.

Glad he was doing it right, Evanor decided to add something more. Dipping his head, he licked her nipple once again. Another sigh escaped Mariel; her hand rose, cupping the back of his head. Encouraged, he did more, savoring the taste of her skin all the way around. When he caught the peak of her breast in his lips, gently tugging on her flesh, she moaned again.

The thought of pleasing her, of leading her up the slope of her desire and dipping her over the edge of her passion, was an exciting one. Evanor stroked a little faster, suckled a little stronger. She pushed at his cheek when he did so, though, murmuring, "Not so hard . . ."

Gentling his mouth, he continued to stroke through her folds with his fingers. She didn't object to the firmness of his touch there, but she did lift her hips into each downward stroke, dipping the tip of his finger into her opening. Curious, he curled his two middle fingers inward the next time she lifted herself up, stroking farther. She gasped and pushed higher into his hand, clearly liking it. Shifting his hand, Ev slid those fingers into her and brought his thumb down to tease and rub against the little peak of nerves, ensuring it wasn't abandoned. Inside her body, his fingers fluttered upward against her flesh, toward his palm.

"Oh, Goddess . . . ohhh Goddess—ah, *Goddess*!" Bucking up into his touch, Mariel let herself go, let herself shatter on his talented fingers. He was just as good at this as she was—even better, in fact, since he had the length of arm to touch her comfortably, and the length of fingers to touch her well. Clutching at the back of his head, she groaned, bucked a little more, then quivered and let out her breath in a shudder.

Thankfully, he eased his ministrations, sliding his fingers free until he was cupping his hand against her loins. A second shiver raced through her at the gentle yet possessive touch. Mariel couldn't help making a comparison between Milon and him; Milon had always removed his hand after doing something similar, rather than letting it linger. Then again, Milon had usually touched her like this to arouse her passion, not to complete it. Not without doing other things at the same time, or shortly thereafter.

That made her aware of the hardened flesh poking into the side of her thigh. Sliding her hand free of his soft locks, she lowered it between their bodies, seeking his erection. To her surprise, Evanor hissed and shifted onto his stomach, rolling closer and protecting himself from her touch. *"No, no . . . this night is for you. Not me."*

No innocent, Mariel knew he had to be aching; the length of his masculinity was pressed against the bedding now, rather than digging into her, but he was surely still hard and ready with need. Yet he didn't want anything from her. At least, not tonight. It puzzled her. "Why not?"

Dipping his head, Evanor kissed her softened nipple. *"Tonight is reserved for you. Don't worry, it'll go away."*

"What if I *want* to give you pleasure?" Mariel asked him. His forehead dropped to her breast, resting there. A hiss of breath escaped him; she guessed it was meant to be a rough groan.

Pulling his palm away from her groin, Evanor turned his head sideways. Breathing deeply, he inhaled her scent, then suckled his fingers. Another night, he would taste her more directly. Tonight . . . this was as far as he would go. It was a piece of advice his next-youngest brother had once given him. Back before their exile, when there had been plenty of potential bed partners available, Trev had told his brothers that women enjoyed a man who took his time in seducing them. Even if it drove them crazy at the same time.

In fact, Trevan had said that women loved being driven crazy, so long as they were eventually satisfied in full. Since the fifthborn brother was the acknowledged lover among them, Ev was willing to heed his advice. However, since he was leery of exposing himself to Mariel's touch until he wasn't quite so painfully aroused, he stayed where he was rather than retreating. Pulling up the blanket, he covered what he could of her body, then wrapped his arm, damp fingers and all, around her ribs. Trevan had also claimed that women complained how most men didn't cuddle enough after lovemaking, and Evanor was quite willing to cuddle right now.

It also ensured she couldn't move the arm trapped between them, since his groin was pressed into the bedding down by her thigh and her hand was caught against her hip. His erection would go away. In time. If she kept her fingers to herself and didn't try to reach any lower.

Still not quite sure why Evanor wasn't seeking his own pleasure, Mariel watched him press a kiss to her breast through the blanket that was sheltering her flesh, before laying his head on her chest again. The arm he had wrapped around her felt nice, even cozy. Bringing up her free hand, she stroked her fingers through his blond locks.

"Evanor . . . are you sure you don't want me to . . . ?" she offered.

He shook his head. *"Tomorrow night is soon enough."*

Mariel could finally accept that. He hadn't said it in a way that demanded reciprocation tomorrow night, so much as his whisper—toneless though it might literally be—had hinted at the feeling, if she was still in the mood to reciprocate, he'd likely be in a mood to accept. But until then, he seemed quite content to just cuddle with her. Equally content, flattered by the self-control that showed he considered her pleasure paramount this evening, she stroked his soft hair. The fire died down, and the room grew cool again, until the thin wool blanket wasn't quite enough to combat the chill.

Since her host was lying on the bedding he had folded back earlier, she had to move him. To be fair, he *was* providing a very nice source of warmth, but only for her left side. And to move him, she had to wake him, for Mariel realized he had fallen asleep at some point.

Nudged, Evanor woke with a touch of disorientation. Not expecting to wake holding a woman in his arms, he blinked a few times in confusion, then lifted his head. *"Yes?"*

"It's growing cold," she murmured. "I'd like to get under the covers."

"Ah. Yes." Nodding, Evanor shifted off the bed. No sooner had he stood than he sank back onto the edge of the feather-stuffed mattress, feeling his head pounding from the sudden change in position.

"Are you alright?"

"Just a little dizzy—I stood up too quickly," he dismissed, turning to see her pulling the covers into place. Taking the gray blanket from her, he helped arrange the others, then flicked the gray one over the top. It pleased him when she sat up and kissed him before settling back down again. He smiled at her. *"Goodnight, Mariel."*

"Goodnight, Evanor. Sleep well," she said. Then smiled somewhat shyly, adding, "And it's definitely my turn to please *you*, tomorrow night."

Flushing with pleasure at the thought, Evanor retreated, grinning. Then he scurried sheepishly back into her bedchamber, snatched up his forgotten boots, and left again.

ELEVEN

*H*ello, Uncle. *You're looking rather fat and bald, as usual."*

  No . . . no, not again . . .

  "Insolent brat! I wondered why your magics didn't come to me, when all my magics said you were dead."

The part of Evanor that was separate from his dream struggled against it, struggled to warn and defend his earlier self.

  "An oversight I will correct—"

NO!

  "Skaren skaroth!"

Evanor flung himself between Alys and her fire-ringed uncle, even as Evanor flinched back from his nightmare. An arcing blade of light slashed straight at him, while his throat tightened. The spell grabbed his shoulder and woke him with a start and a hissed yell—

Ev blinked, jolted upright on his bed. The room was cold, the lighting gray and dreary, but he could see a short, curly-haired body to his left, half leaning on the edge of his bed with one hand and staring at him with wide, curious eyes.

"Are you all right?" Mikor asked him, lowering his other hand; apparently the boy had shaken him awake.

Drawing in a shaky breath, Ev tried to clear his head. The terror of his nightmare was too much, though; exhaling in a shudder, he curled over his legs, bracing his elbows on his knees and his forehead on his palms. *"No . . . no, I'm not all right. Thank you for waking me."*

Mikor leaned both hands on the mattress and asked with the mild curiosity only someone young and innocent could have, "Was it a bad dream?"

Evanor managed a nod.

"Oh. I didn't know adults could have bad dreams, too."

There was something in the youth's voice that said he'd just had a foundation in his life disturbed. Quickly realizing the boy needed some reassurance, Ev uncurled his left arm. Hooking it around Mikor's waist, he urged the boy onto the bed next to him, and gave him a one-armed hug.

"Even adults get nightmares, when bad things happen to them," he explained carefully, grateful Mikor was leaning into him. The boy was giving *him* comfort, in a way. *"My brothers and Kelly and Alys were going to be hurt. I knew I could stop the fighting—and I did—but in doing so, I lost my voice. But because I Sing my magic when I use it, like your mother does, I lost not only my voice, but all of my powers . . . and there's not a very big guarantee I'll get them back, even if my voice is restored."*

Mikor snorted at that. "My mother can fix lots of things . . . not *everything*," he admitted quietly, his tone sad. "She couldn't fix my father. But then, he fell down the mountain and broke a bunch of stuff, including his neck. I wish she could've, but she couldn't. But she can fix you. She's said she can, and my mother *never* lies."

Despite his natural skepticism at an endorsement from a child, Evanor smiled. Mikor's faith in his mother was touching, even encouraging. *"Never, huh?"*

"She also said she likes *you*," Mikor added, glancing up at him. "An' *you* said you like *her*. Do you lie?"

Evanor answered honestly. *"Only to very bad people, when it's absolutely necessary and will help save my family and friends from their enemies. But never to my family or friends . . . and since you and I are friends, then I will never lie to you. We* are *friends, right?"*

It wasn't easy, putting emphasis into words that had to be whispered, but Mikor's nod reassured Evanor. "An' if you and Mother get married, then we'll be family, 'cause you'll be my next-father."

"I think I'd have a better chance at winning your mother's hand if I nagged you about saying 'because' instead of ''cause,' since she thinks speaking properly is very important," Evanor dared to observe. Even sitting sideways to each other, he could see Mikor rolling his green eyes and gave the boy's shoulders a squeeze. *"Mikor, don't you think that if I'm to be your next-father, I should at least agree with your mother on how to raise you? Right?"*

"Right," Mikor agreed. Somewhat reluctantly—but only somewhat.

"Now, what brings you in here, without being invited?" Evanor asked, lifting his hand from the boy's shoulder to his head, so he could briefly rumple those brown curls.

"Oh! Right. Aunt Serina says she's not feeling well, so you have to set the table for breakfast. She says she's not contagious, though, and Mother agreed. She also laughed, for some reason," Mikor added. "I knocked on the door, but you didn't answer, so I opened it. And when I saw the inner door was open, I thought you'd left your room, but checked anyway, and you were still in bed asleep. You didn't look happy. But that was because of the bad dream, right?"

Evanor nodded.

Hesitating, Mikor offered, "Mother said I wasn't to come in here without permission, but she also says when it's important, you can interrupt someone. Setting the table is kinda important, right?"

"Kind of important, yes," Evanor agreed. *"Though it's not life-and-death important. If you hadn't saved me from the rest of my bad dream, I might've been upset with you for invading my privacy . . . though I would only have been a little upset,"* he added, noting how Mikor's expression fell a little at the admonishment. Giving the youth's shoulders a squeeze, Evanor nudged him back onto his feet next to the bed. *"Off you go. I have to rise and dress before I can set the table."*

Considering Evanor wasn't even wearing under-trousers beneath the bedding pooled around his lap, it was just as well that Mikor nodded and left so agreeably. Having been a bachelor in his own quarters for so long in his island exile, he had gotten out of the habit of wearing nightclothes. Mindful that Mikor might decide to wake him up again for some other semi-important chore in the future, Evanor resigned himself to digging something suitable out of his storage chests.

More important, he knew, slipping out of bed and padding toward the refreshing room, *I should get into the habit of it for when Mariel and I are joined in marriage. She'll undoubtedly want to wear some sort of nightgown, in case her son visits in the middle of the night, needing comfort from some nightmare of his own . . . and if and when we should have more children, we'll need nightclothes for that, too.*

Picking up the pumice stone his next-youngest brother had imbued with a shaving charm, Ev sighed at his reflection in the scrying-blocked mirror over the sink, before rubbing the rough stone over his jaw. *You'll have to pay attention to such things right away, you know. If you take on Mariel, you take on her son as your own, and that confers instant fatherhood into your lap . . .*

Strange, how that thought was exhilarating, yet more nerve-racking than the nightmare of losing his voice.

How odd, Morg thought, eyeing the whiteboard and the woman drawing on its surface. *For three days, she leaves 44 on the board, and now she changes it to a 41?*

A noise interrupted his thoughts. Turning away from the cheval mirror—set just to scry, not to pass objects, as usual—Morganen eyed the sheet-draped oval mirror hanging on his workroom wall. Faintly, he heard his voice reassuring the caller that their call was important and to leave a message. Smirking, he started to turn away as the gong sounded, but the angry words of Councilor Consus of Sea Commerce penetrated.

"Dammit, if one of you doesn't answer my calls immediately, I'm going to march into that Council Chamber tonight and tell them what I saw, the last time I talked to one of you Jinga-be-Damned idiots! Or rather, who!"

Kelly. The Councilor had seen Kelly among the brothers, the last time they'd chatted with the man. Morganen was not ready to let *that* secret out, so he lunged across the room, yanked the cloth off, took a scant second to compose himself, then tapped the rim of the mirror, changing it from its peach-colored recording mode to an active communication link.

Thankfully, it looked like Lord Consus was in his office, not the Hall of Mirrors, where anyone could be summoned to answer other mirrors at any moment, and thus be there to overhear this conversation. Reasonably sure the man was alone, Morganen gave him as pleasant a smile as the younger mage could muster. "Hello, Councilor. How may we of Nightfall help you?"

Consus narrowed his brown eyes in suspicion. Running a palm over his thinning, gray-streaked, light brown hair, he composed himself visibly. "The Council, and the King," he stated after drawing a deep, steadying breath, "are concerned at the unusual list of supplies you and your brothers have been requisitioning. They are concerned that these non-normal items might indicate the presence of *women* on the Isle. Which, as you well know, has been forbidden."

"Are you alone?" Morganen asked him, rather than answering the questions buried in the other mage's statements.

"Of course!" Consus snorted. "I even spell-sealed the door to my office and scry-locked my other mirrors. For all *I* care, the lot of you can go hang yourselves from trees until you turn into Mendhi monkeys, but Council and King would have a conniption fit . . . which is why I didn't report the presence of that woman. But the purchasing of objects women like to buy is jeopardizing Katan's neutrality, and with it, the Empire's safety. *It is drawing their attention,*" he emphasized. "If Katan gets involved, we could be dragged into your Gods-be-Damned Curse!"

At that, Morg choked on a laugh. Shaking his head, he grinned at the older mage, who was scowling at him for the insult. "Sorry . . . but it was *your* refusal to aid us in the previous matter that *fulfilled* the Disaster, milord."

"What?" The Councilor stared at him.

"Just as Prophesied, Katan failed to aid," Morg clarified. "In specific, you failed to aid *us*, when we requested your help."

Consus gaped at him through the mirror, his jaw falling slack enough to droop his middle-aged mouth open. "Katan . . . *failed to aid*. Jinga's Tits!"

"Mm-hmm," Morg agreed, smirking. "That's right. *You* were the instrument of the Seer Draganna's Prophecy. At least, for that part of the first verse. I've been keeping my eye on the other verses, but none of them should pose a threat to Katan. So long as Katan does not pose a threat to *us*, that is."

The other mage narrowed his eyes sharply. "What do you mean by that?"

"Since Prophecy *is* being fulfilled, Mage Consus," Morganen reminded him, "there is more than one woman on the Isle by now. And more yet to come. I will also remind you that the last duchess of Nightfall predicted that the Isle would be repopulated after a certain Curse of her own, engendered by the destruction of the Aian Empire, forced the people living here on Nightfall to flee the island for the mainland when the island could no longer support the thousands that used to occupy this land. *That* Curse will be lifted by having *its* conditions fulfilled—conditions which are now coming true in conjunction with the Curse of the Sons of Destiny, I might add. The island *will* be repopulated in short order, Councilor."

"Are you sure of that?" Consus asked him warily. "I haven't studied that particular Curse myself, but from what I heard, it seems highly unlikely that it'll happen anytime soon."

"I remind you, it is *my* Destiny to study certain Prophecies. I am *very* certain of it," Morganen chided the other man, his tone cool. "Now, because the weight of Prophecy is handed down by the Gods Themselves, I suggest you continue your know-nothing stance with the Council, allowing Destiny to attend to itself."

Consus sat back in his seat, one of his graying brows arching upward. "And what do *I* get out of this?"

Morganen quirked one of his own eyebrows. "You scratch my

back, I scratch yours, is that it? Do you have something specific in mind?"

Consus hesitated, giving Morganen the impression that the older man honestly didn't know, for a moment. But only for a moment. "Information, of course," the Councilor stated smoothly. "I want to know exactly what is going on out there. If the others find out I know *something*, they'll assume I know *everything* and hold me accountable. I want to know what I'll be presumed to be keeping secret."

Folding his arms across his chest, Morganen rubbed his chin. "I don't know . . . That's a *lot* of information. Scratch for scratch—you keep *me* informed of what the Council is doing, in regards to Nightfall, and I'll keep you informed as to what is happening out here."

Consus snorted. "I thought you were Destined to be 'the Mage,' the best of us all. Or are your powers not strong enough to spy on all that we do?"

Morganen shrugged eloquently, arrogantly, despite the content of his reply. "I'm but one man; I can only watch so many mirrors at once, and scry in so many locations, before needing to eat, sleep, and bathe. What I would get from such a situation is piecemeal, picked at from a distance. You're immersed in the Empire's politics; you would understand background motivations for conversations, which a scrying spy would only catch in uneducated pieces."

It was the Councilor's turn to fold his arms across his chest. "Now *you're* asking for more than I should give. Value for value, Son of Corvis."

"Son of Nightfall," Morganen corrected. At the Lord Councilor's puzzled look, he smiled tightly. "Nightfall no longer recognizes the authority of the Katani Empire . . . by your own cognizance, I might add. You did say that the Empire would disavow all responsibility for us, and you *are* a duly appointed member of its ruling body."

The epithet that floated through the mirror linking them in communication would've cracked the glass, save for two things: one, Consus hadn't put his magical energies behind the vulgar oath; and two, the mirror was protected to some degree against the possibility.

Not completely, of course; the only magic in all of their world that was unbreakable belonged to the Prophecies handed to the Seers, in divine foresight given to them by their patron Deities. They were highly subject to vast and varied interpretation, yes, but they invariably came true. Shattering the frame of the mirror, however, was quite possible, *if* the Councilor were upset enough to throw something at it.

"You stole away our birthright, *Councilor*. We gave in to your demand for exile, because I knew it was necessary," Morganen reminded him. "*I* was the one who convinced the others to go quietly, if you'll recall. A war between my brothers and the Council would have torn Katan apart far faster than any Prophetic misunderstanding. We went into exile, yes, but do not delude yourself that we will *stay* in exile."

"If you want the Corvis coronet restored to your eldest brother—" Consus argued.

Morg waived that off with a flick of his hand, dismissing it as negligible. "That was our old life, Councilor. This is our new one. Nightfall is now our home, as Prophesied. By rights, we *should* have been receiving profit from the familial holdings, if Broger of Devries hadn't sucked it all dry, either through unnecessary expenses or outright lies on the County's profits. But we haven't seen more than a hundred gilders of Corvis profit in the three-plus years we've been exiled out here, and most of that was in the first two months.

"No doubt his son and heir, Barol, is doing much the same, since we have received nothing in recent months from him, either. But do you see us demanding our fair share? No. We are striving to be self-sufficient, here. To *avoid* entangling Katan unnecessarily in our affairs."

Consus grimaced. "That reminds me. Lord Broger and his brother, Donnock of Devries, have gone missing. As has Lord Broger's ward . . . what was her name . . ."

Morg ignored mentioning his sister-in-law in favor of the bigger question. "Broger slaughtered his own brother in order to open up a Dark Gate between some secret lair of his and this island. That was part of the foreseen Disaster," he added, silently enjoying the way the older mage blanched. "We enacted a justice-death upon him, cast back upon him his own lethal magics, and the Netherhells accepted his soul as eternal payment for sealing the apertures . . . which were both here *and* on the mainland.

"If you want to count what is owed to anyone, Katan *owes* us for sealing that Dark Gate, which cost us several injuries to enact—and I'd suggest tracking the residual traces that may still exist, to locate that lair," Morg warned the Councilor. "The apple that is Barol of Devries didn't fall *that* far from his father's tree . . . and there are several magical beasts unaccounted for that we know Broger of Devries was constantly setting against us. Beasts which were not used in the final confrontation with him, beasts which he had been breeding and sending against us for nearly three years. Beasts that are being kept in direct violation of Katani law. Beasts which you neglected to search hard enough for, the last time we tried to complain about it to you."

The older mage narrowed his eyes speculatively. "What proof do you have of this violation?"

"A member of our late, unlamented uncle-in-law's own household was forthcoming on many details when we came in contact with this person, though the exact location of the menagerie's lair was unknown, as it was accessed solely by mirror-Gate from somewhere in Corvis Castle to somewhere on the Devries estate up until a few months ago," the younger mage explained. "Now, I have given you more than enough information for an equitable exchange. Tell me what the Council plans to do about us, at this point."

"*Not* enough information," Consus countered. He held up his hand as Morg drew breath to protest. "*Almost* enough information for the exchange, I'll grant you that. Tell me what happened with that woman I saw, and I'll let you know what the Council has planned for you at this point in time. Is she still there, among you?"

That made Morg grin. Clasping one arm over the other, he shrugged. " 'That woman' is still living safe and sound on Nightfall, yes."

"And the Curse?" Consus asked shrewdly. "If you have a woman on the Isle, then one of you must have bedded her by now. Logic suggests that would have been Count-in-exile Saber, presuming she was a maiden, of course, and presuming the first verse indeed speaks of him, as the firstborn."

"She was, they did, and it was before we contacted you, for a situation which has since been resolved. There is no more Disaster looming over Nightfall," the younger mage asserted calmly. "No Disaster, no Curse, and no reason whatsoever to ban women from approaching the Isle. Nor any reason to bar them from settling here. Now, what is the Council up to?"

"They're concerned about the possibility of women being on the island, and they won't be easily convinced that their concerns are no longer valid. *They* want to know what the nonstandard objects you are purchasing are being used for. Embroidery floss, silks, and fine linens," Consus stated, picking up a piece of paper from the desk beside him and reading from it. "A silver set of hairbrush, comb, and hand mirror. Replacement parts for a loom. New place settings for a table in a very large amount, more than just the eight you and your brothers would need. Essential oils that could be used to make perfumes. *Dairy* cattle. One would think that the woman I saw was pregnant, and in need of milk for nursing in the near future," he added scathingly, tossing the paper back onto his desk.

"No, she isn't pregnant," Morganen retorted. "Not for lack of trying, of course . . . to the discomfort of those of us who haven't found our own wives, yet."

Lord Consus smirked. "Good luck finding seven more brides. It doesn't matter that I, personally, don't care if you had seven times seven women for each and every one of you. The *Council* will not permit you to 'import' any from the mainland. They are upset about the money being charged for the salt and algae blocks, they are upset about the strange purchases, and they are growing concerned that you will raid Katan, looking for women. They're holding off for now, but some of the Council is willing to consider a possible deployment of the Department of Conflict Resolution at some point in the future."

"Who said we would fetch them all from Katan?" Morganen countered mildly, arching a light brown brow in mock-skepticism.

"And who said we wanted dairy cattle for the impending feeding of infants? Even adults can enjoy a fresh cup of milk from time to time. You're skirting the issue, Councilor. What is the Council's next move, aside from your current efforts to pester us, and for now setting aside any future attempt to chastise us? What are they focusing on next, in our list of 'crimes'?"

Dropping the last traces of his smile, Consus stated bluntly, "They are pursuing an inquiry into your demand to be paid for the salt and algae blocks, that's what. You have no right to do that!"

"If the effort is ours, then the profit is ours," Morg stated reasonably. "I don't see what the problem is."

"Effort?" Consus scoffed. "I've seen the reports. There's no more effort involved producing that salt than there is in yawning! The island's waterworks produce freshwater, which spills of its own volition out of the faucets you use, and that in turn automatically generates the salt blocks."

"You oversimplify the matter, Lord Councilor. The blocks must be moved from their creation ramps to the warehouse, and from the warehouse to the ships that visit. Protective spells must be cast to guard them during shipping against weather and grime—the Council knows full well the value of those spells, as it regulates the set-price for certain standard magical services," the younger mage stated coldly. "Every time in the past that we have cast those spells, *we have not been paid for them.*

"We have also put a lot of effort into cleaning up the fountains so that they flow freely, increasing our daily block production by more than sixfold, with plans to expand production," Morg continued. "When you disavowed any responsibility on Katan's part toward helping Nightfall in our hour of need, we had to claim that responsibility for ourselves. Had you *aided* us, lent us your protection and your assistance, you would still have had some claim to the commodities produced by this place . . . and I don't mean just the recent crisis wherein you disavowed us. I mean your lackadaisical attitude toward our near-weekly invasions by that menagerie—and it was *we* who uncovered that fact, exiled though we were and lacking all the vast resources that the Council has at its command. Your efforts *were* poor, in comparison.

"But we asked you for help, and you refused to grant it—a refusal, I point out," Morganen added, cutting off the older mage as he started to protest, "that *began* when the Council demanded that we be exiled far from our home and our normal sources of assistance and protection, demanding that we be cut off from most forms of contact and interaction . . . and with it, cutting us off from our rights as Katani citizens to be protected. Katan failed to aid us long ago.

"I'll remind you that when we first started being attacked by those mage-beasts, the Council chose to call it a 'cry for attention' and ignored our requests for assistance. We were 'exiled' and therefore no longer worthy of your efforts, because it wasn't a 'Disaster' that threatened the rest of the Empire," Morganen pointed out bitterly. "It was just someone trying to kill off eight highly inconvenient, mostly powerful mages. Rivals for the Council's power."

"And some visit from these Mandarites constitutes a Disaster that would have encompassed Katan?" the Councilor of Sea Commerce challenged him.

"It would have, if they had managed to establish a colony, taking Nightfall away from Katan, and dragging the Empire into a war in order to reclaim it," Morganen informed him. "But you ignored us, yet again, despite the very real threat these people represented. In doing so, you *broke* the covenant between a government and its people. If you wish to rule over a people and expect them to heed the rules of your guardianship over them, then *they* have a right to *be* guarded. By refusing the responsibility to guard us, you refused the right to rule over us."

"So, what, you're saying that you've declared independence?" Consus scorned.

"If those who have pledged to protect a people fail to follow through on that pledge, then it is up to the people themselves to provide that protection."

The Councilor narrowed his hazel-brown eyes again. "Now it is *you* who are being obtuse. Have you, or have you not, declared your independence from the Empire of Katan?"

"Define *declared*," Morg countered warily.

"Have you Rung the Bell?" Consus asked him impatiently.

Not wanting to lie outright, Morg replied merely, "We're working on it."

"What does *that* mean?" the older mage asked, arching one gray-salted brow.

"It means that it is not yet time for anyone else to press that matter . . . but if you or the Council *do*, we are ready to ring it ourselves," Morganen warned him. "Right now, if needed."

The Councilor for Sea Commerce blinked at that, slumping back in his seat. He frowned in the next moment. "You would risk doing that? Invoke the awakening of a new God? There's only nine of you on the whole island, including that woman!"

"Careful, Lord Councilor; you don't actually *know* how many are living on this island, these days. Nor even if all of my brothers are still living here, now that we've rejected Katani authority, and with it, your demand that we stay exiled . . . though I wouldn't count Nightfall as defenseless, if I were you. As I said," Morg hedged neatly, bluffing the older man, "if you push us, we'll ring the Bell ourselves. *Your* best course of action would be to delay the Council's interest in this island for as long as possible, because you won't like what will happen, otherwise."

"Those salt blocks are the property of the Duchy of Nightfall, and thus belong to the Empire of Katan!" Consus argued.

"The last duchess is *dead*," Morg snapped, "and the Empire can go sodomize a pookrah, for all the care and consideration it's given us! Those that *do* the work get the profit! Those that actually *care* get the benefits. You keep your Council off this island, Lord Consus," he ordered, "and we'll be *suitably* grateful. Bring them here in an attempt to enforce any sort of authority over us, and you will *not* like the results."

"Is that a threat?" Consus demanded, sitting forward in his chair.

Morganen deliberately folded his arms across his chest, looking as belligerent as his eldest brother sometimes could, despite his lack of extra muscles. "That is a *promise*, with the inexorable weight of Prophecy to back it up—*more* than one Prophecy, I might add, from more than one Gods-ordained source."

Silence reigned between the two men. The battle of wills clashed wordlessly as they stared each other down, waves of willpower struggling for dominance over a single stretch of sand . . . then the conflict ebbed on one side. Consus breathed deeply, then let it out slowly.

"What am I to tell them, then? They *will* expect a report on the whys of your purchase and your demand of payment for the salt and fertilizer blocks."

"Tell them the fripperies were for spell components, the cattle are for food and drink requirements, and the salt and algae blocks are being sold to compensate for an utter lack of income from our ancestral lands," Morganen instructed him. "Inform your colleagues that they should investigate the actual produce and commerce versus the reported produce and commerce of County of Corvis for tax purposes, if they wish to recoup any money that was lost . . . because if we didn't receive the moneys we were due, then it's equally sure the government never got its taxes, either.

"Half of the post-tax profits *should* have been shipped to us, to help sustain us in our exile," he reminded Consus sharply when the older mage drew in a breath to argue. "As they were not, yet Corvis undoubtedly still remains a prosperous expanse in spite of the Gods know what our loathsome kinsman may have done to it, ask your fellow councilors to investigate where our missing funds have gone. If they want to investigate *any* breaches in their precious laws and enforce anything, they can start with what my brothers and I have been rightfully due for the last three years. Due, but *not* received—as recorded by *your* department's transaction records."

Consus eyed the younger mage through the mirrors linking them. "Until then, I take it I'm to tell them you'll be selling the blocks to make up for the deficiency?"

When the younger mage nodded, he ran a hand over his thin, graying hair.

"Then afterward . . . *if* your rightful income is restored, if it hasn't been squandered away by natural causes, droughts, floods, plagues among the sheep and cattle . . . what do I tell them then?" The Councilor let out a mirthless sound somewhere between a laugh and a scoff. "Because somehow, I don't see the lot of you giving up a single inch of whatever you may have gained."

"We'll deal with that trouble if and when we come to it," Morganen told him. "I suggest you leave the implication dangling, though not confirmed. Now, if you don't mind, I have other business to return to. Good day, Lord Councilor."

"A *good* day? *That* would make a nice change," Consus muttered before flicking his hand at the mirror, turning it blue, then shutting off the link, leaving Morganen to watch his own reflection sigh and sag with relief.

One confrontation with the Council had just been successfully navigated, at least.

TWELVE

W ait," Mariel interjected quickly, straightening from her toe-touching exercises. The other three women paused as well, though it was Alys the Healer addressed. "I'm confused. *You* say that you're related to this 'Uncle Broger' person, and yet the *boys* have said the exact same thing—doesn't that make your marriage to Wolfer a bit . . . you know . . . ?"

Alys blushed, Serina quirked one of her pale brows, and Kelly laughed. None of them objected to Mariel calling their husbands and siblings-in-law "the boys"; this was a women-only moment, after all. The redhead lifted her chin at Alys, grinning. "*You* explain that one. While we finish our stretches, ladies? Stretched muscles are limber muscles."

Balancing her bare feet on the felt-padded floor, arms stretching over her head before windmilling around her body, Alys rolled her eyes and explained as shortly as she could. "Wolfer's mother was named Annia. Annia had a sister, Sylvia. Sylvia married Broger. Broger had two brothers, Donnock and Tangor. Tangor was my father . . . so we're related by marriage only, through my Uncle

Broger and their late Aunt Sylvia. Well . . . I suppose Uncle Broger's son, Barol, technically links us by blood," she added thoughtfully, "but we're not related *directly*. It's not as if my father married their Aunt Sylvia. He married my mother, Glyssa, who isn't related to any of them."

"Right . . . and you said that your Uncle Broger took over the County after the boys were exiled?" Mariel asked next, leaning over as far as she could sideways to stretch out her rib muscles.

"First, Lord Daron of Corvis took it over. He was Saveno's younger brother, and in the direct line of succession, what with the boys exiled all the way out here," Kelly explained for Alys, who was a little red in the face from leaning over so far. "But then Broger had him secretly killed off, so that he, as the next most powerful mage, could take over the governance of the family County. Since it was only a pro tem position while the brothers were in exile, he didn't have to be directly related by blood."

"In fact, technically my uncle was holding it on his son's behalf, since Barol is the one who's related by blood," Alys continued, straightening and lifting one foot, doubling back her leg so she could stretch out her thigh muscles. She wobbled a little, catching Mariel's shoulder for balance. "His plan was to steal not only my own powers if and when he killed me, but to steal the boys' powers, murdering them to send those magics into his son, and then kill his own son to transfer those energies to himself, to become the most powerful mage in Katan, and thus become our next king."

"Sounds like a true bastard-by-nature," Serina grunted, having bent over one foot again. She swung her body so that she leaned over her other foot. That made her long, platinum-pale braid slide across the layers of felt serving as a cushioning pad underfoot. "I'm glad he was swallowed into a Netherhell. I don't really get along with my mother or my sister, but I'd never try to kill either of them—even at my most annoyed!"

"I'm glad he's dead, too," Mariel agreed. "I don't think I would've liked him, much."

A moment later, Kelly laughed, staring at her hand. Serina eyed her askance. "What's so amusing?"

"Oh, it's a cultural thing. When we went up against him, I used an enspelled mirror to bounce back one of his spells," Kelly explained, holding up her hand. "But his protections caused the mirror to burst, and that literally tore off this finger, the middle one. I was going to say, 'I definitely didn't like him, not after he tore off my finger,' and I was about to hold it up all on its own to indicate which one . . . but culturally, holding up just the middle finger is a *very* rude gesture, where I'm from. Not that he didn't deserve it, of course . . ."

"Morganen did a very good job of reattaching it," Mariel admitted, nodding at it. She had already examined Kelly's finger, not to mention Trevan's shoulder. Some extra Healing work had been needed on the wound garnered by the copper-haired mage, which had literally torn all the way through his body, but none on the strawberry-haired woman. "A finger is nothing to mess around with, even if it's not quite as complex as a whole voice box."

"Speaking of which, when will you start your work with Evanor?" Alys asked her. "More than half the chickens you chopped into are healed already."

"Mm, chopped chicken. Sounds delicious," Kelly joked. Serina joined her in a laugh, but Mariel frowned.

"Just because they're nasty beasts destined for the oven does not mean we should be so carelessly cruel in our attitudes toward them," the Healer chided both her hostess and her best friend. "Natua gave us chickens to eat with the understanding that we would be *grateful* for their sacrifice."

Kelly shook her head quickly. "No disrespect for their sacrifice was intended, honestly. I'm just . . . hungry? So. We're all stretched out, we had a good workout, the rainstorm has passed, and we have about two hours before we have to be back here for lunch. Anyone interested in going down to the eastern beach?"

Alys was the first to express her enthusiasm, but then she had already visited the shoreline; Mariel was just as interested in getting off of the castle grounds, so she quickly agreed. Serina pressed her hand to her stomach, wrinkled her nose, then nodded cautiously. "So long as the cart doesn't go too fast, or over too many bumps,

I should be okay . . . but I don't want to be gone too long from my work. Perhaps I should stay up here."

"Exercise is good for you," Mariel countered, not taken in for a moment by her friend's supposed caution. She knew all too well how much Serina would rather play with her arcane formulae than play with sun and sand. "Besides, didn't you whine about how much you missed being near the shore, all that time you were up at the Retreat?"

"Yes, I do miss it, but my work on the cell phone spells is very important," Serina protested. "I should get that done, before I allow myself time to play."

"As your queen, I decree that even *you* must take a couple hours off from your chalkboards," Kelly asserted, joining Mariel's side. "And to make it absolutely fair, since I know Mikor will throw a fit if we go outside the walls without him, I'll invite him and Evanor to join us. We can all get back to work after lunch."

"Maybe we can get Evanor to bring a gittern or lute?" Alys asked, looking at the others. "I mean, he's lost his voice, yes, but *he* didn't lose any fingers, so he should still be able to play for us, right?"

Kelly stuck out her tongue at the younger woman, an un-queenly display that made Mariel laugh. Serina grinned and nudged her friend's shoulder. "Why don't *you* ask Evanor to come and play for us? I'm sure that he'd be all the more eager, if you made it sound like you were encouraging him to court you."

Blushing, Mariel gave Serina a mock-stern look. "I don't *need* to encourage him . . . but I will ask him all the same."

"In the meantime, ladies," Kelly ordered lightly, "let's stop teasing each other, pick up the two boys, and go looking for a cart big enough to drive us all down there. Otherwise, we won't have any time left to play."

They *what*?" King Taurin asked, his tanned face pinching from his incredulity. He set down the King's Sphere that had ordered silence out of the turmoil that had erupted.

"They demand that we investigate why they never received more than a hundred gilders of Corvis income in the entire length of their exiled stay, when that County has been one of the more prosperous holdings in the Empire," Consus repeated, outwardly neutral and calm, but flinching internally at being in the hot seat. "Until a thorough investigation into the actions of Count Pro Tem Broger has been conducted and suitable reparations have been made, they will not consider revoking their demand of payment for the salt and algae blocks.

"*Furthermore*," he stressed as the others started muttering again, "they bring allegations against Lord Broger of Devries, charging him with the harboring of the very same magical beasts they complained were being sent against them since early on in their exile, claims which we discarded after a cursory examination. They add the allegation that Count Broger had murdered his own brother, Lord Donnock of Devries, in the quest to open a Dark Gate to the island, that he attacked them, and has subsequently been killed in a justice-slaying, successfully closing down said Dark Gate . . . and that if we were to investigate any remaining traces of that foul magic, we should be able to find the location of the menagerie we failed to uncover in our previous, 'lackadaisical' examinations.

"It was pointed out to me that *they* finally uncovered who their mystery attacker was, while in exile on an island, and without using any of the vast resources this Council possesses," Consus stated sarcastically. Then found himself adding, "They charge us with failure to uphold our promises to *them* as their government, to protect them in times of trouble . . . and they refuse to allow the blocks to be given away for free, implying that it is a way of recompense for our deliberate and willful negligence of them."

The noise that erupted at that, filled with shouts of how the Corvis brothers were in exile and the definition of exile *was* supposed to be negligence, covered the Sea Commerce Councilor's nervous blink. He hadn't *meant* to say that. He hadn't meant to hint at anything that came close to the truth, that Nightfall was preparing to formally break away from the Empire. *That* would have been far more volatile a subject than what he had already said.

As it was, he had barely skimmed free of that particular implication with his last words. But something within him had forced him to say it. *Kata, don't tell me I'm developing a conscience now, of all times. I'm a bureaucrat! I'm supposed to be favoring Your and Jinga's kingdom, not some bid for independence away from You . . .*

The King's Sphere rapped once, quieting the chamber. King Taurin eyed Lord Consus, as silence fell once more. "You said they will refuse to consider revoking their demand of payment for the salt and such until we have investigated their allegations against the missing Count Broger and the income of County Corvis?"

"That is correct, Your Majesty. They want a *thorough* investigation, this time," he added, again prompted by that internal urge he really didn't want to acknowledge. "I should point out that my department has found evidence of only enough shipped income to equal one hundred gilders, almost all of it from the time of Lord Daron's few months of holding the County in pro tem, the rest tapering off rapidly. A preliminary investigation did find a few 'natural disasters' that accounted for the tapering off of taxes accrued from that holding . . . but that shouldn't have affected the income of the area for three whole years.

"I respectfully suggest that Councilor Thera of Tax Collection investigate these allegations," he added, glancing at the woman in question, her icy expression unmoved by the outbursts of the others. "Since, if Broger of Devries was indeed holding back the truthful income the brothers were due by law as exiles, he was holding back that extra income from being properly accounted and taxed by the Empire. *If* we investigate these allegations thoroughly, the Corvis brothers have hinted they would be quite amenable to renegotiating their stance on the salt blocks . . . *without* needing to resort to the costly expense of invoking a conflict resolution."

That was a jab at Duke Finneg, who was clad in red and gold. He addressed that comment. "It might not be cost effective in the short term, but if they can think to hold us financially hostage once, they'll think they can do it again and again . . . and then the next thing you know, they'll be demanding we ship them women, not just 'unusual spell components'—unusual spell components, Jinga's Ass!"

"Councilor!" Queen Samille snapped reprovingly, blue eyes glaring in affront. "Language!"

"Apologies, Your Majesty," Finneg muttered.

"Relax, Finneg," King Taurin commanded. "We received news this morning that the border conflict between Baron Selon of Karlton and Viscountess Jania of Peloma has escalated into outright warfare, and that Her Excellency has acquired the Baroness of Waunderi as an ally. Your office will have plenty of conflict resolution opportunities in the near future. We will continue to look for peaceful solutions to the Nightfall problem. Until then, you'll have plenty of time to work on the Peloma-Karlton conflict."

Somewhat mollified, Duke Finneg relaxed back into his seat. Consus smoothed the front of his sea green tunic, trying to settle his nerves along with the lay of the velvet. He was grateful the conflict-eager duke would be very busy with that little fracas, and thus very distracted for a while.

"Lord Consus," the king continued, dragging everyone's attention back to the older mage. "While the Department of Tax Collection is busy investigating these allegations by the exiles, I think it is best if you continue to keep in contact with the Corvis brothers. Do what you can to find out what exactly those spell components were used for and anything else that may be happening on the Isle. Subtly and politely . . . but find out what is going on out there. And instruct your trader captains to ask that list of questions we presented to you at the start of this meeting. What they might not tell a Councilmember, they might let slip to the captains they interact with more frequently.

"Now, let us move on to the subject of that asinine conflict between Karlton and Peloma . . ."

Consus resumed his seat with relief. Now the Corvis brothers would have a few more weeks of peace in which to do . . . whatever it was they were doing. Eventually, things *would* come to a head, and conflict resolution might have to be enacted. But the Council had been warned, however obliquely. At least he now had official orders to keep an eye on the situation. Hopefully, he would be able to find a way to mitigate it before anything got out of hand.

Feeling his stomach roil with nerves, Consus debated finding a Healer to give him a calming draught. Preferably something not addictive, since the Councilor suspected he would need a fair amount of it before this whole mess was finished.

Nervous about the preparations Mariel was making in his tower workroom, since Morganen had advised her to incorporate the resonances of his own eight-pointed wardings, Evanor finished instructing his twin on what Dominor was to do. *"And double-check the chores board I got from Serina; do it every single day. If anyone has to trade off a chore, make sure it doesn't throw off the whole schedule for everyone else. She helped me schedule it for a full four weeks out, last night, but I was very tired by the end of it."*

So tired, in fact, that if Mariel had come to visit him last night for a backrub, he didn't know it. He had lain himself on his bed after taking off his footwear, but before taking anything else off, he had a vague memory of pulling the covers up over his shoulder. The next thing he remembered was waking up in the cool morning light with wrinkle lines all over his body from his trousers and tunic bunching the wrong way.

"I'll check the chores board," Dominor promised, his expression polite, but his tone hinting at hidden, inner eye-rolling.

"And keep an eye on Mikor," Evanor ordered his twin. *"He's a handful, and—"*

"I *know*," Dom retorted, giving in to the urge to roll his blue eyes. "I was the first of us to spend any time with him, remember? Everything will be *fine*, Evanor. We'll all keep an eye on Mikor, and on the chore roster, and on keeping the palace clean and its occupants fed. It's not as if you won't be able to nag us via chalkboards and parchments, if we forget!"

"She said there's a slight chance that I could lose even the urge to write, when she dampens my urge to communicate," Evanor whispered, worried about the prospect.

"A *very* slight chance," Dominor reminded his twin. "Stop worrying, Ev! This is the way to get your voice back, and with it, your power. This is what you have to endure. At least it's only for three weeks, and it has the highest probability of restoring your ability to Sing—Serina ran the calculations for it, and *she* says it'll work. Morganen says if we do it in your workroom, he has a spell to 'prime' your Voice-magic by using the residual resonances that linger in here, to aid in your fullest recovery. *He* says it'll work. With two geniuses in the family, you'd think you'd stop being so Gods-be nervous!"

Evanor stared at his twin.

". . . What?" Dom asked defensively.

"You didn't call yourself a genius? Are you feeling alright?" the blond mage whispered, concerned.

Dom flashed him a rueful smile. "Being confronted by true genius—and all the pains in the backside it entails—has made me appreciate my limitations. And the limitations of someone who actually can claim the title. I'd rather be a vastly superior generalist than a super-genius specialist—and I *am* still vastly superior, as a generalist."

"Thank you," Ev sighed, as much in true relief as in teasing. *"For a moment, I wondered what had happened to the arrogant brother I knew."*

"If you two are finished chatting, I need Evanor to strip to the waist," Mariel instructed them. "Dominor, braid his hair back out of the way, shave his throat and chest all the way from his cheeks down to the middle of his ribs, and then scrub all the way around his neck, including the base of his ears and the tops of his shoulders. Use that sink over there, and don't splash anything near the runes and wardings. And don't let him do it himself."

"I can shave myself, woman!" Evanor protested in as loud a hiss as he could manage.

"Not for this, you can't. You can't see under your own jaw all that well, even with the help of a mirror. I need the area as clean and stubble-free as can be managed," the petite Healer asserted, joining them, "and to do that, I need someone to prepare you properly for the procedure." Pressing a vial into Dominor's hands, she gave him a warning look. "Make sure you scrub your own hands thoroughly as well, including around and under your fingernails, before opening this bottle and using its contents. Anoint your fingers once they and he are completely clean, and use them to smooth it all over his throat, from ear to ear and from chin to clavicle.

"Once you're ready, Evanor, lie down on the table at the center of the octagram. You'll be more comfortable if you're horizontal—you're lucky I warmed up the room, and put a pallet on the table for padding," she added briskly, as Evanor drew in a breath. "No arguing, young man. You're not dealing with the woman you're courting, right now. You're dealing with a fully trained Healer. If you want your voice back, you will do everything I tell you to do."

"And if you tell me to stand on my head and cluck like a citizen-chicken, am I supposed to do that?" he challenged her.

"Don't tempt me," Mariel retorted. "Especially if you try to be as ornery as one of them. Get him cleaned up, Dom, and don't forget to wash your hands."

Ev and Dom both glanced over at Morganen, who was busy marking runes on the floor in different colors of chalk after having marked up the walls, but the youngest mage merely flashed them a cheerful smile and continued his work.

"He is far too happy at taking orders from a woman," Dominor muttered, setting the vial aside so he could help Evanor remove his long-sleeved tunic.

"My woman, at that," Evanor agreed.

"Where is his dignity, for Jinga's sake?" Dom demanded under his breath. "Almost three and a half years without a woman, and now that there's four on the island, he's practically turning himself into their slave—and they're not even his!"

"That's because I *like* women, whether or not they're 'mine'; it has nothing to do with courting, and everything to do with friendship," Morganen chided his brothers, shifting over to their side of the room in time to overheard Dominor's comment. "Not everyone in this family thinks with their gonads—stop groaning and start scrubbing!"

Exchanging wry looks, the twins complied. Evanor braided his own hair back out of the way, securing it with a bit of string from a nearby workbench. As soon as Dominor was done scrubbing his hands, Ev sat on a stool, tipping his head back so that his twin could apply a depilatory charm. It stung, but it removed all the hairs from the indicated area of skin, even the fine, downy stuff along his collarbones, and at least half the faint blond hairs scattered across his torso.

Dominor eyed Evanor's stomach, wrinkled his nose, and shook his head. "That just looks wrong—like one of those poodle-dogs Kelly told us about. Not that you're that hairy, Ev, but I'm taking it all off, down to your navel. It just looks *wrong* . . ."

Before Evanor could protest, his twin applied the depilatory charm to the rest of his skin, denuding him of the pale scattering of body hair. Not that there was much, but he did have a slight, blond treasure-line. At least Ev's twin did stop at the top of his belly button, and when Dom handed him a hand mirror from one of the workbench drawers, Ev had to agree he would have looked odd with his chest only half-shaved.

It didn't take long to scrub the skin, after that. Dom took the time to rewash his hands, while Evanor blotted himself dry with a clean towel, then the elder twin anointed his fingertips with the oily liquid contained in the vial. It looked bluish green with yellow undertones on his skin, clear but viscous. However, within a minute of letting it touch his flesh, his skin turned a sort of grayish lavender. As did his twin's neck. It allowed him to see where he had missed anointing Evanor, at least.

"Mariel?" Dominor called out. "What is this stuff?"

"It's called *muristhel*; it's a recipe from Guchere, where I studied. It functions as an antibiotic and an anodynic," she replied, busy doing something with a set of bottles.

"I take it I just apply it until the whole area is purplish gray?" the thirdborn mage asked.

"Correct. You should have plenty in the vial."

"I did. I'm done. Chin to collarbone, ear to ear," he stated, stooping and craning his head to double-check. "All of it's colored."

"Good. There is a jar of removal cream on that table there. Take it with you elsewhere, and find a place to wash your hands," the Healer instructed him. "Whatever you do, don't come back until all the discoloration is gone, or you'll risk losing the feeling in your fingertips. Presuming you want to be here while Evanor's undergoing the treatment. If not, go wash your hands at the palace; you don't want to be within hearing range once I start Singing."

Evanor gave his twin a pleading look. He might be a fully grown man, twenty-seven and independent . . . but this was a major magical procedure. Dom shook his head, rolling his eyes.

"As if I'd abandon you. I'll be back before she starts—you *will* wait for me, won't you?"

"Of course," Mariel reassured him. "I'll be applying more of the ointment internally while you're gone. It's a tricky spell, since I have to be careful not to expose the ointment to a lot of extraneous magic, so if the door is still closed, don't walk inside; wait for me to open it."

Nodding, Dominor picked up the jar and left.

"*Is it safe to talk?*" Evanor asked, watching Mariel mutter soundlessly to herself, flicking through the pages of a book so brand-new, he knew it had to have been a copy made specifically to hold the relevant spells.

"What? Oh, of course, yes," Mariel reassured him, returning from shutting the door in Dominor's wake. "The *muristhel* is activated by magic. Not until I enchant it will it numb your speech ability. But since I need to do that, would you please come over here and sit on the table, now?"

Nervous inside, Evanor padded into the center of the octagon inlaid on the floor, careful to avoid smudging the runes his youngest brother had chalked. Hitching himself onto the table that sat in the center of the eight-sided ward, he watched Mariel pick up a jar and tap it on the outside, near the base. The jar started to vibrate rapidly, first buzzing, then whining, until finally it rang like a struck bell. The liquid inside sloshed, splashed . . . and vaporized.

Carrying the corked bottle over to him, she spoke loudly over the whining of the glass. "In a moment, I am going to stop the buzzing. At that point, I will soften the glass, and you are to inhale and exhale *shallowly* twelve times. Inhale and exhale very shallowly twelve times, *not* deeply. You do not want this to go into your lungs, but you will be able to feel how deeply it goes, so breathe very slowly and cautiously each time. Once you've done that, you need to take the bottle away and breathe very slowly until I count to one hundred, though you can breathe deeply once the bottle has been taken away. Got that?"

Since he couldn't be heard over the sound of the vibrating jar, he nodded. She struck the bottle, which stopped it from ringing, then muttered a short phrase and popped the cork, lifting it quickly to his mouth. Fitting it to his lips, Evanor inhaled and exhaled in short little breaths. It helped that he could *feel* what the atomized potion coated. Not wanting it to get into his lungs—Jinga save him if he was too "numbed" to remember how to breathe—Evanor only let it coat just down to the bottom of his throat.

It was an odd sensation, like extra mucus in his throat. Resisting the urge to cough, he finished sipping and exhaling the viscous mist, then took the bottle away and breathed as slowly as he could. Deeply enough to ensure he got sufficient oxygen into his lungs, but slowly, so that it wouldn't stir the stuff now coating his throat and tongue.

"One . . . two . . . three . . . Lie down on the pallet, if you please; I'll count silently, and let you know when you can breathe normally."

Taking some comfort in her soothing tone, Evanor carefully swiveled his legs up onto the thin pallet covering the tabletop, then eased himself down onto his back. Adjusting the lump that was the end of his braid, he stared up at the ceiling.

"Ninety-eight, ninety-nine, one hundred. You may now breathe normally, if you need it," Mariel added, her tone gently teasing. Evanor did just that, drawing in a nice, deep, full breath, then letting it out in a sigh. She bent over him—as much as she could, given she wasn't exactly tall—and prodded his throat, humming a diagnostic tune. "Very good. You did a good job of not breathing in too deeply. I only have a couple of spots to clean up, inside your bronchi. This may feel a little weird. Don't move. *Sonovocharo . . . morado maikiul . . .*"

Her fingertips traced halfway up his sternum while she Sang the words, tickling his flesh. Not just on the outside, but on the inside, too. Dutiful to her admonition not to move, Evanor restrained himself, including the urge to cough. She stopped and removed her touch, patting him on the chest.

"Slow inhales, then hard exhales as you cough."

Obedient, Evanor expelled the dryness in his chest carefully.

Morganen came up to his side, leaning over the table. He eyed the grayish lavender stain on Evanor's throat and flashed his elder brother a grin. "That color doesn't look too bad on you, Ev."

Evanor snorted, rolling his eyes expressively.

"Hey, save that for what I'm about to tell you. Remember that half-finished song box of yours?" Morg asked him. When Ev nodded warily, Morganen grimaced ruefully. "Well, it's going to be drained, by the time this is all over. The actual pieces won't be destroyed physically, but I've set up a 'recovery' spell, to recapture your vocal-magic and send it back into you."

"*My work tools—*" Evanor protested, starting to sit up. His youngest brother pushed him back down with a hand on his shoulder.

"Relax, Ev, most of my chalked runes were to *protect* your enchanted tools. The energy making them useful Artifacts will remain. The excess energy from your enchantments, which seeped into the stones of your tower over the last three-plus years, some of that will be funneled back into you. Mostly from your wards. But most important is the song-based magic, not just Song-based, in those music-box squares," Morganen reminded him. "That, in conjunction with Mariel's regenerative spell, should repattern your Voice, aiding in its full restoration. It's possible that the sacrifice of your uncompleted work isn't necessary . . . but I'd rather have the brother-mage I know and love back in one magically melodious piece."

Patting Ev's shoulder, Morganen moved away from the table. If Evanor didn't trust his youngest brother's skills at warding so much, he might have been more worried about his work tools. As it was, he would have to start all over again, or at least nearly from scratch with that music box, once he got his powers back. Mentally reviewing what steps he would have to take, he didn't hear the door open again. His twin's baritone murmur brought him out of his thoughts, though.

"I presume I removed it all?"

Craning his head, Evanor saw Mariel inspecting Dominor's fingers. She nodded after a few moments. "A thorough job. Now, you're not going to be squeamish about the sight of opened flesh and a little blood, are you? Fainting might disrupt the warding runes."

The haughty look Dominor gave the Healer made his twin smile. "I am willing and able to endure nearly anything, woman. I do not faint."

"Good. Go hold your brother's hand. We're ready to begin—the other side, please," she directed him. As Dominor moved to stand at Evanor's left, wrapping his fingers around his twin's palm, she moved to the recumbent male's right side. "Okay, here is the progression of events; I'm not one of those Healers who thinks an ignorant patient is a happy patient, but I'll try to spare you the gory details:

"Step one, I put you to sleep, Evanor; this will help to immobilize you for the procedure," Mariel stated briskly. "Step two, I enchant the *muristhel* to numb your speech abilities; you should still be able to communicate, but you won't have the slightest urge to do so verbally or vocally—even mouthing the words will be completely out, but you should be able to communicate via gestures and writing, once you've recovered from the initial disorientation."

"Disorientation?" Evanor asked her, interrupting.

"Yes," the Healer agreed. With her curly, light brown locks pulled back from her face and her curves swathed in a plain, almost dull, green tunic-dress, she looked far more efficient than lover-like, almost intimidatingly so. "We'll get to that in a moment. Step three, which is after your speech ability has been numbed, is the application of the amulet Morganen has constructed, which will keep the *muristhel* active and keep you numb for the full duration of your regeneration."

"I'll be gluing it to your chest with a three-week-and-one-day spell," Morganen informed him from somewhere beyond Evanor's field of view. "Along with erecting the sterilization shields right afterward, in step four. You'll have a little circle of silver right about the same place Alys has her diamond."

"The length of the enchantment on the amulet will allow the *muristhel* to last two days beyond the projected regeneration time," Mariel continued. "That's in case we have to go back in and rework the regeneration. I won't check it until the day after the regeneration is due to be complete, to keep from interfering with the process, and will remove it at that time, if all goes well.

"Step five, once you are completely numb, is to use a bloodless incision to penetrate your throat, examine the exact extent of the tissue region to be regenerated, and then implant the regeneration spell. That step will take approximately one hour, maybe a little longer. Step six, imbuing the regeneration spell with the energies recaptured from this workroom of yours. That will help to further empower the regeneration spell, patterning it to restore everything that you lost . . . with any luck."

"Step seven," Morganen continued for her, "is the closure and bandaging of the incision, which will regenerate seamlessly within a few days as the spell laid inside your trachea takes root—using a spell runs the risk of causing scar tissue, which we're trying to avoid, but the *muristhel* will numb the incision along with your voice, so you shouldn't feel any discomfort. And step eight is returning you to your quarters where you will be monitored as the sleep spell wears off. I get to do the levitating for that, since Mariel will be a bit tired by that point."

"Tired, but still functional. Kelly and Saber have graciously offered to keep my son busy for the rest of the day, so that I can have my full attention free to watch over you and help you adjust to the disorientation of not being able to communicate verbally," Mariel told him. "Some patients experience panic attacks out of the fear they'll never be able to speak again, while others seem to go into a dreamy state wherein they don't do much *but* cogitate, and yet others find themselves acting entirely upon impulse, as if even the inner monologue of their thoughts had been silenced as well as their physical ability to formulate words. They become creatures of pure instinct, a state that has to be monitored for your own safety, but which isn't as scary as it sounds.

"Once we know which is which for your situation, we can deal with it. Now, for the most important bit," she stated, squaring her shoulders. "Do you, Evanor of Nightfall, consent to the Healing procedure I have outlined, with the understanding that no major Healing is one hundred percent guaranteed, though all possible care will be taken to encourage and hopefully ensure a positive outcome?"

"*I consent*," he whispered, feeling Dominor squeeze his palm in encouragement.

"Then we begin with a lullaby," Mariel stated, and with that, began humming a gentle, rocking tune. Gradually, the power pouring into the sound of her voice increased, until it wrapped around Evanor's mind, enfolding his awareness and lulling him into sleep.

THIRTEEN

❦

Awareness returned after a while, seeping into him like a slowly drawn breath. His eyes opened slowly, too, focusing gradually on the butterflies drifting overhead. It had no context, but that didn't bother him. Noise and movement to his left tilted his head that way, making him aware of the pillow under his skull, of the bedding over his body, and the mattress under his back.

Something annoying had been wrapped around his throat. He lifted a hand to paw at it, but other hands came up and clasped his, stopping him. Their touch was accompanied by noises, and so he returned his attention to their source. Her. The most beautiful woman in his life.

His woman.

He accepted it as he accepted the air he breathed. She was making more noises at him, a query in her hazel gaze. It wasn't important. She was. For a moment, when he tried to get up, she pushed on his shoulders. Then she gave in and helped him up, making more noise with those beautiful lips. He needed to kiss them.

The change in position put pressure on his bladder. Forgetting for a moment about those lips, he pushed to his feet. It pleased him when she slotted herself under his arm, snug against his side. Supporting him. Yes, that was right, and proper. They were meant for each other, so it was right and proper that she should support him when he needed it. As he would support her, if she ever needed it. Perfectly natural.

She helped him to the refreshing room, made noises at him, then hesitantly withdrew. Guessing that she wasn't sure if he needed help, he managed the few steps to the sink on his own, then nodded; the strength was coming back into his limbs. He could manage the rest on his own. And he did so, attending to nature, washing his hands, staring for several long moments at the face in the mirror, until he realized it was *his* face, and that the annoying thing around his neck was bandaging. Since she wanted it left there, he left it there, drying his hands and exiting the room.

Having waited by the door for him, she slipped back into place, this time on his other side. The faint look of worry pinching her brow just a little pleased him; not that he wanted her to worry, of course, but that she cared enough to be worried, that pleased him. Wanting to show his pleasure, and to ease the little pinched mark on her forehead, he leaned over just as they reached the near side of the bed and kissed her. Right on the forehead.

She blinked, startled, and more noise escaped her. The way her lips shaped the sounds fascinated him. Her forehead had smelled and tasted nice; now he needed to know how her lips tasted. Since one arm had been conveniently looped over her shoulders and she had stepped back a little, turning to face him as she made those noises, smiling just a little, it was a matter of moving his hand just a few inches. Once he did, his fingers were buried in the curls falling free around her pink-clad shoulders. And once they were there, he could tip her head back just far enough for him to close the gap between forehead and lips, and kiss her again.

This time, her noise was startled. And muffled.

She tasted delicious, however.

Her lips weren't the only things he explored. Pulling her closer with his other arm, he hunched his back a little—she really was a bit shorter than him—trying to pull her closer. It wasn't enough for their mouths to meet, to angle and nip and taste, though it was very nice to feel her responding, nibbling in return. He had to touch her all over. She was his, he was hers, and it was utterly required between them.

Unfortunately, he was still wearing a pair of blue trousers, and she was wearing one of her tunic-dresses, pink with cream-colored hose. The clothing interfered with the touching of their bodies. So, the clothing would have to go. Perfectly logical.

Except she slapped lightly at his hands when he tried to pull the gown up over her head. Stepping back, she made more noises at him, trying to frown . . . but he saw the blush in her cheeks, the flattered excitement in her eyes . . . the budding tips of her breasts, excited enough to press through the front of her dress. She had backed up a few small, hesitant steps; he closed the distance in one large step, dropping to one knee. Before she could avoid him, he had flipped up the front panel of her skirt, ducking his head underneath.

That put him on a level with the waistband of her hose. A tug on the string with one hand, a looping of the other arm behind her thighs so she couldn't back up, and he had the knit material tugged down just far enough for him to kiss the deep dimple of her navel. Not just a kiss, but a taste, too. Her forehead, her lips, and now her belly. Which quivered with a sound, a familiar sound . . . what was it? Ignoring the pressure of her hands on his shoulders, the squeaky noises she was making in between the other sound, he licked her again.

She spasmed again, and that was when he knew what it was. Laughter. He was making her laugh, a very good thing to do. Grinning, he licked her again, then tugged her hose right down to her feet. She gasped and squirmed, making more noises, the non-laughter ones. Ignoring them, he tugged off her soft suede shoes, and with it, her leggings.

Unfortunately, by allowing her to cooperate in shifting her weight while he divested her of her lower clothes, she managed to step back out of his arms. Whereupon she skipped back a couple more steps and gave him a half-stern look. This time her noises were low, not high, and she held out one hand between them, warding him off. Aware that she wasn't too happy with him, he shuffled forward on his knees, caught her fingers in his, and kissed them in apology.

Even her fingers were tasty.

There was a certain unfairness in that realization. Here she was, very tasty all over—as far as he had been allowed to tell, that was—and she wasn't letting him taste the rest of her? Unfair. Utterly unfair, in fact. Keeping her hand in his, he tasted it thoroughly. Not just her knuckles; he turned it over to lap at her palm. Then suckled individually on each finger, just to see if there were differences between the pinky, the middle one, and the thumb.

This time, the noises she made were low, but drawn out. The look in her eyes was dazed, and something more. Something that made him ache. Desirous, that was it. Filled with desire. That was a good sight to see in his woman. Desiring himself to see more, he lapped at her inner wrist, nibbled his way to the soft flesh in the curve of her elbow, then nipped his way up her bicep, shuffling closer.

Catching her other arm, he started all over again on her other hand, laving it with the attention she so clearly enjoyed. Since it was exactly what he wanted to give to her, he saw no reason not to give it to her. By the time he reached her bicep on that arm, she was not only making low noises, she was panting heavily. That was fair and reasonable; she was stealing his breath, too, making it hard for him to breathe fully.

But it was time to take advantage of her distraction. Switching his kisses back to her cloth-draped stomach, he slid his hands up under the back panel of her skirt, kneaded the soft, copious flesh waiting for him beneath her undergarments, then rose steadily, kissing his way up her body. With his rise, stealthily, came the lifting of her dress. The subtle combination of distraction and action was successfully played; she only realized it when he had to end the kiss that had landed on her mouth so that he could pull the fabric over her head.

She cooperated, lifting her arms so that her limbs wouldn't tangle in the fabric, but gave him an exasperated look as soon as she was free. More noises, non-laughter noises, and she snagged the dress with her fingers, tugging it toward her vest-snugged breasts and undershort-clad hips. She was resisting being undressed. This was not natural.

Giving her a firm, chiding look of his own, he tugged the cloth out of her hands, tossing it to the floor. She planted her hands on her hips and made noises at him, her tone and stance a clear challenge to his right to love her properly. She was *his* woman—if she would only stop thinking about it, she would resume enjoying it! Before she could retreat farther, he stepped close and scooped her up in his arms. That startled another higher-pitched noise out of her, but at least it got her to clasp her hands around his neck.

Pleased, he carried her back to his bed. She tried making noises at him again, which was beginning to get a little irritating, since there were hints of some sort of a pattern now and again, but it was just noise, nothing important. Laughter, now there was something important. And that low, elongated stuff . . . moaning, that was it. He liked it when she laughed, and he liked it when she moaned. Determined to make her do more of both, he dipped his head over her belly even as he released her on the bedding . . . and blew a noisy raspberry on her belly.

That made her shriek and laugh, then squirm with the need to protect herself. Mainly because he took advantage of her distraction to tickle her, and in tickling her, yanked loose the drawstring to her undershorts. As she squirmed on his bed, gasping for air and trying to tickle him back in retaliation—a man with seven other brothers learned very early how *not* to be ticklish when attacked—he managed to tug those shorts down. Until a shriek let him know that she'd caught on to his hidden game.

Since the shorts were tangled around her calves, he pushed her legs up, doubling them over her soft stomach. That helped pin her in place, preventing her from squirming free. It also put him in a very good position, requiring just a little bit more tickling, to distract her from all that thinking and noisemaking she was doing, stuff that was preventing her from enjoying him properly.

She smelled rich and divine, thick with the musky perfume of a fully flowered womanhood. Like a bee or a bird, driven by instinct, he kissed her there as he had kissed her elsewhere. Drank in her perfume, lapped at her nectar, supped on the sweetness of her flesh . . . burrowed into her, tasting everything regardless of less important matters, such as catching an occasional breath.

The annoying noises went away, and that lovely moaning came back. She squirmed a little after a few minutes, annoying him, until he realized she was just kicking off her undershorts. Then she squirmed again, this time loosening and freeing herself from her undervest. Pleased she was finally willing to start enjoying everything in full, rather than continuing all that unnecessary fussing, he returned to his task, trying to figure out how to draw out the best moaning sounds from her. She was his woman, after all, which meant her pleasure was his priority. As was only proper.

A few minutes later, two fingers caressing her from the inside, his tongue laving her on the outside, he was rewarded with the loudest, longest moan yet, one accompanied by laughter-like quakes of her muscles, only without actual laughter. Very pleased, he soothed his touch for a little while, then tried that particular combination again. Fingers buried themselves in his hair, tugging on his braid, then on his scalp. The moaning and panting came back faster than before, dragging his own excitement along with it.

Freeing his hand, he licked his fingers somewhat clean, then returned to savoring her flesh. A couple tugs loosened the lacings on his own clothes; a bit of squirming shoved them off his legs, though whether they landed on the bed or the floor, he didn't know, or care. The important bit was being naked and ready. Very ready. Reluctantly, he gave her warm core two last, suckling kisses, then pushed just far enough away to crawl up between those beautiful, soft thighs . . . so soft and delicious against his waist, his hips.

This time, her noises were encouraging in their tone. She even wormed a hand between them, catching his flesh and positioning him herself. Deeply pleased with such an eager invitation, he let her heels bounce on his backside, ensuring that he burrowed into her—and from the second nudge of her calves, he suspected he wasn't burrowing fast enough. No matter; they were becoming one, and all was becoming right in the world. That was the important thing, joining with her.

Lowering his torso to hers, he breathed deeply when the soft curves of her breasts brushed against the harder, oddly hairless muscles of his chest. Her throat wasn't wrapped in bandaging gauze; hunched over her, he was just able to nibble on the curve of flesh below her ear. Her light brown locks tickled his nose, crisp with delicious curls. How long he would have stayed there, just breathing in the scent of her, he didn't know. The third thumping of her heels on his rump let him know *she* was not so content to let him breathe instead of move.

Compliant with his woman's desires—now that she was no longer denying them—he moved. Pulled slowly out, almost all the way, then pushed back in again. The heavily breathed moan in his ear, a sort of humming sigh, intrigued him. It sounded happy, yet hungry. Another slow thrust inward fed it, made it louder. A grin curved his mouth. Shifting his weight just a little, putting it mostly on his elbows and knees, he thrust in and up, faster than expected. She gasped, then moaned loudly, right in his ear.

It was a bit uncomfortable, being rather loud, but rather satisfying to hear at the same time. Repeating his thrust, he enjoyed her moan and the gasp that followed it with his third thrust. Her eyes flew wide with that one . . . and it was then, falling into her hazel gaze, that he succumbed to his own successful seduction of her. *He* had put that glazed stare in her eyes. *He* had put that passionate flush in her cheeks. *He* was buried to the hilt in her delicious, searing wetness.

Instinct took over; he retained enough control to not hurt her, but he did burrow his hands under her back, curving his fingers up over her shoulders so that he could keep her from being pushed inch by inch up the bed from his need to thrust, and thrust hard. Following the pounding of his heart, reveling in her gasping moans, feeding the desire that drugged his sense and his sensibility, he pursued both their pleasures down to the dregs, drinking it in with his bottom lip caught between his teeth.

As was hers, until her body convulsed, and she released her lip to shout his name.

"Evanorrrr!"

Mariel—!

Arching his head back, he released his passion into her, shuddering hard, breathless, thoughtless. His whole body twitched, passion wringing his muscles, knotting his bones, until it gradually uncoiled all that lovely tension in thoroughly requited satiation. Her body trembled, shuddered, relaxed, and eased, both sets of her limbs entangled around him. Slowly, slowly, he drifted down from the pinnacle, savoring every nuance.

Muscles ached, quivered, relaxed, then sagged, until the only thing keeping him from potentially smothering her was the careful positioning of his elbows and knees, still bracing part of his weight over her. But their bodies were one, joined in sweaty, flushed, trembling union.

Delightful, blessed union.

As much as he had just claimed her, he had given himself to her. Completely. With the ebbing of his passion came the recollection of her shouting his name, of her name ringing through his mind . . . and the remembrance of what had been done to him. He could not *tell* her that he loved her beyond all measure, but Evanor was fairly certain he had just *shown* her, and shown her thoroughly how much he cared.

Just in case, he resolved to show his Mariel very thoroughly how much he loved her. He had three whole weeks of enspelled silence in which to wait before he could *say* it, after all. That was much too long to wait. *And I'll roast in a Netherhell next to my unlamented uncle-in-law, if I'll wait three weeks before coaxing her back into bed with me. Or let her say no, if she's only going to refuse out of propriety alone.*

If she wants me, I will give her no reason to refuse me; not when she can have all of me, he asserted silently. Aware that she was beginning to rouse from her passion-driven daze, he shifted off of her, onto his side next to her. But not to abandon her. Cupping her head, he gently turned her mouth just far enough to meet his, propping himself up with his other elbow.

Ev gave her a kiss to finish waking her from her blissful daze, another to silence any protests about what they had just done, and a third to rearouse her interest in another session. Doing so evoked a soft, willing moan and another, much quieter release of his name when he released her lips. That was what those noises had been. Words, which he had forgotten how to recognize and use for a little while. Forgetting them—thanks to the *muristhel* ointment—had shown him how words weren't always necessary, though, not when actions and tones spoke far more eloquently, and quite agreeably.

When she kissed him back, rolling her lush curves against his frame, Ev knew he had "spoken" eloquently himself. Enough to convince her to try another wordless dialogue in his arms. Which, in his opinion, was perfect.

Somehow, she made it all the way to the kitchen. All the way to one of the tall stools at one of the worktables. That was as far as she could go, though. Collapsing onto the seat, Mariel gripped the table with fingers that trembled and waited for her leg muscles to stop quivering. Across the table from her, Serina glanced up briefly from the Natallian-style pocketbread she was stuffing with greens and meat.

"You look like you've been in a minor war," the arithmancer observed dryly. "How is your patient? Is he giving you any trouble?"

". . . Abawa," was all Mariel could manage. She sagged forward, propping her elbows on the table and her forehead in her palms.

Serina arched a pale brow at her friend, bemused by that odd sound. "'Abawa'? That's not a spell-word . . . wait . . . Flushed cheeks, healthy glow, glazed eyes, trembling limbs . . . you *didn't*! Tell me you didn't pounce on him the moment he came out of the sleep-spell, Mariel!"

Mariel shook her head, her tangled curls sliding over her shoulders.

"Not *while* he was asleep, surely?" her tall friend added warily.

She shook her head again.

"But you *did* . . . ?" Serina needed to clarify.

"*He*," the Healer enunciated carefully, "pounced on *me*."

"He did?"

"Three times. *Three times!*" she repeated for emphasis, then groaned and dropped her arms, folding them so she could rest her forehead. Mariel's voice was muffled as she added, "I've never had a man who could . . . for *three times* in a row! Bright Heavens, I ache in muscles I didn't even know I had—and I'm a Healer! I *know* every muscle I have!"

The chuckle that escaped her tall friend was unrepentantly amused. Mariel lifted her head just enough to glare at Serina, but her friend was unfazed. "Three times, you say? Huh. And here I thought Dominor and Evanor had nothing in common, despite being twins."

Groaning, Mariel dropped her head back onto her forearms. "I didn't need to know that, Serina!"

"Hey! You twitted *me* over my project, both before and after I bought Dom for it," Serina chided her. "And if you're not going to be nice and let me have a bit of fun at your expense, I *won't* be nice and fix you a pocketbread."

"Food?" Mariel asked weakly, since that was why she had dragged herself all the way here from Evanor's bed.

"I gave in and made some to help quell my stomach from all the midday nausea I've been suffering, since *you* said any flat, unleavened bread is supposed to be good for quelling it," Serina agreed. "Ironically, I finished them just in time to finally be ravenously hungry again—why is it midday nausea?" she asked her Healer friend. "I thought it was supposed to be *morning* sickness. I've only been sick once in the morning, so far, but for the last week, it's been lunchtime nearly every single day!"

"It's only called 'morning sickness' because it happens most frequently in the morning to most women. I had morning sickness with Mikor," Mariel offered, rolling her head so that her cheek rested on one bicep. She was too tired to bother sitting up just yet, but at least her voice was no longer muffled. "My mother had evening sickness, with every single one of us kids. And my sister had middle-of-the-night heartburn. Are you really being nice and making me up a pocketbread?"

"One for you, and one for Evanor. And one for me, of course. With spell-melted cheese," Serina added with a little flourish of her

hand. Setting the two completed bread halves on a plate, she muttered over it. The plate rose up off the table, levitating. "There.
Now you don't have to carry it, just push it ahead of you. The spell
will end when you've pressed it onto a flat surface. Would you like
some juice to take with you?"

"No, I have a pitcher back in the room that's still half full. I
brought it up there when I settled in to wait for him to wake up."
Pushing herself mostly upright, Mariel smothered a yawn. "Presuming I can distract him with food and drink, I think he'll be staying in
his room overnight, then be well enough to come down for breakfast. I hope. Kelly and Saber were kind to take on Mikor all day today, but I can't expect the others to watch him every hour of the
day."

Serina chuckled again. "You may have twinges of guilt over it,
but I remember how grateful you and Milon were to let me play
'aunty' with Mikor, back when I first arrived at the Retreat. I don't
think anyone will begrudge you a day or two with your new love,
now and again."

Milon . . . Mariel realized abruptly that she hadn't once thought
of her late husband, today. Not that she still thought about him
every single day, she had been widowed for two years, after all . . .
but in her past liaisons with casually interested men . . . she had usually compared them to her late, beloved husband, and found them
wanting.

Those had been strangers, of course; she couldn't have known
any of them long enough to make accurate comparisons. But even a
quick study had given her plenty of reasons to dismiss the possibility
of sticking around long enough to see if they were worth her time.
They just hadn't compared. One was too fat, one was too loud, one
was too dull . . . outside of a bed, that was. All sorts of reasons to
keep things casual, temporary.

Yet somewhere along the way, she had stopped making constant
comparisons between Milon and Evanor. There would always be
something that made her think of the differences between the two
men, but she wasn't comparing them as much, anymore.

The question being, is that a good thing, or a bad thing? she wondered, gathering her energy to stand. Serina came around the table to give Mariel a hug, then pushed the floating plate into her hands, turned her around, and nudged her toward the hall.

"Go on, he's waiting for you . . . and if nothing else, eat some of that food on your way there, so that *you'll* still be going when he faints from half-starved exhaustion." One last nudge, and Serina sent a grateful but thoughtful Mariel on her way. Until the arith-mancer spoiled it by adding cheekily, "Don't do anything I wouldn't do. At least, not without allowing me to take notes!"

An exasperated groan escaped the Healer. Serina's unrepentant laugh followed her out into the hallway.

Since she could easily push the floating plate with one hand, that left her other hand free to pick up one of the stuffed pocketbreads. One bite, and Mariel's eyes watered. Serina had slathered a little too much peppersauce on the inside of the flatbread. But it was good, sweetened with honey, it cleared the sinuses nicely, and she took her time to savor the meal while negotiating her way back to the south-west wing of the sprawling palace. Attention on her food, she almost tripped over Morganen, who was seated on the bottom step of the stairwell nearest Evanor's suite.

"Oh! I'm sorry, Morganen, I didn't see you," she hastily apolo-gized, setting down her pocketbread and pushing the plate to one side so she could see him better. "I didn't hurt you, did I?"

Extending his suede-clad foot, he wriggled it and smiled. "Not even a bruise."

As much as she liked the young man, Mariel didn't know why he would want to sit on the bottom-most step of a spiral stairwell. "Um . . . is there any particular reason you're sitting here all by yourself?"

His smile faded a little. Those aquamarine eyes, framed by lashes the same light brown as his hair, looked at her a little oddly. Warily. He quirked a brow after a moment, shrugged, and lifted something from his lap. A folded packet of paper, slightly yellowed with age and sealed with a blob of green wax. "This is for you. And before you ask, I've held on to it for more than four years, so I received it *before* we were exiled here. Long before we met."

Bemused, Mariel took the paper, turning it over in her hands. The words, written in Natallian, didn't make her eyes twitch, unlike the books she had been reading lately. Even so, it took her a few moments to realize the import, not only of the words, but of the handwriting.

Her late husband's handwriting.

"To be given to Mariel the evening that she Heals, before she returns to him."

Before she returns to him . . .

Stunned, Mariel flipped the letter over, examining the seal. She *knew* that seal; it was the one her husband often used for his Prophesies. Seers were different, all around the world. Some sang or spoke in rhythm or rhyme, swept up in the vivid yet cryptic language of poetry. Others had visions or went into trances, and spoke to whomever was listening, requiring that they be followed around by scribes most of their prophetic lives. Some burst into fits of Prophesy when in the midst of fits of passion, whether it was from anger, joy, or grief. Others, like her late husband, were often struck strongest while writing, finding the pen dancing across the page under the guiding touch of the God or Goddess commanding them.

Sometimes her husband had known it was happening and retained an awareness of it. Other times . . . he hadn't known until after the fact. He hadn't known about his trip down the mountain, two years ago, wasn't aware *why* it was necessary, but he *had* known that it was necessary, and so he had ridden down the mountain, until his mount had slipped and the pair had plummeted to their deaths. To receive one of his Prophesies now—and *here*, of all places—was both unexpected and uncomfortable. Almost unwelcome, given what had happened just a short while ago.

Almost.

Ignoring the mage seated at her feet, she cracked open the seal with trembling fingers. Unfolded the sheet. Within it was another letter, also sealed. Upon it was written the words, *This is for Mikor, for when he would deny what is to be.* Puzzled, Mariel looked at the paper that had enfolded it, seeking an explanation. His handwriting marched neatly across the page, even as it greeted her with his favorite salutation.

My Most Beloved Mariel,

    You are forbidden to feel any guilt or regret. While the Gods have veiled from me the details, I do know that you will be incredibly happy where you are now, with the man whose company you enjoy. He is a good man; were he anything less, I would have fought what the Gods have decreed, but he is worthy of you. I insist that you continue to enjoy his company, and to share with him the love that is growing within both of you. Some women are lucky enough to know a second love after losing the first, and you will be one of those women.

    As for myself . . . it will have been necessary; I cannot give the details, because They will not allow them to be spoken at this time. All I can tell you is that Glory and Communion will be returning to our world, gracing our soil once more. You are a part of that; you and the man now at your side. We each have our place in the universe; your place was at my side, and I was grateful to have you in my short life. Now your place is elsewhere, and the Gods have assured me that you will know great joy, in spite of our own parting's sorrow.

    I was the luckiest man alive when you said yes to me for marriage, and the luckiest to help create and raise our wonderful son. I do not regret a thing, even knowing it was only for a while. Now it is another's turn to be the luckiest husband and father a man can be, and he will be even better in many ways, and for a lot longer than I could ever be—a whole lifetime's worth.

    An amazing Destiny awaits you and those around you. I have Seen that much in advance, though it is all I can tell you.

    All my love, and my blessing,

    Your Milon

One hand abandoned the sheet of paper. It covered her mouth. It also allowed the age-creased sheet to fold back on itself, but that was all right; her eyes were closed against the sting of tears. The tumult of emotions held her silent for several long moments, until she felt a hand gingerly touch her elbow.

"Are you all right?"

Opening her eyes, blinking back the liquid that had welled into them, Mariel focused on Morganen, still seated on the steps at her feet. She looked from him to the paper and back, then unfurled the sheet and stared at that first sentence, and the second to last.

"Did you . . . read this?" she managed to ask, her voice low and husky.

He shook his head, light brown locks dancing across his chest with the quick movement. "It wasn't for me, so I didn't open it."

"How did you get it?" was her next, even more important question. "*How* did you get your hands on a letter written by my husband? My late husband," Mariel corrected herself, since that was more accurate. Two years ago, even a year ago, she would have damned the Gods for that truth, but now she had to put this letter into some sort of a context, in order to put its message into context.

The wry look the young mage favored her with wrinkled his nose and twisted his lips. "So long as you promise to not tell the others, I could let you know, I suppose. I'd rather they didn't know."

"Know what?" Mariel asked him, confused.

"Well, I *am* the Mage. It's my Destiny to use my powers to arrange wives for my brothers," Morganen reminded her, stretching out one leg and bringing the other up higher, looping his arms around his blue-clad leg. He looked younger when he did that, younger and more vulnerable, somehow. Not that he was vulnerable, but normally the youngest of the brothers seemed impervious to the twists and turns of his and his brothers' lives.

"And . . . ?" she prompted him.

"I was scrying farther and farther afield, looking for anything of interest, anything to help me in my task . . . just looking, really. And . . . I saw your husband. He was in the library of that place where you were. The Retreat at Koral-tai. That's how far afield I sometimes scried." He shrugged his shoulders, dismissing his efforts despite their improbability. "I have enough power to do that, on a good-aether day. And so I saw him, writing out one of his Prophesy attacks. I didn't know what it was, at first. But then he finished and sealed the one letter in your hands, wrote out and sealed the first letter, the one you just read, addressing each, then sealed *that* in a third piece of paper, and wrote *my* name on the outside, and the words *reach through the mirror and take this now, and keep it until it is needed.*

"Then he set it aside, turned . . . and *looked* at me." Morganen shuddered; it didn't look like an affectation to Mariel. The experience *had* bothered him. "It was like looking into the eyes . . . no, the echo of a God. Fathomless and not entirely *there*. And he said, 'Don't worry—we'll be working together, until *she* comes back.' It was the strangest thing . . ."

"She, who?" Mariel asked, curious about that part.

Morg shrugged again, unfolding his other leg so that it stretched out, too. That left her standing between his calves. "I presume he meant you. I sent a small mirror so I could open a dialogue with him, he seemed to recover some of his . . . normality, I suppose you could call it, and we chatted about how he knew the Gods had something in mind, something that would involve him assisting me in my ordained quest to match-make my brothers. I would then check on him at regular intervals, spaced about every two weeks or so . . . or rather, we had worked out that I'd check on his desk in a specific spot, and if he had anything for me, he would leave it there and mark it with my initials.

"Sometimes it was just a short note; other times he had a couple of different letters bundled together. And I knew from our few conversations, that he knew his wife would find her way to another man."

"Did you know—" Mariel interjected, irritation rising within her. Morg cut her off with a quick shake of his head.

"Who you were destined for, where you were going, and how you would be split from your husband? No, no, and no," he quickly denied. "It made sense that you might find your way here at some point, since he made a point of asking me to keep an eye on you . . . but I didn't know which of my brothers you would be suited for." Morganen paused, then smiled wryly, "Except for Wolfer, of course. His match was fated the day he literally swept her off her feet at the tender age of three. And . . . well, I knew that Saber's mate would be an outworlder, thanks to your late husband. Though it was one of those times where he didn't consciously remember what he had written, so I never discussed it with him."

Mariel considered his words. It was not impossible that her husband had teamed up with a mage to manipulate the Destinies of others a quarter of the way around the world. Improbable for most mages to be able to scry that far . . . but then she hadn't thought it was possible to link a mirror-Gate spell through a Font, either. Yet she and Mikor had traveled all the way here through one.

Looking down at the letter in her hands, she knew that things were not the same, anymore. She wasn't married to Milon, wasn't living in the Retreat . . . wasn't lonely anymore. Though it was still early, she knew she not only cared about Evanor—she *cared* about most of her patients—she also *liked* him. That was the telling difference; she could care for someone without liking them more than mildly at best, and she really, really liked Evanor.

It was still early, and she didn't want to leap into a relationship without considering everything, but it was quite possible that her husband's prediction of deep happiness would come true between them—between her and Evanor. It helped a little that Milon had included the observation that Ev could and would be a good father to their son. Who was seeking a next-father, clearly missing his own father's presence in his life. Her son was an important consideration when contemplating any man becoming a part of her life.

But to know that Milon knew *I'd be* here, *of all places . . . that I would have . . . well, no,* she amended, checking both sides of the note again. *He doesn't specify that we've just made love. He just says "before she returns to him," and . . . hmm. Never calls Evanor by name. I wonder if that's because he never knew, or because he didn't want to know? Either way . . . I'll never know.*

There were lots of mysteries she had endured as the wife of a Seer: things only half-explained, things *never* explained. It had both developed and taxed her patience to the utmost, at times. Now she had her loving, late husband's *permission* to be happy—for a moment, she started to get angry. How dare . . .

Then the old habits kicked in, and Mariel let it go with a deep breath. The Gods proclaimed, and Milon obeyed. Thus was the life of a Seer.

At least he did *foresee happiness for me* . . . Happiness, and a half-eaten pocketbread. And a mage whom she had never known about.

"Will you be alright, now?" Morganen inquired. He had seen her emotions chasing through her face, until reaching a state of equanimity with the knowledge he had given her. When she nodded, he relaxed inside. "And you'll keep my secret, for now?"

Mariel glanced again at the age-creased paper. Her mouth quirked up on one side. "I will . . . but at a price. Nothing too terrible."

Morg narrowed his aquamarine eyes warily. "What price?"

"Babysitting. If I am to fall in love with your elder brother, I'll need at least *some* uninterrupted time with him."

"Don't think to hold it over my head forever," he warned her, folding up his legs so he could push to his feet. Towering over her once he stood, Morganen gave the petite Healer a warning look. "I'll not be your permanent provider of child care. I have three more brothers besides Evanor, and my own happiness to arrange, and the Gods have ordained that I *will* arrange it."

"Then you'd better keep this," Mariel stated, handing him the letter that she had opened; she would keep the one addressed to her son until she figured out what the part about "denying" meant. It wasn't easy to part with the letter addressed to her; it was her late husband's last message to her, even if it had been written two years before his death. "If Evanor sees it, he might react one of two ways: either wondering why I hadn't opened it earlier, considering its undated nature . . . or he'll consider it freedom to skip all the stages of courting me and assume that I'll fall into his hands like an overripe fruit."

Chuckling at the idea, Morganen took back the letter, folding it carefully along its creases. "I'll hold on to it. If and when he has any doubts, you can get it back from me and show it to him, to prove Milon himself had no doubts about my fourthborn sibling's right to occupy the rest of your life. Until then, I'll bid you a good night."

"Morganen . . ." Her use of his name stopped him before he had stepped past her, heading for the corridor. She held out her arms. "Thank you."

A shy smile curved his lips, and he bent a little, giving her a hug. Letting him go, Mariel turned back and headed up the stairs.

Then cursed and tromped back down before she had done more than gone halfway up the first flight, in search of the forgotten, floating plate and its half-eaten food.

FOURTEEN

❖⊰❊⊱❖

A voiceless, wordless Evanor was an oddity, his family discovered. Though he had recovered the power of communication via one of Serina's lap-sized slates and a piece of chalk, he rarely used it. He listened to conversations, but didn't participate in them. Instead, he just did things. Mariel mentioned she wanted to gather such-and-such herbs from her garden to supplement Serina's sometimes spotty diet, and the Healer found Evanor already gathering them.

Koranen mentioned he was running out of high-quality sand for the creation of the crystal towers, and Evanor came back after an hour with a wagon filled with bags of the high-grade silica they had purchased from the mainland the month before and stored in the salt block warehouse, since there was so much of it. Mikor mentioned to his mother that he was bored and wanted to go "outside," meaning beyond the castle walls, and Evanor had a wagon and a basket of lunch ready as soon as she made up her mind . . . but without her having to actually ask him.

It was fun for Evanor to figure out what people wanted. Never had he been so aware of body posture, of tensed or relaxed muscles, of the quirk of an eyebrow, the pinch of a pair of lips. He learned that Saber, despite his constant cautionary notes, had faith in his wife to be their queen; Saber was proud of her. He was also prepared to step in at a moment's notice to give her support in case she stumbled.

Evanor learned that Kelly was nervous about making herself into a queen, but not the least bit intimidated, a subtle distinction. She hid her nervousness, but it was there. She just had no problems pushing up her tunic sleeves and wading into any problem that came along. Alys was still more shy than bold, though she was slowly gaining enough confidence to reach out and grasp whatever she wanted.

Wolfer was feeling a little left out of the construction of the cell phone Artifacts; he could add magical energy when appropriate, but not the skill that some of his brothers could apply. So he contented himself with overseeing the harvesting of the island's fruits and wild-grown vegetable and root crops. Evanor could tell his second-born brother knew his gratification would be delayed until much later, when his family would notice and reveal their pleasure at the bounty of spell-preserved foods he was gathering. Yet the thought of such delayed gratification didn't seem to bother the largest of the brothers.

As for Evanor's twin, when he wasn't helping his brothers on the communications problem, Dominor chased after his wife, making sure she rested and took care of herself. Dom felt satisfied to have a task that no one else could do better, and which no one else needed more than his Serina did. In fact, Evanor had never seen Dominor so relaxed and calm. Upon reflection, the silenced mage decided it was because Dominor had been confusing both competition with challenge and feeling worthy with feeling needed. Serina needed someone to manage her life. That challenged Dominor and in turn made him feel complete.

Serina, who admitted candidly she tended to over-focus on her fascination for her work and freely agreed she was completely besotted with her husband . . . also truly cared about Mariel and her son, Mikor. There was no doubt in Evanor's mind that she and Mariel had adopted each other as sisters as well as best friends. No doubt, either, that Mikor loved his honorary aunt in return. For all that she tended to ignore the world, Serina was actually quite mindful of the boy's moods and his needs, just as his mother was. The slender mathemagician also suffered more than she let the others know from her midday version of morning sickness; it was just at its worst around noon.

Mariel . . . he loved her. Evanor found himself helpless in the face of that realization. It didn't just come out in the urge to pleasure her, but in the urge to *please* her. With most of his attention focused these days on body language, instead of words, he was finding ways to do that, based on how she tensed and relaxed when doing some chore or speaking about something. Though she didn't come out and say it, she enjoyed his attentiveness—that much was clear.

She certainly enjoyed it when he joined her with one of his lutes, or his lap harp, and played softly in the background while she worked in her corner of the gardens or the herb room. Though he couldn't sing to her, he could play, and he picked melodies that he hoped would convey his affection and admiration. Judging from the relaxing of her muscles, from the under-the-lashes little glances she gave him and the occasional smile that graced her lips, he was doing exactly what she wanted.

Mariel let him know she thought his insistence on joining her each night was a bit high-handed, but she didn't deny him the opportunity to curl up in bed with her. She was also visibly grateful that he came to her wearing sleeping trousers. It was a good thing, too, that he made sure to re-don them if they were removed for any reason. On the sixth night of his voicelessness, after they had made love, redressed, and fallen asleep together, Mikor came into his mother's bedchamber, upset by a bad dream the boy couldn't quite remember.

It surprised Mariel when, upon seeing the blond mage in his mother's bed—for Evanor reached up and gently rapped the lightglobe into a dim glow, allowing them to see their intruder—young Mikor abandoned her and went all the way over to Evanor's side of the bed, climbing into the covers next to *him*, rather than staying with her for comfort. Giving Mariel a wry look, Evanor had settled back into bed, tucking Mikor against his right side, while Mariel reclaimed her place against his left.

It wasn't until the next day that Ev explained to Mariel via his slateboard that Mikor probably trusted him to understand what nightmares were like, thanks to his own troubled sleep. Mariel accepted that, though it wasn't much of an explanation. And when her own troubles came around, in the form of that time of the month, he badgered Dominor via chalkboard into taking time off the crystal-tower project to brew a batch of the symptom-curing drink they had first crafted for Kelly.

Mariel's surprise and grateful relief were quickly taken over by her Healer's interest, and she badgered Evanor in turn on what, exactly, those ingredients were. Then she promptly passed that information back to the nuns at the Retreat via the mirror in the dining room, along with a promise to gather a large amount of the non-Natallian ingredients involved and ship them to the distant nunnery, in exchange for certain things she wanted shipped out to Nightfall. It made the Mother Superior very, very pleased to still be in contact with the far-flung island, boding well for future trade negotiations.

Next on the list of people Evanor studied was Trevan. He seemed cool and calm on the outside, accepting of the fact that his elder brothers had women to love and to hold, and he had none, but there was a barely perceptible *flinch* each time he came across a loving couple. A tiny wince whenever someone did something loving in his presence, whether it was as bold as a kiss or as innocuous as resting one hand on top of another and giving it a subtle caress. Surprisingly, Evanor noted this latter part, the romantic gestures, evoked a stronger flinch than seeing something more sexual. It seemed his next-youngest brother was lonelier for romance—never mind sex—than he cared to admit.

But it was Rydan whom Evanor studied the longest. Not just because he was the most reclusive and was thus rarely around to study, being a night lover by trait, but because Rydan held himself tightly in control. He was very unsociable, too; if the others were calm and quiet, he lingered after breakfast and supper. But if the others were in the mood to chat and laugh, never mind debate and argue, he invariably left. Even if he seemed to be enjoying the livelier, happier moments, he left.

It was almost as if he either envied or hated the others, yet that didn't jibe with the subtle patterns Evanor gradually learned to observe in Rydan's stiff body language. Rydan did care about his siblings. He even cared about his sisters-in-law, accepting Kelly's deft, calm handling of him with a strange sort of respect, being gentle around Alys whenever she was suffering one of her many shy spells, and daring to tease Serina, just a little bit, for being so smart.

And he respected Mariel. Rydan didn't even try to hide that, though he didn't really talk to her, either. But Mikor made the sixth-born brother nervous, for a reason Evanor couldn't discern. He didn't try to be mean to the boy—he was courteous if pressed into conversation—but he didn't linger in Mikor's presence, either.

Giving up on the ongoing enigma that was Rydan, Ev concentrated on his last two siblings.

Koranen was a bundle of envy and energy. The energy was just how Kor was; he was too closely aligned to fire-magic, pyromancy, to not literally have excess energy to burn. The envy was for his married brothers, who got to retire each night with their wives. Poor Koranen didn't dare take a wife until his pyromantic affiliation was addressed and overcome. He'd tried kissing girls when he was young, as they all had. It was just that, the first time he had gone beyond kissing, back when he was in his mid-teens, he had left reddened, painful handprints on the girl, from his passion literally heating up under her touch.

It had been fairly obvious just where his hands had been and what they had been doing, too, with no way to pass it off as a magical accident. Not when the interlude had left the poor girl forced to wear the loosest blouses and tunics possible for the two days it took the local Healer to cure her reddened, almost blistered skin. Ev remembered Kor being lectured by both sets of parents, since the girl might have been sixteen, but he had only been fifteen, too young by Katani standards. *Almost* sixteen, but almost wasn't quite good enough. They had *all* been forced to listen to a lecture on proper adult behavior from their father, after that little incident.

With that as his legacy, Koranen had not been able to coax another girl to cuddle with him for a few more years . . . and then when he seared *her* with his touch partway into their mutual seduction, he had given up entirely on trying to court a woman, never mind attempting to get one into his bed. Not when he literally burned with desire. Of course, Kor had tried to keep this fact from everyone outside of the family, but rumors had spread. It became one of the factors that had eventually convinced the Council of Mages they were the eight males mentioned in the Song of the Sons of Destiny. Until Koranen found the woman who could literally quench his desire, single he would have to remain. That was his part of the Curse of Eight, and Evanor didn't envy him for it.

Morg was the second-most puzzling person Evanor observed, close behind the reclusive Rydan. He seemed lighthearted, as casual as Trevan, though without his fifthborn brother's flinching over the sight of the first four of them being happy in their own romances. Yet he was as deep as Rydan, with mysteries Evanor couldn't quite plumb, even with the help of this voiceless awareness he possessed. Ev could see it in his youngest brother's eyes, a level of knowledge, of awareness . . . that was it. Morg was *aware* of everything around him.

Even though it wasn't easy to tell *what* he knew, there was a definite feeling about the young mage that Morg knew more than he was letting on, and that he could *do* more than he was admitting he could do. How much more, though, Evanor couldn't tell. It could just be an innate, arrogant belief in himself, or an actual, fact-backed confidence. Ev just didn't know.

He did know two other things about the youngest of them: Morganen was a lot more aware of what was going on in their expanding little family than he let on; and Morg did not like being teased about watching Kelly's outworlder friend, Hope, through his enchanted mirror, something Dominor had mentioned to his twin in passing. Evanor could understand why. It was something that could be exacerbated easily; their group-effort to sketch out and implement the requirements for the communication bracelets and their relaying crystal towers required Morg to contact the outworlder woman several times each week.

Much as he chose to do for Rydan, and did automatically for Koranen out of respect for the second-youngest's situation, Evanor vowed to ease back on teasing his eighthborn sibling as well. Whether Hope was the woman destined for Morganen or not, only time would tell—a lot of time, since Morg's other brothers had to be match-made, first. That was too long and uncertain a span to tease anyone.

Mikor, next to the boy's mother, was the one Evanor kept his eye on the most. Nine years old, he was a bundle of energy and curiosity. Evanor was grateful how his brothers stepped into the breach that he, being voiceless, couldn't fill. Koranen let him watch some of the forge-working they were doing, Trevan let the boy watch him in his woodshop, Saber and Dominor took time out to practice sword work, and even Wolfer offered to help the boy work on his wrestling moves.

Intimidated—despite his protestations to the contrary—it took a week before Mikor accepted. Once he did, and spent a couple hours crawling all over, tugging on, and escaping from the largest of the brothers, much of that wary fear of the overly muscled male vanished. It changed instead to admiration. In fact, Mikor proclaimed at one point that he wanted to be "a shapechanger, too," to the bemusement of Wolfer and the amusement of everyone else.

Evanor didn't feel the least bit jealous that his second-eldest brother had stolen some of Mikor's affections. He knew that what he did, managing the household, wasn't nearly as impressive as hunting and such in younger eyes. It was enough that his fellow adults appreciated it.

The amount of energy coupled with curiosity in the boy made Evanor cautious. Mikor wanted to get into *everything*. He obeyed most rules laid down by his mother and the other adults, but occasionally his curiosity and enthusiasm would overwhelm him, and he'd do something he wasn't supposed to.

One of those things he was curious about was the island outside the palace walls. Some of that curiosity was assuaged by trips down to the beach, but not all of it. As soon as he got his voice back, presuming he got his magic back, Evanor resolved to put a tracing spell on the boy.

Of course, that was assuming he got his magic back.

The allegations posed by the Corvis brothers are true," Councilor Thera reported to her fellow mages. She was clad today in pale beige, making her large-boned body look even more like a wardog than usual. "Count Pro Tem Broger deliberately withheld income information from my department, exaggerating and even falsifying reports of disasters versus estate production. Unless I were to add more manpower to this project, a full accounting will take a turning of Brother Moon to judge, but the estimated taxable income was over five thousand gilders, for the last three years.

"It is interesting to note," she added dryly, "that Count Pro Tem Barol of Devries, the new holder of the Corvis lands, did not bother to uncover this information when he took over during his father's absence. He did not obstruct my office, however, and has agreed to pay the preliminary evasion fines without quarrel or protest.

"The priest-mage accompanying my officials initially could not find traces of Dark Gate energies on Corvis lands," Thera continued. "However, when confronted, Count Barol showed him to a mirror-Gate and said his father often used that to travel. He claimed he did not know where it went, nor for what purpose his father used it. Crossing the barrier, the priest-mage, Ferris of Glyssima, discovered a small mountainside hold in the southeastern mountains, a place filled with pens, pools, and cages suitable for the breeding of illegal beasts. Most looked like they had been abandoned for a few months, but there were still mekhadadaks, grodaks, and half a dozen other kinds, and it looked like someone was still feeding them.

"When questioned under spell, Count Barol insisted he didn't know anything about what his father had been doing over there, nor who had been assisting him with so many beasts. It is possible," the beige-clad woman cautioned, "that he has used some sort of memory-modifying charm upon himself. We cannot, however, test such a hypothesis without violating his rights as a mageborn noble. Not without at least some proof of complicity."

"We will not risk an incident at this time," King Taurin said. "We've had enough trouble with the recent Karlton-Peloma debacle."

He gave his Councilor of Conflict Resolution a brief, chiding stare. Duke Finneg shrugged; as far as he was concerned, he had stopped the conflict cold. It didn't matter to him that his methods had damaged both families' homes. They had garnered results, dismaying both parties into heeding the Council's edict against further conflict.

Finneg did have a question of his own, proving he could keep track of petty details. "What of the Dark Gate? You said you found no trace of it on Corvis lands. What of this other place?"

Consus, seated above and to one side, was relieved someone had remembered to keep track of that detail.

"The traces were old and faded, but there. Priest Ferris investigated the matter carefully and ascertained that the Dark Gate has indeed been fully sealed. There is no threat of a weakening of the Veil between our universe and the Netherworlds," Lady Apista, Councilor for the Temples, stated from her seat near the ground floor of the oval Council Chamber.

"And the location of the Gate's terminus?" another Councilor asked.

"Undeterminable. Had we been able to tell, the aperture would still be there. It was apparent, however," Apista related, "that someone closely related to the casting mage had been slain in order to activate the Dark Gate. Whether this victim was Lord Donnock of Devries, Count Broger's missing brother, was not discernible. If and when we find the terminus of the Gate, we might be able to ascertain that information."

"Was there anything aside from pens, cages, and signs of a Dark Gate at the site in question?" someone asked.

"There were a few signs that a couple of the rooms in the mountain hold had been used for casting magic," Councilor Thera agreed. "One room even had the shelving for a library. However, they seem to have been cleared out at some point. Judging from the layer of dust, I'd say about a month ago. When did the Corvis brothers allege that they were attacked, Councilor Consus?"

"Uh . . . I'm not certain . . ." Consus shuffled through the papers on his smallish table, skimming the notes quickly. He finally gave up and shook his head, strands of brown and gray sliding over his shoulders. "It was never stated when, exactly, these things took place, but . . . I have a note from a conversation with Morganen of Corvis stating that the trace of the Dark Gate was a couple months old—here it is. No, wait, sorry. That was a comment on the information they had garnered on the existence of the bestiary. Their informant spoke with them 'a few months ago,' to quote the conversation I had with the youngest brother."

"Who was this informant?" Finneg asked, dark eyes narrowing in suspicion. "They're not allowed to have any unauthorized contact, so who contacted them, and how did they manage it?"

"The details of the informant were not discussed, beyond that it was a servant in Lord Broger's household," Consus stated, sorting through the pages to make sure of that. "And it is incorrect to state that they aren't allowed to have any unauthorized contact. They are not allowed to have any unauthorized *visitors*. Nor are they allowed to leave the island. By the terms of their exile, they are still free to contact anyone whose unwarded mirror they could scry and reach, if they so wanted."

"Is there *anyone* that these files of yours mention by name?" Finneg asked him sarcastically.

Giving the other man an annoyed glare, Consus set down his papers. "Alys of Devries, ward of Lord Broger of Devries. From what I can tell, she has been missing for the past couple of months. Did anyone think to ask after her welfare during your visit to County Corvis, Councilor Thera?"

The Councilor of Tax Collection frowned. "No. I wasn't aware of any girl I should be looking for."

"She was made a ward of Broger of Devries when her parents died, roughly ten years ago," Queen Samille stated, surprising everyone with her knowledge. "Lord Broger petitioned to have her declared mentally incompetent and made his permanent ward. Knowing her parentage, the intelligence of the late Lady Glyssa— who was a distant cousin of mine—and the genteel reputation of Lord Tangor of Devries, I found that aspect of the report difficult to reconcile. And I have found no official record of her being tested for insufficient intelligence.

"If she was framed for incompetence, then she is a victim of her uncle's machinations. Why has she not come forward, if her uncle is dead? Is it because she fears her cousin? Is it because she, herself, was killed?" Samille continued. "We have only the Corvis brothers' word that it was Donnock of Devries who was slaughtered; it could have been this Alys. If she was not framed, nor slaughtered . . . then we have a woman wandering around the Empire somewhere, one whom we are morally obligated to care for."

"And if she was killed to activate the Dark Gate, then we have Donnock of Devries as our loose end," Finneg pointed out grimly. "I know the man, and I have never trusted nor liked him. As much as I'm not supposed to wish anyone dead—"

Several Councilors choked on that, earning a harsh glare from the duke.

"I resolve conflicts, yes, but I rarely kill, if it can be avoided," Councilor Finneg snapped, irritated. "It's too much paperwork to deal with when that happens, and too many outraged relatives to deal with—so as I was *saying*, as much as I'm not supposed to wish anyone dead, I hope it's Donnock who was killed to open the Dark Gate, and not some addle-witted girl. He's the more dangerous of the two."

"Councilor Thera, how soon will you have an accounting of the exact money owed the exilees?" King Taurin asked her. "I wish the matter of the rights to that salt and algae cleared up as soon as possible—and I want you to come up with a way to *fine* them for daring to withhold what is not theirs."

"Oh, there're ways to fine and penalize them, officially," she returned smugly. "If I pulled in enough workers to question the people of the county, I could have everything tallied within . . . eight days? It would be expensive in terms of extra manpower, and I'd have to push other projects back a bit, but it could be done quickly enough if my department is authorized for it."

"The last ship to the Isle departed earlier today, Your Majesty," Consus interjected. "It will be roughly two weeks before the next one sails."

"We've held back long enough. As soon as we have a full accounting, we will confront the brothers with the results of their 'demands' regarding their rightful income . . . and confront them with an investigation of what, exactly, they are crafting on the Isle," Taurin stated. "Thera, you have the authorization you need. Make enquiries into the history and whereabouts of the missing girl while you're at it, since you'll have your department investigating that region anyway. Go into a deeper investigation of Count Pro Tem Barol, too. His claim to know nothing doesn't sound truthful, and I would not have the Corvis brothers accusing us of not pursuing *all* complaints . . . since their reported complaints of mekhadadaks, grodaks, and whatever else they said had been attacking them seem to have been true.

"Councilor Finneg . . . prepare for a possible conflict resolution on Nightfall. However, you are *not* authorized to exercise your office's powers without Our personally expressed permission," Taurin stated, using the royal "we" for emphasis. He shifted his attention to the side of the chamber. "In fact, none of you will be permitted to discuss where or when we may be headed, in regards to Nightfall, until you are given Our formal permission. Councilor Consus, continue to liaise with the Corvis brothers and try to get more information out of them. Politeness and diplomacy is always cheaper than resolving conflicts . . . and I remind you all that the annual budget will need to be debated soon."

Several muffled, aggravated groans could be heard. Consus wasn't the only one who started massaging his temples in the effort to stave off a headache. Taurin might be their King, but when it came to the budget, *everyone* had an equal voice, and—by law—only ten days to allocate all of the funds. An arbiter was chosen literally by random draw to resolve disputes, but their powers could only be invoked during a tie. And, naturally, everyone thought that *their* department deserved the most money.

"On *that* joyous note, I call a recess for lunch," Taurin stated, cracking the black marble of the King's Sphere against its matching stone holder.

Waiting for most of the others to exit first, Consus gathered his reports, stuffing them back into the divided sections of the leather satchel he had brought from his office. As he stooped over to fetch a fallen paper, he heard someone addressing the warlike duke on the other side of the chamber.

"Do you really think you'll have no problems resolving a conflict with the Corvis brothers, Your Grace?" the younger man was asking. Consus couldn't remember his name, but he knew the dark-skinned mage worked in the Department of Archives in one of the lesser branches, like Consus' own Sea Commerce position.

Finneg snorted. "No problems at all. They'll buckle and bow to the weight of Imperial Law like anyone else I've faced."

"But the Prophecy clearly states—"

"Prophecies are *nothing* more than the twice-lucky ravings of lunatics!" Duke Finneg snapped, losing his temper. "Men were created with free will, and all this manure about predicting the future is just that: *manure! I* rule my life, not the Gods!"

The outburst startled not only the mage from the Archives division, but Consus as well. The Councilor for Conflict Resolution was brash, bold, arrogant, annoying, obnoxious . . . bully his way into another department's problems as he might, Finneg never lost his temper. Conflict resolution was a position that never went to someone with self-control problems.

Aware that he had reacted a bit out of line, Finneg breathed deeply, letting go of his anger with a visible effort. He managed a smile, too. "Let's just say that I refuse to believe the Gods gave us Prophecies that are carved in stone, dictating how our lives will go, with no chance for deviation. It would go against Their first gift to us, after all, the gift of free will."

Stuffing the loose paper quietly into his satchel, Consus watched the duke clap the other man on the shoulder then stride out of the room as if he were clad in his flowing battle cape, head high and shoulders squared. *Drama King*, the Councilor for Sea Commerce thought, disgusted. He met the gaze of the other, younger mage, and quirked his mouth on one corner. It was a wry offer for the two of them to share a touch of humor in the duke's grand-striding exit.

The fellow, his dark eyes thoughtful, came down the steps of the tiers, crossing the chamber to Consus' side. Thannig, that was his name. Lord Thannig, Councilor of . . . Prophecies, Consus suddenly remembered. He felt his skin turn a little clammy, knowing what he did about the brothers' activities. But the other mage didn't seem to notice. Instead, he wrinkled his dark-skinned nose wryly.

"Is it just me, or is His Grace always a royal pain to deal with?" Thannig asked him, reminding Consus that the younger man was newly elected to his office.

Consus snorted. "He's as welcome as a pookrah at a picnic, some days."

The look in Thannig's eyes shifted from sardonic to smirking. "Of course, he has *reason* . . ."

"Oh?"

"I'd like to know a tidbit or two of any information you may have on the Corvis brothers that you might not have shared yet with the rest of the Council," Lord Thannig bartered, proving that he was young, but not ignorant of the ways of politics. "In return, I'll tell you why His Grace has a polearm shoved up his backside, when it comes to Seers and their foresights."

Consus let his skepticism at the value of the proposed trade show in one arched brow.

"Oh, it's quite amusing," Thannig assured him. "And if we're to avert the foreseen Disaster—which *can* be done, Finneg's right about that—it would be wise for my department to know any details you may have . . . overlooked . . . in your reports to date."

Curious in spite of his caution, Consus sorted through what he had gleaned from the brothers and offered a potential tidbit. "It has been suggested by the brothers that the ongoing invasions of Lord Broger were a part of the Prophesied Disaster. They *asked* us for aid, you see . . . as in, they asked *Katan* for aid . . . and we *failed* to aid them."

Thannig blinked, eyes widening enough to show most of their whites in his surprise. "*And Katan will* fail *to aid* . . . A remarkable interpretation. I wonder who came up with it. And who came up with the interpretation that sent them into exile. I should look that up, I suppose."

"It was even suggested that our *sending* them into exile was our first failing to aid them," Lord Consus stated dryly.

"Yes, but *who* made this new interpretation? It's not like any of them are members of *my* department," Thannig pointed out. "I would have heard about it, since anything that averts or downplays a Curse is usually welcomed."

"Morganen of Corvis."

"Of course. The key figure Destined to orchestrate the whole affair, ensuring that his brothers comply with their own Destinies." Thannig wrinkled his nose again, this time in condescension. Folding his arms across his chest, he snorted. "I suppose he fancies himself something of an interpreter of Prophecy, because of this? Amateur."

Consus decided Duke Finneg wasn't the only supercilious person on the Council. Thannig was modestly arrogant, compared to the Councilor for Conflict Resolution, but thinking of it reminded Consus of Thannig's promise. "You have your tidbit. Now, where is my amusement?"

"Ah, yes. Duke Finneg. It seems that when he was younger, around eight or nine years ago, he was his arrogant, brash self in front of a Seer," Lord Thannig informed him. "You may remember her—Seer Pellida, Lord Toskin's wife? Finneg claimed he would be renowned throughout the empire as the best warrior and the best leader, better even than her husband, who held the office of Conflict Resolution for over twenty years. And when she scoffed at this, he claimed he would one day be King of Katan, and that when his time came to reveal his abilities, no man would be able to defeat him.

"His boasting annoyed her so much, she snapped into one of her trance-fits, and proclaimed . . . let me see if I remember the exact wording as recorded by her scribe ... ah, yes: 'Beware, Lord Finneg, no man may be your downfall, but your pride in your prowess will end with the fall of night, when you will eat your own words at the foot of a true leader! Thus speaks the Goddess!'" Smirking, Thannig eyed the older mage. "It seems that the next time the Throne of Katan is up for contention, we'll get the opportunity to see him humiliated!"

Chuckling, Councilor Thannig wandered off, pleased with having spread that little tidbit of gossip. Consus stayed in his seat, the only one left in the Council Chamber now. A smile curved his middle-aged mouth after a moment or two of thought, and Consus finished gathering his papers in a better mood. As unkind as it was to wish for another man's humiliation, Consus would definitely look forward to the opportunity, which only came along once every five years, for the various mages of Katan to vie for the chance to prove themselves strong enough to take the Throne.

If anyone needed to choke on their own arrogance, Finneg was definitely near the top of the Gods' list.

Eyeing Hope through his mirror, Morg watched her change the number to 11. She capped and set down the whiteboard pen, full awareness returning to her vision. Once again, she had altered the number on the board. First it had been 44, then 41, 37, 36, 25, 17, 16, 15 . . . and now 11. Each number corresponded to a particular day in the countdown, but other than that, Morg didn't know what it meant.

She didn't mark the changes every single day, not even on the days that Morganen watched her. Sometimes he would activate the link between their two universes to find the number had changed while he wasn't looking. But something was going on, something prompting her to count down the days like this. And it was something in *his* realm, he was fairly certain, for she only wrote down things meant for *him* to see, on that board. Morg resolved to step up his vigilance in scrying for possible dangers to the island, just in case.

Such as now, when she hesitated a moment, then picked the pen back up with her tanned fingers, uncapped it, and wrote with her normal, easy grace, *How is Kelly doing? Will she and Saber come by for another visit anytime soon?*

Reaching for his transdimensional powder, Morganen readied himself to open the Veil between their worlds. He wished he could step across to her universe for a visit himself . . . but that would leave him stranded in a low-magic universe with little chance of transporting himself back. And he wasn't going to expose himself to more ridicule from his brothers, which would happen if he asked one of them to help him court the outworlder woman.

As the words of the spell thundered out of him, vibrating with pure power, Morganen contented himself that at least he would be able to touch palms with her. It wasn't much, but it would have to be enough for now.

FIFTEEN

wareness filtered into his mind, creeping like tendrils of mist in the gray light of dawn. Sounds came first, the hush of several people breathing, the restless shifting of weight, and a voice. A beautiful, mellifluous voice.

"He's coming around . . . Evanor, can you hear me?"

Opening his eyes, he blinked, focusing on Mariel's face. Her lips curved in a gentle, confident smile, though there were tiny traces of worry in her hazel eyes. She helped him as he shifted to sit up on the pallet-padded table in his workroom. Once he was upright, she gazed at him in encouraging concern.

"Can you speak?"

Evanor flexed his throat muscles, licked his lips, swallowed . . . and lifted his hands to her face. Cupping her cheeks, he pulled her into a kiss. She squeaked a little, startled, but melted into it willingly enough, mating her mouth with his. Only because he was aware of his brothers and sisters-in-law waiting anxiously for the results of the regeneration did Evanor reluctantly release her lips.

Still cradling her head, he looked into those beautiful green-and-brown flecked eyes and said the first and most vital thing he could think of: "I love you."

In his original, smooth, blessed tenor voice.

His brothers cheered. The skin under his palms burned with Mariel's blush. But she kissed him back, a quick peck of her lips, letting him know she accepted his declaration. Forehead to forehead, it was her turn to whisper, though she had not lost her voice, "I love you, too."

Grinning, Evanor embraced her, burying his face in her curls.

Someone tugged sharply on his sleeve. "Hey, Ev—your shirt's on fire!"

Out of old habit, Ev glanced toward his arm. The left sleeve of his light-green tunic was indeed literally on fire. His gaze snapped toward his second-youngest brother. "*Faidek! Tyuroh!*"

The flames snuffed out with the first spell, and the second one shoved Koranen on the shoulder invisibly, pushing him back a few steps.

"He's got his magic back!" Alys shouted—normally shy, reticent Alys—flinging herself at the couple and wrapping her arms tightly around her childhood friend. "You've got your magic back, Ev! I'm so happy for you!"

Evanor grinned and freed an arm from Mariel to hug her, but gave his auburn-haired brother a dirty look over her shoulder. The pyromancer had played that trick on all of his brothers back when he was just coming into his powers. "*Thank* you, Kor . . . though you *owe* me a new shirt, you ass!"

Koranen grinned, utterly unrepentant. "You're welcome."

Mariel whapped Evanor lightly on the chest. "Watch your language. Mikor's in the room."

"My apologies . . . but, Gods!" The blond mage closed his eyes for a moment, overwhelmed by his relief. "It feels *good* to speak, to hear my voice—to *feel* it!"

Both of the women clinging to him hugged him again at that, Mariel on his right and Alys on his left. Ev heard Wolfer clear his throat roughly and opened his eyes again. Wolfer looked pleased to see he was well, but he also looked . . . jealous. His gruff words proved both.

"I'm glad you're well, Brother . . . but I'd appreciate it if you'd let go of *my* wife and cleave to your own."

Evanor rolled his brown eyes. "And *who* was it who told *you* to stop being an . . . idiot, and told you to woo her properly?" Pressing a chaste kiss to his young sister-in-law's cheek, he nudged Alys back toward her husband. "Go on, soothe your savage beast, over there."

She giggled and complied. That left enough room for Kelly to step forward and hug him, followed by a wan-looking Serina, who was still suffering from morning sickness. His brothers embraced him as well, their attentions rougher on his back with all that pounding than the gentler way they treated the miracle-working Healer in their midst.

Evanor waited until Wolfer was hugging Mariel, then leaned in and growled in his brother's ear. "*Mine.* You have your own."

Wolfer grinned, as unrepentant as Koranen had been.

"Alright, alright, everybody," Kelly ordered them as Evanor slipped his arm back around Mariel's waist. "We've been holding off some of the key enchantments to wait for *you* to have your magic back, young man. Even Morg agreed it would be better for you to handle some of the communications aspects of the final enchantments for the bracelets and the towers.

"So, since there's no rest for the wicked, everyone get back to work!" she ordered. "With Evanor once again in fine voice, we should be able to get all of this done within the next six or seven days, right?"

Evanor, aware of the spells awaiting him, nodded. He had to throw in a caveat, however. Now that his magic was back, he could feel the "deadness" of his workroom. Morganen had managed to siphon most of his wards and energies out of the room and into the spell that had restored his power and throat. It remained to be seen just how far that power now stretched.

"Given a day or two to test my powers, and with the hope that they're back at or near their old extent, yes. Which I can test for, if everyone would clear out, please?" he asked. The others obediently headed for the stairs.

Mikor came back, hugged him around the waist, then grinned and dashed off, weaving among the others. Evanor smiled in return. Catching Mariel by the wrist, he detained her long enough to kiss her again. She blushed, kissed him back, and strolled out of his workroom. He enjoyed the sight of her lush hips swaying the panels of her dress with each step, then sighed and rubbed his hands together, looking around his workroom. It had been abandoned for far too long.

It took him two days to get back into full voice . . . but that full voice was more than Evanor expected. Something had changed because of the way his vocal cords had been reconstructed; his power seemed easier to grasp. So it wasn't a case of building himself back up to power, so much as learning how to control that power, to economize so he wouldn't over-empower anything. Once he did that, it was simply a matter of attuning each of the faceted, half-yard-diameter crystals that were to be mounted on stone spires across the island.

A bit of preliminary experimentation by the others had judged that the towers had an effective radius of about five miles, roughly ten miles in diameter. On an island roughly fifty miles long and up to twenty miles wide, that meant if they put the towers in pairs along either side of the north and south mountain ranges and let them overlap just a little to ensure there were no blank spots, that would just cover the island. Serina pointed out, however, that if they put a line along the sharp crests of the ranges and another set down by both shorelines, they'd ensure that anyone on a fishing boat partway out to sea would still have some communications ability.

The construction and pre-enchantment of the faceted spheres themselves was fairly easy, with Serina's mathemagical help to figure out most of the technical aspects through her equations, which otherwise would have taken them a lot more time in the way of experimentation to figure out. They had plenty of high-grade silica, plenty of *comsworg* oil, and a Voice-mage capable of implementing the complex, tonal-based enchantments that would "program" the spheres.

There were, however, twenty-four of the things—twenty-one to form the actual grid, and three more for spares. Most of the spells could be done en masse, with his brothers feeding him energy from behind and the spheres arrayed in tiers before him, but for some of the spells, Evanor had to individually enchant each largish, milky white crystal. That took three days to complete.

Then Evanor got to help finish the enchantments on the bracelets the brothers had made, which also required both mass and individual enchantments. Those had been crafted from a prototype Trevan had designed, with Kelly as his consultant. Each bracelet, cast from silvered steel forged by Saber and Koranen, had a hinged, latched lid that was covered in a translucent, milky white crystal on the outside, a crystal-glazed mirror surface on the inner side of the lid, and little milky white crystal dots for buttons, some inlaid with silver-cast numbers, some inlaid with other symbols.

It had taken a fifth of Saber's steel ingots and roughly half of their silver coins to forge the metal parts—silver to hold the magics, and steel to harden and keep the bracelets from oxidizing against the wearer's skin—but thirty bracelets awaited Evanor when he was done with the spheres. As far as the towers were concerned, it was mostly a matter of enchanting them to detect individual crystal bracelets, receive and forward scry-messages from tower to tower and bracelet to bracelet, and imbuing them with powerful wards for the towers' own protection and with wards and scrying spells that would augment the island's protections.

The bracelets were more complex, on the other hand, though most of the preliminary spell work had already been done by the others. By the time Evanor finished his part four days later, they were complex works of artificing clearly worth their weight in gold. And works of art, in their own way.

The crystal on the outside of the hinged lid was not just the receiver/broadcaster for the bracelet, it also doubled as a light-source, Koranen's contribution to the design. He included a tap-sensitive ability to control the light level, much like the lightglobes, but ensured it wouldn't be accidentally set off by including the requirement that the lid had to be open, first. And if the lid was closed, the light automatically switched off even if it hadn't been double-tapped.

The lid and the oval base with its array of buttons underneath it also rotated directionally, clicking at any one of twelve different stops around its pivot-point, allowing the lid to be lifted and used from any position, for any purpose, whether it was shining a beam of light into an awkward spot from the back of the lid or allowing two or more people to look into the mirror on its belly, without having to twist the user's arm into an awkward position. That was Trevan's idea. He also made the bracelets in different sizes, out of deference to little wrists like Mikor's and thick ones like Wolfer's.

There was a volume control for both sending and receiving communications and for the chimes that indicated someone was calling. There were also a variety of chimes, which Evanor dutifully imbued into the units. They could be selected for individual preferences, to indicate a specific individual was calling, or to sound when the lid was lifted, if there was a message waiting.

The bracelets could record incoming messages if they weren't answered within a certain number of chimes, or they could be recorded mid-conversation, at the touch of a crystal button. Dominor came up with the idea of a feature that not only used the mirror surface to show someone's face, either live or recorded, but also utilized the crystal on the back of the lid for projecting a larger version onto a flat, blank surface via illusion. The image ended up looking a bit thin and translucent, the larger it was projected, but it was a good idea nonetheless.

More buttons gave the option to re-call recently dialed numbers, and there were shortcut keys for the most commonly used numbers, as well as a way for even a nonmage to store those options in the unit. Rydan had included spells to ensure the bracelet and its mirror and crystals were warded against shocks and were capable of functioning underwater. Kelly insisted on an emergency beacon function, something that could track the bracelet and hopefully its owner, if anything should happen to them, and Serina had the bright idea to have it automatically dial another bracelet in an emergency.

And Mariel had the best ideas of all: She suggested that the bracelet have the ability to call *two* numbers in an emergency, in case the first person wasn't around to answer, and that the chiming functions could be shut off so that the user could move around silently, without fear of disturbing others at critical moments such as when they were spellcasting or sleeping.

The last thing each bracelet had to be enchanted with was its individual scrying number. Kelly, with the foresight of a leader, insisted that each be given a six-digit number. Even though they barely numbered thirteen right now, she reminded them that the goal was to make Nightfall its own independent nation, and that the island could, with careful management, sustain a population of several thousand. It would take time to build up their population that high—decades or more—but in the meantime, bracelets might be lost, or simply wear out, which meant they would have to be replaced with new ones. And she insisted on numbers, not names, because it was quite possible that two or more people with the same name might end up living on the island at some point in the future.

The last few spells, and the number-enchanting phase, Evanor tackled with Mikor's help. His brothers and sisters-in-law headed out into the jungles, escorting each sphere to its designated resting site, which Rydan had been preparing at night. But Ev and Mikor stayed up at the castle, the blond mage carefully enchanting each bracelet with its call number and emergency capabilities, and Mikor carefully painting the numbers in liquefied, spell-cooled gold on the silvery bracelets' curving arms.

Each arm was composed of a curved triangle made of four ribbons of metal that wrapped around about a third of a forearm before they conjoined in a rounded point at the underside of the bracelet. On each ribbon of metal, Mikor carefully traced out the number characters of each of the major alphabets of countries in the known world: Katani, Natallian, Draconan, Aian, Fortunai, Sundaran, Mendhite, and Trade Tongue. Ultra Tongue gave the boy the ability to do so. He merely had to glance at books containing the numbers in question and allow the translation potion to guide his brush tip.

The result was a strangely attractive, if seemingly random, patterning. The marks gave the bracelets a final touch of elegance. It also gave Mikor a very important task, and he acquitted himself well. Evanor made sure to give the youth the opportunity to get up, move around, and have an occasional snack, so he wouldn't be too restless, and to give him just enough praise to let him know he *was* doing well.

Having drunk Ultra Tongue himself, Evanor found it a little eye-twitching if he concentrated on reading each individual language, for the spell tried to compensate for how his eyes perceived each set of numbers. But if he just glanced at them without the intent to read, the gilding remained a pleasant bit of ornamentation. With the slightly domed, faceted, milky white cabochon of crystal covering each top, the bracelets appeared to be nothing more than large, unusual wrist jewelry. Yet their potential was amazing.

By the time the pair finished their tasks, so had the others. Everyone else, save for Rydan and Kelly, had transported the crystals to the carefully spaced pedestals Rydan had force-grown out of the granite bedrock of the island at night. As tempting as it was to try to activate the bracelets, none of the crystal towers were completed, nor had they been empowered. Nor would they be, until Rydan had finished his final, overnight enchanting.

While everyone else slept, the pedestals would meld with the bases of the crystal spheres, then rise up into tall, slim spires. Rydan would lift those towers well over the tops of the trees around them, until they stood taller than most buildings. Taller than the peaks of the mountains, too, which—the sixthborn brother had told Serina—meant those spires required shielding and grounding against the possibility of lightning strikes.

More than happy to figure out another equation—or four—she had come back with a tapered, spiraling design that would be stable in high winds and earthquakes, as well as be able to ground any lightning in the tower's vicinity, without damaging the sphere's function or causing the energy to feed back into the island's Fountain. The third arithmantic equation she added at Morganen's request—a set of spells to help detect anyone landing on the island. So far, sheer luck had allowed them to notice the Mandarites' arrival, and for Wolfer to have been near the right beach when Alys arrived.

The fourth spell the mathemagician offered was something they had all nearly forgotten: an encryption enchantment to block non-authorized scryings from any mirror other than the ones linked into the array across the island. That would allow them to keep all of their conversations relatively private, since the bracelets themselves were already enchanted to connect only to the numbers dialed.

Rydan accepted her chalkboards, looked them over, and nodded wordlessly, conceding that he could perform the amount of magic being requested of him. He shook his head at the offers of assistance, since the five shrunken slates suggested he had a lot of enchantment ahead of him, and disappeared after the evening meal was through. The use of the Fountain, a wellspring of pure magical energy hidden somewhere under the mountain range to the north, would permit the sixthborn brother to do in one night what would normally take all of them a handful of days. No, Rydan didn't need any assistance. Of course, neither did he want any, and his brothers did their best to respect his solitary ways.

Bree-deeenng. Bree-deeeenng.

Eyeing the chiming crystal on her wrist, Mariel flipped it open. Her son's face beamed through the surface of the finger-length oval that was the scrying mirror. His voice came through clearly from the resonance spells of the bracelet and faintly from the room across the hall, where half of them had gone to call the others still in this chamber, in order to test the Artifacts.

"Hello, Mother! I made it work! It was really easy," Mikor said excitedly, "and I just followed Aunt Kelly's directions. I pushed your numbers, and the calling button-thing, and it worked!"

"Yes, I can see that," Mariel praised her son, trying not to laugh. It wasn't his fault that his age and enthusiasm were making him hyper. Even her fellow adults were a little giddy, playing with the various buttons to try out their spell functions. In fact, Trevan was projecting his twin's image on the wall near Mariel, which made it interesting to view. The wall was currently painted in a swirling image of scudding gray storm clouds, well suited to the black-clad, brooding Rydan. Since Trevan was standing back far enough to make his twin's body seem full size, if only from his ribs up, the illusion was rather translucent and thus eerie, superimposed on the storm-colored wall.

"I'm going to call Aunt Serina with this thing!"

"You do that," Mariel agreed, and touched the call button to end the scrying link, which was a silhouette of an open-lidded bracelet seen from one end. She personally thought it looked like a silvery spider trying to balance on two pinpoints, abdomen thrust up into the air. A moment later, she heard Serina's bracelet chime and heard her son's voice again, this time overheard more strongly from the other room.

"*Enough*," Rydan's voice, as thin as his illusionary self, asserted. "I am turning off this infernal thing. *You* may live in the daylight, but *I* need my sleep. Stop calling me."

The illusion on the wall winked out. His twin, Trevan, looked a little disappointed, even a touch depressed for a moment. The copper-haired mage sighed, raked his sun-streaked hair back from his face with his free hand, and tapped in another set of numbers. Mariel's bracelet chimed again, startling her. Opening the lid, she activated the call, and found him grinning at her. It was strange, knowing he was just a couple of body lengths away, grinning at his forearm, yet she could see him smiling out of the little oval mirror at her.

"So," he said. "Any chance I could get you to leave my elder brother and consider courting me for a change?"

An arm slipped around her shoulders, startling her. Evanor leaned over, staring into the mirror. "If you would like me to look you in the face and kick you in the rear, I can now do that quite easily, dear brother. Wait for your *own* woman."

Reaching out, he snapped her bracelet shut, then kissed her cheek.

"Sorry if that was high-handed," Evanor apologized under his breath. "I can't wait until his own Destined bride arrives. Then the rest of us won't have to feel so nervous."

Drrreenng . . . Drrreenng . . .

Removing his arm from her shoulders, Evanor flicked the latch of his bracelet, letting the tension of the spring snap open its lid. Mikor's face beamed up at him. "Hi, Evanor! Are we going to have a fighting lesson today? I like your brothers, but I miss spending time with you!"

Pleased at the request, Evanor smiled back at the boy, clicking the oval on its pivot so that Mariel could see her son, too. "Of course. You get another quarter hour—we all do—to play with these crystal bracelet things, then we'll go to the salle, and I'll test you on what my brothers have been teaching you."

"Great! I really like these crystal bracelets," Mikor stated. He frowned slightly, the action kind of hard to see in such a small image. "Crystal bracelets . . . that's a mouthful, isn't it? Crystal bracelets . . . crystal . . . lets. Crystalets? No, that's still a lot to say. Crystal . . . crys . . . *cryslets*!" he exclaimed, loud enough to be heard from the hallway as well as through the bracelets. "Let's call them cryslets! 'Cause they're half crystal, half bracelet!"

Kelly's freckled figure appeared in the image behind the nine-year-old, leaning down as she put her face next to his. "That's a great idea! Did you come up with it, just now?"

Mikor grinned and nodded, twisting his head to look up at her.

"Then congratulations, Mikor, on picking out a good name for these things. Cryslets. I like it!" Kissing him on the cheek, Kelly moved out of view again.

Mariel noted that her son wrinkled his nose for a moment, a possible harbinger that he was about to enter that girls-are-icky stage of his childhood.

"Alright, Mikor, you heard Evanor. Finish playing with your new cryslet, then get ready for a martial arts lesson," Mariel told him. "We'll talk to you in person in a few minutes."

Reaching up, she closed the lid of Ev's bracelet . . . cryslet, rather, and kissed him on the cheek. It helped that he dipped his head a little, accepting her salute.

"Thank you for helping teach him how to defend himself," Mariel told her lover. "He's positively thriving under all this male attention from you and your brothers."

"He's charming. And a handful." Returning his arm to her shoulders, Evanor cuddled her against his side. She turned into him, so he wrapped his other arm around her, resting his chin on top of her curly brown hair. "When the others aren't busy calling us, I'd like to ask you some questions about Natallian marriage practices."

Mariel pulled her head back, peering up at him quizzically. "Natallian marriage practices?"

"Yes. I'd like to know how they compare to Katani ones . . . and I'd like to come up with a version of our own," Ev explained. "If we're going to be an independent nation, we'll have to start inventing and implementing our own customs—"

Bree-deeenng. Bree-deeenng. Bree-deeenng.

Rolling her eyes, Mariel unwrapped her arms from Evanor's waist so that she could answer yet another call. "I'm beginning to see why Kelly insisted on different chimes for everyone's bracelet . . . and why Rydan called these cryslets 'infernal things' . . . Oh, hello, Alys!"

"Hello! I was wondering if us ladies want to get together for our usual prelunch kung-foo-tai practice," the other curly-haired woman stated. "Care to join us in a few minutes? Mikor will be busy playing with Ev and the other boys—hello, Ev!—so I thought it would be a good time to have some girl time."

"Certainly," Mariel agreed, before watching Alys' image swivel sharply downward; the mirror went dark for a brief moment, then became a simple reflection. Looking up from her wrist, she spotted Morganen, youngest of the mages, looking rather pensive. She would have blamed it on his playing with the new Artifacts, except his was closed and latched.

Leaning down, Evanor whispered in Mariel's ear, inadvertently distracting her. He was glad it was only a whisper and not his sole source of sound-making anymore. "Tonight, my chambers, and we both turn the bracelets off. The cryslets, rather. Just in case."

"*Agreed*," she muttered, restraining the urge to roll her eyes. These Artifacts would no doubt be a godsend over long distances, but too much use of them was a potential abuse of them, in her opinion. Certainly her son would be too excited to *not* try to use his cryslet for every least little thing, including a possible interruption or two in the middle of the night.

Better to cut out the chance of that happening, she thought, *than to let . . . what was it Kelly called it? Yes, that was it. Better to cut off the chance than to suffer from* childus interruptus. *She said it was a sort of magical phrase encapsulating the sexual frustration of parents with too-curious, needy children, back where she used to live . . .*

Y̰our Majesty . . . was it really necessary to bind us in an actual spell to not mention our trip?"

Consus waited for King Taurin's answer. It was one he wanted to ask himself, but didn't dare. The brave soul in question was the pudgy, seemingly ineffectual but arcanely powerful Councilor for Weather Implementation, Baron Pover.

"Yes, it was," His Majesty responded calmly, eyeing the baron. "Is there any particular reason why you object?"

The portly redhead wriggled his sausage-like fingers along the edges of his overrobe, making his wedding ring gleam. "Well, you're having us board so *suddenly*," he complained. "I barely had time to pack a change of clothes, never mind give my wife a *proper* good-bye."

The look in Taurin's dark brown eyes echoed the one in Consus' own gaze. Neither man wanted to know what the overweight mage considered a proper good-bye. Not when the rumors of the good baron's proclivities ran to stories of debauched orgies.

"And I didn't have the chance to tell her where I was going!" Pover added petulantly.

"I told everyone to be silent about our intent to visit the exilees, once the tax accounting was completed," King Taurin reminded the older male. "The Council servants then heard rumors about it. That could have been the result of deduction, or it could have been the result of an information leak. None of us wish for the Corvis brothers to be aware in advance of our arrival."

"But, my pretty worries so, when I'm gone without her permission," Councilor Pover protested.

To each their own tastes, Consus thought as charitably as he could, quickly averting the other thought, the one about how the baroness was even more lewd—according to rumor, a nubile, beautiful young woman with a taste for overweight, libidinous males—than her husband. If that were possible.

Consus himself had once thought to wed, but had never found a woman willing to match his yearning for a quiet life. It was at odds with his desire to be a bureaucrat, yes; most potential bureaucrat-wives were the social-ladder-climbing types. To realize that Consus was *content* with his lesser office of the Department of Sea Commerce, and didn't want to make a move for the throne or a higher office, had disappointed more than one would-be mate.

"Couldn't we have brought her?" Pover asked. He gestured at the wharf and the Councilors still lining up to board the ship His Majesty had commandeered for their journey. "There's still time to fetch her by mirror-Gate."

"Though she may possess many . . . charms of one sort," Queen Samille stated diplomatically, joining her husband, "your baroness is insufficiently empowered as a mage to be of use. *And* a bit too . . . well, to be *frank*, a bit too lusty to be trusted on a trip like this. You will note that the only female Councilors invited to go on this journey are those who are either solidly married or solidly uninterested in men, and decidedly not a one of them a maiden."

"With due apologies for pointing out the obvious, Your Majesty," Baron Pover offered with an unctuous bow. "You may be solidly married . . . but you aren't a mage."

"We have chosen to bring Our wife with us, so that at least *one* of us will keep a cool head in the coming confrontation," Taurin stated reprovingly. "Magical ability has nothing to do with wisdom, diplomacy, and discretion."

"Of course, of course . . . but my pretty will worry terribly—when will this spell of silence toward others be lifted?" the baron asked. "When will I be able to scry her, to reassure her that I am fine and well?"

"When we're ready to dock at the island. If you have any further objections as to the duration of this very necessary trip, We can always arrange to have you stand one of the hourly shifts for enhancing our sailing speed with steady-wind spells." The King of Katan guided his wife away from the railing, effectively ending the conversation.

Consus turned his gaze to the last of the Councilors coming aboard. Most of them were powerful mages in their own right. It was hoped that if worst came to worst, the Councilors would be a front-line assault against the brothers. The ship they boarded was a military vessel; its sailors were skilled to some degree in battle magics, and there were two cargo holds filled with spell-braced mirrors, ready to Gate in more mage-troops, should the Corvis brothers prove intractable enough for Duke Finneg to be given the order to resolve any possible conflicts.

It was not a pleasant thought to contemplate. The duke was far, far too happy about this turn of events for Consus' comfort. He turned his gaze to the aft deck, where the duke's teeth could be seen gleaming in the late afternoon light. Councilor Finneg was busy chatting with the captain, gesturing with his leather-clad arms, no doubt outlining how he wanted the crew to follow his orders, should the time come for an attack.

This wasn't the first sea voyage the duke had made, and there were plenty of ways to scry out a target a mile or two from shore, bombarding it with spells flung from afar. With mages standing by to ensure a smooth, wind-powered journey, it wouldn't take them long to reach the Isle, and definitely sooner than a normal, nonmagical ship would be expected to arrive. Duke Finneg crossed his vision again, looking perfectly at home on the gently bobbing decks.

Already in armor, literal and figurative, even though our first line of attack is supposed to be strictly a verbal one . . . Disgusted, Consus turned his gaze back to the mainland once more. Mournfully, the

Councilor of Sea Commerce wondered where it had all gone wrong and whether it could be put back to rights again. *Unless, of course, I can use one of those mirrors below deck to contact Morganen of Corvis . . . No, not one of those mirrors. Half are designed to reach the Imperial Barracks, and the other half to reach only a few miles away at most, the only distance guaranteed to not be disrupted by bad aether conditions . . .*

I'll have to try a scrying from my personal mirror as soon as King Taurin lifts his communications ban. It won't be easy. The one in my office was specifically attuned to the mirror we gave the brothers, just as the one in the Hall of Mirrors was. And every time I've seen the boy's image of late, there have been several different illusions on the wall behind him, an excellent counter-scrying precaution. But despite what else I've seen of the place he keeps, that mirror has been the same . . .

Personal scryings weren't easy, unless the person and location to be contacted were very familiar. One wag of an arcane scholar had quipped centuries ago that it was like trying to grab the fluttering, snapping end of a ribbon dangling from another rider's grasp during the quarter-mile dash of a horse race. But if he *could* manage a scrying link, informing the brothers of what was coming to meet them might help avert an arcane war . . . or start one.

Envisioning a happy ending to this whole expedition wasn't easy, but the Councilor for Sea Commerce tried. It didn't take long before the gangplank was drawn aboard and the bo'sun was ordering the crew about, preparing them to shove off under a touch of magic, since they would be departing against the tide.

SIXTEEN

❧⟐❧

Morganen waited impatiently for the thunder of his words to finish echoing through his workroom, rending the Veil between his tower and Hope's kitchen. All day long, in spite of the excitement of getting the new "cryslets" to work as clever little communication Artifacts, he had been worried about that number 1 hanging on Hope's whiteboard thing. And yet, aside from that, there had been nothing noteworthy all day. No reason for Hope to have marked down the day with such strange importance to her actions.

These outworlder "sigh-kicks" that Kelly and Hope had discussed didn't seem to work in the same ways as the mages and Seers he knew about. A Seer could be questioned about their visions, but most of the time, nothing productive could be discerned. The Gods dictated, they Foresaw, and then often either couldn't adequately explain what they'd Seen, or chose out of prudence to remain silent. With nothing to show for the importance of the matter, aside from the successful activation of the cryslets and their network of transmission spires, Morganen couldn't think of a single thing to account for the countdown of days.

His only hope was to ask Hope herself what the numbers meant. Perhaps these "sigh-kicks" of Kelly's world operated differently, had more of an expressible insight into what they were Seeing.

As usual when she was home, he didn't have to wait long before she skidded into the kitchen, grinning and blushing, and somehow sensing when the aperture of his mirror had opened fully onto her world. Once again, her graceful, tanned hand pressed to her chest, which was clad in an absurdly patterned tunic and matching trouser set. The other lifted outward, facing the intersection plane of the mirror. Flushing with his own pleasure, Morg extended his arm through the mirror, pressing his palm to hers. Warm flesh met warm flesh for a lingering moment, then she lowered both of her hands, grinning.

"You caught me about to crawl into bed," he heard her say, the noise somewhat muted since her realm was so far from his. She flashed him a grin, her teeth white in her lovely, naturally tanned face, and flicked the hem of her rabbit-and-cloud covered tunic. "Bet you didn't expect to see me in nightclothes, huh?"

She struck a coquettish pose, one hand primping her curly dark brown hair, the other planted on her hip. Morg laughed and gestured, lifting the pen on the whiteboard. There was room underneath that 1 to write his reply.

You are lovely, as usual. That pattern, however . . .

He gave her time to glance at the board and read his writing, then lifted the eraser block, wiping away the words before continuing. It was harder for him to project his voice into her universe than it was for him to pick up the sound of hers; he had magic to amplify her voice on his side of the link after all. She had very little magic to assist in the same on her side, hence the clumsy half-written system they used.

I'd think it would give you nightmares from the pattern alone, he dared to tease her. *How very . . . fluffy.*

She read that, whirled, and stuck out her tongue at him, hands on her hips. A laugh, and she let him erase his comment. "They're made from flannel, which is nice and warm, and very much appreciated at this time of the year, since things are getting colder. Now, is there something you wanted? You don't normally contact me this late at night."

Sorry, he wrote in apology, tracing the letters on the board by using the tip of his finger to guide the hovering pen. *But I'm confused and curious by the numbers you've been writing on the board, a sort of countdown over the last month-plus.* He had to write small, and wait for her to nod, before erasing that line and adding another one. *Was there something significant that was supposed to happen today, on day 1?*

"Day 1, of a countdown?" Turning, Hope stared back through the intersection plane. She never quite completely met his eyes, at least not for very long, but she did give him a wry, sardonic look. "Last I heard, 1 was merely the last number before the all-important 0, in a countdown."

Morg could've slapped his forehead. He should've remembered that himself. How embarrassing. *Silly me*, he wrote. *I hadn't considered it that way. So . . . while we're on the subject, what exactly will happen tomorrow, that you've been anticipating?*

Reading those words, Hope rubbed at the nape of her neck under her dark, rib-length locks. "You know, I'm not quite sure. I just get these feelings, at times. But it has something to do with you, and that you'll need to be vigilant. Speaking of which . . . shouldn't *you* be putting on your pajamas and tucking yourself into bed? You'll need your sleep to deal with whatever-it-is . . . though I do hate to tell you to go."

Her wistful admission agreed with his own regret. Still, Morg held out his hand, pushing it through the mirror, so they could touch palms again. Smiling, Hope did something unexpected: She kissed her fingertips before touching hand-to-hand with him. He withdrew his hand before it could tremble and betray how much the gesture affected him.

It was much too soon to think of seriously courting her. Evanor and Mariel might be all but assured—providing whatever-it-was that was supposed to happen didn't disrupt anything—but there were still three more brothers to go through before it was his turn . . . and one of them was notoriously anti-everything. A last flick of his fingers, and the board erased his previous words, leaving behind a simple message.

Sleep well.

To his surprise, she gave the spot in the air where the mirror invisibly crossed her world a saucy wink. "If I knew what you looked like, I'm sure I'd have *wonderful* dreams . . . Goodnight!"

Without bothering to check and see if he closed the aperture again, she sauntered out of his sight.

I t was with a sigh of bliss that Mariel silenced her bracelet. Anyone who called her would receive a polite request for the caller to record their reason for calling between the chimes, spaced roughly one hundred heartbeats apart, hopefully long enough for a caller to leave an adequate message. Thankfully, she had finally gotten it through her son's head that he had to use his cryslet *responsibly*—in other words not pestering his mother, aunt, or next-father-to-be for just any old reason.

Setting the device on the nightstand next to Evanor's bed, she sank onto the mattress with a second, motherly sigh. "I love him more than my own life . . . but he drives me up the castle ramparts, at times."

"I look forward to being just as lovingly aggravated by his antics as you, someday," Evanor replied smoothly.

Tossing his last article of clothing at the hamper, he joined her on the bed. Later, he would don a pair of sleeping trousers. Right now, he wanted to make love to his wife-to-be.

"Now . . . I believe I was going to ask you all about Natallian wedding customs, compare them to Katani ones, and come up with something suitable for Nightfall, wasn't I?" he murmured, gathering her into his arms while she finished tugging the bedding up over both of them. Dropping a kiss on her forehead, Evanor cuddled her close. "I would also like to do a little research into Natallian versus Katani wedding-night practices, in the interest of cobbling together something suitably Nightfall-ish in *that* direction as well . . . if that's alright with you?"

Mariel chuckled, looping an arm around his shoulders. "Why do I have the feeling this is going to be a lengthy research project?"

"Because you have excellent instincts," the blond mage agreed, before cutting off further conversation with a very thorough kiss. Just because he had his voice fully back was no reason to stop communicating without words, after all.

"Mmm, I think I do," Mariel agreed as soon as they broke for air.

"You do, what?" Evanor asked her.

"I think I have excellent instincts. Shall I tell you what my instincts are saying right now?" Mariel teased him, skimming one hand up over his chest. She could feel the crispness of his chest hairs under her fingertips, regrown from having been spell-shaved away for his surgery. Enjoying the feel of the crinkly little strands, she circled his nipples, making him squirm.

"I think I know what they're saying," Evanor retorted, feeling his loins tingle and tighten, simply from the way she played with his chest. He twisted to escape her fingers, not ready to be so quickly stimulated when she wasn't ready herself, but she pursued his writhing body until she straddled him, pinning him on his back, the covers now draped across their lower legs. Her hands held his wrists to the bedding, keeping him from retaliating with any tickling of his own. Surprised by her aggressiveness, Evanor lifted an eyebrow at her. "Maybe I *don't* know what they're saying . . ."

"And maybe you *do*," Mariel purred, confident enough in bed with Evanor to take the lead. Pressing on his wrists, she gave him a brief, stern look. "Keep your hands right there."

"Or . . . ?" Evanor queried lightly.

Dipping down, she breathed on his chest, stirring the fine blond hairs scattered over his sternum with the heat of her breath. "Or I won't play with you."

"Well. If you're going to be *that* way about it . . . may I put my hands behind my head?" he asked.

She pretended to consider the question for a moment, then mock-sighed, sitting up. "I suppose if you must . . ."

Smirking, Evanor tucked his hands behind his head, relaxing into the mattress. Sitting up had shifted her groin onto his. That meant his manhood was trapped beneath her . . . and with a slight squirm of her hips, that meant it was now trapped right between the folds of her core. The heat of her femininity made his flesh twitch, attempting to swell in rising desire. Hints of moisture dampened his shaft; his hips instinctively rocked up into hers, wanting to spread that dampness usefully.

"Evanor!"

"What?" He gave her as innocent a look as he could muster. It was difficult, considering how he wanted to smirk with masculine pride. Another rolling thrust made her roll her eyes.

"Behave," Mariel chided him. "It's *my* playtime."

"What am I doing?" Ev queried again, trying to look and sound innocent. "My hands are behind my head! Exactly where I told you they'd be." He punctuated his words with an upward flex of his elbows . . . and an upward flex of his hips.

Shifting her hands to either side of his head, Mariel dipped down just low enough to brush her breasts over his chest. "You're not only attempting to play with me, Evanor, you're *smirking* about it. Hands aren't the only things that can touch me . . . or touch you."

Bracing her weight on palms and knees, lifting her groin from his, she twisted her body slowly, dragging her nipples across his ribs. Evanor groaned softly, enjoying the warmth and the weight of her flesh. It was more soothing than titillating, but the fact that she was caressing him so inventively aroused him anyway. He almost released his hands from behind his head, but remembered at the last moment. Clutching instead at his hair, he groaned louder when her breasts passed the line of his ribs, brushing over the sensitive skin of his abdomen.

Crawling slowly backward, Mariel revelled in her sensual power. She wondered just how far she could go with this particular experiment and shifted just a little farther down the bed. Her breasts brushed against his shaft, now arcing firm and proud. His breath hissed sharply. Hands flying from his head, he cupped her breasts, moulding them firmly around his manhood.

"Oh Gods—Sweet Kata!" He had heard whispers of such a thing as a younger man, but Evanor had never really considered it as a possibility. Even if he had, he would not have believed how erotic it was, both to see the tip of his manhood peeking out from her cleavage and to feel her flesh enfolding him so sweetly. Now it was all he could do to *not* thrust rudely, inconsiderately. Rocking upward slightly, he enjoyed it for a few moments, until she slapped lightly at his wrists, reminding him that his hands weren't supposed to be down by his hips. "Oh, please—please, Mariel—Goddess!"

Grinning, pleased with his reaction, Mariel gently freed her breasts from his grasp. Scooting just a little bit lower, she kissed his shaft, enjoying his musky-sweet scent. That was one of the things she really liked about him: Evanor bathed nearly every single day, if not every day, and always changed into fresh clothes. He wasn't nearly as fashion-conscious as his twin, but he did make sure he presented a neat, clean appearance whenever possible. For some jobs, such as working in the gardens, it wasn't possible to keep clean for very long. But he would invariably wash up before a meal, even change clothes when necessary, such as after a sweaty workout in the men's salle.

And now it's time for both of us to get very nicely sweaty . . .

Licking his turgid flesh, Mariel dampened it thoroughly, swirling her tongue several times around his shaft. His hands had gone back to clutching at his hair. With his knees splayed out to either side, giving her room to kneel between his calves, she had plenty of room to inch forward again, this time bracing herself on her elbows so that her hands were free to help smother his manhood once more.

Groaning loudly, Evanor couldn't contain his lust. This time, he didn't slow the flexing of his hips. The enfolding warmth of her soft, feminine skin, the cooing chuckles of her amusement as he growled and bucked, the sight of her mounded breasts clasped around his loins—crying out, he came, undone by the sensuality of it. Only when he lay limp and panting on her bed did she release him, rising to fetch a damp cloth. Once again, he had spilled his seed across his belly because of her.

Mariel returned after a few moments, but rather than leaning over him and wiping the cloth in her hand over his chest, she crawled onto the bed. He looked so relaxed, so content and satisfied from his release, she felt both smug in her feminine powers, and just a little irked that she hadn't had her own bit of fun. But she had a plan for that. Shuffling across the bedding, she carefully straddled his head, trying not to pull on his hair.

Waking up from his contented, post-bliss daze, Evanor realized what she was up to barely in time to scoop his blond locks out of the way of her knees. Once his arms were out of the way, she settled back carefully on her haunches, which meant settling onto his face. No fool—or at least a willing one—Ev quickly inserted his hands between her and him, mostly to open the folds of her flesh, but also to guide her just a little farther back. That put her in the perfect position for his assigned task, as far as he was concerned.

Within two or three licks, Mariel agreed it was perfect. Shivering, she leaned over just enough to mop the white streaks from his abdomen and chest, cleaning the evidence of his pleasure before it could dry into a sticky, crusty mess. Once she was finished, she tossed the rag onto the floor, then bent over to kiss the taut muscles she had cleaned.

That shifted her position over his face, stopping each delicious lick. She felt him fumble another pillow beneath his head and repositioned herself just a little, splaying her knees and bracing her elbows so that he could resume his attentions. It left her torso pressed against his, thanks to her shorter limbs and the softness of the mattress, but Mariel knew he liked the feel of her body against his. Reveling in the feel of his own body beneath hers, Mariel licked the dimple of his belly button, circling it with her tongue.

She couldn't quite reach his shaft, limp and quiescent, shrunk from its earlier exertions, but she could imitate whatever he did to the folds and peaks of her flesh by using his navel as a substitute. Her efforts paid off, for his manhood thickened again, twitching and rising. His efforts paid off, too. Because they had already been lovers for a few weeks, Evanor now knew where to lick, how to lick, and when to lick even harder.

Just . . . like . . . that!

"Bright Heavens!" Mariel gasped, shuddering over him. Panting as the wave of her climax swept through and faded, she enjoyed the broad, slow strokes of his tongue, soothing her flesh even as he kept her on the edge of stimulated. He readjusted his grip on her flesh, twisting his head just enough to get the right angle to suckle. "Gods! Oh, Gods, Evanor!"

Freeing one hand, she grabbed him, cupping his shaft gently at first, then with more pressure, squeezing in time with the pleasure he was giving her. The flesh in her palm thickened, pulsing with his own returning need. It was a good thing. As much as she loved the feel of him nibbling all over her loins, licking and suckling her flesh, she needed friction even more.

Pulling free of his hands, Mariel crawled down the bed; her movements were made awkward by the way she straddled his torso, but her goal was quickly reached. Shifting upright, she balanced on one foot and one knee, gripped him in her hand, and sank slowly into place, still facing his feet. *Ohhh, Blessed Natua . . . he feels so good!*

The angle was a little awkward, since his manhood pointed more toward his stomach than his knees, but by rocking her hips forward in her half-kneeling position, she was able to keep him in place. The pressure of that angle was perfect for stimulating her from the inside, however. Added to the desire he had aroused with his mouth, it didn't take long for her to gasp and cry out his name, shuddering over him . . . and popping him free of her body, between the angle and the tightening of her muscles. She had just enough presence of mind left to find it funny, and enough courtesy to not laugh out loud, in case he was too close to his own release. But when she grabbed his flesh again, wanting to return him to his rightful place, Evanor surprised her by removing her hands.

"No," he murmured when she tried grasping him again. "Off. Or turn around."

Twisting, she looked at him over her shoulder. "Off, or turn around?"

"I want to see your face when you ride me, this time," Ev told her, nudging her with a twitch of his hips. "I like it more, that way."

"Oh." Pleased that he wanted to see her, Mariel carefully stood, turned around, and dropped back to her knees, smiling. This time, he gripped his shaft, guiding her hips with his other hand. Sinking onto him, she sighed, content. The hour was growing late, the room was growing chilly, and she wasn't sure if she had enough energy for a third orgasm in her, after all the excitement from earlier in the day. But it felt good to ride him like this, with slow, circling thrusts of her hips.

"Kata, you're so *beautiful*," Evanor whispered, shifting his hands so that he could cup and caress her breasts.

Concerned, she looked down at him, worried that her regeneration spell had suddenly failed. In her fear, her body tensed for a moment, including the muscles sheathing him. The groan that escaped him, accompanying a harder thrust of his hips, reassured her that all was still right in the world. Smiling with relief, Mariel concentrated on giving him his second orgasm. If she had another one—and he would probably do his usual generous best to give her another one—she would enjoy it, but right now, she just wanted to enjoy the way she was making Evanor tremble beneath her.

Smirking, she found herself asking, "Anything else I can do for you?"

"Mm, yes . . . Sing for me."

That took her aback. "Sing? As in, cast a spell of some kind?"

"No, just . . . sing," Evanor directed her, flexing his hips in time with the slow rocking of her pelvis. "I love the sound of your voice."

"What should I sing?" Mariel asked, curious.

"Words don't matter," he dismissed. "Just . . . sing for me. I want to hear your voice as we make love."

"Alright . . . but you sing, too," she told him. "I love your voice, too. It does things to me."

"Mm-hmm," Ev agreed, smirking at her.

Tipping her head back, feeling the tickle of her curls brushing over her shoulderblades, Mariel hummed the first simple tune that came to her mind, a gathering song the nuns had sung while picking the rare herbs they dried and sold. It had an easy rhythm to match to the rolling of her hips, and after the first pass, he joined her midway through the second, first matching as he crooned the melody to make sure he had it right, then harmonizing with it.

The blending of their voices, her light alto and his tenor, sent a frisson of pleasure through Mariel's bones. She gasped out loud, but it was a note, a triumph of surprise a third higher than before. It modulated their impromptu duet, allowing Evanor to take the melody, leading her into the notes of one of the songs enchanted into that music box thing of his.

There hadn't been time yet for him to make a second one, but thankfully his sister-in-law Kelly wasn't in a big hurry to reclaim her wedding present. A corner of his mind not caught up in their fusion of flesh and voice wondered briefly if that was Kelly's way of encouraging a match between the two Singers, but the rest of him couldn't really care at the moment. Her voice was caressing him, stroking his thoughts, fondling his aural nerves—the sound of a woman in her ecstasy was a good sound, but a woman *singing* her pleasure was beyond stimulating.

Their bodies insisted on upping the tempo of their carnal tune. Now it was her turn to croon, his turn to gasp—the melody vanished, though the music remained, rhythmic and hard-driving as it pounded through their blood. Clutching her hips, Evanor thrust up into her, crying out with each stroke at the feel and the sound and the sight of her bouncing above him in her own abandon.

It was too much, and not enough, and just enough to be perfect. Mariel keened, tightening around him as his body pounded into hers. Collapse was inevitable, if ragged; he still thrust into her as she dropped to his chest, muscles tensing in orgasmic spasms. Crooning into his chest, Mariel encouraged him, loving the sweaty feel of her lover, her beloved.

"Come for me . . . sing for me . . . *sing* for me!"

"*Mariel!*"

Back bowing under her sated weight, Evanor slumped back into the bedding, lungs heaving and heart racing. He could still feel liquid heat pulsing out of his body, urging his groin up into hers with each fading spasm, but most of him now felt limp and deliciously sated. Relaxed and ready to sleep.

Except they were both still naked, and they did have a nine-year-old bump of curiosity sleeping in the suite next door. Nudging the woman slumped across his chest, Evanor got her to roll onto her side. That freed him to take enough air into his lungs to find the energy to sit up.

From there, he found the energy to stoop over and pick up the rag she had discarded on the floor. Wiping at himself, he rose and padded toward the refreshing room on unsteady legs. A rinse of the scrap of cloth, and he came back to the bed. Mariel roused enough to take the rag from him for her own use. By the time she was finished, he had donned his sleeping trousers and offered her nightdress.

While she struggled into the soft fabric, he pitched the washrag at the laundry basket, then straightened out the covers rumpled by their lovemaking. Once she was decent, Mariel double-tapped the lightglobe into darkness and felt him climb into bed next to her. Twisting so that she faced away, she scooted close to him, their bodies bumping awkwardly together before he chuckled and pulled her into better alignment, both of them on their sides.

Evanor's lips brushed her shoulder along the edge of her sleeveless nightdress. "We still haven't discussed marriage rituals."

"No," she agreed, amused. "But we certainly discussed mating rituals."

He laughed into her curls, hugging her close. "That we did. But we can talk about it"—he paused to yawn, snuggling closer—"in the morning."

"Goodnight, then," she agreed, smiling into the dark. Then impishly added, "A *very* good night."

He chuckled. "Indeed."

Despite the excitement of the previous day—or perhaps because of it—Mikor woke very early, yet feeling very refreshed. Full of energy. The first thing he did after tapping the lightglobe mounted on his bedpost was to snatch up his cryslet and fit it around his small wrist. One day he'd be big enough for an adult-sized model, but for now, the small bracelet would have to do.

Climbing out of bed, Mikor hurried to dress in suitably warm clothes, woolen hose, a linen undershirt and a felted split-tunic in shades of green. It was so early, he could barely hear the first twit-terings of birds through the windows of his bedchamber. That was alright, though; his cryslet had that neat light-casting spell on it. And since he'd been told days and days ago that if he wore one of these communication-Artifacts, it would be *safe* to let him roam around the island—Her Majesty, Kelly the Freckled, had *said* so—he was going to do it.

Before breakfast, and hopefully before his mother woke up. If she wasn't around to ask him where he was going, she wouldn't be around to spoil his fun by saying *no*, after all. Or worse, assign chores. With that piece of logic firmly in his mind, Mikor eased out of his suite, careful to close his door quietly and tiptoe all the way to the nearest stairwell.

That was the easy part. The hard part would be figuring out a way to get out through the big doors forming gateways into the palace compound. One lay to the east, which he was familiar with, and one lay to the west, unexplored territory. He wanted to explore westward. If nothing else, he knew from his explorations along the ramparts of the outer walls—he could go onto those walls, just not into the towers ringing them—that the ground outside the walls had been cleared of everything for more than the length of a tree trunk, all the way around.

If he found a way out the east gate instead of the west one, he'd just trot all the way around to the west one and take that mysterious western road all the way down to the harbor where the trading ships were supposed to come. The next ship wasn't due for a few more days, if he remembered right. Mikor knew he wasn't supposed to go down there when there was a ship visiting the island, but there wasn't going to be one today. Wearing his bracelet, he should be per-fectly okay to go down there. Even if he would probably have to argue the point with his mother, when he got back.

*E*kles." The last of the sacks of high-quality sand settled into the bed of the wagon on top of its companions. The brothers had used up a lot of their shipment, along with a good portion of the

comsworg the Mandarites had traded to them in exchange for kidnapping Dominor, but Koranen still needed to make more lightglobes.
More lightglobes meant more income for the island. Jumping onto
the driver's seat, Rydan picked up the reins, guiding the magical
vehicle out of the warehouse.

A wave of his hand, another muttered phrase, and the warehouse
locked itself behind him. Not that anyone visited the island, aside
from the merchant captains, but there was always a first time. When
the wagon turned onto the main road, Rydan glanced over his
shoulder, checking the western cove. Nothing but scudding clouds,
the blue-white twinkle of stars, and a clustered, yellow-white glint
of light on the horizon.

He yanked on the reins of the cart and stomped on the brake
lever, a move that would have made a mortal horse snort, but only
made the wagon wheels lock and skid under the momentum-
propelled mass of the bags of sand lying behind him. A cluster of
yellow-white lights on the horizon, too unnatural and unusual to be
stars. Lightglobes, no doubt. As he sat there in the chilly, damp,
predawn air, he watched those lights slowly glide and shift, signs of
a ship tacking into harbor.

It wasn't the scheduled arrival date for the traders. That was a
few days off, still. Which meant it was likely that someone among
the captains had finally decided to sneak past the Council's edict for
a bit of illicit trade and profitable smuggling. Sighing roughly, Rydan released the brake and stepped on the accelerant lever, guiding
the wagon up the hill at a rattling pace. The sooner he got the sand
back to the castle, the sooner he could scry upon the traders and decide whether or not he should wake his brothers early, or just inform
them of the unscheduled arrival at breakfast.

An insistent, soft chime dragged Morganen from his rest. Bleary-
eyed, fuzzy-minded, he struggled to focus on where the sound was
coming from, and what it meant. It wasn't his cryslet-thingy, though
he knocked that accidentally to the floor in his attempt to find the
source. It wasn't until Morg sat up and breathed deeply of the chilly

morning air in his bedroom that he recognized the chime pattern. Unlike Trev's odd attempt with location-based summoning bells, Morg had long ago created a system of pattern-recognition that made more sense, both musically and situationally.

This chime-based melody contained the musical phrases for "sea," "ship," "west," and "unknown." That woke him up rapidly. The last unknown ship to approach the island had been the Mandarites, coming in from the east. He had stayed his hand, then, letting Kelly and Saber decide what to do about their Prophesied Disaster. This was something else. Hoping it was the traders, Morganen flung on his clothes and headed for his workroom.

Once there, he pulled the shroud from a rectangular mirror, quickly enchanting it to focus first on the palace itself, and then . . . he zoomed back to the castle compound, focusing on the western gate. It stood partially open. Morganen frowned thoughtfully; for a moment, he thought he had seen a shadow slipping out of the compound, but it was still too dark to tell. The brothers sometimes had a habit of leaving it open if they went down to the warehouse in the seawater processing compound and intended to come driving back up with a load of something, and Rydan was no exception. Undoubtedly he had gone down to fetch up more high-grade sand to replace all the silicate used up in the manufacturing of the bracelets and towers.

With a trader ship sneaking into harbor, now wasn't the time to leave the doors open, however. A clenching gesture of Morg's fist closed the gate. Rydan would just have to open it when he got back. Hoping his older brother noticed the ship and stuck around by the harbor to watch it come in, Morganen turned his attention to the ship itself, refocusing the mirror off to the west.

He found himself looking at a slightly blurred patch of night air. In fact, he had to pan several times across the horizon before he spotted that blurring. When he realized what it meant, he smacked himself lightly in the forehead. Of *course* the traders would approach under a cloaking spell that would prevent anyone from scrying their location. Illicit, illegal smuggling operations weren't conducted out in the open! If he was actually down there on the one surviving dock, Morganen probably would have seen the ship approaching, but not through a mirror.

Of course, there were ways to break through and remove such anti-scrying wards. With Hope's admonition to be extra-vigilant today, Morganen set himself to find the ingredients he would need to augment his efforts. It *might* be traders . . . or it might be the Mandarites, back for another untimely visit.

P repare the advanced scouts for launch," King Taurin ordered Councilor Finneg. "They are to secure the dock and its immediate area for two hundred yards into the shore, but are not to range any farther inland, nor to provoke an attack. Their purpose is strictly to ensure our landing is unhindered and that this ship stays secure."

Nodding, Finneg passed the orders to the crew. There was a bit of bustle and confusion on the decks, with the Councilors still in the stages of waking and dressing and coming up out of the depths of the ship while its crew were organizing the initial landing party. A pudgy figure pushed his way through to the king's side.

"Majesty, *now* can I call my pretty and let her know I'm alright? Although there's *nothing* alright about being cramped in a cabin with three other men, all of whom snore like monsters . . ."

Rolling his eyes, Taurin muttered the release-words. "*Feles vocanu.* There. You can speak of our arrival on the island. Finneg! Launch the landing party."

Nodding, Finneg activated the mirror that had been brought up on deck, focusing it on the surface of the sole surviving dock. Barking a spell-command, he cast powder onto its surface. As soon as the glass finished rippling, the first wave of Katani soldiers leaped through, abruptly appearing and landing on the dock in the distance.

It was hard to see them, since the sky was only beginning to hint at turning lighter beyond the double-range of sharp, silhouetted peaks in the distance, but about a dozen figures clad in the dark greenish blue of the Katani military scuttled toward the shore, ready to secure it and the dock for the ship still sailing their way. At the same moment, the spell-stirred winds that had been pushing them shoreward eased, allowing them to approach at a slower, more manageable pace.

Yes! The moment he felt the restrictions easing, Consus focused his personal, palm-sized scrying mirror on the room where Morganen of Corvis had been located, of late. With real luck, the eighthborn brother would actually be there, even this early in the morning. The Councilor for Sea Commerce only needed a smidgen of luck, though—enough to ensure that Morganen had set some sort of alert-cantrip on the mirror to let him know when Consus would be calling him next. He needed the younger mage to respond quickly, since he didn't know how long he would be uninterrupted.

There! Swaying back from his enchanting, Morganen grabbed a cloth to wipe at the sweat that had escaped his headband. These were some of the toughest anti-scrying wards he'd faced, layers of them interspersed with warning spells that would tell someone on board the ship if its wards were breached. Paranoid thanks to Hope's warning, Morg had carefully disabled each and every spell, preventing whomever was on board the ship from realizing they were gone. It was a feat of counter-enchanting that would have impressed even Dominor, the most competitive of his brothers, and one that required Morg to take a brief breather before actually scrying the ship itself.

A chime rang, making him jump and yelp at the unexpected sound. Once again, it took him a moment to recognize what it was for: the oval mirror hanging on his wall. Reaching it before the answering spell kicked in, Morg pulled down the shroud, tapped the frame, then blinked and jumped a second time, confronted with an extreme closeup of the slightly balding, gray-and-brown-haired Consus, Councilor of Sea Commerce.

"Lord Consus! What—"

"Shh! The Council's about to arrive at Nightfall," Consus hissed at him. "I'm below decks, alone at the moment, but there are enough mages on this boat to make a serious dent in your exiled home. Not to mention the war-happy Duke Finneg is the one leading them."

"They've come to invade?" Morganen repeated, carefully keeping his voice pitched low despite his instant concern.

"They've come to *speak* first—but if they don't like what they hear, yes, they've come to invade! Either hide that woman, or be prepared to Ring the Bell today—and I hope to the Gods you can back it up."

"We can back it up," Morganen assured the other mage, though he himself wasn't entirely sure. "How many Councilors?"

"About half the whole Council, including suboffices with those strong enough to make a dent in your defenses, should it come to a fight. Frankly, I don't see how you'll be able to escape one, even if you *say* that the Prophesied Disaster has come and gone."

"It has not only come and gone, Prophecy will continue to guarantee that all of us will go on the same as before," Morg returned, taking comfort in that fact. He didn't know *how* it would, but he had faith that it would. "And we *will* be independent, no longer forced to grovel under the heel of the so-called leadership of King and Council."

A strange look rippled across Consus' spell-enlarged face—he had to be using a small scrying mirror, for the distortion to be that strong in Morg's portrait-sized one—then the Councilor eyed the younger mage speculatively. "You know . . . if you're going to be independent, you're going to need a leader. Do you *have* a leader—a *true* leader?"

"I believe we do. Why do you ask?" Morg inquired.

"Well, I heard a Prophecy a few days ago, about Duke Finneg. I thought it pertained to the leadership of Katan. Here are the words, as best I recall them: 'Beware, Lord Finneg; no man will be your downfall, but your pride in your prowess will end with the fall of night, and you will eat your own words at the foot of a true leader! Thus speaks the Goddess.' If the 'fall of night' refers to Nightfall Isle . . ." His mouth twitched upward slightly, though the distortion of the mirror made it stand out. "Well, it isn't politically correct to admit I'd love to see that arrogant idiot taken down a peg or two, and have it done very soon. He's ambitious enough, he'll probably cause problems during the Council's attempt to talk with you."

"I'll think about the possibilities. Thanks for the information," Morganen added.

"Just keep this situation from blowing the Empire apart!" Consus hissed as someone knocked loudly on a door somewhere at his end of the connection. The link was cut before Morg could eavesdrop on more than a few words, something about advanced scouts. Not bothering to redrape his mirror, Morganen hurried out of his tower. He would have to stop at the palace library to pick up a book on Katani protocols, before heading up to the suite perched at the top of the donjon dome.

Her Majesty desperately needed to know a few things about what all went into the Ringing of a Bell, and the raising of a new kingdom on this world.

Exploring the western road was fun. The gate had been standing partially open, surprising Mikor, but after just a couple of switchbacks, he heard the rattling of a wagon coming up the road. He had just enough time to shut off his cryslet light and hide behind a tree trunk, before seeing the black-clad brother, the one who didn't seem to like anybody very much, rattling up the road at a good clip. Rydan must have left the gate open, allowing him to get out.

Those dark eyes were fastened on the roadway, however, not its verge. Confident he hadn't been seen, Mikor turned the cryslet back on and slipped back onto the road and continued downhill, sure no one else would be down around the cove until later. The youth wanted to delve into the mysteries of the jungle-thick forest, but knew he had to wait until daylight. Still, there were enough birds that chirped sleepily and a few insects that fluttered past the beam of light pouring from his cryslet to let him know he wasn't alone in the night.

So intent was he on playing with the flashlight portion of the enchanted bracelet, peering at bits of ruined, foliage-entwined buildings and fallen arches lining either side of the road, that he didn't really register his approach to the western cove as more than a rushing sound of waves curling and slapping against the shore. It had a different sound than the eastern beaches, but he knew the western cove had a long, stout stone seawall for most of its length, with bits of age-broken docks jutting out into the bay, and a single, solid, surviving quay for ships to dock at when the traders came.

When he finally became aware of how close he was to the bay, he turned his light in that direction—and yelped, shocked as the light caught the figure of an entirely unfamiliar, blue-green-clad man. Whirling, Mikor scrabbled back up the road, sprinting for the safety of the castle.

"Hey! You! Jinga's Bollocks—*Somnoloca!*"

The stunning-spell caught him in the back of his head, knocking Mikor to the ground. The last thing he could see before unconsciousness swept over him was the lid of his cryslet being knocked shut, ending the light-casting spell.

Rydan eyed the shimmering rivulet of magic, mouth twisted up on one side. He watched his youngest sibling's efforts in stealthily taking down the last of the wards on that inbound ship. It was good that he didn't have to do such painstaking work himself. The sixth-born brother could have done it, but if Morg wanted to go to all the trouble . . .

A touch of his finger to the surface of the stream shifted its focus; he wanted to see how close the ship was to the quay. When he did so, he spotted a cluster of dark-clad bodies. Adjusting the focus of the Fountain's viewing-stream, he narrowed in on the figures. The eastern sky was beginning to lighten, and the ship was near enough to begin furling its sails, but it was still hard to make sense of what he saw.

Two figures stood on either side of a third, and the third was

carrying something . . . no, not something, someone, Rydan realized. A *small* someone. Focusing the stream's reflection as the figures shifted, talking among themselves, Rydan caught sight of a
mop of dark curls. A familiar mop of curls. The shadowy edge of
a nose showed it turned up slightly at the tip, proving the owner's
identity.

Mikor.

"Kata's Ass!" he hissed. The Healer's son had been kidnapped!
The gate had been closed when he came back up, but he had assumed it was one of his brothers' doing. Either Mikor had slipped
out when he'd carelessly left it open, or someone had gotten into the
palace grounds . . . No, not the latter—they had too many wards
and telltales to prevent anyone unknown from creeping into the
compound. But not nearly enough wards to let them know when a
certain young someone decided to creep *outside* those walls.

Now he was in the hands of strangers. Rydan focused on the
ship, glad Morganen had divested the last of its protections. It
gave him a clear view of the people on the deck. Not the crew, who
were busy lashing the last of the sails to their yardarms and preparing the lines and cushioning bales of straw that would keep the ship
snugged to the dock without damaging her hull, but the ones trying
to stay out of the crew's way. It didn't take long for him to recognize
at least three Councilors.

From the fanciful dress of the others, he guessed at least a third
of the Council had finally decided to pay the exiled Corvis brothers
a visit, if not more.

Cursing again, Rydan banished the image and set certain wards
firmly in place. The sanctity of his halls would *not* be violated, if he
had anything to say about it, even if he had to take on the Council
by himself. He wouldn't have to, of course; his brothers would be
fighting alongside him to keep the Isle and its Fountain free from
outsiders. But that thought checked him; there was someone else
who had a higher-priority score to settle with the Council.

Tightening his self-control against the coming turmoil, Rydan
moved away from the Fountain, intending to wake Evanor. If the
fourthborn of them was Destined to wed the Healer-woman,

Mariel, he was also Destined to be a father to young Mikor. It was thus up to Evanor to have a hand in rescuing the boy.

Or rather, a Voice, now that his powers were back.

A boy?" King Taurin asked, puzzled. Since everyone else around him was just as confounded, he cupped the unconscious youth's face, noting the boy's features: the level eyes, the slightly snub nose, the dark brown curls that had flopped back from that rounded, lightly tanned face that was so clearly not Katani in origin. "Can anyone tell me what a boy this young is doing on Nightfall Isle?"

"It must be the child of one of the brothers!" someone offered near the back of the crowd of Councilors. Consus recognized it after a moment: Barol of Devries, Count Pro Tem of Corvis, had been invited to join the Council's expedition for the portion wherein they explained what had happened to the missing money the exilees were due, the "diplomatic" half of their mission.

"Don't be an idiot, Count Barol!" Duke Finneg retorted. Unlike Barol of Devries, Finneg was there to be the "undiplomatic" half of their visit, should diplomacy fail. The man excelled at non-diplomatic solutions. He also demonstrated he had a mind under all that testosterone-soaked armor, adding an explanation for his insult. "The brothers have only been exiled here for about three and a half years. Even if they miraculously found a woman to dally with the very first day they were left alone on the Isle, any child they conceived would only be two and a half at most, not nine or ten like this one obviously is."

Taurin gestured at the boy in the scout's arms. "Well, wake him up. We'll only find out who he is, where he's from, and why he's here if we can question him."

The mage-soldier muttered the counterspell, rousing the boy.

Mikor blinked up at the circle of strangers around him, disoriented and unable to make sense of it. Three seconds after he awoke, he stiffened with the shocked realization there were *strangers* on the island. One second later, scout, king, duke, and the others had a squirming, yelling child on their hands.

"Let me go!—Let me *gooo*!" Twisting around, Mikor managed to remember one of the escapes Evanor and Wolfer had taught him. That thumped him to the wooden floor underfoot, allowing him to scramble among the legs of the people crowded around him. Someone grabbed him by the back of his tunic, someone else tried to grab him by the front of it. Mikor bit the second hand, and when its owner yowled and let go, used another wrestling move to twist himself free of the first one.

Shoving and squirming, he got all the way to a wooden railing . . . and gasped, seeing nothing but heaving waves ahead of him on its other side. Mikor couldn't swim. If he was stuck on a boat, he couldn't get away!

"Got you!" The accent was like the brothers' words, translated through the Ultra-Tongue potion Mikor had drunk. But the man who yanked him off his feet by his belt was dark-skinned, armor-clad, and utterly unfamiliar.

Another man, one with a scalloped gold circlet on his head and cradling one hand in the other, glared at both of them. "Take the boy below decks and interrogate him!"

"Yes, Your Majesty."

Mikor yelled and squirmed again, managing to kick the armor-clad man in the knee. He grunted, muttered something, and Mikor felt the same blackness as before swoop up and drag him down again.

The banging on the door roused Saber with a grumble. Untangling himself from his sleepily muttering wife's arms—something about off with their heads—he grabbed his trousers from the laundry basket, pulled them on in the rising gray twilight of dawn light seeping through the blue velvet drapes shrouding the room, and yanked open the door. Morganen pushed his way into the room, startling his eldest brother into a scowl.

"Morg, what are you doing?" he demanded, following the darker-haired mage.

Morganen marched straight to the bed, where Kelly was carefully making sure the bedding covered her to her armpits, between puzzled looks at the youngest brother. Thrusting out a book, Morg made her take it. "You'll need to read this as quickly as you can, Your Majesty. I've marked the important section."

"You woke us up, barged into our bedroom, and all for a *book*?" Saber demanded, taken aback by the absurdity of it.

"Not for just a book—the *Council* has come to Nightfall," Morg enunciated, making sure their sleep-muddled minds grasped that fact. "They have come to argue against our bid for independence. *You*," he told Kelly, "need to read what's in that book, if you want to have a hope of understanding the situation we're now in. I'm sorry I didn't think of getting it to you sooner. *You* need to help me get the others up and awake, Brother, so that we can all figure out exactly how we're going to handle them. Like we did the Mandarites, or in some other fashion."

Puzzled, Kelly sat up carefully and cracked open the book to the spot marked by a scrap of ribbon. *"Chapter 21: Rites and Rituals of Ringing the Bell and Raising a New Land . . . ?"*

"Read," Morg ordered her. "I'll wake Trevan and Koranen, if you'll wake Wolfer, Evanor, and Dominor," he added to Saber, who grumbled but nodded.

Kelly rolled her eyes, tucking the bedding more firmly under her arms. "Don't be ridiculous, Morg. Just ring the carillon bells! That's why we installed them, to alert everyone when anything unusual is happening."

Both men stared at her, then Morg smacked his forehead. "Of course . . . We've been without Evanor's Voice too long and got used to doing things without him. He has his voice back, but he doesn't have his sing-and-hear spells set up. But we can ring the bells and wake them all up—we really need to work up a set of protocols on what to do in situations like this, where to gather, who to seek out . . . I'll go ring the bells for the donjon—and make sure they aren't heard outside the compound. The last thing we want is to precipitate an attack from the Council before we're ready for them. Get dressed and read that book!"

SEVENTEEN

❦

The banging on the door, loud and sharp, woke Evanor and Mariel with a start. The light through the curtains was dim, but suggested morning was on its way. Mariel, grateful they had donned their nightwear after making love, sat up and called out, "Come in!"

The tall, black-clad figure that entered was *not* her son, as she had expected. Rydan inclined his head politely enough to her, though his expression was tight and grim. "Wake up, Brother, my lady," he stated, the most polite she had ever heard him speak. "We have a problem."

Smothering a yawn behind his hand, Evanor eyed his younger sibling. "What problem?"

"Two things. One, the Council has come to the island. And two, somehow your son woke up, left the castle grounds, made his way down to the western cove . . . and ran into the Council's guards. They've taken him to their ship."

"Natua!" Mariel gasped, panicking. "Mikor!"

Rydan flinched, raising his hand. "Relax. He was unconscious, but not injured. And if he is . . . we will deal appropriately with them. Get dressed, Ev. You have a son to rescue."

"I'm coming with you!" Mariel asserted, shifting to swing her legs out of Evanor's bed.

As much as Evanor wanted the help, as much as she had a right *to* help, he knew it wasn't possible. Catching her wrist to prevent her from rising, he met her gaze. "No, Mariel. Your job is to stay here."

She narrowed her hazel eyes at him. "Are you telling me that Mandarite nonsense that, because I'm a *woman*—"

"You are a *Healer*, Mariel," Evanor countered firmly. "*The* Healer. The only one we have on this whole island, aside from a few cantrips for cuts and scrapes and the occasional broken bone or severed finger. The Council is composed of the most powerful mages in all of Katan. They are *dangerous*. Woman or man, I cannot allow our only Healer to risk herself when someone else can go."

"If anything happens to you, *we* cannot fix it," Rydan pointed out, adding his own voice to the argument. He started to say more, but the clanging of several bells cut him off. They rang out the clunky notes meant under the old system to gather everyone in the donjon hall, paused, then rang them out again. Rydan waited through a third repetition, a few extra seconds to make sure they wouldn't ring again, then continued. "Go to the others; speak with them. We will rescue your son."

"We most certainly *will*," Evanor promised, climbing out of his bed. Glancing at Mariel's face as he passed the foot of the bed, on his way to the refreshing room, he crossed to her, cupped her jaw, and kissed her. Pulling back, he looked into her eyes. "I will *not* let anything happen to him. I love him almost as much as I love you, and I already accepted the responsibility that would come with being his next-father."

Another kiss—hoping she didn't mind the hint of morning breath—and Evanor headed to the refreshing room, while Rydan retreated tactfully to the sitting room of Ev's suite.

*E*rvaka!"

"Mm . . . mmuhhh—*lemme go!*"

From enchanted unconsciousness to squirming spitfire in two

seconds flat. Having slipped himself into the duke's cabin on the grounds that visitors had to reach Nightfall by sea, which was a part of Sea Commerce—meaning it was *his* hide on the line for explaining how the boy had come to the island—Consus was impressed with the youth's ferocity. This was the third time they had awakened him. The first time, he had kicked and squirmed and wrested himself free long enough to escape out of the cabin and down to one of the mirror-stuffed holds.

To the Councilor's surprise, Duke Finneg seemed reluctant to actually bind the boy. This time, when the youth got as far as the door, the Councilor for Conflict Resolution snapped out a highly unusual charm. *"Kintertermin!"*

With a yelp of surprise, the boy was flung back into the corner of the small room, onto the stool resting there. Consus was impressed a second time. He hadn't known the bachelor duke knew the time-out spell used by mage-born parents everywhere. Certainly it had been around long before his own parents had used it on him, decades ago. Despite the foreign cast to the boy's face and clothes, it was clear that *he* knew the spell, too, for he slumped on his impromptu seat with a sullen look, crossing his arms across his chest, not bothering to struggle in some futile attempt to free himself from the stool.

"Now, boy, you are going to tell us your name and how you came to be on that island," Finneg instructed him.

The youth said nothing, just tightened his arms over his chest. He squirmed a little, adjusting the wrist clad in a silver bracelet set with a large, shallow, faceted cabochon of some off-white crystal, then glanced down at it. A moment later, he blinked and glared up at the armor-clad duke . . . and stuck out his tongue.

"You will *tell* us your name, boy!" Finneg ordered him. "Answer me!"

Squirming around on his seat, the boy faced into the corner of the small, cramped cabin, hands in his lap. "I'm not allowed to *talk* to strangers!"

It was all Consus could do to keep from laughing at the sour expression on his fellow Councilor's face. Gesturing to Finneg as the boy squirmed a little more, no doubt trying to get comfortable, Consus offered sotto voce, "Perhaps if we introduced ourselves? A little honey to entice yonder fly, rather than an excess of vinegar and spice?"

Finneg snorted, but accepted the advice. "Boy, face us again. *Please*."

Mikor, carefully lowering the lid of his cryslet just far enough that it would look almost shut, but not cut off the emergency call he had just pressed into its buttons, hoped that his mother or his aunt would see what was happening to him. Well, not *see*, since the mirrored side was almost closed, but maybe they would *hear* what was going on, once they opened the link on their end. He had fiddled with the buttons that would keep it from chiming on his end, but not from projecting sounds to others, so they would hear it.

Unfortunately, doing so meant letting his mother and/or aunt know what was going on, and that meant facing the men and talking with them. Squirming back around, he carefully didn't fold his arms across his chest this time. Instead, they went into his lap, with his braceleted wrist positioned just so.

Visibly relieved that the honeyed approach was working, Finneg touched his chest. "I am Duke Finneg, Councilor of Conflict Resolution, and an official of the Katani government. This is Lord Consus, Councilor of Sea Commerce for Katan. Unauthorized visitors are not allowed upon Nightfall Isle without the expressed consent of the Council and King of Katan. Yet we find *you* on the island. Who are you, and how did you get on the island?"

Green eyes blinked slowly at them, lit partly from the lightglobe netted overhead, and partly from the slow brightening of the approaching dawn glowing through the porthole next to him.

"I know you understand me, boy. *What* is your name?"

A brief look of cunning flashed through the boy's face. He lifted his chin arrogantly. "You didn't say 'please'."

Biting his inner cheek, Consus could have sworn he heard the duke's eyes rolling behind their briefly closed lids. "*Please*," the

Councilor for Sea Commerce offered politely. "Now that you know who *we* are, would you do us the courtesy of telling us *your* name?"

The boy deliberately hesitated, then lifted his chin again. "I'm Mikor, son of the late Milon, Holy Seer of Natallia, and son of Healer Mariel Vargel. And you're gonna be in *big* trouble for kidnapping me!"

The two adults shared bemused looks, though Finneg's expression was more skeptical and cynical than Consus', not being privy to what the older mage knew. "Are we, now?" Councilor Finneg challenged him. "Unauthorized visitors are not permitted on Nightfall Isle, and I *know* that the Council did not authorize any 'Mikor, son of the late Milon' to disembark on this island, never mind authorizing a ship to transport you here. What makes you think that *you* aren't in 'big trouble' for *that*?"

Mikor just blinked at him.

"Answer me!" Finneg ordered.

Consus cleared his throat. "Perhaps if you used smaller words, Your Grace? He *is* only a boy."

"And *politer* ones," Mikor added impertinently.

The duke buried his face in his dusky palms with an aggravated groan.

Mikor shifted a little on his stool, mindful of the partly open cryslet on his wrist. It didn't seem like they were going to hurt him, but they did want him to talk, maybe even needed him to talk about what he knew of the island. He had overheard the adults saying how it wasn't safe for the mainland to know there were women on the island at the moment, but they hadn't mentioned little kids in specific.

Of course, a part of Mikor regretted sneaking out of the palace without telling anyone where he was going, but another part pointed out that he would've gotten into a little trouble anyway, since adults weren't clearly logical about things like rules and such. Or at least not consistent. Aware that the time-out spell *had* to wear off after a while—at least, the one his mother used always did—he knew it was only a matter of time before he'd either be free to move again, or the others would have organized a rescue for him.

Hopefully both. Mikor *was* trapped on a ship, and though he was fairly sure he could get *off* the boat, he still didn't know how to swim.

When I get my hands on him, I'm going to turn that boy over my knee for not *telling* anyone he was leaving! He *knows* better than that," Evanor muttered, following his younger brother out into the western courtyard.

The night was now ceding space to day, leaving them lit in half gray light, half fuzzed shadow. The sun wasn't going to be visibly up for a little while here at the pass between the two mountain ridges, nor would it clear their crests and touch the harbor for a while longer, down at sea level, but it was bright enough to see the wagon Rydan had left abandoned just inside the closed western gate. Evanor swung toward the bench, intending to leap up and grab the reins of the magic-powered vehicle, but a hand wrapped around his wrist, tugging him away.

"Not that way, it takes too long," Rydan muttered, pulling him under the shadowed arch of the thick-walled entrance. "We go *this* way."

Evanor didn't have time to ask his younger brother what that meant. Instead, with a strange lurch, everything streaked abruptly around him, reversing colors in a very odd way so that light was dark and dark was light. He stumbled as they emerged once, twice . . . the third time, they made it onto solid footing, only to have Rydan jerk him still, hissing under his breath. The warning was well-timed, for Evanor realized they were now somehow inside the weathered boat-house that served as their storage place for fishing nets and such, down on the sole surviving quay.

As much as he wanted to ask his sibling *how* they had arrived here so fast, Evanor kept his mouth shut. Just beyond the window-panes, silhouetted in the grayish light, was the figure of a man too stocky and short to be one of the Corvis brothers. Though the cracked glass of the window was dirty from neglect—Kelly had yet to extend her preferences for cleanliness and good repair beyond the palace walls, never mind all the way down to this dingy, overgrown shack—it was easy enough to recognize that teal-like shade the man was wearing. The last time Evanor had seen it was when the Council had ordered them dumped on this island, and impersonal soldiers had dumped their belongings on this very dock along with some basic supplies, then leaving them stranded on Nightfall Isle.

There was another window, one that faced out to sea, and it showed the bulk of a large sailing ship. Rydan shifted to go to it, but the boards creaked under his feet; it was Evanor's turn to grip him by the arm. The Voice mage hummed under his breath, projecting a subtle field of soothing energies. Nothing overt, nothing to trigger personal wards into reacting. A glance at the first window showed the guard peering inside, then shrugging and looking away.

Ev didn't allow himself to relax until he had muttered a footstep-muffling spell, something to keep the weathered floorboards from creaking with every step. A nod, and he let Rydan take the lead in picking their way to the window facing the ship. Once there, the two brothers peered at the hull, the rigging, the sailors, the Councilors . . .

It didn't look good.

Searching for anything they could use, Evanor spotted a possibility while eyeing the outline of the hull against the plane of the dock. He caught Rydan by the shoulder, forgetting for a moment that his brother hated being touched, and pointed at something just to one side. "The tide is low," he murmured under his breath. "Some of the portholes are below the level of the docks."

A twitching shrug of his black-clad shoulder freed Rydan from Evanor's touch. "We can go under the docks there," Rydan whispered, pointing at the double doors set in the floor. "I'll cast that water-glass spell Morg used."

Evanor didn't have to ask him when that particular spell had been used; it had been part and parcel of the actions surrounding their confrontation with Broger of Devries a few months ago, and the unforgettable loss of his own vocal cords. Morg, Trevan, Rydan, Saber, and Wolfer had all fallen into the bay by Morganen's abrupt translocation spell, while Evanor, Koranen, and Kelly had wound up on the dock, with Alys fluttering down a few moments later from her spot high in the air, still in her bird form at the moment of translocation. Only Dominor had missed out on that final confrontation with the man who had tormented them for years with mage-beast attacks, but then Dom had been a kidnapped prisoner of the Mandarites at the time.

Once the brothers who had fallen into the bay had recovered from their shock, Morg had solidified the water to a surface they could use for climbing back onto the quay. To use that same spell now would be fitting, in a way. Then, it had been used to rescue his siblings. Now it would be used to rescue his son.

Ev nodded, humming once again under his breath; their footsteps might be spell-muffled, but the hinges on the trapdoors on the bottom of the boathouse were encrusted with the reddish haze of salt-etched rust. Projecting the same subtle aura of nothing being different, nothing being wrong, no sounds or sights the least bit alarming, he nodded to his brother when the vocal spell had saturated their surroundings.

Despite the spell's sound-muffling qualities, both men winced when Rydan forced back the latch bolt and dragged one of the panels up with a squeal. Evanor hummed a little harder, though not louder, glancing toward the windows. Short-and-stocky was still there, increasingly visible through the dingy windows with each moment the rising sun lightened the sky. The man didn't move, allowing the brothers to relax a little in relief.

Muttering his spell, Rydan wriggled his fingers; steps rose up out of the water, solidifying into a greenish gray glass occluded with bits of sea foam, algae, and plankton. Together, they descended. The spell covered the water directly under the boathouse, and most of the space under the broad quay. Overhead, footsteps creaked the planks as the Council's scouts moved about, and water swirled with the fluctuations of the tide just beyond the edges of the parts that had been stilled. It allowed them to creep to within half a meter of the ship, using the pilings as a means of additional cover, just in case anyone inside the vessel peered out at the wrong moment.

Unless Mikor was on the deck somewhere, he would be below

decks, undergoing interrogation. Hopefully in a cabin where they could see him through the rounded windows. If not, they would just have to risk a more direct search of the ship.

With Kelly's nose buried in the book of protocols that Morganen had brought her, it was up to Saber to organize everything. Especially with Mariel's disturbing news. "Are you sure Mikor's been kidnapped? Have you checked his rooms?"

"Yes, I checked them," the petite Healer agreed, biting her lower lip in worry. "I wanted to see if he'd taken his bracelet . . . cryslet thingy," she corrected herself. "As far as I can tell, he has. But he hasn't contacted me."

"We don't dare call *him* through it, but so long as the Council doesn't know what it is, they'd probably not think to check a child for magical Artifacts," Trevan offered. The coppery blond mage rumpled his sleep-tousled hair even further, then rubbed his face. "I knew we should've made children's models with tracking and scrying abilities . . . tracking and scrying upon *them*, it should be said."

"He's a smart kid. I *know* he inserted our numbers into his cryslet for the emergency calling spell," Serina added, worrying apart the end of her long, platinum braid with restless, nervous fingers.

"He hasn't called you?" Mariel asked her friend.

"No, I haven't . . ." A sheepish look crossed the mathemagician's face, flushing her cheeks with embarrassment. "No, I left my cryslet in my workroom. I'll go get it!"

Amused, the shorter woman watched her friend depart in a hurry. "Well, at least *I* didn't—oh!"

Mariel smacked her forehead, then quickly flipped open her cryslet's lid, frowning as she struggled to remember which buttons to push. Once she did, it chimed at her. She muttered a frustrated curse, since her son wasn't around to hear it.

"Damnit—I am *such* an idiot! He kept calling me and calling me yesterday, and I finally told him I was turning it off last night, so Evanor and I could . . . well . . . you know . . . Oh—I have messages!"

Hunting and pecking, she managed to get them to project themselves, angling the images at the polished granite floor of the donjon hall, for lack of a better surface. The others gathered around the slanted illusion. It showed a pair of men's legs in boiled-leather armor, and a shelf-like bunk in a small wooden room. Probably a cabin on that ship in the harbor. The view jiggled, and they heard voices speaking dimly. Mariel increased the volume on the recorded image.

". . . *without the expressed consent of the Council and King of Katan. Yet we find you on the island. Who are you, and how did you get on the island?*"

Silence greeted those words, though the image shifted a little, as if its wielder was restless.

"*I know you understand me, boy. What is your name?*"

Mikor's voice, crisp and familiar, came through more clearly. And impertinently. "*You didn't say 'please.'*"

They could all see the tension in that armored body as it twitched, despite the limited field of the angled view.

"*Please,*" another voice stated, more mellow and conciliatory than the first, more strident one. "*Now that you know who we are, would you do us the courtesy . . .*"

The recording ended there. No sooner had it ended than her cryslet rang, startling everyone. Saber caught Mariel's free hand before she could answer it. "Don't answer it. We don't know if he has the projection volume on his end turned down or not. If they hear us, they'll know he's contacted us."

"But . . . he's my *son*," Mariel protested.

"Yes, and you told us that Evanor and Rydan have gone down to rescue him," Saber soothed her. "Put your trust in them. They'll get him free themselves, or come get more of us once they've scouted the situation."

The cryslet started projecting the incoming message, recording and relaying it as one. ". . . *want to help us,*" one of the mages was stating, a middle-aged man in purple and blue clothes, not clad in brown-and-red leather. His image jostled rhythmically, as if the cryslet sending the image was being rocked steadily. "*We don't want to hurt you—*"

"*But we will, if you don't cooperate,*" the other, first voice from earlier growled.

"No, you won't!" Mikor's voice piped up, confident to the point of a sing-song tone.

The mage in purple and blue—seen only from his left side, since the cryslet's view had shifted in the rhythmic jouncing, making the watchers up in the donjon wonder if Mikor was swinging and kicking his feet—gave the boy a puzzled look. *"You seem rather confident, young man. What makes you think we won't hurt you?"*

" 'Cause you'd have done it already. But you're not gonna, 'cause then you'd be bullies picking on a little defenseless kid, an' nobody likes bullies. An' if you're from a government, then you're not supposed to be bullies an' pick on little kids, 'cause that's against the law."

Half of leather-clad-man was now in view, and the adults up in the palace watched him shift from glaring at Mikor to glaring at his companion. *"If he doesn't start—"*

A horrific crash made everyone jump, from Mikor and his interrogators to the six brothers and their ladies watching the scene. The two mages inside the ship's cabin jerked around, staring at something beyond the cryslet's limited field of view—and at that moment, the timed nature of the cryslet's recording spell cut off the illusion. Mariel shook her bracelet, desperate to see more. "Bright Heavens! What's going *on* down there?"

"What? What did I miss?" Serina demanded, her braid almost completely undone from her nervous dismay as she hurried back into the broad, domed chamber, cryslet in hand. It chimed in the next moment, startling everyone a second time.

It seemed Mikor's cryslet was still enspelled to automatically dial either his aunt's or his mother's cryslet numbers.

By the time they had worked their way around to the far side of the ship, Evanor was getting more than a little worried. So far, they hadn't seen any signs of Mikor. What they had seen gave him and Rydan the chills: a long cabin full of mirrors. Man-sized mirrors in cheval stands, of a kind suitable for making one-way mirror-Gates. Whatever reason had brought the Council here to Nightfall—and hopefully it was just to talk—they were clearly prepared to do more than just talk.

"Hsst!"

Tearing himself away from the porthole, Evanor hurried to join Rydan. He was standing to one side of a porthole, carefully not blocking any of its light. Curling his finger, he pointed at the angle he had, then pulled his head back, allowing Evanor to lean forward just enough to take his place. The sight that met the blond mage's eyes warmed him with knee-weakening relief. A small, short, curly-haired body, with a child-sized profile boasting a nose somewhat similar to its owner's mother.

Mikor.

"Thank Kata!" Evanor sighed, eyes rolling briefly up in his head. He felt Rydan shifting, watched the younger man duck carefully under the porthole, then rise up on its far side, peering cautiously into the room from the other angle. And watched his black-haired brother jerk back again quickly.

Rydan held up one finger, then lifted his hand, so that his palm was level with the temporarily glazed surface of the sea underfoot, stopping it at about ear level. One adult, then. Evanor pressed his ear to the bobbing hull, knees dipping and swaying to keep contact with the planks—the ship itself was not mired in glazed water, just the narrow band they stood on—and listened with his magic. He held up two fingers after a moment; there were two adults in the cabin with Mikor.

Evanor wondered if he should try to enhance his hearing further, but wasn't sure what sort of magic-detecting spells were woven into the ship's protections. Even using the water-glass spell might have been too much magic, except no one had noticed them, so far. If they had, the Council surely would have reacted, maybe even attacked. How Rydan could cast it so blithely so close to the hull, he didn't know.

A glance up showed Rydan had snuck ahead to the prow of the ship, leaning past it. A gesture of his fist, and he stayed like that for several long seconds, crouched close to the ship to keep under the shelter of its curved side. His hand swayed, as if catching something, and he snuck back again, dipping low under the portholes that varied between forehead and mid-chest in height, thanks to the motion of the ship.

Displaying what he had caught, Rydan grinned at his brother's confusion and crept back toward the stern, back to the nearest porthole into that long cabin that held all those mirrors. Twisting to follow him, Evanor found himself shooed back toward the rounded window in front of Mikor by an impatient flick of his brother's pale hand. Muttering over his fistful, Rydan blew a breath into his curled fingers, shook their contents, and flung them at his chosen porthole.

The half-dozen pebbles bashed through the circle of glass and careened through the long cabin on a wild, enchanted, destructive spree. Evanor quickly put his ear up against the side of the ship, muttering under his breath; if there were any wards around to detect him, the shattering of all those mirrors would distract everyone. He hoped.

It didn't take him long to hear the two men leaving the room; the door banged shut behind them, and one of them cast a locking spell on it. Leaving Mikor alone.

Mikor didn't know what the crashing was about, but the distraction was more than welcome. It sounded even worse than when Aunt Serina was in one of her frustrated, vase-throwing piques, upset with whatever arithmantic equation might have failed to calculate just right. Sitting there, doing his best to annoy his captors and delay telling them anything important, without making them *too* mad, Mikor had felt the tingling compulsion to stay in the corner vanish a couple of minutes ago.

He wasn't stupid, though. Getting up would show that the time-out spell had worn off, and they'd just re-cast it on him. Instead, he had stayed on the stool in the corner of the cabin, swinging his legs to offset his need to get up and escape. But now they were racing out of the little room. The moment the door slammed shut behind them, he jumped off the stool, twisting to face the porthole. He might not be able to swim, but if the ship was like a Natallian vessel and was carved on its sides—

Evanor! His fingers fumbled at the latch, surprised by the sight of the blond mage. Evanor was standing right there, outside the ship—and on the water side, where there was no place for anyone to stand!

Hissing a spell of his own, Evanor unlocked the porthole, moving in front of it just in time to see Mikor fumbling for the catch. Together, they got it open, and when the boy hopped and squirmed up onto the rounded brass ledge, Evanor caught him by the arms and pulled him free.

He almost lost the squirming boy, not only out of his arms but almost off the narrow strip of glass-hardened water, but all Mikor got was a single foot wet before Evanor had the boy righted. Rydan jolted into both of them, his arms wrapping around the two, and then that squeezing, inverted sensation came back. They stumbled out of dark-turned-light literally on the edge of the wharf, where the dock joined the mainland. Rydan dragged them forward, into the archway of a half-ruined building—and they lurched forward again.

Three more times they jolted through that strange other-place, a rougher ride than the first time Evanor had experienced, then staggered back into reality a body-length from the cliff-face illusion someone had activated to hide and protect the palace gate. Mikor staggered away from the two men, dropping to his knees, panting heavily, his expression green enough to suggest he was struggling not to retch. Evanor felt like joining him. This trip had *definitely* been rougher than the first time, and his stomach longed to rebel, complaining that it had not only been left behind, it had been mangled in the attempt to catch up with the rest of him, too.

His stomach lurched for another reason. They were temporarily safe, over a mile from the coastline and probable discovery. But the whole rescue wouldn't have been *necessary* if his impending son had stayed in the castle! Righteous rage built within him. Evanor *knew*

Mikor had been told he wasn't to leave the castle grounds without an adult to accompany him, yet the boy had done so anyway! And in doing so, had gone down to the western side of the island, where he had been *expressly* told he shouldn't go—and he had gotten himself kidnapped by Council forces, endangering his life!

Drawing in a deep breath to yell at the boy, with nothing to be held out of his tone but his magic, Evanor choked it back at a gasp from Rydan. A quick look showed his sixthborn brother pale to the point of looking white, his face pinched with horror and his brow glistening with sweat. Rydan flinched back from his glance, holding up a hand as if to ward off a spell. But all he said was, "Don't—!"

And fled in a blur of . . . something.

Taken aback, Evanor stared at the jungle around them, turning in a circle. The sun was almost ready to crack its way over the eastern horizon, so there was plenty of light to see their surroundings. Nothing rustled, no broken branches showed where Rydan had fled, no sign of bird or beast that he could have shifted into in order to retreat. He was just . . . gone. Yet another mystery to annoy Rydan's sibling.

The sound of Mikor retching reminded Evanor of his concern for the boy. He was still angry, yes, but not furiously so. Ashamed of his urge to lay into Mikor as if he'd been a wayward adult, Evanor crouched by the youth, scooping those brown, chin-length locks back from that small face. *Children aren't the same as adults; they don't understand actions and consequences. Not fully. They don't think about potential dangers. And this one has been cooped up in the compound too much . . .*

He probably thought that, with a crystal bracelet to call for help, he didn't need an adult to accompany him, Ev thought, grimacing at both the boy's assumption, and the scent of bile. Thankfully, there hadn't been much in Mikor's stomach. It looked like he was done retching. Since they needed to get inside, Evanor scooped Mikor off his hands and knees, cradling the boy, as he faced the illusion of a rugged, slightly curved cliff face.

"Come on, back inside with you," he grunted. Mikor was young and small, but he was nine, a bit old to be carried far. A mutter of the spell-word that opened the gateway parted the rock face. Normally, it looked like a wall with a stout wooden gate, but when the castle's defenses were raised, it looked like just another piece of terrain. Not that it would fool the Council for long, but it would keep them out for a little bit longer.

Mikor wrapped his arms around Evanor's neck, burying his face in the mage's shoulder. "Thank you," he whispered, still feeling a little ill. "For rescuing me."

Biting back what he *wanted* to say, which was to ground the boy for a full turning of Sister Moon, Evanor settled for a more diplomatically phrased admonishment.

"When this is all over, you and I are going to have a talk about how to behave responsibly. You didn't behave responsibly this morning, and your error was worsened when you got into a lot more trouble than anyone—including us adults—expected you could. Right now, I'm going to take you back to your mother—*shalashoul*," he added over his shoulder, closing and sealing the gate, "*pele saddana!*—and you will *apologize* to her, and you will stay in the palace itself, exactly where we tell you to stay, until we say you can move around again.

"Those men who were with you are part of a big group of people who are very dangerous. You will stay out of their way until they are gone, and that means you will do as your mother and I say. Do you understand?" Evanor prodded him.

Unhappy but glad he wasn't being yelled at—yet—Mikor nodded his head.

"Good. You and I *will* have a talk, later today . . . but for now, you're not completely in deep trouble. Provided you do what you're told."

Once Mariel had taken her son away, alternately examining him for injuries and chastising him—though at a word from Evanor, she confined it to threats of having a *talk* with him later, since they really didn't have time to sit the boy down for a good, solid lecture—Kelly moved the meeting from the donjon to the council room with the

V-shaped table. Morganen fetched a couple of mirrors to watch both the ship and the road up from the harbor, and Rydan was fetched via cryslet.

Whatever odd fit he had suffered outside the palace gates, the sixthborn brother had recovered his usual brooding demeanor by the time he returned, joining the others. He returned just as Mariel did, holding the door for her with silent civility before taking a seat at one of the very ends of the table farthest from the apex. It was an appreciated gesture, since she arrived with a platter stacked with pocket bread stuffed with cold meats and greens.

"I've ordered Mikor to stay in his suite and packed him in there with a plate of pocket breads to eat. I've laid some safety wards on his rooms, but if one of you could add some more?" she asked the others, who had paused in their discussion of how to handle the Council to snag the makeshift breakfast she had brought.

"Of course," Morg reassured her, swallowing quickly. "Trust me, the last thing we want is the Council endangering anyone, especially someone who cannot fight back."

"It's just that this whole situation is exacerbated by the fact that we are technically still in exile, and are thus—by the Katani Government's way of viewing it—not allowed to have any visitors," Dominor explained to her. "Having women on the island compounds our sin."

"*We* know that the foretold Disaster has already come and passed," Evanor added. "But *they* don't know."

"And frankly, they don't *want* to know," Wolfer rumbled. He didn't brood like Rydan did, but he didn't speak up very often, either. It made his words impact all the more when he did offer them. "To do so would prove that they overreacted, three-plus years ago."

"I don't think we can hold them out of the palace," Saber stated bluntly. "Not without a major war. I *think* we could hold our own against them, but it will come at a cost. Damage to the palace, potential injury to ourselves . . . This is not going to be pretty. We're going to have to be very creative, to get around the formidable training the Council possesses."

"Diplomacy, as my people say," Kelly interjected, interrupting the discussion, "is the art of saying 'nice doggy' while reaching for a big stick. Or, as I believe Wolfer once said to me, 'nice jonja' while reaching for your biggest spear."

"Something like that," the secondborn brother grunted, amused that she had remembered that little tidbit.

"My point, gentlemen," she continued, her attention still mostly on the book laid open before her, "is that we shall make nice, invite them up for tea and biscuits, and"—flipping back a few pages, she checked the notations—" 'display to any doubters the civilized extent of the incipient kingdom they are visiting.' To my thinking, that means we pull out all the stops, exactly as we did for the Mandarites. From the color-shifting banners hanging in the donjon throne room, to the throne itself, to even the illusionary courtiers and servants populating the place. *And* the guards on the walls, naturally.

"We shall give them a show of strength coupled with a show of courtesy and civility." A pause as she flicked back to her last reading point, and she looked up at the others. "This is not a discussion, ladies and gentlemen. Prepare the palace for the arrival of our important, *foreign* guests."

"They're moving!" Morganen warned the others, turning the mirror braced in his lap to show to the rest of the table. It was focused on the gangplank of the ship and on the parade of people, some in fanciful clothing, others in the bluish green uniforms of the Katani military, assembling on the dock.

"We'll need someone to get down there as soon as they can, invite them up here, and then delay their arrival," Kelly stated quickly. "The rest of us need as much time as possible to prepare, but a nice, slow walk should suffice."

"I'll go." The others looked at Rydan. Evanor gave him a wary look, though Rydan seemed to have recovered from his earlier oddness—odd for Rydan, that was. The black-haired brother shrugged. "I can get there quickly . . . and they don't know I'm a Fountain Guardian. If they try to capture or harm me, so long as I'm touching the local soil, they won't succeed."

Kelly nodded, accepting his offer. "Go. The rest of you, get the palace polished up."

Rising, Rydan bowed to her and left the room.

Alys grimaced. "Wolfer and I need to get the cattle milked. It'll be an hour early, since we normally do it after breakfast, but better an hour early than to risk them being thrown completely off their schedule."

"Hurry through it," Saber ordered her and his twin. "We'll probably need everyone on hand to deal with the Council once they get here."

Wolfer smirked, rising in tandem with his wife. "We'll leave the chickens unfed. If nothing else, we can always sic them on our foes."

"You're lucky I haven't instituted any laws against cruel and un-usual punishments yet," Kelly half-joked. "I'm tempted to take you up on that offer. Go on, everyone! Get out those banners we used when the Mandarites were here, and unpack the courtiers-in-a-marble. And don't forget to change into nice clothes!"

"A moment of your time, Kelly," Morganen interjected. Saber arched his brow at his youngest sibling, but Morg only made a shoo-ing motion and whispered something in her ear. Her eyes widened, she pulled back and blinked at him, and he nodded. Then straight-ened. "If you'll excuse me, I have work of my own to do."

"What did he want?" Saber asked his wife, watching the light brown–haired mage hurrying out of the room.

"Just . . . to give me some advice," she dismissed, distractedly returning to her reading task.

EIGHTEEN

A third of the mirrors were destroyed, Your Majesty . . . and the child is now missing," Duke Finneg admitted gruffly. His skin was too dark to see if he was flushed with embarrassment, but a muscle twitched in his jaw all the same. "I was unable to ascertain what he was doing on the Isle, who brought him here, or even if he was staying with the exiles. Your Majesty, this was a blatant attack against the Council, and I—"

"It was *not* a blatant attack," Queen Samille chided him, interrupting the Councilor of Conflict Resolution. "Well, it is, but it is *not* the sort of attack sufficient to invoke your department in full. Frankly, we're lucky that *all* they did was smash several of our mirrors. They could have harmed lives, not mere Artifacts—and they have a *right* to rescue a child. If *your* child were snatched up by complete strangers and held prisoner for unknown reason and purpose, wouldn't *you* do whatever you could to ensure his safe retrieval?"

The duke rubbed the back of his neck, clearly discomforted by her demand. He hadn't been too happy at having to interrogate a mere child in the first place. Samille took pity on him by shifting her blue eyes to the others, even to her husband's impassive face.

"For that matter, how do we *know* the Corvis brothers were responsible? The duke has admitted he didn't have enough time to ascertain whether or not the child even knew the brothers," Samille stated.

"Yes, why *didn't* the duke ascertain that?" a voice asked. It belonged to a youngish man. Count Barol, pro tem in charge of the Corvis family lands, eyed Finneg speculatively. His words were blunt, even if his tone was gentle, nonconfrontational. "You do talk about how effective you are at conflict resolution, Your Grace. At how swift and decisive your actions are. You had several minutes with the child; surely you learned something we can find useful?"

"He's the son of some Natallian Seer, someone deceased. And the son of a Healer. Now as to where his mother is, I didn't get that far . . . but I suspect they'll know up at that wreck of a palace," Councilor Finneg stated calmly. His jaw muscle twitched twice, but he kept his tone calm. "I would suggest, Your Majesty, that if we are to ask our questions . . . we should stop asking *ourselves* and march on up that hill to ask the brothers themselves. What say you?"

"The Council shall gather on the dock, arranging itself in order of precedence, and then we shall march upon the Corvis brothers and demand many explanations from them," King Taurin stated, lifting his wife's hand in his. "And if their explanations are not satisfactory, We just might call upon your department's services, Councilor Finneg."

The others quickly parted, bowing in deference, as the King of Katan led his Queen off the ship, then hustling to take their places—with a bit of jostling—behind their sovereign.

Despite a few pointed mutters and glares, the Councilors knew their various ranks and ascendancies. Some of it was based on department and office importance, but some of it also depended on the individual and collective strengths of the mages filling those positions. Consus found himself up near the front, though not the very front of the assembling parade.

The dock was certainly wide enough for the maneuverings; it

had been designed to allow cargo to be offloaded directly onto its planks with room to spare. For a moment, Consus wondered if the age-worn boards would remain stout in the face of so many bodies, since they creaked underfoot, but no one plunged into the water. A pity; it might have been briefly entertaining to see one of his colleagues drop, arms and legs flailing, embroidered and trimmed finery fluttering, only to end in a soggy wet plunge—provided no one got hurt, of course.

Once Duke Finneg had a dozen guards arranged around the column of people, ostensibly providing a ceremonial escort, though mostly an additional show of force for the brothers, he joined the parade, nodding at his king. Taurin nodded back and strode forward. Consus concentrated on not stepping on the hem of the head of the Commerce Department, his superior in bureaucratic skill, though merely his equal in power.

The cortege moved a little raggedly, with some people lagging behind for a chat with one person, or hurrying to keep up with another, but they reached the foot of the dock quickly enough. Only to stumble to a halt as a dark-clad figure stepped out of an archway almost directly across from the wharf. Shock silenced the murmuring Councilors; they hadn't expected to be met by anyone. Only the soldiers flanking them reacted appropriately, some grabbing for sword hilts, others lifting hands, readying protective spells.

The pale-skinned, black-haired, black-eyed man gave the procession a single, penetrating look. King Taurin returned his regard steadily. "You must be Rydan of Corvis."

"You are expected," the newcomer stated, neither confirming nor denying the label even as his curt statement cut off whatever else the ruler of Katan might have said. "Come."

Exiting the shade of the half-ruined archway, he turned sharply at the crumbling corner of the building and started up the road. Without waiting for the others to agree to follow him. Duke Finneg bristled at the arrogant maneuver. "Identify yourself! Stand and face us, man!"

The black-clad man spun on his heel, facing the others; his hair, swinging with the movement, crackled audibly with energy. As did his clothes, fine-spun wool trimmed in black silk ribbon, difficult to discern despite the bright dawn light. Glancing at his colleagues, Consus noted the only one not impressed by the display of power was Councilor Pover, the pudgy little mage in charge of Weather Control.

"You are expected," their guide repeated curtly. His hand cut sharply through the air, gesturing up the road he had been following. *"Come."*

Consus wasn't completely sure, but as the other man whirled back around, he thought he saw a hint of an amused smirk on Rydan of Corvis' face. *It has to be him.* He looked too much like his brother Morganen, and Rydan was the only one who had the coloring and the temperament to fit what Consus last remembered of the brooding youth. *Smashing the mirrors might have been excessive, but Consus couldn't blame whomever had done it. The deed had provided the perfect distraction needed to rescue that boy, Mikor.*

It had apparently allowed plenty of time for the Corvis brothers—or whoever now shared the island with them—to also figure out how to deal with the Council's arrival. Good or bad, Lord Consus was stuck with a front-row view, watching Fate unfurl Their distant, Threefold plans on soon-to-be-ex-Katani soil. Somehow, he had the feeling this visit might not be quite so tedious as he'd feared.

Still dangerous, yes, but tedious . . . hopefully not.

Saber watched his wife as she finished slipping into her aquamarine silk outfit, the strange yet strangely elegant combination of blouse, corset, trousers, and skirt-like wrap, short in the front but long in the back. It was her version of practical outworlder style meets traditional Katani clothes. She did so with the book of Katani customs and protocols laid out on their bed, her attention more on the pages than on her sleeves and skirting. She even struggled into her ankle-high boots with her nose centered over the tome.

"Kelly, are you going to stop reading that when the Council gets here?" he finally asked her.

"Depends," she muttered, straightening up just long enough to tighten the lacings on her corset-vest and adjust her breasts for comfort. "If I still need to read, I'll still be reading. But that's alright."

"It is?" Saber asked her dubiously.

"Yep." Marking her spot with the ribbon bound into the book's spine, she quickly checked her reflection in the magic-warded cheval mirror in the corner of their broad bedchamber. She grimaced at her strawberry blond hair, swiped at it with a brush, then gave up. There wasn't much that could be done for hair that was only just now beginning to grow past shoulder length.

"Well?" her husband prompted her.

Kelly dragged her mind back to the task at hand, scooping up the book from the edge of the bed on her way to the door. "If I take the lead from the start, the Council will realize they're interacting with a female. A real female. They'll go—pardon my language—ape-shit over it, and probably attack us or something, out of their fear over that silly misinterpretation of the Prophecy. Instead, *you* are going to be my front man, while I assess the situation from the background, just one more illusionary courtier-marble among many."

Pausing just long enough to make sure that his own hair and matching aquamarine clothes looked presentable, Saber followed her out the door, down the enclosed stairwell that connected their suite to the rest of the palace. "And what, exactly, does that mean?"

"They're no doubt expecting you, as the eldest and former Count of Corvis, to be the one in charge. Don't disabuse them of that notion. Ask lots of questions," Kelly instructed him. "Avoid giving straight-out answers. You know, stall for information. That sort of thing." Hefting the book, she showed him where the ribbon was. "I have at least a dozen more pages to go in this thing, and it's been long enough, Rydan should be at the castle gates very soon. So *you*, being the head of the family, if not the nation, shall stand up, draw attention, and see what you can do to diplomatically avoid caving in to their demands.

"When push comes to shove, *that's* when I'll step in."

"I'm not sure about this," Saber muttered as they reached the topmost balcony ringing the broad, domed hall of the donjon.

"What, you don't think I can do it?" Kelly asked him, letting him guide her to the left, toward the eastern stairwell down to the ground floor. "You don't think I can face down, out-think, and out-leader the Council?"

"No, I'm pretty sure you can do that. I'm just not sure about how *safe* you'll be, while doing it," her husband countered. "You're my wife, and you're our Queen, but you're not a mage. These people are. It's what defines their right to political power, in Katan. They're not going to respect a non-mage, not without a very good reason."

"And *that* is why I need to finish reading this thing," she returned mock-tartly, lifting the book in her hands. "I think I have an idea or two, but I'll need to read all of the details to make sure I can pull it off properly. Besides, I'll be sitting on our throne-bench, which means I'll get to ogle the lovely view of your—"

"I do *not* need to hear that, Sister," Koranen muttered sharply, alerting them to his presence.

He was carefully hooking one of the long banners in place, letting the material flutter almost to the floor forty-plus feet below. The black silk had been coated with a variation of the color-changing paint adorning the palace walls, but where the scenes on the walls shifted randomly, if slowly, from one image to the next, these banners cast the illusion of the fading colors of a sunset behind silhouetted mountains and trees. Four of them had originally been made, positioned to cover the stone pillars that helped support both the tiers of balconies and the broad, domed roof. This was the third one that Koranen had hung so far.

Restraining the rest of her comment to a mere smile, Kelly nodded politely to her fellow redhead and continued toward the stairwell, accompanying her husband. "Anyway, the object is to throw them off the scent of what's really going on with a semblance of what they'll be expecting. But only a semblance. They may want you brothers to bow, scrape, apologize, and fall into line with whatever threats and blandishments they've come prepared to deliver—"

"—But we're not going to," Saber agreed. "Not that we'll be rude . . . provided *you*, O voluptuous virago, do not lose your temper."

"Like I did with the Mandarites?" Kelly asked, having the grace to give him a sheepish look. "I'll try not to. But I don't think the Council will irritate me like they did. Your people aren't a bunch of misogynistic braggarts. Or at least, you and your brothers aren't."

"Milady, I resent that remark. I *am* a braggart, thank you very much," Dominor interjected as they emerged at the ground level. Judging from the movement of his hands and the accompanying haze in front of his palms, he was using a cleaning spell to scrub away any dust and grime in front of his palms, freshening the floor and walls at ground level.

"Ah, but *you're* not a misogynist. You're an equal opportunist when it comes to your arrogance," Kelly joked back, grinning at the thirdborn brother. "You look down on both genders, if they're not up to your exacting standards."

Giving her a mock-bow, Dominor continued his work. "Flattery will get you obsequity, Your Majesty. And I started cleaning over by the throne, so it's ready for you. Don't ruin my efforts."

"Thank you," Saber replied dryly.

The pair angled toward the bench, skirting around Evanor, who was pulling inch-sized glass marbles out of a chest and activating them, turning them into instant courtiers. Some held only the most basic enchantments; those he rolled toward the corners of the room before invoking the spell, essentially making them crowd fillers. Others were capable of doing more than just smiling and saying hello; these he activated nearby, instructing them to fill in the edges of stone floor next to the carpeted runners.

There were four main runners, each leading in from one of the four main wings of the palace, and a fifth one leading to the throne bench. The red velvet underfoot had once upon a time been curtains hanging around the palace. Now they served as carpeting leading from the four main wings to the dais. The bench on that dais had been crafted by the fifthborn brother, Trevan, out of a local, gilded hardwood, and padded with cushions made from the same aquamarine silk as Kelly and Saber's wedding finery. They sort of blended in when seated on it, but it looked good all the same.

"What about that outworlder crown you wore, last time? You didn't return that, did you?" Saber asked her.

Kelly shook her head. "No, I just returned the gun. It's bad enough that the Mandarites developed their own version of them, in this universe. I didn't want to keep another one. The crown got put up in the attic along with the people-marbles, but those got brought back down again when Broger attacked a few months ago. I never got around to bringing the crown back down, so it's probably still up there."

That earned her an impatient look. "Kelly, we have literally *hundreds* of linear yards of attic space in this sprawling lump of a palace, never mind all the width that goes with each wing. *Which* attic is it in?"

She lifted the book in her freckled hand. "Saber, forget the crown for right now. If the Council challenges us to Ring the Bell, then according to this manual, it would be an affront to already have one *before* Ringing said Bell. We got away with it with the Mandarites, because they weren't challenging our right to have our own kingdom; we were challenging *their* right to try to take our home. What we *need* is a bell to ring. According to this thing, a sanctified bell. Last I checked, none of us was a priest."

A bird fluttered down, landing between them. It shifted shape as it touched the ground, turning from a reddish-golden feathered hawk into the reddish-golden haired Trevan. "If you're looking for a bell, I think I recognized Councilor Apista of the Temples Department in the little parade headed for our door. Which will be at the western gate in about five minutes."

"Rydan?" Saber inquired.

"Looking unhappy to be up and about, trudging all over the place after the sun has risen, but otherwise fine and well. Or maybe just annoyed to be leading so many Councilors up to our home. I've got to get back. I'll open the gates when they actually get there, but I wanted to ask if you want me to challenge them. You know, have Rydan announce who they are and why they're there, give 'em an impression of law and order," Trevan offered.

"Some law and order, yes. But don't give them as hard a time as we gave the Mandarites," Kelly decided. "The Mandarites, we needed to impress with signs of strength and arrogance. The

Katani, we need to impress with signs of civility and politeness. Oh, and ring the bells in the carillon when it comes time for them to enter, so we'll know when they're inside the walls."

Trevan covered his heart with one hand and gave her a mournful look. "You take *all* the fun out of my life . . ."

Before anyone could respond to that, he turned and launched himself back into the air, transforming with swift wing-beats that lifted him back up the way he had come.

"Well, you heard the man—five minutes to showtime!" Kelly warned the others, before dropping onto the bench seat and cracking open the book in her lap. One hand lifted in a distracted flutter, most of her attention already focused on the pages. "Places, everyone. Evanor, if you could give us a little music to make this place sound as well as look civilized . . . ?"

The ascent up the side of the mountains wasn't too steep, nor was the pace set by Rydan particularly arduous, but more voices than just Baron Pover's could be heard complaining by the time the tall, rugged, granite cliff came into view. King Taurin called out to their taciturn guide, who had refused to answer any of the questions the others had thrown at him during the first half of their walk. The second half, most of the Council had been a bit winded by the climb.

"You, there, Rydan," the mage stated as the road finished leveling out. "How much farther have we to go?"

A voice called out in reply, but it came from ahead of the cortege of Councilors. Leaning on the edge of the weatherworn escarpment was a man with golden-red hair that, backlit by the rising sun off in the east, formed a halo around his head. The owner of that voice also did not address His Majesty directly. "Greetings, Lord of the Night! I see you have fetched us some guests. Care to tell us their names, so they may be introduced properly?"

Rydan flicked his arm. "King Taurin, some of his Councilors, and an *escort*."

The deepening of his voice on that last comment shoveled doubt and other, less salubrious things onto the word.

"Well, I'm afraid there won't be enough room for all these Councilors *and* their escort in the donjon. They may wait in the courtyard, if they wish, or in one of the side halls. Provided, of course, that they do wish to enter Nightfall Castle. Your Majesty of Katan, do you and your gentle lords and ladies wish to enter Nightfall Castle and partake of our hospitality?"

"Of course we do," King Taurin responded. "What farce is this?"

"The farce of polite, civilized behavior, of course," was the lightly mocking reply from the man on the wall. His voice deepened a little, hardening. "Know you, Majesty of Katan, Citizens of Katan, that in requesting the right to step within these walls, you would place yourself under the laws and jurisdiction of this island. You may, of course, refuse to enter. But know also that Nightfall is generous and hospitable to those who enter as our friends.

"So enter, and be welcome!"

The cliff face split open, revealing a deep archway and a broad, granite-cobbled courtyard beyond. Bells rang out, startling everyone; they rang in a welcoming, almost triumphant melody before fading away. Waiting impassively until the doors were fully open, their black-clad escort strolled inside, not even bothering to glance behind to check to see if anyone followed him.

Sighing audibly, King Taurin took Queen Samille's pale hand in his tanned grasp, and led the way into the compound at a determined pace . . . only to slow and stare as the scope of Nightfall Castle impacted on both of them. His Majesty tipped his head up, looking past the immediate view of the V-shaped wing in front of them to the dome at the center, carved from white granite blocks and tiled in blue ceramic. A craning glance to either side showed just how large the entire compound was, thanks to the curving outer wall, and there were hints of other wings, though the angle was awkward for viewing.

Spinning around to walk backward, he eyed the drawbridge-spanned walkways that connected the third level of each wing to the ramparts of the outer wall . . . and the bodies of midnight-blue clad guards, far too many to be the eight exiled brothers, standing at attention at regular distances.

"Sweet Kata . . . *Illusions!*" the King of Katan exclaimed after a moment. "They've rigged this place with illusions!"

Duke Finneg cursed under his breath, breaking rank to trot quickly back outside again. Consus, worried, stepped to one side and craned his head, trying to see what the duke was up to. The younger mage's lips moved, his hands made sweeping passes . . . and a scowl darkened his face. He hurried to rejoin the others, moving up close to the king. Consus did as well, wanting to hear what was happening.

"It's not just illusions, Your Majesty, they've managed to place some very complex anti-scrying wards on this place," the Councilor for Conflict Resolution stated grimly. "Any attempt to scry an exterior view will be very difficult. There's a distortion warding laid on the outside of these buildings."

"What kind of distortion spell?" King Taurin asked him.

"The farther away you are from the exterior, the worse the distortion is, but it's wrapped up in an illusion that makes this part of the island look like every other part." Finneg grimaced. "The mirrors would have to be right outside these walls to be able to transport anyone into the courtyard. The only good news is that this particular distortion field can only be applied externally. We'll have better luck picking a starting point for a scrying somewhere within the actual walls of this place. *How* in the Names of the Gods did they wind up in a palace?" he demanded, visibly frustrated at the finely tended gardens, the splashing fountains, the neatly swept flagstones underfoot. "They're supposed to be in exile, living miserably in some crumbling old ruin, not living gloriously in something nearly the equal of the Royal Palace!"

"Your Grace has forgotten his history lessons," someone stated from farther back in the procession. "Nightfall Isle was once a very important—and thus very wealthy—trading port. That was how it merited the rank of 'duchy,' despite its relatively small landmass and population size."

"Yes, but they should be living in a hovel, not a castle!" someone else groused.

"Did anyone say they *couldn't* move into the palace? Or forbid them from fixing it up so that it looked nice?" Queen Samille asked the others, and received only silence and averted, embarrassed looks in reply.

Consus was honest enough to admit, "No, Your Majesty. We just dumped them and their belongings on the dock, gave them the list of rules not to break, and left. Shelter and so forth was their own problem, at that point."

"And no one visited them, in all this time? Other than the merchant captains bringing their supplies?" she asked. Again, negatives were her reply. "Then I don't see by what right any of us have to complain. Not if no one bothered to check if there *was* adequate housing for the exilees."

They had reached the short steps leading up into the castle. The door stood open, and the black-clad Corvis brother could be seen ahead of them, still leading them onward. The corridor, broad and somewhat tall, was illuminated at regular distances by a profligate use of lightglobes, allowing everyone to see that the walls were richly decorated in an astoundingly realistic mural of green meadows, mossy rocks, forested hills, and falling water farther up the hallway. The view was dappled in patches of sun and shadow cast by a source that drifted literally overhead, filling the ceiling with an illusion of blue sky, white gray clouds, and flocks of equally fluffy, white, gray, and black breeds of sheep that grazed on the patches of grass to either side.

And a sheepdog that charged into view, rounding up some of the sheep from the right-hand wall to the left, where they joined the flock as it moved toward a road that skirted the edge of the waterfall. The dog's mouth opened, and his body jerked, tail wagging, but no sounds greeted the stunned Councilors. Every detail was distinct and clear, interrupted only by the carved wooden frames and panels of the doors interspersed along the length of the corridor.

Consus was deeply impressed. He muttered a divination spell, probing the nature of the illusion, then shook his head. "It *seems* like just a highly complex illusion . . . but it's a property of the paint itself, which is doing the changing. Not some external projection."

Taurin eyed the walls, as did Finneg and several others. The

King called out to their guide. "Is this meant to be an insult? Comparing our arrival to the herding of sheep?"

Spinning on his heel, Rydan arched one black brow at the foreign ruler, then marched back to a door between the two of them and gestured. Without being touched, the door flung open. A second curt gesture invited His Majesty to peer inside. When Taurin did, he blinked, pulled back his head with a thoughtful frown, then moved up to the next door, where Rydan had retreated in order to fling it open magically as well. The others bunched and knotted as they passed the two doorways, wanting a peek of their own.

The walls of one, a storage room filled with racks of aging mapscrolls, had an impressive aerial view of snow-blanketed hills painted on its walls. It took everyone a few moments to realize a snow hare was hopping cautiously through the trees, pausing now and then to twitch its nose, scenting for predators. The other room, a sitting room, was a little disorienting, since it seemed to show a slowed-down version of a bubbling mountain stream . . . from a viewpoint half-submerged in the water. Consus was just as glad to leave that one alone. By contrast, the vista with the sheep—which had disappeared in the distance—was far less distracting. But when he glanced behind them, the paint seemed to have a fog rolling over its surface, obscuring the view.

He didn't have a chance to linger and see what was happening. King Taurin and Queen Samille had been stopped by the black-clad man, Rydan of Corvis. The mage had stopped by another door that had flung itself open, and now gestured within.

"Your escort may wait in here, along with any other members of your party who would seek a moment of comfort. There is fresh water and fruit on the table, and a refreshing room in the corner." His brisk tone didn't alter by much, though it did pick up an edge of warning when he added, "Kindly do not wander elsewhere in the palace. This is not your home, and to do so would be the height of rudeness.

"Rudeness is not tolerated on Nightfall."

"Does that include *your* rudeness?" King Taurin challenged him.

The younger man's mouth quirked up at the corners, the first sign of a sense of humor in him. "I am rude only at my liege's leisure. The rest of me is merely . . . efficient."

Substitute the word ruthless, *and it would be more the truth, with* that *tone of voice*, Consus thought, pursing his lips in a brief, soundless whistle. His King didn't take it kindly, either, but even as Taurin drew in a sharp breath to argue the matter, Rydan of Corvis spun on his heel and stalked to the archway at the end of the corridor . . . where the Councilors realized several finely dressed bodies milled, chatting quietly among themselves. Soft lute music filled the air, a soothing melody plucked by someone buried in the crowd.

Far too many bodies to comprise the eight brothers, just like the outer wall had held. Councilor Finneg muttered, gestured, and smiled grimly. "*More* illusions, Your Majesty. They seem to be putting on quite the show for us."

"Some of them seem to be illusions of women," King Taurin observed, shifting to follow their guide.

"I'm not surprised, Your Majesty," a voice stated, making the sovereign turn to see who had spoken. It was Barol, Count Pro Tem of Corvis. "Exile eight men to an island without any women," the young man explained dryly, "and they're still eight grown men with *needs*."

"Not to mention a lot of power at their disposal," Duke Finneg muttered. "Majesty . . . with the way this paint keeps changing, I don't know if we can focus the mirrors for an internal scrying, either. If we had the mirrors already linked on this end . . . but we do not. I'm afraid that, if things turn ugly," he murmured, just barely loud enough for Consus to overhear, "we will be forced to attack from the ground. Not from afar."

"We are here to *talk*, Councilor Finneg," Queen Samille chided him, pinning the duke under her cool gaze. "If talking fails, *then* we will consider your services . . . and We will be watching to make sure no one on *our* side sabotages the chance for a peaceful discussion in the coming moments."

She stepped forward, all but dragging her husband with her, and thus missed the slight rolling of the King's eyes.

Everyone hurried to shift back into position. There were a few last-moment jockeyings for position, then the cortege of Councilors swept into the hall, and fumbled, trying to make a sharp right turn. The red carpet crossing the hall continued on into what looked like three more wings to the north, south, and east, but here, in the center of the large, domed hall, a fifth runner had been laid into the northwest corner.

A small dais had been erected in front of the glazed windows in that corner, no more than three steps high; on its velvet-carpeted surface stood Saber of Corvis. It could be no other: his proud bearing and his honey-blond hair marked him in the memories of those who had met the ex-Count in person and raised echoes in the memories of those who had met his late father, Count Saveno of Corvis.

More than that, to one side of the windows hung a neatly framed portrait of him. An *embroidered* portrait, stitched with exquisite care and shading, Consus realized. Of course, the ex-Count in the picture was smiling, and the one on the dais wasn't, but the resemblance was clear. On the other side of the window hung a second embroidered portrait, of a red-haired, freckled-faced, unfortunately familiar woman.

A woman who lounged on the double-wide chair placed behind the ex-Count—literally lounged, for she had one trouser-clad leg braced on the edge of the bench, keeping her nestled into the corner of the seat while at the same time providing a backrest for the book in her lap. All three were clad in matching aquamarine silk, ex-Count, woman, and bench-throne.

The last time Consus recalled seeing the woman, she had looked thinner, less healthy. She had also bothered to look at him, the last time. Now, her attention was focused on the tome in her lap, as if the arrival of half the Council of Katan was of no real importance to her.

Maybe it wasn't. Between the wall-paint, long banners showing the shifting shades of a silhouetted sunset in yet more color-changing paint, and the opulence of the illusion-courtiers—and the profligate waste of magic it must have taken to create them—these Nightfall exiles didn't seem to be the least bit concerned with the fact that they *were* exiled here.

"What is the meaning of this?" Taurin demanded, flipping his hand at the courtiers crowding the non-carpeted portions of the hall. "You're in exile! You're not allowed to create your own court, as if you were setting yourself up as some sort of king!"

"I haven't set myself up as a king," Saber countered calmly, the lute music coming to a quick, graceful end, leaving only their voices to fill the octagonal hall. "Now, who are *you*, to be making such accusations in the heart of my home, without even the courtesy of an introduction?"

Consus quickly stepped forward, literally and verbally sensing a potential altercation that he desperately wanted to avoid. "Saber of Corvis, this is King Taurin of Katan, who won the last five-year contest for the Throne of Katan, which was two years ago. Next to him is his beloved wife, Queen Samille of Katan . . . and behind them are about half the Council. Your Majesties, fellow Councilors, this is Saber of Corvis, ex-Count, and head of the Corvis bloodline."

"Saber of Nightfall," the man on the dais corrected. "You are all bidden welcome in the name of Nightfall . . . provided that you abide here in peace and friendship. We currently have no quarrel with you. Please try to keep it that way. Now, why have you come unannounced to Nightfall?"

"First of all, you will clear this hall of all of these . . . magical *dolls*," the King of Katan ordered, flicking his tanned fingers once again at the illusions around them.

Saber folded his arms across his chest. "Perhaps no one told you, but it is *rude* to make demands in another person's home. Even if you are a king, you are still a guest. Guests do not make rude demands."

Quickly touching her husband's arm, Queen Samille interjected politely, "Then we *request*, politely, that you clear these illusions so that we may have more room for everyone to see you, and for you to see them. Would that not be more hospitable on your part than crowding us into this narrow path?"

Saber arched a brow, but dipped his head, acknowledging her point. "Reduce the unnecessary ones. Courtiers, move back and give the Council room to stand comfortably."

No one on the carpeted strips could see anyone actually doing anything, but within a short period of time, the number of illusionary courtiers in the back ranks had thinned to the point where the front rows had shifted back, allowing the procession to expand into a crowd. Taurin looked around at the remaining illusions, both men and women, and arched a brow. "I thought I said . . . *requested* . . . that *all* of them should go away."

Keeping his arms folded, Saber gave the other man a sardonic look. "And *we* requested that your escort wait in the sitting room set aside for their comfort."

"We have a right to an escort, to guard us against an unwarranted attack," Duke Finneg retorted.

"As do we."

Consus quickly stepped into the breach. "Saber of Nightfall, this is Duke Finneg, Councilor of Conflict Resolution. Your Grace, this is Saber, eldest of the Nightfall brothers."

"Of Nightfall," the duke scoffed. "How pretentious!"

"The Council stripped us of our rightful home, our rightful land, even our rightful *lives* and dumped us here, and you object that we have chosen to make this place our new home?" a voice asked from the side.

NINETEEN

❧✦❧

Many of the Councilors knew the figure who stepped up next to the dais, with his dark brown hair, blue eyes, and formal velvet clothes in a deep shade of blue. For the sake of those who didn't, Consus once again stepped into the opening. "Everyone, this is Dominor of Nightfall. Milord, this is . . . everyone."

It was a bit lame for an introduction, but even the most protocol-picky Councilor would surely agree that naming everyone would be too tedious.

King Taurin looked around the room. Aside from Saber and Dominor, it wasn't readily apparent who else was present. "I presume the rest of your siblings are here, lurking behind your play-toys?"

Dominor snorted at that. "Play-toys . . . how amusing. It's good to know the new King of Katan has a sense of humor. What happened to King Dethor? I thought he was more than strong enough to keep competing."

"Heart attack," Consus admitted. "Nothing serious, and the Healers fixed it, but it convinced him he should retire and enjoy his remaining years with far less stress."

"How wise of him to know when it is best to retire, rather than when it is forced upon him," someone else stated, moving up on the other side of the dais. His pale gold hair and the lute now slung over his back gave Consus the clue he needed to introduce him.

"And this would be Evanor of Nightfall, Dominor's twin."

Evanor dipped his head in acknowledgment.

A shriek startled all of them, cutting off whatever might have been said next. It was a shriek of outrage, not one of fear, and it came from one of the Councilors near the back. Heads craned toward the woman, who stalked her prey with a livid expression, teeth and fists clenched.

"How dare they?! How *dare* they mock me like this!"

"That would be Baroness Felisa of Novella," Consus stated, glancing at the trio of brothers, "who is now the Councilor of Health Management."

"Trust us, we remember her," Saber muttered, watching the woman stalking her almost identical twin. The illusionary version was clad in a trouser-and-skirt combination, like the woman lounging on the dais bench, still more or less calmly reading from her tome, though even she had glanced up at the Councilor's outburst.

"I *demand* you disenchant this . . . this *mockery* at once! Immediately—or I'll have your heads for this insult, this outrage! Like I *should've* had your heads three years ago!"

"King Taurin, I suggest that you have your guards remove her—the real one—from the donjon and ensure that she waits in the sitting room set aside for your comfort," Evanor asserted, his words cutting through the woman's shouts as she shoved at her illusion. Which promptly barked a word and vanished, startling the real Lady Felisa into silence. That allowed Evanor to continue gently but implacably, his words dropping into the sudden quiet. "Or we will be forced to deal with her appropriately, for daring to disturb the peace in a most uncivilized manner."

"Councilor Felisa, resume your place," King Taurin instructed her.

Red-faced and glaring, she marched back to join the others, muttering under her breath.

"Do not think you have the right to order us about," Taurin added, facing Saber again. "We are here on official business. You have posed allegations of neglect by the lawful government of Katan and have accused the Count Pro Tem, Broger of Devries, of withholding the funds you are lawfully due for your upkeep, even in exile. You . . ."

He trailed off, staring at Saber. Consus eyed his liege nervously, wondering what Taurin was thinking. Only the Gods—and, it was said, sometimes their Seers—had the power to read a man's mind, though. Taurin's dark brown gaze shifted from Saber to the woman on the bench and back, then to Dominor. From there, he looked out into the crowd, a frown pinching his naturally tanned brow.

"You married your own *illusions*?" The demand caused a stir in his Councilors. Taurin pointed into the remaining crowd at a tallish woman with hair so pale, it almost looked white, then back at the woman on the bench. "Look—they're wearing matching marriage torcs on their necks, there, and there! Are you so desperate for female companionship that you've married *enchantments*?"

Finneg muttered and cast his illusion-scanning spell. He wasn't the only one, but he got his results first. "Majesty—they're real women! At least three of them are in this room!"

"No, four," someone else observed quickly, gesturing at the four true females not standing within the cortege of Councilors. "That woman is real, too!"

The one on the throne-bench snorted. "Of *course* we're real. Marrying an illusion would be like marrying a wastebasket."

One of the women giggled, quickly raising her hand to cover her mouth. It drew attention to her from several in the Katani half of the room, even as Finneg exploded, "Dammit, I *knew* they were violating their oaths! No women are to be allowed to travel from Katan to this island!"

"Ah, but *I'm* not from Katan," the tall blonde stated, moving up to stand next to Dominor. Her gilded crystal wedding-torc matched his, though her choice in clothes didn't quite match most of the other garments being displayed. Rather than Katani corseted dresses or the odd trouser-skirts that seemed popular here, she had on a light green, sheath-like dress with long slits up either side. Her smile was somewhere between benign and smirking. "Thus I am not bound by its laws."

"Neither am I," said a woman who was her antithesis, short, plump, and curvy, with tight, light brown curls framing her face and shoulders. She was clad in a similar outfit to the one the tall one wore, though hers was a deep green.

The woman in aquamarine shrugged eloquently, as if to agree with their declarations of non-Katani origins. She did not, however, pause more than a moment in her reading in order to do so. The casual way she sat on the bench, ignoring most of the proceedings, was almost an insult. Consus wanted to groan, wondering how badly the manure had just hit the aeration charm with this revelation.

"Cousin! What are *you* doing here?"

Oh, the flying fecal matter . . .

Barol of Devries stepped out of formation, drawing everyone's attention to him, and to the woman at the center of his focus, the one who had giggled at the comment about marrying a wastebasket. Barol turned and faced Taurin with a half-smile quirking up one corner of his mouth. "Your Majesty, this is Alys of Devries, my missing cousin!"

"Seize her!" Finneg ordered. "Bring her here!"

"What?" she exclaimed as a couple of Katani soldiers shifted forward to do so. She craned her head over her shoulder, then looked up at the throne.

"Councilor, you overstep your authority," Saber stated coldly.

"Hardly," the duke snorted as the young woman was hauled up next to him. "First of all, now that her uncle is dead, she is a ward of the state—"

"A ward of the *state*?" Alys challenged, eyeing him as if he'd suddenly turned from nut brown to blanched white.

"You may not remember in your delicate condition, but you were declared mentally incompetent by a government-certified Healer and placed permanently in your uncle's care," Finneg reminded her bluntly.

She paled, then flushed, shoving off the hands of the guards. "*Mentally incompetent?*"

"Be silent, woman, or be silenced. As I was saying—"

Alys, normally shy, diffident Alys, lost her temper. "*Kai, lusai!*"

He instantly stiffened, armored shoulders back, chest out, face forward . . . though his eyes rolled sideways to try and keep her in sight. A strangled sound escaped him, but no actual words.

"What has this madwoman done to my Councilor?" King Taurin demanded as the guards re-seized her arms. He shifted closer to free Finneg from her spell, muttering a common countercharm; the duke slumped within moments, breathing deeply.

"*Madwoman?*" Alys retorted, skepticism raising her brows. "Which is the greater madness, a woman who defends her honor, or a man who bribes government officials to have her declared incompetent, just so she can be treated as chattel and sold to the highest bidder against her will? Let go of me!"

The book slapped shut, loud enough that the *bang* of the pages slapping together startled everyone. Rising in a single, smooth motion, the freckled redhead in aquamarine glared at the Katani guards. "Get your hands *off* my citizen!"

"Your what?" King Taurin asked, confused.

"You heard her! She said, let go of me!" Alys demanded.

They didn't comply fast enough. Impatient, Alys twisted and shoved, using some of the techniques she had been taught, and threw back both of the guards a few staggering steps, surprising them. Finneg grabbed her by the arm, clearly intending to restrain her where his guards had failed—no one quite saw what she did, but she did it quickly enough to whirl around, under his arm, and fling him over her hip . . . sending the startled duke sprawling on the floor. The woman on the dais smirked and sat back down again, opening her book and flipping through it to find her last reading point.

Dusting off her hands, Alys glared at Finneg, at the two guards, and stalked back off to the side. Then she halted and swung around, pointing at her cousin. "Not only do you dare to believe that I'm *mentally incompetent* on the word of the very same bastard who had been plaguing the Corvis brothers for the last three years—plagues that *you failed* to investigate and prevent—you bring *this* viper onto the island!"

"Cousin, you are overwrought—"

"*Kai, lusai!*" she snapped at Barol of Devries, halting her kinsman before he could touch her. He, too, assumed a stiff posture, forced to stare straight ahead, past her shoulder. "Didn't expect *that*, did you? Using the very same Obedience Hex *you* taught me, specifically for use on your father's pet pookrahs! Not to mention all the other beasts you and he were breeding together."

With Barol locked into stiff attention, he was unable to refute her charges. To be absolutely fair, the silently watching Consus felt *he* had to address them. Everyone else was too busy gaping at the unraveling of sanity in the room. "What proof have you of this? He has already testified under spell that he has no memory of anything his father ever did. Where is your proof of his complicity?"

"First of all, you can Truth Spell me to the Netherhells and back—I'd *love* the opportunity to spit on my uncle's festering soul," she retorted. "I know almost everything about the ill and outright evil deeds performed by Broger of Devries, and probably half of what his son, here, has done over the years. I was bound as his virtual slave by several highly illegal spells, until I found a way to neutralize them and escape. And yes, I came *here*, because the Corvis brothers were the only ones I knew I could trust to keep me safe from my own uncle.

"Second of all, faking a lack of memory is one of the oldest tricks in Barol and his father's book. He simply removed all the pertinent memories and temporarily locked them in a Memory Stone."

"A *Memory Stone*?" Queen Samille asked, confused. From the blank looks of several of the other Councilors, they hadn't heard of the term, either.

"It's an Artifact that looks like an egg carved from a piece of opal. It won't be very big, not much larger than your littlest fingernail, but it can hold quite a lot." That came from the youngest of the Corvis brothers, Morganen. Consus had wondered where the younger mage was—now he knew. He was standing behind the procession of government officials. In fact, all of the brothers were scattered around the room, flanking them.

Alys nodded, confirming it. "My unbeloved cousin will either be carrying it on him, or he'll have it hidden somewhere around his quarters—probably in plain sight in a jewelry box. Shatter the gem, and the memories will come rushing back into him. Then you can cast all the truth-enforcing charms you want on him, and they'll work."

"Majesty," Councilor Pover stated, "I can see a ring on his little finger from here. It does seem to be set with an opal of something close to the indicated size."

"How do we know you're not just trying to damage a valuable gemstone out of spite . . . or instability?" the King of Katan challenged her. "Opals only come from Shattered Aiar, far to the north. If we break that thing, and it's not what you claim it to be, then you'll have made us smash something extremely valuable and hard to replace."

"Oh, please," the platinum-haired woman on the other side of the room snorted. "If you want assurance that we can *afford* to replace the damned thing if it's not what she says it is, *I'll* pay for it myself. Pound for pound, in rainbow pearls!"

Taurin eyed her skeptically. "*You* own a rainbow pearl? Who in Jinga's Name do you think you are?"

"Allow me to introduce my wife," Dominor interjected. "Councilors, Your Majesties, this is the Lady Serina Avadan, formerly the Guardian of Koral-tai in Natallia, and daughter of the Inoma of the Moonlands . . . which makes her a princess, as her mother is the equivalent of a queen in that legendary land. A land that also happens to be the source-point for the equally legendary rainbow pearls."

A *crunch* sound made everyone flick their heads back to the eastern side of the large chamber. Alys lifted her foot from the floor, revealing the ring she had removed from her cousin's finger and smashed while the others were distracted. As she did so, a wisp of multicolored light rose from the shattered stone. It hovered in midair for a moment, then darted up into Barol's head, making him jerk a little, spasming, despite the way her spell still held him tightly at attention.

"Jinga's Tits—guards, clap him in spell-chains!" Finneg ordered, on his feet once again. He faced her, a muscle twitching in his jaw. "I . . . apologize . . . for doubting your sanity. However . . . you *are* on Nightfall, as are the other three of you ladies, and while *you* may not be mentally incompetent, the penalty for real women existing on this island is death. Guards—"

"*Enough!*"

The angry shout made even the Katani soldiers fitting rune-carved cuffs onto Barol's hands jump, as did the second slamming shut of the book in the redheaded woman's hands. Bounding up from her seat with more anger than grace this time, she slapped the book on the bright blue green bench cushion, stalked off the dais, and walked up to Finneg. He was a few inches taller than she, but she glared up at him as if his armor and his status didn't matter, pinning him with a furious aquamarine glare.

"You have no authority on this island to order *anyone's* arrest. If you attempt to usurp that authority again, or speak in *any* way that is disrespectful of Nightfall, I will have you bound, gagged, and tossed into the dungeons! Do I make myself *clear*?"

Finneg swayed, flinching back from her snapped words. He started to sway forward, to draw in a breath and argue, but swayed back quickly as she poked at him with a sharp finger.

"It was bad enough when you *kidnapped* and interrogated a child—a *child*!" She flipped her hand, stalking away from him. "But, I will admit he has been safely recovered, and restitution for *that* particular crime has already been made, so we can be generous and forgiving." Turning crisply, she was in front of the broad throne once again. Dropping back onto the bench, she scooped up the book. "I would suggest you be very careful how you tread, from here on out. *All* of you. I will not be so *tolerant* a third time, should you seek to transgress."

Flipping open the pages of the book, she sorted through them, put one foot up again, and settled back into the corner of the bench seat to continue her reading.

"I would also suggest, ladies and gentlemen, that you concentrate on your original business for coming here," she added calmly, if pointedly. "Restitution for the kidnapping of a child has cost you several enchanted mirrors, but then kidnapping a child is something we take *very* seriously. Restitution for the missing funds from the Corvis estate and the utter lack of *aid* from Katan, throughout the last three-plus years as well as most recently in the brothers' hour of need, is another matter. That, too, will cost you. Do not compound your folly, for it will only raise the interest that is already accruing."

"Who in the Gods' Names do you think you are?" King Taurin demanded.

Rolling her eyes, she looked down at him. Her leg dropped to the floor, her body levering upright on the bench, though this time she didn't rise. "Who am I? I am the Maiden to my husband's Sword. I am the living proof that you—the lot of you—*cannot* stop Prophecy. I am the woman at whose heel Disaster was foretold, a Disaster that came *and went* months ago. I am the one who listened to the plight of the Corvis brothers, how they had *repeatedly* asked the government of Katan for help in thwarting the madman who was plaguing them constantly with magical attacks meant to maim and kill them . . . and I am a witness to the Katani government *refusing*—and thus *failing*—to aid the brothers when the Mandarites came to the Isle several months ago, seeking to conquer this land in the name of their asinine, misogynistic prejudices. A level of idiocy I have only seen surpassed by *your* treatment of these brothers.

"Who am I?" Kelly demanded, sitting forward as she answered his challenge. "I am the woman who pointed out that the responsibility of a government is to protect and lead its citizens . . . even the ones in exile," she added bitingly, "and I am the one who pointed out that Katan has *neglected* to fulfill those responsibilities. To the point where you would clearly rather kidnap children and decree the slaughter of women who would travel here, than bow to the demands of what *your own Gods* have decreed Must Be.

"Who am I?" she asked, rising from the bench seat one more time. "I am the scion of the family Doyle, and beloved wife to Saber of Nightfall. I am the *first* person who gave a *damn* about these brothers, whom *you* condemned simply for the crime of *being born*.

"Who am I? In the Names of *all* the Gods of this world, I am Kelly, Sovereign Queen of this land!"

Casting the book at his feet with a skidding thump, Kelly lifted her chin, quoting from it as he and the others from the mainland gaped at her.

" 'When, in the course of action *or inaction* of a nation, it becomes self-evident to the people of a particular land that they *must* rise up and form a government of their own to survive and thrive, or perish under the weight of perils and unchecked anarchy thrust upon them, it is the *right* of the citizens of that land to select from among themselves a true and just leader to become their ruler.' Thus we, the citizens of Nightfall—a palpably neglected and clearly imperiled land—have done so in the face of your *willful* inaction," she pointed out literally, jabbing a finger in King Taurin's direction. "Page 242. Go ahead, look it up. There's nothing you can do to stop it—and everything you have already done to *start* it."

One of the guards picked up the book, offering it to his sovereign. He narrowed his eyes in a wary frown and opened the volume, flipping to the correct page. It took King Taurin only a moment to read the passage, before passing the book to his wife. She read it, frowned, and passed the book to Duke Finneg's outstretched hand.

"If you *have* Rung the Bell, there would be proof of it," King Taurin challenged her. "I see no proof."

"We haven't Rung the Bell yet, because the Council stranded the brothers with neither a sanctified bell nor a priest to bless one—and in doing so, you have deliberately hamstrung their spiritual well-being, injuring them further," Kelly added tartly. "That, too, is grounds for a secession from Katani rule—which should be on page 238. You are *bound* by that very crown you wear, King Taurin of Katan, to ensure that your people have just and reasonable means of expressing their worship of the Gods who are their Patron Deities. You didn't send them a holy servant once, let alone enough times out of the year to tend adequately to their spiritual needs!

"You and your predecessor willfully neglected this aspect of the

Corvis brothers' most basic, fundamental rights as Katani citizens. Rights which even an exiling cannot abrogate. You and your Councilors have set in motion the breaking away of Nightfall and the raising of a new kingdom. *You* have done this, so-called leaders of Katan."

Taurin reddened beneath his tan. "This act of rebellion is utterly illegal, and I will have *you* bound, gagged, and—"

"I call upon my right, as an unjustly treated inhabitant of this land, to Ring the Bell!" Kelly asserted loudly, formally, cutting off King Taurin mid-tirade. "Bring forth a Sacred Bell, one from the very land which has neglected us, as it is written by the laws of Katan, and the laws of all lands. Let the God Jinga and the Goddess Kata hear these allegations, that They may answer these accusations according to the very Laws They have mandated for all of Katan. Let our voices be heard by *all* the Gods in Heaven—*bring forth a Sacred Bell!*"

Her words echoed off the balconies, dying down into silence. Nobody moved for a long moment. Consus finally lifted his hand to his mouth, coughing delicately behind it. "We don't *have* a Sacred Bell to . . ."

A hand nudged him on the shoulder. It belonged to Lady Apista, Councilor for the Temples of Katan. Her fingers were wrapped around a handbell, her littlest finger holding the clapper silent. She jiggled her hand to make sure everyone saw what she held; the bell made no sound, but it was blatant what she was offering. She shifted forward, stepping around her king; it was clear from the look on Taurin's face that he wanted to stop her, but knew he couldn't.

"Oh, Jinga's Bollocks!" Duke Finneg snapped, first glaring at his fellow Councilor, then at Kelly and the brothers who were visible. "Fine. You want to play it that way? Well, there *is* something we can do to stop you—and it's *in* the book. Page 247. I challenge you for the right to claim the leadership of this land!"

"I *accept* your challenge," Kelly shot back.

"What? Kelly, no!" Saber countered, whipping around to look at her.

"Too late," Finneg snapped. "She's accepted! Prepare your magics, woman—"

"*Wrong.*" The hard word cut him off. Kelly nodded at the tome in his hands. "According to that very book, the challenger may give the challenge and state a time for it to take place. The challenged may accept or refuse. If he or she refuses, the Bell cannot be Rung for a year and a day. But if the challenged party accepts—which I have done—it is the *challenged* who states what the weaponry will be for the contest.

"Name your time for this challenge, Duke Finneg, Councilor of Conflict Resolution, and I will name its form," she ordered him.

"Right here, right now!" Finneg asserted. "Or are you afraid to face me?"

"Kelly, *no!*" Saber countered at the same time. "Name *me* as your champion—Jinga's Ass, name *Morganen!*"

Morganen slipped behind Dominor, grabbed Saber by the elbow, and whispered in his ear. The worried frown on the eldest brother's face shifted slowly into a look of incredulity.

Finneg paged quickly through the book. "I invoke the clause of . . . Natural Leadership! As is my right. No substitutes or champions may be named!"

"In return, *I* invoke the clause of Terms of Victory, as is my counter-right," Kelly stated quickly.

The duke's tightly triumphant smile faded a little. Those two choices were optional, unlike the first two clauses . . . but like them, if one person chose one, the other choice defaulted to the other person in the challenge. By claiming the right to refuse either side a champion, he had just given up the say as to whatever act would end their bout. It had to be a decisive victory, but that could be anything.

Up to and including death.

Kelly glanced quickly at Saber. His hand had risen to cover his mouth, his elbow supported by his other arm. His steel-gray eyes were wide but inscrutable, as Morganen finished whispering whatever it was he had to say. For a moment more, he stayed that way, then shrugged and dropped his hands.

"As you wish," Saber said, his tone light but fatalistic. He even shrugged and retreated to the bench, seating himself seemingly with no further concern. Which confused everyone else in the room—save for maybe Morganen—and not just his freckled wife. She turned to Morg with a questioning gaze, and he quirked up one corner of his mouth, then looked at the Councilor of Conflict Resolution. Realization dawned in her aqua eyes, and an answering smirk curled up the corner of her own lips.

"Name your terms and the weapons to be used, woman," Duke Finneg prodded her, drawing Kelly's attention back to him. "And make your prayers to the Gods. As soon as the rules are set, we will begin."

Gathering her wits with a double-blink, she addressed the Councilor. "The form of weaponry shall be unarmed, unarmored, magic-less combat. Nothing is to be used but what our bare hands, bare feet, and physical bodies can do. Without protective armor, though for decency's sake, we may retain our clothes. No weapons of any other kind, and *no* magic."

Duke Finneg snorted skeptically. "No magic? You call *that* a test of leadership?"

"A true leader can lead without any tools or props," Evanor stated, speaking before Kelly could. Having spent many hours working beside her since her arrival months ago, sewing and cleaning, cooking and gardening, he could guess the point she was trying to make. Ev studied the dark-skinned Councilor. "If your hands were to be bound in the same sort of antimagical cuffs that were slapped on Cousin Barol over there, if you were stripped of all of your weapons and armor, Your Grace, and reduced to the bare state of a prisoner . . . would you still be able to defend your king?"

"No weapons, no armor, no shoes . . . and *no magic*," Kelly repeated, stressing that last part. "Either agree to bare-handed, physical combat, or withdraw your challenge. Any breaking of these terms will be declared a forfeit, with your name dishonored and your self banned from this land for two years and two days, according to your own laws.

"Either way, if you withdraw or if you cheat, we'll still Ring the Bell. As is our right."

"*Sazal, sazal, sa kouda! Sazala!*" Opening his arms as he chanted, the Councilor for Conflict Resolution enchanted his boiled-leather armor. Straps wriggled free of their buckles, pieces floated off, and the lot stacked itself at his side. He had to stoop to unlace his boots, since the spell hadn't removed them, but the dark-skinned man managed to look graceful even while balancing on one foot and tugging on the other. "I don't cheat. I don't have to. *I* don't lose. Prepare to meet the Gods!"

"You haven't heard the Terms of Victory, yet," Kelly countered smoothly, folding her arms across her chest. "Evanor of Nightfall is correct. A leader must be able to lead under all circumstances. He or she must be able to win a fight even when his or her normal resources have been stripped away. But a leader also needs to understand the value of the resources still at hand. That includes preserving the lives of those around him or her . . . even if that life is currently an enemy. An enemy always carries the potential of becoming an ally.

"So the Terms of Victory will be exactly this, no less and no more: We fight to the yield."

Finneg wasn't the only one giving her a puzzled look.

"That means we do *not* attempt to kill each other," she enlightened him. "It also means we do not attempt to injure each other. No maiming, no broken bones, no shattered joints, and no knocking the other person unconscious. *To the yield.* One of us must say 'I yield,' for the other to win the bout . . . and by this, I mean no spells may be used that would prevent either of us from speaking that yield. Nor biting out our own tongues, nor swallowing them. *That* would be cheating."

"As I said, *I* don't cheat," Finneg retorted, lifting his chin. Turning, clad in a quilted, sweat-stained tunic and worn trousers, he swept one arm out. "Clear a space for us to fight," he ordered his fellow Councilors, before glancing back at Kelly again. "*My* terms are that we alone fight . . . to the *yield* . . . here and now. Just you and I. Interference from anyone else will not be tolerated."

Dropping back onto the bench, Kelly tugged off her boots and socks, while the Councilors cleared out a space roughly twenty feet in diameter. "No one on *my* side will interfere. They have faith in me and will not be disappointed when I win."

"When *I* win," Finneg countered, tugging off his own socks, "I will take command of this island, disband this farce of an attempt at independence, and have *you* bound and gagged."

"Bring it on!" Kelly snapped, bounding to her bared feet on the dais.

That paused her opponent out of confusion. "Bring *what* on, where?"

Rolling her aquamarine eyes, Kelly stepped down onto the stone and velvet of the floor. Some days, Ultra Tongue just didn't manage to translate certain colloquialisms. ". . . Just prepare to eat dirt, okay?"

Finneg arched one of his black brows, backing up to give her room to enter the cleared section of floor. "We're inside where there's no dirt. But if you like, I'll toss you out into the gardens, where I'm sure you'll be as happy as a pig wallowing in its sty."

She flashed him a grin. "I'm glad to see you approve of my high standards in housekeeping—oh, any time you're ready to lose, you may begin."

That earned her a smirk. "I *cannot* lose. The Gods themselves de-creed it!" Lunging, he grabbed at her. She dodged, but he managed to snag her wrist, striking faster than anticipated. "Yield!"

A whirling twist allowed her to yank her arm out of his grasp, levering it free. He followed her—which meant following right into her back-kick. Finneg grunted and staggered back, rubbing at his thigh. She advanced on him, and he blocked her darting hands, re-turning a punch of his own. Side-stepping it, Kelly shoved him twice, first with her hand on his shoulder and an instant later with her foot on his hip. He almost went over, but recovered.

Another exchange had him backing her up almost to the dais be-fore she whirled around him, slipping out of being boxed in by the edge of the low platform.

"Oh, stop playing with him!" Serina ordered.

"Yeah, put him out of his misery!" Alys of Devries added.

"Don't you mean, out of *her* misery?" the petite Healer asked, moving up beside Evanor.

Finneg glared at them, shuffled close again, then jabbed at her rapidly, trying to punch and grapple through her defenses. Some-how, the freckled woman managed to block each blow with slapping moves of her hands and a few knee-lifts when he tried to kick her, too. They broke apart after a few more moments, each eyeing the other, gauging what they had just learned about each other. The duke smirked.

"Had enough yet?" he challenged her, not even breathing hard.

Kelly smirked. She was breathing deeply, herself, but evenly. "Nope."

"Good!" He skipped forward, feinted, and struck hard and fast—and found his limbs inexplicably bound by an entangling block of her own arms. A short, rapid recalculation pause, and he pulled back—and leaped back in, kicking low, then punching high, expect-ing her to leap over his leg.

Instead, she wrenched herself into a flip. She wasn't effortless at it; she spotted herself with one hand, collapsing into a tumble that rolled her over her shoulder, tumbled down her spine, and thrust her body upward, this time with another back-kick. It was an awkward move, but her heel struck him on the shoulder, as he tried to grab her.

He grunted, but his fingers snagged her overskirt by its long back hem. Being silk, it didn't rip—even the ties lacing it in place were made from silk. Which meant it yanked her back by her stom-ach. Stumbling, she found herself hauled within the gloating duke's reach.

"Yield, woman!"

Collapsing, Kelly dropped, twisted under his arm, rose up as she completed her spin, and did two things simultaneously—she thrust with her right leg, kicking his legs out from under him, and swooped her right arm around under his chin, knocking him back as hard as she could. Though it wrenched muscles from her arm to her groin, and especially her side, she changed the kick to a knee lift . . . which altered the whole move into a flip, not merely a double shove.

Finneg, literally spun head over heels, landed on his face with an audible, meaty *thud*. Several Councilors flinched, as did a few of the Corvis brothers. Alys and the other two Nightfall ladies cheered, throwing up their hands. Not finished, Kelly grabbed her opponent by his arm—for it was still tangled in the hem of her skirt—spun over his body, and twisted the limb in her grasp.

Her left foot stomped down fast—though not hard—and pinned his cheek to the floor. It wasn't in quite the same spot that she had once pinned Dominor, nor was the donjon floor anywhere as dirty as it had been back in the first week of her arrival on this world, but the position Duke Finneg was now trapped in was just as inescapable as the one the thirdborn brother had suffered all those months ago. Struggling to control her breathing, since her ribs were definitely strained, Kelly shook her hair back from her face, studying her fallen foe.

"*You* yield."

"Never!" he managed, though her heel was pressing into his jaw, making it hard for him to talk.

"Never is a long time," Kelly retorted. "I could hold this position all day, you know."

"I'll never yield to you!" Finneg growled.

She twisted his arm a little more, but he didn't even gasp. Irked, Kelly sought a way to make him give up the fight without having to dislocate his arm . . . which was against her own choice of victory conditions. She couldn't hold him forever; eventually, she would get hungry, thirsty, and . . .

Wincing in sympathy even as a chuckle escaped from deep within her chest, Kelly shook her head slowly. Ruefully. "You really *should* yield, Councilor. I *could* hold you in this position all day, quite easily. You have no leverage to get yourself free, trapped like this. But I did have a nice, *big* mug of fresh-squeezed juice with my breakfast. And while I could hold *you* all day, I'm afraid my bladder wouldn't be—"

"*I yield!*"

The squeaked shout that escaped him probably hadn't been that high in pitch since puberty. Smirking, Kelly released him, untangling his fingers from the hem of her skirt so she could step back. From the darkened hue of his face, he was blushing furiously at such an ignoble, ignominious method of defeat. He shoved to his feet, glaring at his fellow Councilors, daring them to say one word, to snerk one snickering laugh about his defeat.

Kelly lifted her hand, quelling the others with a hard stare of her own. "Do not mock him, *any* of you. He was a worthy opponent. Honor him for that . . . and if you would not, then think carefully about what *you* would have chosen to do, in his place."

"This changes nothing," King Taurin dismissed brusquely, shifting to step between her and the dais, when she moved to return to it. "You don't have the right to break away fr—"

"I don't have the *right*?" Kelly interrupted, incredulous. Jabbing a hand at the duke, who was dusting himself off, she continued, indignant. "I was informed today that His Grace, here, was Prophesied to *not* be defeated by any man, yet that he was also to learn humility at the heel of a true leader. Here I stand, *not* a man the last time I checked down my blouse, having just had him yield after literally being under my heel!

"There is more going on here, Your Majesty, than the *whims* of a government. The Gods of this world have *quite* clearly decreed a place for me, here in this universe, and it is that of a true leader. If there *were* anyone who could defeat me, you'd think someone would have mentioned that by now, as well!"

"I accept your challenge!"

Kelly's wasn't the only head snapping to the side, fast enough to cause whiplash in more than a few necks. They had all forgotten about Barol of Devries. It was true that Alys had locked him into the rigidity of the Obedience Hex. But the Katani soldiers had locked antimagic cuffs onto his wrists. Enough time had passed to allow his cousin's spell to drain into the cuffs, neutralizing it as well as his own magics.

"Swords, to the death!" the young mage snapped, charging her. "*Pyratis!*"

A longsword popped into Barol's hand. Kelly yelped and dove out of the way. Everyone else scattered. She heard Saber and his brothers shouting words, saw more magically summoned blades appearing out of the corner of her eye as she tumbled to her feet just in time to dodge another lethal swing—and remembered her wedding gift from her husband, her own enchanted blade.

"Son of Sting!" Barely having enough time to reverse her grip, she parried the next slash with her summoned dagger, skipping back farther from the dais. He was driving her back, away from the others; with that much longer blade of his, Kelly couldn't fence properly with him. Nor could she get close enough to be inside that long sword's effective range, where her much shorter dagger would have the advantage. He was too quick with the blade, and she was far more familiar with weaponless fighting than this hack-and-slash stuff.

"Kelly! *Name* me!"

It took her two more wincing, nearly lethal clashes of steel on steel to realize what he meant. "Saber—my champion!"

Barol whirled to confront the eldest of his cousins. In a furious swirl of steel, Saber knocked his opponent's blade aside and rammed the tip of his own longsword through the younger mage's gut. It pierced the far side of his body with a grunted shove from the older man.

"Never threaten my wife! Especially not with the blade *I gave you!"*

An upward yank cut deeper into his cousin's body. Lifting his foot to Barol's hip, Saber jerked his scarlet-streaked blade free. Blood welled up and spilled over; Barol dropped with a wet gurgle to the floor. A burbling exhale was followed by stillness and dulled, unfocused gray eyes.

Kelly wasn't the only one who winced and looked away. Swallowing hard, she looked at the others. Shock, dismay, and disbelief filled many faces, Councilor and brother alike. Mutterings could be heard about how shameful it was for kin to attack kin, even in a situation like this. Mariel had hidden her face in Evanor's shoulder, her Healer's sensibilities overwhelmed by the violence and death. Some of the Councilors, however, bore expressions twisted with outrage at the slaughter, including the King of Katan.

Alys gasped, diverting their attention. Scrabbling at her neckline, the younger woman reached inside her corseted blouse. A moment later, she pulled out something black, flat, and diamond-shaped. She brushed it between her thumb and fingertips, and bits of it crumbled into dust. "I'm free . . . I'm free. I'm finally free!"

Only the Nightfall contingent knew what she meant, knowing that her late uncle had tied her magics into her bloodline so that all of her powers—and those of the eight brothers—would drain into her cousin upon their deaths. Broger of Devries had originally intended to kill the brothers and her, then kill his own son, collecting all of the resulting compounded energies for himself. That blackened diamond had once been a heavily enchanted piece of silver, magically welded to her flesh to neutralize all of the spells Broger had bound into his niece, trapping her at his side. Now she was free of all of it, every last snip of her uncle's enchantments.

"Enough!" King Taurin growled, drawing in a breath to yell at the lot of them. "First you violate the laws against women arriving on this island, which was foretold to bring down a Disaster, then you withhold the resources that are rightfully ours, like highway robbers. You try to thieve away a part of our sovereign kingdom, and now you slaughter one of our nobles—whether or not he may have been a criminal in the end—"

"Yes, *enough*," Kelly retorted, pushing aside her horror at having seen death firsthand. Later, she would deal with her feelings and memories. Right now, she had more important things to manage. She stalked forward, tossing her summons-enchanted dagger from her right hand to her left. Undoubtedly Barol had managed to summon his sword the same way she had summoned her dagger; the magic was in the *blade*, not the person. "You come here, threatening, bullying, *stealing*, and utterly failing to *be* a government to the people on this island, and *you* say you've had *enough*?"

Snatching the bell out of the hands of the lady-mage still holding it, Kelly raised it high, glaring at her royal counterpart . . . and snapped down her arm.

"I Summon Jinga!" CLANG. "I Summon Kata!" CLANG. "I Summon *all* the Gods and Goddesses of *all* the lands!" CLANG

CLANG! "By the full and free will of the people who live within the boundaries of this land, called Nightfall Isle, and by the right those people have granted *me* to govern it, I demand the Gods prove Their Approval and Patronage of an Independent Kingdom of Nightfall!"

CLANG *CLANG* **CLAAAANG!**

The final, hard ringing of the bell in her hand deepened abruptly. It shouldn't have. It was just a handbell, no bigger than a clenched fist, but in Kelly's hand, the sound of the bell deepened, growing louder and more vibrant, like the mounting brilliance of a rising sun. If it hadn't been such a pure tone, everyone would have been forced to clap their hands over their ears, but it wasn't unpleasant. It was powerful. Then it faded, just . . . faded, whispering away within a matter of heartbeats.

But the glow remained. And it came, not from the eastern windows, not from the morning sun, but from the northwest corner of the octagonal, broad chamber. From behind King Taurin. Slowly, warily, he turned, glancing over his shoulder. A step to the side permitted Kelly to look as well.

The source of the glow wasn't the sun. Nor was it the sun's reflection. Nor was it a lightglobe, nor a torch, nor a candle, nor even the flashlight-spell on a cryslet. Instead, a golden circlet floated above the aquamarine-covered bench.

It was formed from several graceful, almost abstract lines swirling up and down in random little peaks. There was a dip just to either side of the center, before the metal swept up into a single, sharp point. A few moments were required before the witnesses in the donjon hall realized the thick filigree actually formed the silhouette of mountains. Two mountain ranges, to be precise, with a dip for a certain saddle-back pass. The sharp peak in the center of that abstract pass no doubt represented the very palace in which they stood.

The King of Katan and his Councilors apparently knew when they were defeated. Still, Taurin turned back to Kelly, a challenge of a different sort in his eyes. "Well. It seems even the Gods agree that you should be independent. Or rather, should have the right to *try* for independence.

"Name your Patron Deity, and we of Katan will release this island to its fate."

Kelly winced. Taurin arched one brown brow.

"Surely you can name your Patron Deity, right here, right now?"

"We're *working* on it," the freckled outworlder muttered. "We have a year and a day, by your own laws. There's nothing that says we can't wait for a full year before making the announcement—either way," Kelly continued briskly, "Nightfall is no longer under your jurisdiction."

"*Only* for a year and a day, if you cannot manifest a Patron," Finneg warned her, joining his sovereign. "And if you cannot . . . your head is *mine*. The Prophesied Disaster will be *yours* . . . and Katan *will* fail to aid you!"

"Oh, please. The Disaster foretold in the first verse of that old Song came and went *months* ago," Kelly snorted. Then gave him a speculative, mocking look. "Unless you refer to *your* personal Disaster, which indeed came at my heel just now?"

The duke flinched at the unwelcome reminder.

"Relax, Your Grace. You did what you had to do, just as I did what I had to do," she countered. "We each were compelled by our loyalty to our own people. Now, if the lot of you will *promise* to play nice, to not block the migration of selected people to this island—and we *don't* want a flood of people who aren't willing to put in hard work to make this island livable and profitable again," Kelly added in warning, "—and to be polite neighbors, I'm willing to consider a peace agreement between our two lands, plus the potential for trade agreements as well."

"*Trade* agreements?" King Taurin repeated, taken aback.

"Of course. It would be disadvantageous for the merchants of Katan to suffer from high import taxes . . . which we would have to impose in order to start filling our coffers, in anticipation of fulfilling the needs of our first annual budget," Kelly stated. Then waved her hand dismissively. "But that's mostly a discussion for my Exchequer and your Councilor of whatever the appropriate office or department may be."

"What could you possibly have that *we* could want?" the King of

Katan scoffed. "Even the salt and algae blocks can be ignored in favor of mainland goods."

"*We* have trade with Natallia, to the far east," Kelly enlightened him. "And a means of shipping goods to and from that land that bypasses the usual risks of trying to sail ships through their war-torn waters."

"We also have trade contacts within the Moonlands," Dominor stated from behind Taurin. "Which is the source of the *myjiin* powder used to create the Ultra Tongue potion."

"Ultra Tongue is just one of the advantages a potential citizen of Nightfall can earn, if they're willing to put in enough effort at making the rest of this island inhabitable," Morganen added. "Even if you won't trade goods with us, word will get out regarding the advantages of Nightfall citizenship, and we'll still have people trying to come here. You cannot postpone the inevitable."

"Plus a loyal customer base. We're still some of the most powerful mages in this corner of the world," Saber said; he still held his sword, but had used a cantrip on it to clean the blade. "People will still be wanting their summoning-enspelled swords, and their lightglobes, custom enchantments . . . Artifacts made on Nightfall will be all the more popular as a commodity, now that we've Rung the Bell and are seeking our independence."

"Call it the lure of the exotic, or the lure of the infamous," Kelly finished. "Heck—call it scrambled eggs, if you like! It is our *Destiny*. There is nothing that you can do to stop it."

"We can stop people from coming here," Finneg retorted. "Without enough settlers on this island to strengthen and manifest a Patron, you'll only have a year and a day of independence."

"Are you *trying* to make me pity you?" Kelly asked him bluntly. "Because if you are, it's working. You've *lost*. Give in gracefully, while you still have your dignity left! We have more ways of importing people than you have of blockading us, from more lands than just Katan . . . and you are forbidden *by law* to go to war with us, for a full year and a day, starting today. According to that book of Katani law and protocol, your own God and Goddess would rise up and paddle your butt, if you tried!"

Consus cleared his throat, drawing attention to himself, hopefully for one last time. "Milords, miladies, Majesties . . . I suggest we withdraw peacefully and refrain from making further fools of ourselves? Too many Destinies have woven themselves together this day for us to even begin to unravel. The Song of the Sons of Destiny, Duke Finneg's own Prophecy . . . I suspect Councilor Thannig's department will have months' worth of analysis to perform on what has happened here, today."

King Taurin gave his Councilor of Sea Commerce a dirty look, but said nothing in protest, allowing Lord Consus to continue.

"We *cannot* stop what has happened, nor can we stop what will come, even if we wanted. If this island is Destined to become a nation, then no amount of blockades or threats can stop it. As your Councilor for Sea Commerce," the middle-aged mage added pointedly, "I would strongly advise *against* blockading this island. It would *not* be profitable . . . and as Your Majesty pointed out not that long ago, the yearly budget is almost upon us. If we cooperate, we'll have that much more income from trade sales and import-export taxes with this place. If we do not . . . we will have that much *less* money to apportion among our departments."

More than one of his fellow Councilors groaned under their breaths at the reminder. A muscle worked in Taurin's jaw, then the King of Katan sighed roughly. "*Fine*. We won't discourage the settlement of this island, or its fair and reasonable trade. But neither will we *encourage* it. You want to stand on your own two feet? Fine. Stand or fall on your own two feet. We're leaving."

"You forgot something." The voice belonged to Alys. The curly-haired ex-Katani woman nodded at the body of her cousin. "Take his body back with you, and run it through a full disenchantment, then bury it where you will."

"*And* you will pick out a much more suitable steward for both the Corvis *and* the Devries estates," Saber instructed the Council. "That steward will send three-fifths of its net profits to us. As we are no longer citizens of Katan, we are no longer in exile . . . but we are still landowners by inheritance. Foreign landowners are still entitled to sixty percent of the net profits of an estate if they do not reside within the Empire's borders. And you'll leave behind an accounting of all that was due to us during our exile and a down payment on the missing funds, if you don't have the full amount. Which you were supposed to discover before contacting us again."

Taurin wasn't the only one to redden with outrage at the idea.

"I think it's best if you leave now," Kelly offered with a wry wrinkle of her freckled nose. "Before the others come up with even more nitpicky details they've been wanting to have a word with you about over the last three years. We wouldn't want to tax you with too many grievances all at once. It makes it all the more difficult to consider friendly negotiations later on. Thank you for coming to Nightfall. It's been enlightening," she added politely. "One of the brothers will show you back out of the palace and down to the dock—Morganen, would you care to do the honors? Don't hesitate to assist them as they leave, should they need it."

"I'll gladly show them to their ship," the youngest of the brothers agreed. "Milords, miladies, back that way, if you please . . ."

Not really that pleased, the Councilors complied, re-forming their original procession. A handful of their escort guards bundled up the body of Barol of Devries, one of them even going so far as to scrub the blood off the flagstones before following the retreating Councilors. This time, the view painted along the eastern corridor was that of a wheat field in the sun, rippling in golden waves under the effects of an unfelt wind.

Only when they had vanished from sight did Kelly exhale and slouch. "Well. *That* was exciting . . . and I think I'll have a nervous breakdown, now. If nobody minds?"

"Get in line, Your Majesty," Mariel quipped. "I'm still shaking inside from Mikor's little escapade, myself, never mind all the rest of it!"

"*Little* escapade, Jinga's Sweet . . . Face," Evanor muttered, amending his words when Mariel glanced up at him quickly, still tucked into the curve of his arm, her own wrapped around his waist beneath the neck of his lute. "He's in a *lot* of trouble for leaving the palace like that."

"Make sure you *explain* why he's in trouble, Brother. Do not just yell at him for his wrongs," Rydan quietly stated, recalling his brothers' attention to his presence. He looked at Kelly next, ignoring the others. "If you have no further use for my services, Your Majesty, it is now well past my bedtime, and I would prefer to retire before I have to endure any more headaches."

"Goodnight, Rydan," Kelly told him. "And thank you for your help. Thank *all* of you."

"Don't thank us just yet," Serina warned lightly. "Becoming a new nation is the most complex calculation one could possibly attempt. There's still a very long way to go, not to mention finding a suitable Patron Deity."

"Well, I'm thanking you for now," Kelly amended. "And I'll still thank you all later. Trevan, go keep an eye on the Council, along with Morg. I want the two of you to make sure they leave the island. Mikor can be let out of his room once they're on board their ship. In the meantime, Mariel, I seem to have pulled a few muscles, making that fellow 'eat dirt'—and will someone *please* tell me what I'm supposed to do with a glowing crown that's floating smack-dab in the middle of the air over my throne-bench? Anybody . . . ?"

TWENTY

・ЭЄ・

"A re you all right?" Evanor asked Mariel softly, when she had finished humming over Kelly's side and was ready to go back and check on her son. His future next-son. He had set his lute aside since it wasn't needed anymore, and was waiting only for her to be finished so that he could escort her back to Mikor and the lecture that awaited the boy.

"I will be," Mariel sighed, grateful for his presence. She slid her arm around his waist, matching the arm he cupped around her shoulders. Evanor checked his longer stride to match hers, allowing them to walk comfortably side by side as they headed down the southern corridor, and she loved him for the courtesy of it. "I learned *tai*-fighting so that I could defend myself and keep in good enough shape to chase after my son, but I'm not a violent-minded sort. I'm a Healer. I fix people. I don't like seeing them being broken . . . or being destroyed, however necessary."

"I wouldn't say that Saber likes killing, though he does like knowing he's capable of defending those he loves, if he must. But he does have the strength of will to survive what it does to a person,"

Ev offered. "Today, it was necessary for him. Better him, I think, than Kelly. She *could* have done it. She has that strength within her . . . but . . ."

"It would've changed her," Mariel finished for him. "I knew my husband when we were both young, before he was touched by Natua to be one of Her Seers. After his first Prophecy resulted in a death . . . he agonized over it, and something in his gaze had changed, even after he had accepted it. But the Goddess chooses, and mere mortals obey."

"Exactly. There's enough of sorrow and grief in our outworlder Queen's eyes, enough loss from what she suffered in her previous life," Evanor agreed, releasing her so that she could mount the spiral steps of the staircase at the fork in the southern wing. "Now, about the sorrow and grief your son caused . . ."

"*Our* son," Mariel corrected him gently, turning to face him when she had mounted the first step. That put their heads closer, though he was still a little taller than her. The corner of her mouth curled up. "You've been researching marriage customs. Eventually, you'll need help in putting theory to practice, and I'm presuming that means you'll be marrying me."

"I do have some sort of wedding in mind," Evanor agreed, stepping close enough to clasp his arms lightly around her waist. "And then afterward, a life filled with a few scattered sorrows, a rare sprinkling of excitement, and a surfeit of domestic contentment, seasoned now and then with bits of bliss. All of it with you and me living together as husband and wife. And some half-siblings for Mikor to alternately tease, torment, defend, and play with, as any good sibling should."

Mariel, her hands in the act of lacing together behind his neck, pulled back a little with a dubious look. "You don't predict a life full of nothing but loving bliss?"

That made Ev chuckle. "With your honorary sister and my own twin as examples of the argumentative side of relationships? They make debate an art form, when they go at it. Saber and Kelly, too. Wolfer and Alys sometimes argue, but not nearly as often as the others. You and I are of their ilk, the calmer, quieter types . . . but *calmer* isn't the same as *calm*. Complete calm is boring. *You* are far from boring. And your . . . *our* son is even farther."

It was her turn to chuckle. "Have you finally noticed that?" Her mirth faded, and her nose wrinkled. Hazel eyes met brown. "He deserves to be punished for leaving the palace compound without telling one of us where he was going, and for going down the western road, and for being anywhere near the dock, which he was told he couldn't approach if there were ships in the harbor. But . . . he has gone through a bit of a fright."

"Mariel, he knows better. Adding a lecture, a grounding, and some distasteful chores on top of his fright will teach him to *think* his actions through, and pick a more responsible course. I was a boy like him, at one time. He probably had some reason for doing what he did that he *thinks* was justifiable, and we should listen to his explanation, but it was still the wrong thing to do. He needs to learn that actions have consequences. Privileges have responsibilities. He needs—"

Eyes gleaming, Mariel interrupted him gently, touching his mouth with the fingers of one hand. "I love you. And I think you'll make a fine father."

"Provided I keep my rare temper in check," Evanor mumbled against her fingertips, recalling how angry he had been just a short while before, once Rydan had somehow transported them to the top of the road.

"*You* have a temper?" Mariel challenged him, tipping her curly head in skepticism.

Evanor nodded, dislodging her hand. "When my loved ones foolishly endanger themselves, it seems I do. I much prefer being mild-mannered and civilized, though . . . which means instructing Mikor on how to behave in a civilized manner, so that his unthinking actions don't cause me to become uncivilized."

"And what sort of a reprimand would you give him?" Mariel asked, curious. "You mentioned a grounding. For how long?"

"A month."

"A full turning of Brother Moon?" she wanted to confirm. "Isn't that a bit harsh? I'd give him two weeks, myself. One for slipping out without accompaniment, and another for going to the west side of the island."

"Because he slipped out of the compound without permission," Evanor reminded her, "I agree with your reasons for the first two weeks. But in the course of rescuing him, Rydan and I ended up smashing roughly a score of the Department of Conflict Resolution's mirror-Gates. On the one hand, that cut down on the potential threat of an invasion of Katani soldiers. On the other hand, the Council is *not* going to forget or forgive such a costly destruction anytime soon.

"Since we won't know what the fallout from that will be for months, maybe not even for a few years, I wouldn't assign Mikor a truly harsh punishment. Like grounding him until he's sixteen," Ev stated dryly. "But he does need to be punished. Someone also could have been hurt during the rescue. Whether it was a Nightfaller or a Katani doesn't matter; Mikor's actions precipitated the whole thing."

"I see what you mean, now. A month is a bit harsh, but . . . not that unfair, everything considered," Mariel conceded. She hesitated a moment, then eyed her beloved. "I think you should be the one to tell him he's grounded. He wants a next-father, and he needs a next-father. A good next-father doesn't flinch from disciplining his new child, if it becomes necessary. In this case, it is. And since I don't think you're the type who thinks a beating solves problems—"

"—It doesn't," Evanor quickly agreed. "It only teaches violence. My parents always explained our actions, their consequences, and why they were wrong. Mother's method of punishment was to have us make reparations if we could, doing dozens of chores instead of having time to play if we couldn't make amends, as well as confining us to the castle. And, of course, apologizing to everyone we wronged . . . and we dreaded seeing Father's disappointment. That's the kind of father I hope to be—one who leads by example, shames by disappointment, loves without hesitation, and teaches right from wrong."

She smiled. "I think you'll succeed, Evanor of Nightfall."

"Ev," he coaxed her, smiling. "I refuse to stand on formality with my wife-to-be."

"Ev," she agreed. Then gave him a mock-frown. "But if you call me anything but Mariel, I'll be very cross with you."

"What, I can't call you 'beloved,' or 'dearest,' or 'voice of the divine'?" Evanor quipped.

Rolling her eyes, Mariel sighed. "I meant, don't shorten my name. My aunt's name was Mari, and we never got along very well."

"Then how about I just call you 'mine'?" Ev compromised. And kissed her, right there in the stairwell, ensuring she couldn't deny it.

Trevan fluttered down out of the sky, landing in his human form next to his youngest brother. The gangplank was being lifted onto the ship, and the stout ropes were deftly being untied. Every overt sign stated the Council's ship was getting under way, headed back to the mainland.

"Amazing thing, the eyesight of a hawk," Trevan muttered to Morganen.

"Indeed?" Morg commented.

"I can see the smallest details, when I peer through them."

"Ah. One of these days, I'll take up shapeshifting myself," Morg agreed. "When I get around to it."

"Did you know it also helps to be able to read lips, sometimes?" Trev added.

"An admirable skill for a Lord Vizier and chief spy to possess," his youngest sibling professed.

"Exactly. His Majesty—who currently resides in that cabin over there," Trevan stated, nodding at the stern of the ship, "is trying to figure out how to balance the need to blockade the island with the need to garner revenue from it. He was only facing the window half the time, but I get the feeling Nightfall goods are going to be slapped with a hefty import tax, on the mainland."

"Then it's a good thing we've already discussed alternative routes of trade with the good Captain Thorist," Morg returned. "I believe Captain Reganon's ship is the next one due into port. I'll have to remind Saber to have him discuss the new, formally independent status of Nightfall and the profits to be made in circumventing the usual channels for Nightfall-made goods—ah, here comes the King of Katan now."

Trevan squinted at the man moving up to the railing nearest the docks, his dark hair ruffling in the breeze, and sniffed disdainfully. "*Our* sovereign is cuter . . ."

Morg burst into laughter at that.

King Taurin heard it and thought it was for something else, given the way he projected his words at the two brothers on the dock, standing next to four metal chests filled with the monies they had been due all along. The last of the lines were being unlashed, but it seemed the ruler of Katan had to have one final word. "Laughing at our presence will not make us more amenable when it comes time to negotiate what you will be allowed to trade . . . and who will be allowed to visit."

Trevan made a disgusted noise. Morganen folded his arms across his chest. The ship was slowly beginning to move, the last of the sailors having released the last of the ropes and caught the dangling rope ladder, swarming up the departing vessel's side.

"Majesty, I grow weary of all the blusterings and the threats," Morg called out, pacing toward the end of the dock to keep up with the ship. "You seem to think that a year and a day from now, you'll be able to wage war upon our land. You think that you can insult us and blockade us and treat us rudely with impunity. I think you have forgotten just who you are dealing with—though I want you to know I do still respect you, even as I must chide you for your arrogance."

"You think you can chide me?" Taurin challenged him, gripping the railing. "I am the King of Katan, the strongest mage in all the land!"

"In all of Katan, yes. But not in all of *this* land," Morganen drawled. "If you may recall, my Queen bade me to assist you as you leave. Allow me to speed you on your way."

Unfolding one arm just far enough to free it, Morg flicked his fingers in a shooing motion. Two linear sprays of water hissed up, slashing high overhead. Thunder *cracked* through the air, rumbling through the planks of the dock and ruffling the waves of the sea.

Trevan blinked. The ship was no longer visible on the horizon, save as a line of falling water stretching into the west.

"How . . . No, scratch that," the redheaded mage corrected himself. "*Why* did you do that? I don't know how you did it, but you just proved you have the power to shove a ship of that massive size halfway back to Katan, and you did it faster than the speed of sound. At least, I presume it's halfway back, and that you didn't damage the ship or its occupants—Morg, exactly how strong *are* you?" he finally demanded, glaring at his youngest brother. "And no evasions, this time!"

"Hopefully, I'll be strong enough for what lies ahead—and that's the best answer you'll get out of me," Morg stated firmly, cutting off his fifthborn brother. "Trev, we have a pantheistic sovereign, a very small number of inhabitants from an increasingly varied number of cultural and theological backgrounds, and a year and a day—now lessened by an hour or so—in which to raise ourselves a Patron Deity. I may have the weight of a Prophecy or two to help guide me *roughly* in the right direction, but I'm not a Seer, and I don't know yet what it'll take to pull off the miracle of maintaining our happy little independence, in addition to gaining happy little love lives. Which, I must remind you, is all I'm *promised* to pull off via Prophecy.

"As for why, it was meant to be a warning that we of Nightfall are not to be taken lightly, and not to be treated lightly," the youngest of the brothers continued. "I held my hand over three years ago for two reasons. Warring with the Council would have damaged Katan, and because being exiled put Katan into the position of willfully failing to aid us. But things have finally changed. Prophecy is being fulfilled. I do not have to hold my hand anymore . . . save that I will hold it to whatever our lovely leader commands.

"Now stop asking questions I don't have time to answer," Morg chided his older brother, "and start praying to Whomever will listen that I can pull it all off, alright?"

"*You* are annoying," Trevan retorted, poking his finger at his youngest sibling in his irritation.

Morganen spread his arms. "Hello? That's what little brothers are for!"

A wooden-sword-wielding, curly-haired figure of fury attacked as soon as they opened the door. With a yell of, "You're not gonna hurt me!" Mikor flung himself at the intruders. "You're not gonna—"

Evanor flung up his hand, using the Voice of Command. "**Hold!**"

The boy froze midswing, practice sword tilted over his head and the toes of one foot still touching the floor. Mariel blinked in surprise. "Sweet Natua! I didn't even know you could *do* that!"

"Anyone with the Voice can, but it only lasts a handful of seconds," Evanor admitted, stepping forward and carefully prying the hilt out of the boy's hands, careful to not hurt those young fingers in doing so. "And it's thwarted by most personal shields . . . and it doesn't work on the deaf."

No sooner was the sword freed than Mikor shuddered and finished lunging forward, hands still hurling downward in what might have been a reasonably devastating overhand blow. He staggered and almost fell, thrown off balance, then recovered, blinking and whipping his head back and forth between the two adults. "Mother? Evanor? I, uh . . . I thought you were those bad men, from earlier—you didn't knock!"

"You're right, we didn't, and we should have. But, rights of privacy aside, young man," Mariel stated crispy, taking him by the shoulder and turning him toward the nearest chair, "you are in *big* trouble."

"I didn't know it was you!" he protested, allowing his mother to push him to the chair. Seating himself, he gave the two adults a pleading look. "I wouldn't hurt *you* . . ."

"We're not talking about that," Evanor dismissed, folding his arms across his blue-clad chest. "You had the right idea in defending yourself just now, though the wrong persons as your target. But earlier, you had the *wrong* idea. Do you know what that wrong idea was?"

Judging from the blank look in Mikor's green eyes, he didn't have a clue.

"You left the palace compound without permission," Mariel enlightened him.

Mikor blinked at him for a moment, frowning, then protested. "I had permission!"

"From *whom*?" Evanor challenged.

"You said that when we got these cryslets, I could be free to go all over the island, and you wouldn't worry about me!" he protested. "Even Aunt Kelly said that—and she's the Queen!"

Mariel stared at her son, then covered her eyes with one hand. Evanor wasn't nearly as impressed. "To be precise, she said she would rather you had one *once* we decided to let you go wandering all over the island . . . but you didn't stop to *ask* if we were going to let you do that."

"But if I'd asked you," Mikor protested, "you would've said no!" Then he widened his eyes and clapped both hands over his mouth when both adults stiffened at his inadvertent confession.

Arms still folded across his chest, Evanor loomed over the boy deliberately. "And for *that* reason, you just got yourself into even deeper trouble. You're not old enough to be allowed to wander out and about, Mikor. Because you don't *think* about the consequences of your actions. Now, you may have thought about being told 'no,' but you didn't think about why you would have been told no. Can you think of why you would have been told no?"

Lowering his gaze, Mikor folded his arms over his own smaller chest and glared at the floor. "Because you don't want me to have any fun!"

"Wrong. Because you don't think all the way through. You knew we wouldn't let you go out on your own, but you didn't stop to figure out why . . . and *that's* why you aren't allowed to go anywhere."

Wrinkling both nose and brow, Mikor frowned up at the older male in confusion. "What? I don't get it!"

"You're not old enough to figure out the consequences of all of your actions. You may know that fire is hot and you shouldn't put your fingers into a candle flame," the mage stated, "but you didn't think about what would happen if you touched that anti-fire sigil my brother Koranen made for you and your mother. He told us you burned your fingers on it. This is the exact same thing. You went against our wishes and left the palace. You only thought about the fun you would have.

"The result of that fun, the *consequences*," Evanor lectured, "of leaving the palace without permission from an adult, of going down the western road, which was forbidden to you, and of getting anywhere near the western harbor—which you were told was a dangerous place for you to go without an escort—were that you ran into the Council of Katan. Who do not like the fact that we have new people living on this island. Who could have *killed* you, not just kidnapped and interrogated you—you're incredibly lucky those men who were holding you weren't interested in hurting you in order to find out what they wanted to know. But there *are* those in the world who would, Mikor! *You didn't think*. Not of the bigger picture."

"Well—how was I supposed to know they'd be there? It wasn't the same time of the month as the traders come by!" Mikor protested. "I knew the traders weren't gonna be down there!"

"*Going* to," Mariel interjected, correcting her son's grammar out of habit. "But that was why you were to ask an adult. We would have checked first, scrying the bay from afar to make sure there weren't any ships in sight. *Then* we might have escorted you down there."

"That is the responsible way to handle such a request," Evanor confirmed. "When there is a possibility of danger, you check first to see if it is actually dangerous. You didn't check. You didn't ask someone else to check. You didn't think. And *because* you didn't think, you endangered not only yourself, but Rydan and myself," he emphasized, leaning over the boy a second time, "when we had to go rescue you!

"In addition to that, you put a whole ship's worth of people in danger, because we could've had to fight the Council openly in order to rescue you. If we had been forced to fight the Council, they would have been very angry with all of us and would have attacked in force, and *that* would have put all of us in danger. Not just *you*," the blond mage emphasized. "Mikor, you put your mother in danger, because you went where you weren't supposed to go—when you knew you weren't supposed to go there—and the Council found you.

"As it is, rescuing you required Rydan to smash about twenty expensive enchanted mirrors in order to distract the men holding you. Which the Council will still be mad about, and they will blame us for a long time. They may even demand that we replace those expensive, enchanted mirrors." Straightening, Evanor looked down at the boy. "To that end, you will be taught the value of just *one* of those mirrors. You will be grounded for a full month. You—"

"A *month*?" Mikor protested. "Mother's never grounded me for more than two weeks!"

"*I* am not your mother," Evanor returned pointedly, looming over the boy one more time. "I am going to be your next-father, and as I am going to be your father, I am grounding you for a month."

"You're not my real father! My *real* father wouldn't ground me for a month, either!" Mikor accused. "You're just a big bully, and I don't want you in my life!"

"Mikor!" Mariel snapped, making him look her way. "He is going to be your next-father, and you had better get used to that right here and now, because I am going to marry him, and you are going to obey him . . . and I'll remind you that you wanted him to be your next-father. Well, *this* is a part of being a father, first or next!"

"I don't want him, anymore!" Folding his arms tightly across his chest, Mikor scowled at the floor, shifting away from the side of his chair where Evanor stood. "I thought he was nice, but he's just a big bully! He's not my father, and he's never gonna *be* my father!"

"Deny this all you want, Mikor, he's still going to . . ." Blinking, Mariel trailed off. Both males glanced at her. She blinked a second time, then straightened. "I'll be right back."

Both Evanor and Mikor watched her hurry out of the sitting room. Turning back to the boy, Ev studied him. "Being a father, next or first," he continued, choosing to follow that thread of Mariel's argument, "means teaching you right from wrong, as well as teaching you how to read, write, and all the other things, like wielding a sword, and how to calculate numbers. I don't know how things may have been in Natallia, but you're on Nightfall, now . . . and that means you're going to be raised at least partly by the Katani method that I learned.

"At the age of four, our children are old enough to learn how to help with the easier household tasks, such as picking up after themselves. At the age of six, they are sent off to be schooled. At eight, they are old enough to learn weapons-practice if they wish. At ten, they're old enough for the responsibility of their own chores, taking care of them on their own without having to be supervised every moment. At twelve, they're usually judged old enough and responsible enough to be allowed to go where they will . . . but *until* that age, they aren't old enough to think about what they intend to do. *You* are only nine.

"You may be bright, Mikor, with the potential to be every bit as smart as your mother, maybe even as smart as your aunt, but you aren't ready for the responsibility of taking care of yourself. Which is a lot more complicated than something like feeding or milking the cows," Evanor stated, holding the youth's gaze, brown eyes pinning green. "When I asked your mother to be my wife, I was also asking her—as she is the person responsible for your well-being—if she thought I was capable of taking care of *you*. She said yes. When you are twelve, you will be given the opportunity to start proving you're mature enough to handle taking care of yourself . . . but you will still be a child, and you will still be under our care.

"Only when you turn sixteen does Katani law state that you are free to do as you will, because by then you will hopefully be old enough to know right from wrong, and how to gauge whatever you want to do, versus the risks of doing it. And that's presuming that Kelly will keep the legal age of adulthood at sixteen," Evanor added. "She once told me that her people wait until their children are *eighteen* before they're considered to be adults. That means you would have to wait another nine years. You're lucky I am reasonable, and I haven't grounded you for that long . . . because if we'd had to hurt anyone in rescuing you, rather than just smash a bunch of mirrors, it could've caused nine years' worth of trouble for all of us on Nightfall.

"*Now* do you understand the consequences of your actions?"

Tightening the arms across his chest, Mikor turned farther away from Evanor, sullen and silent. The door to the hall opened, and Mariel strode back inside, a folded letter in her hand. Mikor glanced at her in curiosity, though he didn't lose his scowl entirely.

"This is for you, Mikor. I'm sure you'll remember your *real* father's handwriting," she added tartly, passing him the wax-sealed page.

Taking it, Mikor turned the folded sheet over in his hands. He frowned softly, reading the words aloud. "*This is for Mikor, for when he would deny what is to be . . .* "

Cracking it open, he unfurled two pages' worth of writing and read the contents silently.

First he frowned, then his eyes widened. His cheeks paled, then flushed. His eyes watered, and he blinked rapidly, but they spilled over. Finally, Mikor covered his face with his young hands and drew in a shuddering breath, letting the papers fall to the floor.

Evanor scooped up the letter, turning the sheets around so that he could read the small, neatly scribed Natallian characters himself.

To My Beloved Son:

    The man who will marry your mother is going to be your father. He will be your father for four profound reasons. You won't appreciate them in full right now, and you won't understand the depth of them until you have children of your own, but these reasons are the only reasons needed, in all of the world.

    Reason One: He is a truly good man. He will be an exceptional role model for you to follow, teaching you how to be strong without being a bully, how to be gentle without being weak.

    Reason Two: He loves your mother. This means he will care for her, and take care of her, as he would take care of himself. And for her sake, he will take care of you, to ensure that she knows he is equally concerned for everything that she thinks is important in her life.

Reason Three: He loves you, too. For your own sake, because you are—usually—a good boy, and because you have the potential to grow up to be a good man, he will watch over you and help you to become that good man. He will encourage and guide you, and yes, discipline you when you have strayed . . . but he will also point out where you went wrong and show you how to find the right paths to take in life. You do not have to wait for him to learn to love you, for he already loves you. He shows it by his concern for you, his willingness to risk himself when protecting you.

Reason Four: Because I love you, too. Because I knew the Gods have decreed my life will be short, and because—and only because— the man I Foresaw would come into your and your mother's lives to replace me as husband and father was a better man. As much as it pains me to admit this, half of my life has been dedicated to the Gods . . . and thus only half has been free to love and care for my family. He will give you more than half of his love for the rest of his life . . . and together, your mother and he will give you siblings whom you will also love, help care for, and protect . . . and I love you so much that I couldn't deny you and your mother the opportunity to have the family you deserve, when the Gods demanded I give up my life in Their cause.

For nothing less than a truly good man who loves you and your mother, I would not have obeyed. I would not have gone. I would not have left either of you willingly. But he is your father now, by the promise of the Gods Themselves . . . and by my permission and approval. You will always have my love for you, and your mother's love, but you will now have his love, too.

Your Loving First Father,
Milon

Silently, Evanor handed the letter to Mariel, letting her read her late husband's writing. It was good to know that the late Seer didn't object to Evanor's presence in this little family. Crouching by the youth, Ev touched Mikor's shoulder. The boy sniffed hard, scrubbing at his eyes, but didn't quite look at him.

"As I was saying," Evanor stated quietly, "you are grounded for a month. For the first week, you will do nothing but chores and lessons between breakfast and supper, and you will have one hour each day in which to play. Between supper and breakfast, you will stay in your room. If you are good, the second week you will have two hours in which to play. The third week, if you are still good, doing your chores and your lessons, and obeying your mother and me—and the other adults here in the palace—you will have three hours each day for playtime, and in the fourth week, again if you are good, you will have four hours. If you are not good . . . you will have only one hour to play, until the next week, and if you have been good for a full week, you will have two hours, and so forth.

"To teach you the cost of *one* enchanted mirror, you will be told how much each day's worth of chores is worth, of scrubbing sinks and chopping vegetables, of helping to feed the cows and sweep the halls, just as if that were your job, as if you were getting paid like any adult would be paid. You will write down each day's number, and you will add together the whole month's worth of chores at the end of that month.

"At that point, you will compare how much you earned in a month of chores to the price of an enchanted mirror, which we will give you at that time," Evanor explained quietly as Mikor sniffed again. "Once you understand how much one mirror is worth, then you will figure out how much twenty mirrors are worth and figure out how many days and months—and quite probably years—you would have to work at those chores to pay for that many mirrors. This is the only way you will see just how much trouble your decision to go down to the western side of the island without waiting and asking for permission may have cost this family."

More tears welled up at that, spilling over Mikor's cheeks. Evanor was not immune to the boy's remorse. Moved to comfort his soon-to-be next-son, he shifted onto his knees and put his arms around Mikor, holding him close. To Ev's relief, the nine-year-old leaned into him a little.

"Understand that I do love you, Mikor. For your own sake, as well as your mother's. *Because* I love you, I care about you, and that means caring about the things that you do. If you do the wrong things, you need to be shown the right way. If you want to do something, you need to learn to think about how what you want to do could affect yourself and others . . . and when you do things that you *know* are wrong, your mother and I may punish you, but we do it to teach you the value of discipline."

"You knew it was wrong to leave the compound without our permission," Mariel added, touching her son's curly head. "That's why you avoided asking us, because you thought we'd say 'no.' Mind you, there *was* a chance we would've said 'yes.' We didn't know that the Council's ship was coming . . . but we would have checked to make sure there wasn't anyone in the harbor or on the horizon, and if there hadn't been anyone, we might have said 'yes.' If we had said 'no' . . . then there would have been a good reason for saying 'no,' whether it was a ship, or because we have our own chores to do before playtime for adults is allowed, which is when we could have escorted you.

"Do you understand now why we're grounding you?" she asked her son, stroking his dark curls back from his forehead. "Adults have to be able to discipline themselves, in order to be considered adults. In other words, responsible and mature. Children don't know why it's important to have self-control, and they haven't learned how. No one is born with self-control, Mikor. It's just like reading: You have to be taught how to do it. But then it becomes natural."

Sniffing a third time, Mikor asked in a quiet, subdued voice. "But . . . a whole *month*? Does it have to be a whole month?"

Evanor looked up at Mariel, silently conferring with her. Not to lessen the time, but to keep it that long. She nodded slightly.

"Yes," he stated, making Mikor pull back in his arms to look at him warily. "A whole month. Consider it a lesson for the future. Next time you're tempted to do something that seems like it might be fun—like tossing a ball around a room, where you might hit and break something—you'll know how long it would take to replace what might be broken."

Offering a lopsided smile, Mariel added, "Of course, you might go ahead and decide the fun of playing with the ball is worth more to you than the cost of replacing whatever might break, but that's another lesson for another day. First you have to learn the value of something, and being punished like this will teach you that lesson."

"Now, you've had a bad scare, being carried off by those men and having to escape them," Ev stated, rising from his knees. "You need to blow your nose, wash your face, and tidy your clothes. And then you get your first chore of the day."

Mikor sniffed and scrubbed at his cheeks again. "What's the chore?"

"For each main corridor of the outermost wings you sweep, for each floor, you'll get to tally one copper coin on your sheet. Starting with this floor. I'll show you where the pushing-broom is kept for this wing, and I'll show you how to use it and the dustpan."

"When you get tired of pushing a broom, you will do your lessons," Mariel instructed her son. "So if Evanor or I see you just standing there with the broom, we will assume you're ready to sit down and write a report on what you've learned so far about the art of tanning leather and fur. Your one hour of play this week will start one hour before supper. And you will only get to count each chore if you do the full chore. Go on," she urged him. "Go wash your face . . ."

Rising, Mikor headed for his bedroom and the refreshing chamber beyond, head and shoulders bowed. Evanor watched him go. He enjoyed the way Mariel slipped her arm around his waist, cupping his around her shoulders, but waited only long enough for Mikor to be out of earshot before muttering under his breath, "I feel like a heartless monster, watching him slump away like that."

"All parents do, unless they *are* heartless monsters," the petite Healer comforted him. She leaned her head against his shoulder with a soft sigh. "You did good, Evanor. Very good. You'll make an excellent father."

"What if I mess up?" Ev asked her. He lifted his chin at the partly closed door. "Raising him—raising any child—is a huge responsibility. What if I do something wrong?"

"Don't be afraid of doing something wrong. Just be an adult, admit that you were wrong, apologize for your mistake, make amends where appropriate . . . and in doing so, show our son how to be a real man. The man I know you already are," Mariel added, turning to wrap both her arms around him.

Evanor faced her, warmed by her faith in him. Cupping her cheek, he kissed her forehead, then her lips, before wrapping her in his arms for a hug. "I'll try to be the best man for you that I can be."

"Evanor . . ." Mariel asked after a moment, pulling back her head and frowning softly.

"Yes?"

"How did you know I was your destined bride? I mean, why *me*?" the Healer clarified.

"Would you believe that I took one look at your smile, and my heart leaped into your hand, forcing the rest of me to follow?" he quipped. She gave him a brief, mock-chiding look for being silly. The blond mage looked down at her, answering her seriously. "Mariel, it was Destiny. My brothers and I are fated to fall in love, one by one.

"You are the fourth woman we have had contact with since our exile . . . no, wait, the fifth, but the second woman is actually the eighth . . . I think . . . um . . ." He laughed helplessly at her confused look. "It's a little confusing, but Morganen's already met the woman I think will be his Destined bride, but he cannot claim her until all the rest of us are blissfully wed."

"Ah," she observed, letting that sink in for a moment. "Hmm. Well, as I do like your youngest brother, shall we go see about putting him that much more out of his misery?"

It was Evanor's turn to look puzzled. "How so?"

She rolled her hazel eyes. "By coming up with a Nightfall marriage ceremony?"

"Ah, yes. That. By all means, let us pester Her Majesty," Ev agreed.

The inner door opened, and out trudged Mikor, freshly washed and ready, however reluctantly, to begin his chores. The boy eyed the two adults still in his sitting room, sighed heavily, and waited patiently to be told where the nearest broom was kept. "Well?"

"Head toward the donjon. Three doors from here, there should be a supply closet on the left," Evanor instructed him. "You should find a broad, flat, rug-broom, good for sweeping large stretches of floor. You can use that one, instead of a straw-broom . . . so long as you understand it doesn't get into the corners very well, and you'll have to spot sweep with the straw-broom to do a good job. The better the job you do, the more you will be paid for it. Now, go on."

Sighing, Mikor trudged out the door.

Evanor watched him go. "Kata help me—or whatever God we end up with—to be a good father to him . . ."

"And any others that might come along?" Mariel asked.

Blinking, he pulled back a little, looking down at her. "Are you . . . ?"

"No, of course not," she dismissed, shaking her head. "But one of these days, I think I'd like another one. A little girl or a little boy to raise up into a young adult. *But*," she asserted, freeing a hand long enough to poke him in the chest, "*not* until we're married. Which means figuring out what kind of marriage ceremony we should undertake, as brand-new Nightfall citizens."

"Then I'll just rush downstairs right now and ask our brand-new Queen to approve of something that's quick and easy," Ev quipped, and hugged her close when she laughed.

Song of the Sons of Destiny

The Eldest Son shall bear this
*   weight:*
If ever true love he should feel
Disaster shall come at her heel
And Katan will fail to aid
When Sword in sheath is claimed by
*   Maid*

The Second Son shall know this
*   fate:*
He who hunts is not alone
When claw would strike and cut to
*   bone*
A chain of Silk shall bind his hand
So Wolf is caught in marriage-band

The Third of Sons shall meet his
*   match:*
Strong of will and strong of mind
You seek she who is your kind
Set your trap and be your fate
When Lady is the Master's mate

The Fourth of Sons shall find his
*   catch:*
The purest note shall turn to sour
And weep in silence for the hour
But listen to the lonely Heart
And Song shall bind the two apart

The Fifth Son shall seek the sign:
Prowl the woods and through the
*   trees*
Before you in the woods she flees
Catch her quick and hold her fast
The Cat will find his Home at last

The Sixth Son shall draw the line:
Shun the day and rule the night
Your reign's end shall come at light
When Dawn steals into your hall
Bride of Storm shall be your fall

The Seventh Son shall he decree:
Burning bright and searing hot
You shall seek that which is not
Mastered by desire's name
Water shall control the Flame

The Eighth Son shall set them free:
Act in Hope and act in love
Draw down your powers from above
Set your Brothers to their call
When Mage has wed, you will be
*   all.*

—THE SEER DRAGANNA